Spirit of the Sea

SPIRIT OF THE SEA

Georgina Fleming

ROWAN

A ROWAN BOOK

Published by Arrow Books Limited
20 Vauxhall Bridge Road, London SW1V 2SA

An imprint of the Random Century Group

London Melbourne Sydney Auckland Johannesburg
and agencies throughout the world

First published in Great Britain in 1991
by Century Hutchinson
Rowan edition 1992

1 3 5 7 9 10 8 6 4 2

Printed and bound in Great Britain by
Cox & Wyman Ltd, Reading

ISBN 0 09 985610 7

To Brand. With love.

BOOK ONE

KERRY

ONE

The first thing Kerry Penhale could remember was the frenzied eye of a plump, white chicken staring at her from where it hung upside down from a beam in her attic room.

Closing her eyes didn't make it go away.

Hot, she was clammy-hot and swollen-tongued with fever. She tried to call for water but was answered by a croak that mimicked hers. She was frozen into silence by the look in that chicken's eye. The specks of blood on its poor, featherless body were as scarlet as the dots that itched her own.

Obscene and terrible in its nakedness, nevertheless the bird was there for her, and it didn't matter how many times the apoplectic parson exhorted his flock to turn from the old ways. The measles rash, Mamma said, would move to the chicken and when it died – hanging there accusing her – she would be better.

'Parson Fox, 'e means well poor soul but 'e's out of 'is depths when it comes to the livin'.'

Kerry lived. She was lucky. Nelly Carne next door, aged four like herself, died.

And Missy – gentle, sloe-eyed, silver-haired Missy. It was through feverish eyes that Kerry was first introduced to 'Missy', or thought that was the name she gave in that sing-song way she had of speaking. Vaguer, distant memories drenched in lavender told her that Missy had always been near.

For it had not been Mamma who came with cool rags to wipe her forehead, or give the wet cloth to suck

9

between parched lips. No, Mamma's way of caring was much more brusque. 'Mamma! Mamma,' Kerry had moaned, and the maiden, strangely dressed and older than the child, had calmed her saying, 'It's not your Mamma, Kerry, it's Missy ... Kerry, sweetheart, please don't die. Don't die, for don't you know I'm goin' to need you!' And Kerry had called her Missy from that day on. And Missy called her Sweetheart. And it was to Missy, not Mamma, that Kerry went through childhood to confide all those things she felt but couldn't adequately say.

Parson Fox said that when you died your soul went to Heaven, and Kerry was so much better by the time the chicken squawked its last that she was able to watch from between the wide holes in her homespun blanket to see if she could see its soul departing. Furtively, guiltily she watched, aware, even in her childishness, of the sacrifice. She was disappointed.

But perhaps that's why the vivacious, curly-haired child flung herself so avidly into life from then to ever after, dangerously sometimes, those that watched her said. Remembering, maybe, that the bedraggled fowl had died for her and that she would be letting it down if she allowed one minute to go by without living it to the fullest.

Or maybe her love of life had nothing to do with that, but was merely the result of such a close encounter with death.

The cottage where Kerry Penhale was born looked out upon two wrecks. Between them was the place where, at the end of each day, the sun dipped, majestic, defiant, or forlorn and pale, according to its mood. The main topmast of the wreck on the right still showed

10

above the waves, a tremulous cross, and the ship's bell rang a ghostly angelus at high tides, eerie in the gloom.

Of the wreck on the left there was no sign but for the rock, the Spur, malevolent and black, surrounded by a perpetual maelstrom. The *Seagull* had hit the rock with such force that she broke in two. From the wreck on the right all hands had perished – from the one on the left had come one survivor . . . The Boy.

The one on the right had happened before she was born, but the one on the left took place on the very night her mother, Cath, went into labour. And they told her, they told her in quiet, story-time voices what had happened. She was told it so often she came to believe it was her own, special wreck. They remembered it with bonfires on her birthday.

It was only on her birthdays that she saw blue corpse-lights flickering round the Spur rock, and twice she heard a nightjar sounding as if it called from the sea.

They told her that on her birthday bodies had come ashore like flotsam from the storm and were carried in ant-like procession up steep, muddied tracks – thighs, legs and the odd hand, too – to unhallowed ground, to a mass grave in Fensome's field, famous for enormous turnips after that. The more that were found, the better, for lost bones call from the sea on dark nights – 'which Parson knows well as any man in spite of what 'e tells 'e' – and brothers, fathers, sons, once loved and trusted, change into monsters that roam narrow streets, shackled and hobbling about with dubious intentions. Oh yes, it was important that every last body be found, every last scrap.

Men had followed Cornelius Fox the parson as he plunged onto a terrifying catwalk of floating planking, wild-eyed, wet-haired, shrieking above the clamour of

11

wind and waves, *'For the love of God help me save these poor souls!'*

It was clearly too late. There was the parson, crazed as a bug on a burning log, when falling rigging and monstrous splinters from the shattered hull had already maimed and broken any who survived the first impact. Others were trapped below and drowned, and still more crushed cruelly on the rocks.

'I's'd follow 'e into the jaws of Hell, Parson, God knows I's would, but I's'll not follow 'e into that,' muttered the wily-faced landlord, Jessop, as he scuttled, slipping and sliding, back to the shore. Two less cautious men had perished, overcome by the fervour of Parson and moment. But Jessop and seven other men from the village were awarded silver medals for bravery 'in the face of overwhelming adversity'. Jessop's was nailed, unashamedly, above his beer-soaked bar. The ramshackle tavern that faced the sea was as frayed and wind-pocked as its owner. It teetered above fish-cellars rammed into cliffs, cellars that concealed a secret but more profitable trade.

And following the bodies came the booty, one hundred and fifty cases of brandy and eighty-two casks of wine, to be buried in attics, outhouses and byres, and certainly in fish-cellars, until such time it was thought prudent to share it out.

In the morning, in quiet waters, Maudie Carne found The Boy. He was in a common sea-chest padded with oilcloth. She claimed him. Around his neck was a tag which told her his name . . . *Tristan*.

Maudie Carne, who had already lost so many of her children.

So later, when men came asking, the villagers of Porthclegga shook their heads and said with one voice, 'No, Sir, there wern no survivors.'

TWO

'*Hevva! Hevva!*' Mazey Jack on the Point, waving his furze bush and leaping up and down, red-faced.

The pilchards! Kerry couldn't help that rush of excitement, that leap of the heart. She wanted to run with the rest towards the sea where the silver shoals were massing in their thousands, to haul to the surface the leaping fish as the men in the seine boats heaved in the tucking nets.

She wanted . . . ah . . . she wanted to belong! But it was no longer to do with her. She was not part of this community any more . . . or wouldn't be . . . from tomorrow.

It was cruel, yet somehow appropriate, that the shoals should arrive today. More than anything else the coming of the pilchards conjured up the images of childhood. They came now, so sharply to mind, that Kerry caught her breath and her eyes brimmed with tears. Because nothing was the same. This summer, for the first time, her father, Jake, was not there, shouting himself hoarse and hauling with all his sturdy strength, hairy black arms putting themselves to any work there was to be done. Calling to Gregor whose first time it was . . . 'Where's 'e to? Where's 'e to? I's put 'e there now bliddy well stop wheere I's put 'e!'

This summer her older brothers, Samuel and Rory, with their gleaming smiles and quick wit that set anyone around them falling about sore-ribbed with tears in their eyes, they were not there. For so long they had desperately tried to be men, so proud when they were able to leave the women and children to

14

their work on the shore and take out the nets with the fishermen. And Tristan was not there. Tristan had been gone for five seasons.

So all she did now was adjust her position and cast her black eyes to the cove below, where a flurry of boats was being launched to a cacophony of excited shrieks and shouts as the seine was shot.

Down there a gaggle of some thirty white-washed, red-roofed cottages clutched and nudged at each other in an effort to maintain position on the natural ledge in the cliff. There they seemed to hang, perilously close to the edge but high enough so the worst winter seas wouldn't touch them. The way to the top was by a tortuous, winding path, treacherous in winter and breathy work in summer. You could choose your way to the bottom and take either of the crab-pincer paths that meandered downwards and met again at the jetty where heavy iron rings were set in stone.

When she was little Kerry sometimes sat on the cottage step and contemplated those paths – the ones that trailed down the cliff in front of her, down and down onto the very floor of the ocean if you cared to follow them there; and at the path behind her – the one that led to the light and up and up to where Heaven was. And she wondered which way her own life would go. For she saw her childish life as static, to be taken by circumstances one way or the other, not knowing that when she was grown up she would feel just as helpless, just the same.

Suddenly, uneasily she noticed she was not alone up on the cliffs with Mazey Jack dancing over there, signalling the movements of the pilchards, jerky as a cut-out man before the glinting sea. No, she sensed the other on the opposite hill, sullen, silent, his pale hair black against the sunlit water as he trained his brass spyglass upon her. She was disconcerted. She'd thought she was alone.

Kerry gave a wry smile, but felt her own cheeks paling. Fear not, John Yelland, there may be few of my family left, but I will pay the debt. I am not going to run away. A bargain is a bargain . . . *but I am not yours until tomorrow.*

Everyone, even Parson Fox, doffed their caps and deferred to Yelland. He walked, he talked, he breathed like a man of power. He exploited his birthright to its full potential. He had once come dangerously near to losing it.

Born to a weakly mother who died soon after his birth, John was the son of Roger Yelland, a mean and cruel man who terrorised the countryside with his rough and ready justice and twisted ideas of religious morality. He had been converted to Methodism at an open-air meeting during one of John Wesley's visits to Cornwall. He had gone there to mock. He came out a changed man.

But unlike his more menial converts, Roger Yelland took what he wanted from Wesley's fiery message, leaving out the charity and love and choosing instead what suited his dark, brooding temperament best . . . the hell-fire, the brimstone, the lamentations.

Behind his back the villagers called him Satan because, 'Nobody is more likely to turn a man from 'is God than 'e.' He sat on the bench as a magistrate once a month in Truro, merciless as a barbed-beaked gull trawling for offal. Before him the hardiest felon twitched and quailed. He sat in his hall chair at home once a day in judgement on his small son. The effect he had was longlasting.

Sundays at the big house were turned into doom days. No work, but no play either, no reading other than the Bible. As a small boy John had been forced to sit in semi-darkness, summer and winter alike, and listen to great passages of print he did not understand while his fanatical father ranted and raved at his captive congregation of servants, housemaids and grooms. He died when John was seventeen, leaving his son his estates and his wealth, although rumour had it that he had tried to cut the boy off as the result of a violent quarrel. But the old man had fallen prey to consumption, become enfeebled and unable to change the will in time.

Some said it was over a girl the young man fancied. Others said it was because of the son's lack of respect for the father's bigoted ways. Whatever it was the quarrel was violent enough for the two never to speak, or eat or ride together in that last year of old Roger's life. There were even darker rumours that John had hastened his father's end to prevent him from changing his will.

The general consensus was that John Yelland was capable of anything.

Freed from the grip of his austere parent, the young John Yelland set about reversing everything his puritanical father had stood for. The lights burned long and late at Trewen: hurling, wrestling and cockfighting – they all went on, the dubious sports of the tinners. There was gambling and whoring, drunkenness and debauchery which the villagers at Porthclegga loved to hear and gossip about, stiff-necked, tongues clicking with righteous contempt. But while John Yelland could reverse the superficial lifestyle he had so rebelled against, he had inherited his father's dark, cruel nature, and the stories that came from Trewen, true or exaggerated, were not the sort of stories for women and children to hear.

Developments at Trewen would hardly have touched

17

the Penhales had not Kerry's father Jake, three sheets to the wind at Jessop's tavern, taken it into his head to build himself a new boat. Times were hard, but in spite of Cath's pleadings he had worked out that over ten seasons he would pay for it and had gone to Yelland for the loan. He wanted the boys to be able to make a living without leaving the village. They were up and coming now, they would soon take wives and it was necessary for them to have a boat of their own.

Jake's plans had not worked out. He had not been able to repay the loan. His sons would never need the boat, the materials for which still lay, smelling sadly of freshly-cut oak, on the jetty side.

Kerry untied the bow of her cap and let her curls tumble loose, immediately feeling them rise to the wind on release. She threw back her head the more to enjoy the sensation and let her coal-black eyes rest on the village below. Memories – Yelland could not take those away. The truth, it was important she remember the truth, for already she felt a compulsion to see it as she wished it could be and not how it was. All she had of the place she loved were memories. She cast her mind like a net and let it fill with memories, fresh and bountiful, memories that, like the fish, would have to be dried and salted, packed and stored, to last her through the winter of her future life.

A life that was promised to Yelland.

THREE

Everyone but Kerry had called Tristan The Boy.

Kerry was never lonely. She had Missy and she had
Tristan. But at least other people could see Tristan.
He was substantial. She could touch him. Whereas
Missy . . . At first she used to talk to her friend quite
openly and happily, until Mamma started tapping her
head and opening her eyes wide in alarm. 'Doan tell
me yous touched same as Mazey Jack,' she said. 'Chun-
terin' away to someone who isn't really there Lord help
us! That's all we's need in our family just now.'

'Missy *is* here,' argued Kerry. 'She'm here as well
as yous an' me. Carn yous smell the lavender?' But
Mamma wouldn't have it and eventually Kerry learned
to be prudent, to speak and laugh with Missy only
when she was alone.

Throughout their childhood she and Tristan had
wanted no one but each other. But her guilt over the
years had not lessened. She would always carry it with
her, because she was sure it had been their behaviour
that had contributed to Maudie's madness and to Tristan's eventual banishment from the only home he knew.

It seemed that the cottage next door, the home to which
Tristan had been taken by poor Maudie Carne, was
blighted.

With the artless cruelty of children, Kerry and Tristan had planted a toad on the step. Thoughtless, but
perhaps trying to provide a belated reason for the misfortune which seemed to have settled on the Carnes
like a low sea fog that no wind came to shift. Those

19

children that survived childbirth died later of fever. After Nelly's death came Jasper's, then Saul's, the twins dying together of the smallpox. Tristan had found the toad reclining under a stone in the stream that cut through the village and fell down the cliffs to the sea. But the idea of putting it on the doorstep had been Kerry's.

'We's carn.' All over, Tristan had the honey-gold colours of Gypsy Jayne's palomino colt. Tense and alert, and yet with the same gentle eyes. Tristan's long, blond curls were bleached to platinum by the sun, but his eyebrows and lashes were dark. They framed and emphasised his amber eyes. From habit, or when nervous, he puffed the hair from his face. Barefooted, as Kerry was, his breeches were too small and scarcely reached his knees. Sinewy brown forearms came scarecrow-like from his shirt. His hands round the toad were gentle. Long-fingered hands, shiny and hard. Kerry was always impressed by the coolness of them.

'We's can! Yous owe'e some favours anyways.' Kerry was dark as Tristan was fair, excitable as he was calm. And she hated Ned Carne, for in a questionable attempt to prevent his wife from further heartbreak, the man was bringing up his adopted son the hard way. 'Hardening 'e off. Too soft with them she is. No wonder the first puff of wind blows the childer away.'

So Ned, a simple but spartan man, showed not the slightest affection towards him and The Boy seemed to accept this for the most part uncomplaining. Against his wife's entreaties Ned insisted on taking him out in the boat 'to earn 'e's keep' from the day he was seven years old.

Life in Porthclegga was far from cosy for children at the best of times. In their first three years they were cosseted and spoiled. So many people to make a fuss of them. So many older ones to pick them up as if they were dolls, naked in summer, blanketed in winter, and lug them about from cottage door to cottage door precariously near to the edge of the cliff, feeding them bread and jam and scones made high with thick, yellow cream. Sometimes the tinies were wheeled along in fishcarts, packed together, their faces shiny and grinning as the pilchards' were. But after three they could get about and had to take their place among the rough and tumble, had to take their chances never knowing who was meant to be in charge, accepting cuffs and kisses from all.

Tristan, forced to grow up faster than most, owed his father many 'favours'.

But neither child had been prepared for the reaction, which heralded the start of Maudie's madness.

Maudie, a big and docile woman freckled all over, came out with a basket of washing, saw the toad on the step and fainted clean away. Then came Ned. Dour, silent, heavy in his long thighboots, he had taken one glance at the gulping toad, looked at his wife and said, 'Silly old faggot.' He'd returned to the house for a pointed steel gaff, pierced the toad in one liquid action, raised it to eye-level as if he considered popping it into his mouth, spat on the ground and, stepping over his wife, had gone back indoors and thrust it on the fire.

Maudie, weeping and shaken back to consciousness, scolded, 'I's been telling 'e for years and now even yous can see we's has been ill-wished. 'Tis Mother Carrivick, I's tell 'e. 'Tis always been her by back.'

Mother Carrivick must always be passed with eyes averted. The crone inhabited a hovel called Kergilliak up behind the village, and was generally accepted by the villagers to be a witch. But because she wove useful spells, too, provided herbs and potions for the barren and the lame and laid out the dead, she must be toler-

21

ated and treated with caution. For fishermen, behind the parson's back, were superstitious folk.

Kerry and Tristan, hiding behind the outhouse door, were horrified by what they had done. Maudie sat rocking by the fire for the rest of the day, loudly and horribly mourning her lost children. Ned, afflicted by gout, was grim-faced and angry, and a good deal freer with his blows than usual. And as for the toad . . .

''E trusted us,' said Tristan. ''E wern doin' anyone any harm. Then we's came along and 'e's fate was decided.' He spoke with anger, sad eyes scowling.

'But we's didn't know,' sobbed Kerry.

'We's should have known,' he replied in the weary, grown-up way he had of talking. 'They . . .' he flicked his curls towards the house, 'they know nothing!'

Four weeks later they lay in sparse grasses when the work was done, scattering seeds between their fingers and spying on Mother Carrivick. From up here the village below was merely a crack in the rocks. At low tide it smelled of hot pitch, seaweed and the rotting shells of little crabs. Up here the individuality of all the tiny pungencies distilled and left only the greater aroma of sea.

Tristan knew all about Missy, knew how she sounded and what she looked like with her long silver hair and her strange, black clothes under white cap and apron. Beautiful she was, in a pale, pearly way. And she wore boots and long wool stockings, different from the fishergirls who went more lightly clad. Tristan never laughed, even when Kerry interrupted conversations sometimes to talk to Missy. But he couldn't see her like Kerry could although, when pressed, he sometimes admitted that he 'felt' her. They used to dream, Kerry and Tristan. And then Kerry felt Missy very near.

'Maybe yous came from the French. Maybe yous the son of a great French prince.'

Tristan lay on his back, lifted his legs in the air and she watched him bring the hard white balls of his heels together.

Nine years old and he was well on his way to loving Penhale's daughter. As yet it was a sweet, protective, showing-off sort of love, but not any the less for that. Kerry's elfin face was often scowling . . . she felt things too deeply . . . she spoke out too readily. She was all hair and eyes, her face seemed to disappear under the load of black she carried. Her limbs poked like sticks from an oft-mended shift. He didn't want to be French. She pacified him, 'Or Italian . . . or even Spanish.'

'Too fair,' he said, the straw of grass bending between his teeth. 'Yous look more Spanish than me.'

'They'll come to fetch yous away one day.' It was Kerry who loved to speculate. 'They'll take yous away an' ply yous with jewels an' make yous live in a castle.' She watched him out of the corner of one eye. 'An' yous'll forget all about me,' she said.

Tristan spat the grass from his mouth and rolled into a sitting position. He clasped his knees and stared at the sea with eyes that matched the wave-tops.

'I's'll go away, but no one'll come for me. I's'll go on my own. I's want to see the world one day. I's woan be content to spend my life here on the boats, not knowin' what was going on out there. I's doan want to end up like old Pengelly, sittin' knockin' a pipe against the bollards, scratchin' an' starin' out with blind eyes at the sea.'

He spoke with passion. Kerry was silent. She was sure Pengelly was a happy man, with a string of grand-children and a daughter who adored him. She was hurt. He had not responded to her coy entreaty for compliments, and she didn't understand this need of his to leave the village. For her it was inconceivable that life could possibly be different. And deep inside she felt aggrieved because he had been taken in by 'her' people and yet was so ungrateful as to want to leave them.

But then he turned to her directly and caught her eyes unguarded. 'An' then I's'll come back,' he said, 'to fetch 'e.'

She tossed her shaggy head. She was the one that flushed and felt embarrassment. He didn't play the games she did. He was unnervingly direct in his actions and his speech. He often undermined her like that.

So she turned on her stomach and looked away. She whispered, horrified, 'She's comin'! Mother Carrivick is out an' comin'!'

Too deep in conversation they had not noticed the dark door opening and the bucket gone from the side of the wall. Now the old crone was almost upon them, struggling, muttering, bringing water to her tethered cow. If it was discovered in the village that they had been annoying Mother Carrivick they would never be forgiven. They would be blamed for illness and poor catches. If bad weather prevented the lobster pots from being collected, angry eyes would be cast in their direction.

Kerry quailed inside. She imagined the force of her father's arm as it knocked her flying across the kitchen, saw the accusation of betrayal in her mother's eyes. She would not feel unfairly chastised. There would be no injustice. She knew her behaviour would not be tolerated and yet she had deliberately flouted the most basic of rules . . . you do not interfere with Mother Carrivick. She pushed her body further down on the mossy ground, feeling the spongy wetness under the dry, and wished that the grasses grew taller and thicker, that she might disappear.

24

Through the grass she saw Tristan's legs, long and brown and strong. He was standing! He had come out of hiding!

'Good morning, Mother!'

He did not hide his voice, either. It rang true and strong across the lichened boulders and stunted bushes, the sworls of deep and pale green grass that lay between them and the approaching crone.

Kerry watched, holding her breath, unable to believe that such a terrible thing was happening. Her teeth dug into her lower lip. Her fists were clenched in front of her. She watched a grasshopper climb to the top of a stalk and bend it. She quite expected Tristan to disappear in a puff of smoke, or be turned into an adder, or look down at her with a face discoloured and pocked by fever. Horrible! Horrible!

She saw the old woman stop, raise her arm against the sun while her lizard-head scanned the landscape to locate the source of the voice. From the bowl of the old black cutty pipe clenched between her gums came evil smokewreaths. The pipe, like the rest of the day, stood to attention.

Kerry heard the grass rustle about her loud as lashing rain on windows. Tristan had not only stood up . . . he was moving . . . not away but towards the hag. 'Let me carry your bucket. It must be heavy.'

Now Mother Carrivick never came to the village except at dusk, carrying grave clothes and unguents with which to annoint the departed. Parents, knowing of her coming, brought their children indoors at such times, 'In with 'e quickly, now in with 'e,' afraid that the evil eye might light upon them as they played their games of hopscotch and five-stones in the evening sun before the cottage doors.

Those that wanted cures for warts or needed recipes for inducing abortion or conception had to pluck up

25

courage and go to her. Some said it was the finding of the courage for such a visit that wreaked the cure, that healed the sick, that cooled down fevers. They said it was the wanting it so badly that made the spell happen. But they said this cautiously behind closed doors so that nobody else would hear them.

So neither Tristan nor Kerry had ever seen the witch before. Now she stood, black-garbed, not yards away, humpity-backed as they said she was, pulled down to one side by the weight of the bucket so her black tatters touched the ground like a broken wing. Her face was brown and walnut-wrinkled, but from it burned eyes like small blue flames. There was one tooth at the top of her mouth and that overlapped her bottom lip which seemed to have caved in so completely that it wasn't so much of a lip as a cleft in her chin.

Her voice, when she answered The Boy, was thin as a curlew's call when it streams with the wind from cliff to cliff. 'Tristan Carne!' she said.

Kerry heard him whisper, 'How does she know my name?' But he kept on walking and Kerry felt like a bird with a parent acting as decoy. She did what any sensible chick would do and laid low.

'An' Kerry Penhale,' called the crone. 'My, my, my! I's is honoured today, I's am, I's am, I's am,' and she swung her head like a posturing snake.

Feeling as foolish as she was frightened, Kerry emerged from the scant undergrowth and, hiding behind Tristan, did what she'd been warned never to do and came nearer to Mother Carrivick. But she was careful to avert her eyes.

'No chores of yers own, boy? I's thinks yous feyther would scarcely approve of 'e coming' up here for an old woman's bucket when 'e's nets to mend an' ribbin' to patch.'

'I's does my share of work.'

26

Mother Carrivick cackled. 'An' more. An' more.' She handed over the bucket and the unlikely party made their way up the steep incline to where a dappled cow with long horns grazed a patch of marsh.

'An' yous, Kerry Penhale, as your mother's eldest daughter, how be yous away from the mindin' of the babes?'

'We's cannot always be working. We's cannot always be at beck and call.'

'An' who told yous that?'

''E told me that.'

'Ah yes . . . The Boy. 'E would, 'e would. Not satisfied, eh, with life as 'tis?'

Kerry couldn't believe they were holding this conversation. Of course she would tell nobody, but if she did they wouldn't believe her. She wanted to ask about Maudie Carne, and what the witch had against her. She wanted to ask about Hettie Pengelly, and if it was true that the old woman had wiped the warts from her face. She wanted to ask many things, but she hung her head and kept silent, believing that one word out of place might decide her fate forever.

'My mother is ailing.'

'Aye.'

'My mother is sick . . .' Tristan stroked his forehead to try and show the old one where.

'She has suffered . . . that one.'

Had he planned to meet Mother Carrivick today? Is that why he had suggested coming to Kergilliak, when they could so easily have gone to the rooks' wood to pick blackberries? Kerry wanted to shout, 'Stop, Tristan! Be careful! Yous cannot completely dismiss what the villagers say!' But she listened with a beating heart and kept silent. For she, too, felt guilty about the toad.

'Is there nothing yous can do?'

Mother Carrivick, bent towards her cow, held her

27

back before rising again to face Tristan. She was smaller than he, and when she raised her head Kerry saw the layers of skin that hung round her neck, mottled and brown like the scaly skin of codfish. So this was what you looked like, if you lived to be a hundred.

'They will bowsenn her . . .' started the witch.

He had the audacity to interrupt. 'An' that will do no good.'

The witch wagged her head and he continued, 'Yes, they will bowsenn her. They will duck her in cold water at Kenack pool. They will push her under again and again until she is exhausted. They will wrap her in blankets an' bring her home, expecting the sickness to go away. That is what yous tell them to do with the mad, an' theys do it! They follow the old ways.' There was anger in him. He did not hide his feelings from Mother Carrivick. 'Theys follow yous!'

'Do yous blame me, or is it yousself, Tristan, with whom yous are angry? 'Twas yous put the toad on yer own mother's doorstep . . . the woman who scooped yous from the water, took yous in an' cared for yous an' loved yous as if youm was her own!'

Kerry gasped. No one knew about the toad. Had the old witch been watching? Could she see all things, even in the dark? Her skin crawled.

But Tristan was not daunted. 'Yous could have saved her! Yous could have saved her children!' Tristan stood straight-backed, his feet planted apart, looking down with scorn at the face of the crone.

The cow drank the water thirstily. Tipping out the little left in the bucket, Mother Carrivick held it under the scrawny udders and squatted, without a stool, beginning to milk. The yellowy white liquid foamed bubbly in the bucket. A cloud of flies rested on the animal's head. It swished its tail and moved an eye but it stood still for her, quite still. Kerry watched

28

intently, for hedgehogs were said to suck from this beast at night, clustered like burrs round the four warty teats.

'Tristan,' said the hag patiently, in the same cooing voice she used for the cow, 'rest easy. 'Tis not the toad that drives yer mother mad. An' remedies are often no more than salves for those of bad conscience, rather than cures for the sick.' She continued pulling the teats, screwing up her eyes as she turned to watch The Boy who stood with the sun going down behind him. 'I's could do nothing for Maudie Carne or her babies. No more could yous. For the weakness she has in her womb her mother passed on to her, an' her mother before her. An' the sickness yous point to in yer own head will become of itself a release from a torment she cannot bear. Would yous deprive her of that?'

'She thinks 'tis yous caused the deaths.'

'Ah,' The old woman sat back on her haunches. It was hard to believe that there was no stool. 'An' yous, Tristan? What do yous believe?'

He wiped his hand across his eyes, not willing to show his other emotion. He shook his head. 'I's doan know! I's doan know!' he said.

'So why did yous come?'

'To find out.'

'An' now then? What have yous found out?'

'Nothing!' he said, with violence, and turned on his heel and went.

Kerry was torn, desperate to go with him, yet terrified of treating Mother Carrivick this way. She fidgeted, watching his tall, lithe figure disappearing from view, feet first, as he went back over the cliff. His white shirt clouded out behind him. Soon just his head would be left and then she would be here, alone with the witch.

The milking was finished, and Kerry felt she should

29

offer to carry the pail back to the house. She didn't want to. She very badly didn't want to.

''E doan mean . . .' she started, and the witch, rising, seemed surprised to see her still there. Kerry twisted the grasses, glad they were there to occupy her hands.

And then Mother Carrivick smiled. It was an awful and peculiar sight, her whole face disappeared in a maze of wrinkles and her one tooth came up in her head like an adder's, pointing.

''Tis not so terrible to be angry with pain,' she chuckled. 'Some people bow beneath it, others rant and rave and accuse. It runs in 'e's family to rant and rave and accuse. They are an accursed lot . . . but in Tristan there is hope of the deep waters flowing towards lighter places. We's shall see . . . we's shall see.' She clamped her lips together stiffly as if she had already said too much.

'I's think I's should carry yous bucket.'

The witch appeared, once again, to have forgotten her. 'Go child,' she said over her shoulder. 'And take yer silent companion with yous. Between yer yous have burdens enough to carry.'

Kerry needed no second telling. Heels flashing, she turned and fled, following the path taken by Tristan. As soon as she was out of range of Mother Carrivick – she turned to check – she called at the top of her voice, 'Tristan! Tristan! Wait for me!' as she must have done a hundred times that summer. For although she was only four months younger he seemed so much older and wiser than she, and she was proud to be his friend.

FOUR

She never forgot her visit to Mother Carrivick. She never went again, although Tristan did, she knew, but he never said so.

When she was small the front door of the cottage was so heavy she could hardly move it. And Feyther had to duck to get through.

Inside, the kitchen was filled by a table scrubbed white the colour of sun-bleached whalebone. Between this and the small open fire Mamma lived, conjuring butter and flour into scones with a flurry of floury spray, concocting a stew from turnips and fishbones, a child under one arm, rolling pin in the other, while all the time she issued her orders to Kerry who felt slow and stupid beside her.

The stew was hung on a hook and chain over the open fire, the scones patted flat on the griddle. The fire, hungry for driftwood, was kept in winter and summer alike for the cooking. It made the bedrooms unbearably hot.

By the fire was an old rocking chair which was Mamma's and nobody else must ever sit in it. Kerry thought it a waste, because the chair was almost always empty. And against the wall was a scarred oak settle, satin smooth, which Mamma called 'that disgustin' old thing' because it had been in Feyther's family, in this same house, in that same place, for generations.

Mamma liked new things but nearly everything in the cottage smelled of age. Each morning Mamma would beat the rug that lay before the fire, a rug she was proud of because she had made it herself from rags; she would doggedly beat it outside the front door with a broom while she muttered, 'That's better, that's better,' as if she was easing something from her system. She beat the rug between the drying nets, the baskets, and the vicious-looking gaffs so often left in the way by Feyther. On bright days, she would fling the bedding from the windows so that it flapped itself fresh and smelt of the sea.

Mamma reigned supreme like the master of a sailing ship in the stone-flagged, low-beamed kitchen. With her white muslin apron stiff with starch she would pass Kerry a procession of dishes and greasy pots which Kerry would dip in the bucket while she sat cross-legged in the sun on the step, chatting to Missy. She squinted back into the darkness and watched the butterfly bow of Mamma's apron bobbing from table to fire, from table to fire. When Mamma went to help salt the pilchards she took her white apron off and wore one made of discarded sacking. Out of her house she looked like all the other women, wrapped in a grey headshawl.

But in the house she was beautiful. Kerry wondered if she ever stopped to realise how pretty she was, with her delicate face and those black curls that wriggled from under her cap, springy as wood shavings. Like Kerry's hair. When Mamma smiled, everything smiled, and her small face twisted into a wryish look of kindness.

Once, up late and forgotten while Mamma mended and waited for Feyther, Kerry had seen her stop and take down the mirror from behind the cookie tin on the mantel and prop it on the table, thinking no one was watching. She was just beyond the circle of lantern-light and the shadows made her bigger than she was. She had gently touched her cheeks before it, staring at her reflection with thoughtful surprise. She unleashed her heavy hair and brushed it – the sound was tearing cloth – turning her head this way and that as she went. Mamma leaned forward, looked hard at herself and said aloud, 'I's thinks that perhaps the nature has gone from my hair.'

So all the time she had known that Kerry was there. Kerry was utterly taken aback. This was the first time Mamma had said anything personal about herself. And now she seemed to expect Kerry to comment.

'I's thinks it looks very nice, Mamma.' And that was the only occasion, apart from when Mamma came creeping in to check the children at night, her face lit from below by the shaded candle in her hand, that Kerry had ever seen her with her hair down.

Still intent on the mirror and catching her watching her Cath had said, 'Now, an' what are yous thinkin' 'bout, sittin' there doin' nothin', midear?'

And Kerry had cautiously replied, 'Nothin', Mamma, just watchin'.'

But that was a lie because she was thinking. She was thinking how lucky she was that she could get away on her own with Tristan, away from the stuffy confines of the cottage, and that there was nowhere her mother could ever be alone.

They crammed the cottage to the rafters. There were ten of them and two bedrooms and an attic room where Kerry slept with her three sisters, Rosa, Cassy and baby Mabs.

''Tis downright embarrassin',' Mamma said one day, inclining her head next door towards the Carnes', where the numbers had tragically dwindled to three. 'That's what 'tis. 'Tis just terrible embarrassin'.' And she clucked her tongue at her own good fortune.

The four boys slept in the room opposite Mamma

33

and Feyther, but they didn't have the view of the sea that Kerry did. She only had to open her eyes to see it first thing in the morning because the window looked straight over it and was down at floor-level next to the comfortable straw pallet on which the four girls slept and which took up three-quarters of the room. The sun's reflection on the sea cast lapping ripples on the ceiling, and there was nothing that made her more want to stay like a lazybones under the covers than the experience of lying on the pillow with her hands behind her head and eyes half-closed, letting that ceiling sea wash her in and out of daydreams.

So small was the cottage and so close were they packed together that it was hard to maintain an identity or to find the freedom Kerry felt she needed to breathe. The kitchen smelt of wet woollen clothing, of broths made from onions, carrots and turnips. When the door was closed the shiny ceiling often dripped with steam. It went down Mamma's neck and she'd give a little scream.

Mamma's moods flashed from high to low in moments. One second she might be stroking your face, the next cuffing your ear. Thin and wiry and small, Mamma never missed. And it was hard to discover exactly the reason for the change.

'Mabs needs changin',' Mamma would say, with her sleeves rolled over her bony elbows. And Kerry would put down Jody, aged two, move to the pulley where the clean strips were kept, see the stew begin to boil, move it over, take Cassy's arm from the churn by the table, and Mamma would say, 'Run to Lizzy Lee's for me for a dip of salt.' And so six-month-old Mabs would never be changed.

'Kerry, take the broom an' brush that dust away from the step.'

She liked to be given the job of filling and trimming the oil lamp because it was the one job that was totally satisfactory to complete. She liked to sit on Feyther's special sea-chest, handed down to him from his great-grandfather the pirate, beside the small, diamond-paned window, place the lamp on the table before her and continue the job right through to the lighting.

'Kerry, fetch a cloth an' wipe that spill,' or 'Kerry, be a good maid an' fetch me some water.'

And clogged in winter, barefoot in summer, Kerry would obediently trot off to carry out the errand. So more often than not she missed the final part and watched with jealous eyes as another lit the lamp.

She tried to imagine as she walked home at dusk before the shutters were folded closed over the windows, she tried to imagine as she saw the lamplight beckoning, what it must be like to have no home, to have no place where you could just slip in and be accepted, clutter and all, safe behind thick walls.

It was not that she was frightened of the wind or the dark or the sea, but she was afraid of the tinners. The inside of the house was bright and warm and cosy, the firelight playing on the pots and Mamma waiting to close the shutters or maybe holding the fork to the fire for toast. But outside – outside lay all that was cold and wretched and lonely.

She pretended to be meek when she reached the door, to be meek and grateful and loving. But that was before Gregor reached for her milk and she slapped him away and took her home for granted again. And when Mamma said, 'Kerry, get off yous backside an' lay this table,' she forgot about meekness and her good feelings vanished completely.

She tried to tell Mamma these things and Mamma said, 'Well hark, she's a thinker, just like her feyther.

Accept, child, accept. Tryin' to work things out does yous no good. No, accept, like I's does.'

Kerry didn't think that Mamma accepted at all. Her life was taken up with fighting every single thing – dirt, hunger, wailing children . . . her aching back, tiredness. Kerry was suddenly worried that Mamma might decide to do what she advised and accept. The world would turn to chaos if she did.

Kerry would sit by the lantern on summer nights and watch the ghost moths come to burn their wings on the flame, throwing themselves against it again and again until they were worn out and exhausted and still they fluttered against it . . . never seeming to learn. Was this acceptance? And she'd think of Maudie Carne and wonder why she kept on having babies when all they did was die.

Kerry would have liked to have proper conversations at home, like the ones she had with Missy and Tristan. You could find out so much from people during a conversation and there was a great deal she wanted to know about Mamma and Feyther. But theirs wasn't a family that went in for conversations. They dealt more in clucking and squawking, she thought, like hens.

During the one time when there might be conversation, when they were at the table, they kept quiet. If you didn't keep your head down and get on with it, it was assumed you weren't hungry and were likely to be given a job like putting the kettle on or fetching more bread, and then you would miss getting your fair share.

When he was home Feyther dominated the household, sitting in his high-backed chair at the end of the table. When Feyther breathed out he sent gales down his nose and he cracked his knuckles like nutcrackers.

The children took it in turns to sit at the table, or

ate on the step, or in winter on the floor by the fire. Feyther's great ham hands tore at his bread and Kerry thought that if it wasn't for those hands and the skill in them then maybe there wouldn't be food on the table.

Feyther announced early on that he refused to learn any more names each time a new baby arrived so he referred to every new black-haired infant as 'monkey'. He had seen one once, wrinkle-faced and brown, chained to a hurdy-gurdy. It had impressed him. He said there was no point trying to remember so he might as well just give up trying.

Nobody spoke, but they listened to what Feyther had to say. And he told stories and gave boisterous accounts of what happened to him in the day, and made them so interesting that no one had any desire to interrupt. And later he would go, unhooking the lantern from a nail on the wall, to sing songs to the fiddle and drink rum at Jessop's tavern.

Kerry could hear the men singing if the wind was low, when she went to bed at night. The candle flame often seemed to dance to the music. She badly wanted to talk at home about something serious. She wanted to ask why nobody seemed to love her in the way they all loved Rosa, who was faery-like and sweet and placid and who got away with anything just by smiling and pulling her feathery, dark hair around her face in the way that Kerry, with her springy stuff, couldn't. Dark and mysterious – Kerry had spent days trying to be like that, but when she got the mirror down and practised her smile she thought she knew why her efforts had failed. Kerry was thin with a pointed chin and angry black eyes and when she smiled that way it just looked silly. Hers was more of a lopsided grin in a pointed face, and she felt she was treated differently because of it. She kept forgetting to stay sweet and always slipped back to what they called her bossy, over-excitable self again. Anyway, Kerry mused to herself, she might be a thinker like her feyther but she looked more like Mamma than Rosa did. She would just have to accept that being the eldest girl, she would always have to bear the sharp edge of Mamma's tongue.

No, there was no conversation in the flurry and bustle of home. Which is why Kerry so enjoyed her precious hours with Tristan.

FIVE

There was something that was never talked about. Everyone knew but nobody said. The women were not encouraged to participate and mostly didn't dare to ask.

But they knew all right. All day they had gossiped with their eyes, shiny-nosed, windblown women with shawls tied round their heads.

But the men talked about it at Jessop's, and the women heard the sounds, listened to plish-plosh dippings of muffled oars on moonless nights, and rag-wrapped hooves, a string of mules, restless, by the jetty.

The boats were going out to a dangerous assignation with the fast sailing lugger *Claire* out in the deep Channel water. Little boats of shallow draft, easily manoeuvred, pointed fore and aft so they rose buoyantly over the breaking seas. Pistols and muskets were gone from nails and left bare imprints of themselves on walls, so long had they hung there.

Feyther might dominate the household, the fishing might dominate Feyther, but the fair-trading dominated even the fishing. It was more profitable.

Earlier in the day she had heard Mamma say to Lizzie Lee, 'They's go wi' Yelland. Anyone else I's could stomach but as for that man, I's carn trust 'e. 'Tis as plain to me as the nose on my face but nobody else seems able to see!'

'They's goes for theyselves,' said Lizzie Lee firmly, a long string of a woman over six feet tall with pendulous breasts that reached her waist. Mamma's head only reached Lizzy's armpits. She looked continually disappointed, Kerry thought, or taken by surprise and these conflicting emotions gave her face that pinched look with which she now regarded Mamma. 'An' because they'm must! The parson trusts 'e! An' Yelland wouldn't let them down at a time like this. It'd be more than 'e's life's worth. Give 'e his due, whatever else yous might think of 'e, 'e's good at organisin' men.'

'An' what does we's do when the excise men come ridin' over the hill . . . or round the point, cuttin' they's off from home? They's will one day, Lizzie, they's will.' Mamma was nearly sobbing.

'Cathy! This is not like yous!' Lizzy Lee's round eyes watched everywhere and she had a privileged view. It wouldn't be good to be seen talking like this. They ignored Kerry. Kerry didn't count.

''Tis come so close to the last one, Lizzie.' Mamma bothered to have conversations with friends. It was just with her family that she held back. 'Sometimes I's doan think I's can take much more! Ah, Lizzie, there's somethin' that nags me so deep I's carn scratch it . . . save to say they's never drank this way 'fore Yelland's time. They's was never so long at Jessop's an' I's is not easy wi' any of it.'

'Time of the month no doubt,' said Lizzie, glad to be safely onto women's matters on which she considered herself, after all her lurid ailments, an expert. And Kerry looked up, wide-eyed while Lizzie sniffed and shook her head.

Everyone waiting for the men's return was anxious. Kerry could feel Mamma's anxiety. It floated up to the attic pervasive as woodsmoke as she snuggled down deep into bed in her flannel nightdress, swearing that she would share Mamma's vigil in spirit and not be asleep by the time the men returned. Kerry shared Lizzie Lee's concern about her mother's state of mind. Mamma was worried about Feyther . . . she thought

40

he might not come back! Incredible! Feyther was as colossally enormous as the sea itself. Indestructable. How could Mamma think he could possibly not come back with the things he had gone to fetch?

Brandy, tea, salt . . . they took it all, to compensate for the iniquitous, newly-inflicted salt tax. The luggers would take illegal tin to Portugal and return with contraband hidden in their holds.

On this night there had been a vermillion sunset. The western sky had filled with clouds floating on scarlet. But now it was black, and Kerry could see nothing.

It was so quiet that over the soft lap of the waves she could hear Grannie Lee across the way, the scrape of spoon on bowl as she mashed and ground her slops to get them past her toothless gums in a jaw that would not open. She spent hours and hours stroking her brown-seamed throat. 'An' me throat's no larger than a bird's,' Grannie would be warbling to herself as she rocked back and forth. 'I's has to work it thin . . . very thin . . . that's what comes of growin' old.' And Grannie looked like a bird. She looked like a tiny old seagull.

Kerry, unable to sleep, plucked up her courage, tiptoed down the narrow staircase and peered into the kitchen to see what Mamma was doing. Mamma had a game – she liked to pretend to Feyther that she didn't care. Kerry often wished she wouldn't play it. Sometimes she played the game with her children, too. Mamma had brought the Madonna to the table and now she sat there stroking it. Carved in wood, this was Mamma's pride and joy and had been washed up on the rocks from a shipwreck. 'She has such a look of serenity in those blank, wooden eyes,' Mamma had told Feyther. 'I's wish my eyes could look as calm as that.'

Feyther couldn't see what she saw in it. 'They will . . . when yous dead,' he said, laughing. 'Those are lifeless eyes, woman, not bright an' alive like yourn.'

'Well, I's think they are contented eyes. This woman has not had to struggle!'

'Well, she only had one child,' Feyther sat back and chuckled. 'That's where yous went wrong. Yous'd maybe look like that if yous could sit back on yer arse all day gazing at the ground like she do.'

'Doan blaspheme, Jake! Yous knows it brings bad luck!'

And now she was sitting, stroking its head. And was she weeping? Mamma never cried. She might shriek and scold or sob with laughter. But not cry, no, never. Kerry was frightened.

Mamma didn't own many things, and those she did, she bought from pedlars and tinks. Most of her purchases – lentils, dry beans and barley for breakfast gruel – went straight into the windowless room behind the kitchen, the larder, where the stone jars of salted pilchards were stored. When she had money she bought pots and pails – Feyther banged extra nails in the wall to take them – calico, thread, and sometimes a beautiful ribbon to cut up and share between the girls. 'Come and chose the colour,' she used to call, excited as if she were choosing for herself. Kerry wished she wouldn't let them choose because they would argue and end up with a colour nobody liked best. They ought to be allowed to take the choosing in turn. Mamma never bought ribbon for herself.

The tinks told them hair-raising tales of tinners, wild, violent men who went about in angry bands armed to the teeth with knives and pickaxes, marching into towns and breaking into houses in search of corn. The fisherfolk went in fear of the tinners as a consequence, and terrible tinners with silver teeth stalked the landscape of Kerry's dreams. Even without closing her eyes she could imagine the ragged, desperate tinners, the wind between the stunted moorland trees screaming out the torment that made them rob and plunder in order to feed themselves and their families. To get the babes to bed Feyther would sometimes say, in a low snarl so awful and full of menace it seemed to shake the house, 'The tinners be comin' . . . the tinners be comin'.' Yes, the tinks and pedlars sold them more than utilitarian necessities. They sold them legends.

Mamma was still stroking the Madonna.

'Youm and yous graven images!' Feyther had scolded her.

The Penhales weren't a religious family but they went to church like everyone else at Porthclegga. It was only a small church set high on the cliff behind the village, and the names of fishermen lost and the manner of their dying was written on tablets in stone walls that rose steeply to the raftered roof.

Parson Fox filled it with the mournful roar of his great voice as he said, 'The church is built of Christian people,' and he slid his hand up the column in front of him. 'Here a man, here a woman, here a child.' And Kerry marvelled that the place was big enough to contain so many human bodies in its walls.

For a long time Kerry didn't connect the gravestones outside with people, for inscriptions could only be read with great difficulty when it was raining and the rain washed the salt from the cracks. But when she found out she was appalled. They would get wet! And see how the boulders tossed and turned out here, as if they were still at sea, trying to cling to something solid!

Lost at sea. Drowned. Lost at sea. She walked round the bleak bit of earth conscientiously before she learnt to read, asking the parson to read out every one. It seemed to her that everything grew eerily here, too green, too grey, and the toppled, weathered stones were pocked and barnacled and the lichen looked like seaweed draped on wrecks.

She didn't want to be visiting Feyther in that wind-swept churchyard.

Kerry stepped down into the room so that Mamma could see her. 'Mamma!'

The knuckle of Mamma's hand where she held it to her cheek was white. With the other hand she went on stroking. She noticed Kerry and sighed. It came as a little shudder. Kerry felt she was imposing on her grief. It was as though Mamma wanted it and wasn't willing to be diverted, as if by willpower alone she could bring Feyther home.

'Shall I's put the kettle on?'

'Yes midear.' But Mamma frowned and Kerry knew that the sound of the boiling kettle might interfere with Mamma's frail connection with the sea. But she put it on anyway and went and sat across from Mamma, looking out at the night. The shutters, she noticed, had not been closed. The men in the boats would be able to see the twinkling lights from the houses from the water.

Kerry, jealous of Lizzie Lee, wanted a conversation. 'Tristan has a jackdaw, Mamma. "E's tamed it and he keeps it on the end of a string. Tomorrow we's are going to find grubs for it under tree bark up at the rooks' wood.'

'Come here, Kerry.'

Kerry went to Mamma, her bare feet padding on the cold stone floor.

44

'Give me yer hands.'

Kerry allowed Mamma to take them and place them where she would. 'Oh! They's cold hands. Yous must take a brick back with yous. I's has one in the fire. Now, put them here . . . that's right, one on each side of the head of the Lady.'

'Like this, Mamma?'

'Now close yer eyes, Kerry, and pray.'

'What shall I's say?'

'Ask God, pray hard to God, that yer feyther comes home safe tonight.'

Mamma's hands were on her arms, tight and hard. They squeezed. And Kerry screwed up her eyes, her whole body, and prayed with all her might, and gave thanks that Mamma had spoken to her about something important at last. She thought it might have something to do with the secret of the jackdaw, for it was a very special secret that Kerry had given Mamma. Tristan had told her not to tell. She didn't often betray Tristan.

'Pray, Kerry, pray!'

'I's am, Mamma! I's am!'

And it was a sort of coversation they were having, just the two of them, with nobody else about.

A cold breeze gusted with Feyther into the house and woke Kerry up. She rubbed her eyes and tried to remember where she was. She was sitting on the sea-chest by the window. She was cold and stiff. She had been waiting for Feyther. She must have gone to sleep and left Mamma to wait alone. She felt ashamed by her weakness and lack of fortitude.

But Mamma wasn't there. She was playing her game again. Her shawl was gone and the Madonna was back on the mantel, sad-eyed, pointing to something on her foot as she always was. Feyther didn't see Kerry there

45

in the pocket of darkness by the window. She didn't dare speak. Mamma must have forgotten her! He took off his boots and put them by the fire. His eyebrows, his hair, were wet and his eyes were red-rimmed. He wriggled out of his coat and, shaking it, hung it on the pulley to dry. He took the lantern off the table and lifted the latch to the stairs.

But before he left the room he looked round nervously as if he'd forgotten something, held his lantern up so it illuminated the wooden Madonna. He wore his most serious expression. He bowed his head and furtively crossed himself with his lantern hand before she heard his footsteps on the stair.

Kerry thought she must remember to tell Mamma that in the morning, but by then she had forgotten all about it and could only think of Tristan's jackdaw and how they were going to search for food. She recalled the small incident of Feyther and the Madonna when it was too late. Mamma had her memories by the time Kerry remembered. She wouldn't want them changed.

SIX

It was surprising how many things there were, as a child, to be afraid of.

There were the forces beyond her power . . . Mother Carrivick, the tinners, the spirits of the sea . . . and then there were the too-numerous things she might do at any time to bring retribution on her head.

Tristan didn't have that problem. 'Yous lucky,' she said thoughtlessly, confiding in him.

'It doan matter what I's do I's get beaten all the same. It just depends on how the mood takes 'e.'

Of course he was talking of Ned, and Kerry felt passionately sorry for Tristan.

'The trouble with yous is that yous never stop to think,' he told her. 'Yous blunder into things. Youm not sly enough. To survive yous must be cunning as a fox.'

But there were so many things! She might spill the milk on her way home, hurrying to finish her chores so she could get out with Tristan. Then she might say, ''Twas Bobby Tremain, 'e pushed me.'

Mamma, unaccountably concerned, would insist on going round to ask Bobby's mother, a cousin of Mazey Jack's, and there the normally stupid Bobby would manage a look of such aggrieved denial that Mamma would believe him and push her all the way home with sharp little bee-sting slaps round the ears.

And next time she spilled the milk she'd know it was because she was trying too hard not to, and that she wouldn't be believed whatever she said and would get punished just the same.

*

She lost a knife. She had toiled up the hill to the knife grinder's wagon with a handful of implements to be sharpened. She was sure there were four knives but on her way down she discovered she had only three. She didn't dare go back to ask the grinder, a swarthy, taciturn man, half-gypsy with pinpoint eyes, of whom she was truly frightened. She couldn't face going home without that knife, either. So she stopped on the track to think about it coolly and calmly as Tristan told her to do. She thought she'd been cunning when she went inside, put the tools on the table and said in her sweetest voice, 'But there wern any knives, Mamma. I's sure there wern. I's had everything wrapped together in the cloth. An' everything I's took is there.'

'But there were three knives, Kerry. I's counted them out myself. I's carn have made a mistake over that!'

Her mother regarded her steadily. Kerry felt her face flush, turned it away but her mother held it there. 'Look at me, Kerry! Now for the love of heaven what has happened to my three best knives?'

How could she tell her that she'd thrown them into the sea? How could she have made such a silly mistake in the first place, and what had possessed her to throw them away?

Behind her she felt Rosa laughing. But when she turned her sister was looking the other way. Both legs stung in anticipation and her mother had not even slapped her yet. But she did, oh she did.

She pushed the cart with Mabs and Jody inside it to the top of the cliff. Well, she might as well be there as anywhere else. She would steal an extra hour with Tristan, spend that hour enjoyably instead of sitting on the step being bored and talking baby-talk. Even as she sweated and pushed she knew Mamma wouldn't see it that way, but she carried on just the same. Now what devil inside her made her do that?

Mamma found her gone and trailed grimly to the top of the cliff to find her. Tristan hadn't been there. The entire enterprise had been a waste of time. Kerry was sitting at the top gathering the strength to come down again when she saw Mamma's head bobbing furiously towards her up the path.

She felt her heart drop like a leaden weight inside her. She realised, at that moment, just what a wicked thing she'd done. And Mamma had more to do than climb the path to retrieve her children . . . children she had trusted to Kerry's care.

Mamma's face was red and puffed up. When their eyes met Mamma was out of breath. Kerry stood up. Her wobbly legs suddenly string-thin. 'The air,' she stammered. 'I's wanted to give them fresh air.'

'Fresh air indeed!' was all Mamma could say. Breathless, she wrenched the cart from Kerry's hands, and Kerry, indignant at not being believed and frightened half out of her wits, tried to snatch it back.

Mamma flung her arm wide and brought it forward so Kerry slipped on the shale and fell. Mamma didn't bother to look. She turned round stiffly and, letting the cart take her, arms at full stretch, proceeded on a wobbly downward course which didn't do much for her dignity.

Kerry lay where she'd fallen and watched, quivering with unaccustomed fury. Where was Rosa? Why couldn't Rosa have been sent to find her? Why couldn't Rosa have minded the babies in the first place? But underneath she knew she was wrong and was desperately searching for a scapegoat. Feyther would be told about this. She would not be allowed to play out tonight. Feyther might hit her. She unfolded one of her own hands as she thought about Feyther's. One winter she had complained about the chapping. Between her fingers the skin was broken and sore. She was sitting in the kitchen with her hands clutched to her chest, sobbing from the pain of them.

'Bring them here, monkey, let me see.'

She had taken her hands and trustingly placed them into Feyther's. Her hands, in his, looked small and smooth, two pink oysters curved in shells much too big. His were broken and cut and red and raw, covered in lines and great callouses. Hers in his looked delicate and fine. With one of his great fingers he stroked the little sore places, up and down, up and down, until she smiled into his face and said, 'Mine are feeling better. But what about yous?'

He wrinkled his brow into a dark brown smile. 'I's wouldn't know my hands were alive if I's couldn't constantly feel 'e! And with dead hands, maiden, where would I's be?'

Feyther's hands would administer no gentle healing tonight. Nor would his smile. So she decided to be hung for a sheep as a lamb and not go back until dusk.

Tristan came and they lay on the clifftop watching the gulls pitting themselves against the wind as they tried to land on the water. The sun flecked the sea, trailing it with silver ribbons.

'I's feel black inside . . . quite black. I's doan think I's'll ever be happy again in my life,' Kerry said as the dread of going home settled on her. 'Mamma will call me wilful an' think that for some reason I's do all I's can to stop her loving me. I's doan, Tristan,' she wailed. 'I's want to be loved. It's just that I's seem naturally to do all the wrong things.'

He turned to her then, she a gawky eight-year-old, he no more than nine, and he said, 'I's love yous. There is nothing yous could do to stop me loving yous.' And suddenly and decisively there on the clifftop he kissed

her. Just a flutter on her cheek. No more than a butterfly kiss. But he kissed her. And for Kerry that made
anything that followed, anything at all, completely
worthwhile.

The blackness fell away. She felt nothing but joy!
She soared with the gulls and knew that, whatever
happened, Mamma loved her, too. It was just that she
didn't dare say so. Mamma had only been frightened.
Mamma was often frightened. Kerry felt big and grown
and able to forgive Mamma.

SEVEN

The following morning Kerry woke to a feeling of relief. Mamma had not told Feyther about her. He had come home too late. She lay in bed, savouring the moment, trying to remember if the kiss had been real while she listened to the lap, lap of the waves and the careless tinkling of the steam drying up. She reckoned that to get water she would have to squeeze the pump handle fifty times today.

The little ones were already up . . . they always woke with the sunrise. But Rosa was still asleep beside her. Kerry propped herself on one arm and stared at her sister. To frighten Mamma Rosa used to say she wanted to be a nun. And Mamma fell for her tricks. She wouldn't fall if Kerry played them.

The only one in the family without curly hair, Rosa made Mamma twist it into rags at bedtime. But it was so heavy it fell in long rolls and made Rosa beautiful in the soft, appetising way ripe fruit is beautiful. Rosa looked refreshing, and her neat little teeth made her looks fizz like elderflower champagne.

Rosa preferred to stay indoors and that's why her skin remained soft as she grew, not battered by wind and spray as the other children's was.

For some unaccountable reason Mamma started saying that Rosa was the poor doer of the family. Why this was so Kerry could not imagine. Rosa had never been ill, far from it. She bloomed, and her breathy way of speaking was only put on.

From early on Rosa's only ambition was to be a

'lady'. From great-grandfather's trunk she took feathers
and lace and paraded with a Chinese silk scarf over
her shoulders while she fluttered a carved fan in front
of her chest, getting in the way of the work, but making
Mamma throw back her head and laugh and say, 'My!
What a fine one yous is! Puttin' on airs! Doan let yer
feyther catch yous in those!' Although she made out
she was cross, Mamma looked pleased. Kerry watched
her.

But if Feyther had caught her he would have laughed
and teased, too. Everyone was gentle with Rosa. They
thought her fragile and beautiful.

Kerry didn't think she was beautiful. She thought
her fat. And her eyes had a look of fatness in them –
big, round, brown greedy eyes that were always searching for something to have.

The boys Kerry hardly saw. She didn't mind. They
teased her. She must have been a very green, naive
child because she was always taken in. When, much
younger, Sam and Rory told her they had pinched off
her nose and showed it to her between their fingers she
felt her face in horror. When they sent her out to catch
a swallow by putting salt on its tail, she went without
suspicion. Gradually she learnt to distrust them, but
theirs was always an uneasy relationship. In the morning they came down early for breakfast while Mamma
scolded and fondled and they teased her back in a way
that Kerry, younger and a girl, could not. They were
rarely back before dark.

But at least their work seemed to finish. Mamma's
never did.

Sam and Rory had always been grown up. They had
gone with Feyther to sea from the age of ten. Gregor,
older than she by a year, spent his days down on the
jetty helping the shorebound men mend nets and giving

53

a hand to Will Trelliss, the carpenter, a dry, thin man like one of his own seasoned planks. Much could be learned from watching Will. When she was little Kerry had gone, mesmerised, to watch him shape pegs for holes and bang them in. Will Trelliss' mouth was full of nails. She suspected he kept them in his beard. She used to count his nails for him, round nails, oval nails, rusty nails and shiny nails. She used to count them out for him into boxes. He never seemed to mind, but Mamma came to fetch her and bring her back to the cottage, 'Always pesterin'! Always in the way,' she said, and she said it, Kerry knew, for Will Trelliss' benefit.

She'd been gratified that Will hadn't laughed as Mamma wanted, but in his slow way had answered, 'The maid was no hindrance, Cath girl. She was a help with her deft little fingers!' But Mamma hadn't seemed to hear, had hauled her away just the same.

Or, for the young lads, there was always the jetty to repair. Great flat, round stones to be found and wedged into place so that when the autumn storms came it would be strong enough to stand. The lifting and the carrying made them grow tall and muscular, like brown young colts.

Downstairs in her pale blue shift, the tiny room felt large to Kerry when the men had gone. After them with their great appetites there were the rest to be fed; Rosa, Cassy, Jody and baby Mabs. While shovelling the fishcakes to prevent them from sticking Mamma said, 'Maudie Carne be gettin' worse. I's off next door this mornin' to give 'er a hand with 'er chores. Kerry, I's want yous to watch the rest. Rosa, yous patch the britches I's put in the basket, an' let Cassy help yous prepare those vegetables. The babes can be wrapped up and put outside.'

Kerry wished she could remember being a baby, a

time when Mamma must have cuddled her, petted her and lifted her around all soft and loving like she was with Jody and Mabs. She couldn't remember. She felt cheated.

'I's saw yous,' said Rosa spitefully, as soon as Mamma had gone out the door.

'Saw me where?'

The morning was warm. The sun was a misty sphere already quarter way up the sky. When the mist cleared it would be hot.

'I's saw yous kissin' on the cliffs with The Boy. I's'll tell Mamma.'

'We's never kissed!'

'Yous did! Yous did!'

'So where was yous then?'

'Wouldn't yous like to know?'

Now Kerry knew that Rosa wouldn't tell Mamma. Even Rosa would have her face slapped for tale-telling, and if Kerry went without supper over it, certainly Rosa would, too. No, Rosa wouldn't tell Mamma. She was merely grubbing for information. Seven years old and Rosa was fascinated by men. She changed completely when there were men in the house, even ancient men like old Pengelly.

She simpered. She dimpled prettily. ''E's blind,' Kerry used to say, furiously. 'There's no need to bat yer eyelashes at 'e!'

And Rosa used to defend herself coyly. 'I's goan to make the most of myself an' what I's doing is practisin'. I's doan want to end up a skivvy . . . a fishwife like poor Mamma!'

Mamma . . . poor? Kerry had never made the connection. Did Mamma, perhaps, think she was poor? Is that why she encouraged Rosa in her fine ways? Was that why she played her games with Feyther? Kerry pondered.

'Yes, yous'll see. I's woan be found dead kissin' a nobody like Tristan Carne. One day I's'll live in a fine house like Yelland's, with housemaids an' grooms an' men to open the front door when I's comes in an' they'll bow to me when I's hands 'em my gloves.' She tossed her head and smiled, regarding Kerry from underneath starry eyelashes. And Kerry, open-mouthed with astonishment, had to believe her.

Afraid of not getting done before Mamma came back, Kerry found herself peeling Rosa's vegetables on top of doing her own work while Rosa daydreamed and dallied, sat deep in Feyther's chair with her legs dangling, taking her time over the patching. But even Kerry had to admit that Rosa sewed beautifully.

It was hot. And when Mamma came home she gave Kerry a basket and told her to look for some fruit.

Now it was Rosa's turn to be jealous. For she had to stay home and finish the mending. There were some compensations in being the eldest.

'How is poor Maudie?'

Mamma shook her head. 'Maudlin', just maudlin! Gettin' worse by the day. 'Er wits is befuddled, she neither speaks nor smiles, just goes on chewin' that darn plug of tobacco. An' Ned says that at night-time she's wicked. Stays down by the fire, woan go to bed, stays down moanin', callin' for 'er babes. Life is a bugger, there's nothing more certain than that! There's no justice. There's that poor soul, now she's never harmed a fly. An' what do she get? Nothin' but heart-ache. An' Kerry . . . doan yous be late back!'

'I's woan be.'

Mamma crammed a broken old straw hat on her head,

'for the sunstroke', and with brazen eagerness the children tried to join her, Jody's fat little legs struggling along beside her. 'Go back,' she hissed, pushing him back through the door. 'I's likes my time alone!' She was afraid Mamma might take it into her head to suggest she take him, too.

Below her in the blueness of the harbour there was gentle movement. Ropes were being coiled, decks tidied, comments bandied back and forth and red, green and yellow boats came and went on swift bow waves of silver. From here baskets of fresh cod and ling caught the sun and glistened. She couldn't see Tristan. Up she climbed, the pathway hot beneath her feet, blue slate brittle and falling behind her, longing to reach the top where she would meet a different kind of cooler air, not so cloying. She was glad she wore only a loose shift so the air could move under it. She passed Maisy Kemp going up, taking her shrimps to town.

'How are 'e, Kerry?'

'Well, thank yous Mrs Kemp, an' how are 'e?'

'Middlin'. Fat as ever. I's get tired of carrying m'self about.'

Kerry had been wary of passing. The fat woman in the voluminous pink dress was as coloured and bent as the prawns she peddled. She took tiny steps and her bottom stuck out very large behind her. She had a club foot. Kerry wondered if you got club feet if you used the path as much as Maisy did. Her basket was covered with a bright, checked cloth.

She passed a group of cheeky-faced boys going down, bloody rabbits flopping over their shoulders. At them she just scowled.

Mamma's larder was already stocked with jars of jam and jelly and bottled fruit. Kerry knew where she was going. She would go right on past the farm, past Kergilliak, and not stop until she reached the ground beside the high wall of Yelland's orchard at Trewen. Last time she did that she came home with a basket of windfalls almost too heavy to carry. She'd found pears, too, dropped from bountiful branches which overhung the wall, pears yellow and leather-skinned, bursting with taste. Mamma would be pleased.

Missy didn't want Kerry to go to Trewen. She wouldn't say why. Missy was often evasive. She tugged at Kerry's dress to pull her back. Kerry was determined. 'I's doan often get to be alone, an' when I's does I's wants to choose where I's goes, Missy,' she said firmly. 'Anyway, if yous doan want to come yous can stay here!'

Missy sulked, and let gossamer tresses of silver hair fall over her narrow face to hide it. Anyway, she must be too hot with all those clothes on.

The air was heavy with bees' buzzings and yellow with sunshine and pollen. In the distance Yelland's cornfields were deep lakes of gold. Men were cutting, bringing scythes backwards and forwards and somehow dictating the rhythm of the day. Those fields looked so different from their cheerlessness in winter when she, along with other girls of her age, picked off stones, their backs bent double to the wind, their hands red raw and their eyes streaming in the bitter cold.

Missy hung back and watched her from a distance, twisting her hair behind her ear. Kerry shivered. She wasn't scrumping but she felt as if she was. If she didn't pick up this fruit then it would be rejected, it would lie rotting and wasted, food for the wasps.

She filled her basket quickly so that it bulged and brimmed. It was heavy. She had to lean nearly right over to get it off the ground. She went ten steps and rested, another ten and rested, blowing away the hot curls that stuck to her face.

She didn't hear the horse immediately. The path was thick and dusty. It was almost upon her before she heard a hoof squeak, then another. She turned, looked up, and saw what she thought must be a tinner . . . a tinner on horseback . . . a tinner who had probably stolen a horse in order to go more swiftly to the riots!

The rider was burnt brown, almost black, and his hair had the colour and flow of stream water. It was tied with a black bow at his shoulders. His fawn-tinged eyes were slits in his face as he gazed down at Kerry. He wore a sleeveless leather jerkin open to the waist, and his brown breeches, she noticed, were leather, too. He must be very hot. Hotter than she.

She'd hardly managed to walk before with her burden. But now Kerry began to run. She was startled by Missy's scream. With a dry mouth and a thudding heart she ran faster and faster, the apples bouncing out of the basket and thudding dully behind her. But the horse strolled after her, not slow, not fast, but in the same way it had approached her before with an even, steady squeak. Eventually, sweating, dishevelled, she was forced to stop.

'Well!' The tinner spoke English! Kerry was surprised. Panting, she climbed off the path onto the scrubby brown grass beside it, hoping that the rider would pass by and let her resume her uncomfortable journey. There was no sign of Missy. Her friend had abandoned her! Her tongue curled guiltily over her top lip as she hoped he would go. Because she'd just remembered what was in her basket.

'Well, an' yous look as if yous done quite well for youssel!' The tinner wiped sweat from his brow and flipped it to the ground.

''Tis not all for me,' said Kerry, puffing, watching the horse's hooves as they trod little pools in the dust.

'An' who *is* it for, might I's ask?'

''Tis for Mamma.' Kerry blushed. She was hot, and felt unreasonably cross with Mamma for putting her in this position. Here she was, a mass of wild black tendrils spraying from her head to her shoulders, and set on top, ridiculous as a cup and saucer, was Mamma's straw hat.

'I's thinks it might be too much for yous to carry home.'

'I's'll manage,' said Kerry, eager to be gone.

'Yous from Porthclegga.'

'How can 'e tell?'

'From yer accent. All yous fisherfolk speak the same. What's yer feyther's name?'

'Jake Penhale.'

'Penhale,' he mused.

'Does yous know my feyther?'

'I's knows everyone round about here.' The man had a cunning about him, a restless shiftiness that went perfectly with his nervous, agitated horse. His voice was warm and slippery as chunks of curd. She knew he was not a tinner because a tinner would have killed her by now. But she didn't like him, no, she didn't like him at all.

He held down his arm and moved beside her. She could smell horse and polished leather. 'Give me yer hand, I'll take yous home. Have yous a sister like youssell?'

'I's has three sisters, all younger 'n me. An' no, thank 'e, I's can get home by myself.' Mamma, she thought, would be pleased she had given that answer.

The man's face broke into a smile. It was the smile of a dog and did not light his eyes. They stayed cold and unpleasant and Kerry remembered winter again and bare fields. He laughed. 'Have it yous way,' he said quite patiently. 'But tell me yer name if I's to remember a maid so determined to refuse my gallantry.'

'My name is Kerry Penhale,' she said, forcing herself to look at him.

'I's good with names,' he said, and then, over his shoulder as he kicked his horse and moved away in a contemptuous spurt of dust, 'I's never forget 'em.'

She walked home alone. Missy did not join her again that day.

'Describe 'e again,' said Mamma.

Kerry did.

''Twas John Yelland,' she told her daughter. 'There's no mistaking Satan's son from that description. Did yous not recognise 'e then, child?'

'How would I's recognise a man I's never seen before?'

Mamma seemed surprised before she said, 'No. No, I's suppose yous haven't. An' yous with that basket of apples! Did 'e say nothing about that?'

'No, only that 'e would carry me home.'

'An' yous refused?'

'Of course I's refused.'

'Kerry.'

'Yes, Mamma?'

'Doan tell yer feyther.' Mamma turned to the sink and went on gutting the fish.

But Rosa wanted to know more. Rosa wanted to know every single thing Kerry could remember about John Yelland. 'Was 'e handsome? Did 'e look strong?'

'Yous would not have liked 'e, Rosa.'

'How do yous know I's would not have liked 'e? How could I's know without having seen 'e?'

'Rosa, 'e's an old man. 'E must be nearly as old as Feyther! How could yous fancy a man twenty years older 'n yous? An' yous just a little girl.'

61

'I's woan be a little girl for long,' replied Rosa saucily. 'An' then I's'll have men like John Yelland crawlin' at my feet.'

'Hush yer mouth Rosa and get to yer bed! Never let yer feyther hear yous talkin' like that. Do yous hear me? 'Tis disgustin'!'

Rosa didn't flinch before Mamma's anger as Kerry would have done. She went from the room straight-backed and smiling, tossing the work she'd been doing on the table behind her. Her face held a secret, remote anticipation.

'Hussy!' said Mamma, pink to the elbows in the bucket. 'She'll want curbin', that one, before she's much older or there'll be trouble! She'll take what she gets like the rest of us!'

But Kerry wished she could see Mamma's face because somehow she knew she didn't quite mean what she said. There was something about Rosa's spirit, her total lack of shame, that Mamma secretly admired.

Kerry sat at the table and started to peel the apples to put in a pie for Feyther to come home to.

EIGHT

Mamma loved a storm when the men were home because she said it made her realise how safe she was. 'Nothin' can budge this house,' she said, as the rain hurled itself against the tiny panes and a violent gust of wind blew down the chimney. Ash was scattered over her precious rag rug, but Mamma didn't worry tonight. The storm, the monstrous breakers that crashed on the rocks below made everyday matters seem small.

It was only one month since her meeting with Yelland. Kerry hugged herself. She knew exactly what Mamma meant. The cottage wrapped itself firmly around them. On nights like these it seemed to rise above time and space. It never occurred to her that their home was not theirs. That one day they might have to leave it.

Even Jessop's was deserted. The men had stayed ashore all afternoon waiting for the weather to break, and had drunk enough. The noise of the approaching storm drowned conversation, anyway. One by one they had put down their wooden mugs and set off for their homes, frowning up at the sky and muttering, 'By Jesus she'll be a cracker when she comes!'

'Feyther, I's scared!' Cassy had never sat up through a storm before, not a storm like this one. 'Maybe the waves'll wash our house away!'

'Doan be such a baby and eat yous supper,' snapped Rosa. Kerry looked quickly at her sister. Her face was suffused with a dull red, and Kerry realised with surprise that Rosa, too, was frightened.

She hitched up her brown calico skirt and started collecting the plates. 'No houses have ever been washed away in Porthclegga,' she told the pale-faced Cassy. 'Have they, Feyther?'

'No, but I's damn worried about the fish-cellars,' he said, wiping a ring from the table with his sleeve. 'There's been some great September storms . . . Kerry's storm was in September.'

Kerry settled herself back at the table, thinking a story was about to be told.

'Must yous bring drink home, Jake?' Mamma's words exploded from her mouth. She had been waiting to say them. Immediately she bent to pat her mouth on a corner of her apron.

'Aye, I's must – in my own home – when I's like!'

''Tis that man Yelland!'

'Say nothin' 'gainst Yelland in this house, woman!' Feyther boomed as he banged his mug on the table. Liquid slopped over the top and Kerry watched it spread, dark brown like fish blood, over the scrubbed white surface. 'We'd be in a pitiful state in Porthclegga if it weren't for young Yelland, I's tellin' 'e.'

Feyther's thick black brows closed in a scowl. His close-cut hair was glossy black. The thick muscles of his neck tightened and clenched where it rose from his open, red-flannel shirt. Feyther's eyes were filled with wormy-red fish bait. Kerry hadn't noticed his eyes like that before.

Something was changing. The house wasn't changing although it had every right to . . . for it was under threat. It stood staunch and square and clung to its neighbours, protecting them as always. The fire wasn't changing, she could feel its warmth from here, in spite of the wind that tried to put it out.

Feyther smelled no different from usual, he smelled

of fish and rum. Kerry looked from her mother's face to her father's flushed and angry one.

'Yous under 'e's influence!' Mamma wouldn't let it go. She rocked urgently in her chair, her head turned unnaturally sharp to the right to face him, stiff and accusing. Every now and then she gave a little tug at her apron. 'Yous like small boys before 'e! I's doan know what 'e's got about 'e that makes it so!'

Cassy's eyes were closing. Kerry, glad to get out from the atmosphere, picked up her sister and carried her upstairs. There she undressed her and put her to bed, neat under the quilt beside Mabs who was sucking her thumb. 'There, there,' said Kerry out of habit. 'Yous'll be safe an' all right an' the storm will pass, wait and see.' But even as she said it she knew it was not the storm that threatened this house. She looked in on Jody before she went downstairs to keep herself away longer. There might not be a storm, so deeply was the child sleeping. She dropped a soft kiss on his face. Jody did not stir. She could stay no longer. Perhaps, when she went downstairs again, the squall in the kitchen would be over.

She heard Mamma's voice as she stood at the door, wanting but not wanting to rejoin the family. She heard the rocking of the chair, wood on stone, protesting.

'But why do 'e pick up the tab? What reason do 'e have for providin' the rum for the men of Porthclegga?' Mamma's voice was high now, whining like the wind.

''E wants to make certain the men do not drink on the nights of the runs.'

'Hold yous tongue, Sam!' said Feyther. 'This is not women's business!'

'But 'tis all right on other nights then, is that it? 'Tis acceptable for us women to put up with men stinkin' an' out of their minds from the bottle?'

'Leave it, Mamma.' Kerry was grateful for Rory's

voice. It was calm but forceful. Mamma would take notice of it. So might Feyther, for Rory, so like him, stockily-built with a stolid, stubborn nature, was his favourite son.

Into the turmoil came another sound, nails in boots, running. Feyther held up a hand so violently the lantern flickered. 'Hark!'

A slapping on the door with the flat of a hand, a voice calling, 'Penhale! Come out! The sea is to the cellars!'

It was Mamma who stood up first, leaving the chair behind her furiously rocking. 'No, Jake, yous is goin' nowhere on a night like this!'

Feyther's chair shrieked as he pushed it back. The iron ring on the door was rattled and all the fury of the night came in with the parson's questioning face. 'Jake . . . come quickly, bring the lads, bring anyone yous can find!'

Mamma rushed forward to plead with the parson. Her skirts were blown back by the force of wind through the door. Water dripped from the visitor's chin and made a pool around him. His hair stood plastered on end, as if he'd come to the finish of a particularly passionate sermon.

'Parson Fox, yous cannot take my man . . .'e is in no fit state . . . look at 'e! 'E will fall into the sea. 'E cannot even see where 'e be goin'!'

The parson looked concerned. He wavered. Behind him came Jessop looking weaselly and scared and even remembering to remove his hat. 'The sea be sweepin' through,' whined Jessop, his eyes twirling in his sockets as if they hung loose there. 'We's stand to lose everything!'

They were not meaning the pilchards. The bulk of the catch had gone weeks ago, had been salted and packed in hogsheads and despatched to Italy and Spain to be eaten during the Lenten fasting. Stacked and pressed in layers of salt by the women, the residue of oil and salt and water that dripped from the pilchards into the stone wells beneath had been made into rich manure, the oil clarified and sold to pay for the seiners next year. No, they were not meaning the pilchards.

Feyther got up and swept the table clear. 'I's'll not be told what to do in my house by any woman!' he said angrily as he staggered to the door, followed by Rory, Sam and Gregor.

The sound of running boots could be heard now outside above the wind, as men, flinging their billowing capes around them, ran to the tavern to climb down the ladder in the trap door, the only way in to the vast sea-swept cellars beneath. There great tongues of water licked through the cavernous breathing holes in the rock to sluice and fall again, cascading down to the rocks below and bringing a scrambled meal of kegs and barrels and sea-chests to the slobbering, salivating ocean jaws.

Another voice, calm, powerful . . . Kerry recognised it. 'Jake Penhale, are yous with us or no?'

'I's with 'e!' Jake brushed Cath aside as if she were a fly on his face. He stumbled as he made for his peg by the door and took down his heavy rubber cape.

The owner of the voice, a good foot taller than the others, pushed past to the kitchen. It was John Yelland himself, but not so panicked as the parson and Jessop, smiling his thin-lipped dog smile again. Courteously he bowed to Cath as his eyes made a quick sweep of the room. He slapped his great, gloved hands together and made a noise that sounded like a lightning crack.

'We's need every pair of hands we's can get,' he said as Mamma clung to Gregor, begging. Gregor, flushed

67

and breathing heavily, turned on her in shame. 'Leave me be, Mamma! I's needed there.'

'You's'll be needed here, son, if anything happens to the men!'

'I's be a man, Mamma, let go of me!'

Anguished, beaten, Cathy turned her back on Yelland and drew herself up straight.

Tristan! Kerry suffered a moment of pure horror, as timeless and intense as a nightmare. Missy pushed her forward, made it possible for her arms and legs to move. Every movement seemed to have stopped and be held in a vice. Words ceased to reach her. With a desperate question on her lips and clad only in skirt and blouse, she flung herself between the forest of arms and legs and coats at the door and stood on the path outside. At once her skirt was flapping wet, her blouse sodden, her mouth forced open, loose as an old woman's, by the force of the wind.

'Tristan!' she called, hanging on to prevent herself from being blown backwards. Grabbing anything firm she could cling to she pulled her way in a terrible reel to the cottage next door. The door stood open and Maudie Carne sat in a stream of wind, wretched by her stove, her shawl blown back from her face.

'Tristan?' Kerry shrieked above the wind. 'Where is Tristan?'

She battled her way into the house, using both arms to pull the door closed behind her. The quiet was shocking.

'Tristan!' she shouted at the old woman who rocked in her madness.

Kerry was quelled by the look in her eyes. For Maudie's eyes were like the Madonna's, blank, lifeless and made of wood.

'Has 'e gone?' She dropped to her knees, pleading

for an answer. She spoke loudly, as she would to Grannie Lee, mouthing the words out carefully so that if she was there, Maudie would hear.

Suddenly Kerry turned fearful eyes to the pegs by the door. She knew the answer before Maudie's head nodded. 'Aye, they's all gone, maid. They's all went long ago!'

Drained, Kerry stood up, easing her neck to a stretch, her arms lifeless, dripping by her sides. Before she left she pulled Maudie's shawl up over her head and picked up the scattered furniture.

Maudie's voice, quiet but far from mad, stopped her as she was about to go. 'Doan close the door behind yous, child. Let the wind blow in. Perhaps it can sweep the death from the corners of this house. I's tried. . . . I's tried wi' mops and feathers . . . but I's carnt find it. Let it in . . .'

Surprised, Kerry turned to object, but Maudie's face had closed again and she spat a gob of chewed tobacco that hissed on the hearth beside her.

Kerry hesitated. But she did as she was bid. She did not close the door.

Missy had gone. Missy had gone to the cellars. Missy could mingle and never be seen. That night it was Rosa who put Mamma to bed. This time there were no games. Mamma had ceased to care.

Mamma might have given up but Kerry hadn't. It was Kerry who stayed up all night, thinking how long and confusing nights were, they had no landmarks like days did. This most adult chore she took over from Mamma, willingly. She knelt on Feyther's sea-chest to pray, wrestling with God for the life of their men, and when her knees ached so she could kneel on them no longer she sat back on her heels and prayed on. When her back ached she prayed on the floor. 'Oh God, oh

God, doan let 'em die!' She felt herself dropping to sleep, and then she would open her eyes and clear the windows, trying to peer out through the darkness. God must listen! He must!

Once she ventured out, barefoot in the fierce moonlight, thinking that outside she might be closer to God, without the barrier of stone walls between her prayers. But had she gone out of the hearing of God by being so wilful and bossy, for having jealous thoughts about Rosa? She hated going to church. She gabbled the prayers, she felt great relief when Parson Fox started on, 'In the name of the Father . . .' Now she beseeched God to forgive her, and in spite of her sins to save those she loved.

Before dawn Kerry saw corpse-lights by the Spur, a blue glow in the water by the rock, and thought she heard the nightjar. She realised then that it was her birthday.

That night they all came home, Feyther, Sam, Rory, Gregor, Ned and Tristan. Every man came home and went to his bed at dawn. Kerry was numb. The relief was almost too great. Under Yelland's firm guidance no one had gone missing. No one had slipped off the edge or been taken by the sea.

But in the morning Mamma said, over and over, 'I's'll never forgive 'e.' And Kerry didn't ask who she meant in case she said Feyther.

Kerry made the same promise, but in secret. And she was sure who her adversary was. There was no doubt in her mind about it. It was John Yelland.

NINE

The seasons changed and changed again. Ten years old and out on the blue sea with Tristan, collecting lobster pots. A time of innocence . . . oh why didn't she realise it would be so fleeting, just a puffball cloud that lingered briefly overhead. With Tristan it was peaceful. Tristan understood.

Tristan rowed, seated on the thwart, while Kerry sat in the stern of the dinghy letting her fingers trail in the water. They clambered onto the rocks, their bare feet hardened to the black clusters of razor-edged mussels. They took their time. Together in the sunshine they watched the life that went on in the rock pools, sea anemones seductive in their endless search for plankton and prawn, trapped starfish hopelessly trying to pump themselves through the water to safety.

Together they gathered seaweed, invaluable for its nutritious and therapeutic uses in the village. From the high ledges above them sea birds watched with inquisitive eyes, heads held high on arrogant necks as if their business was surely the most important. They plumped their white bodies fatly over their eggs, proudly waiting.

Kerry wondered how Tristan could stay so kind and gentle when everyone knew what his life was like at home. He didn't complain to her. When she asked him he used to say, 'Why? Why spoil the day talkin' of things that cannot be changed.'

'But it sometimes helps to share things.' And Kerry felt small because she had spent the last hour complaining of Mamma and Feyther, and Rosa. He had listened,

nodded, continued with his tasks but said little. He
hadn't needed to. Just speaking of it had helped her.

'That's where we's different,' Tristan said. 'Yous
express youssell easily about things that matter to yous.
I's carn.'

Ned had never wanted a son who was not his own. He
had complied for Maudie's sake. His own sons were
dead. He had watched the last one wheeze from life
with pneumonia, had turned on his gouty leg, pulled
up the sheet and had softly closed the door. His wife
was mad, and he was a bitter, angry man. The walls
between the cottages were thin and often Kerry heard
Ned shouting abuse at The Boy while Maudie, she
guessed, would be sitting there rocking, chewing, staring with her curious, blank eyes.

''Tis none of our business,' Mamma said firmly after
they had sat in a wincing silence raising eyebrows at
one another when they heard the sounds of a particularly vicious beating through the wall. ''E's not one of
ours. We must leave well alone.' The inhabitants of
Porthclegga, while intimately concerned with each
other's business, nevertheless were almost patholog-
ically touchy when it came to interference.

But Kerry felt his pain. Kerry wept for him at night.
God knows how he was treated when there weren't
ears to hear, when there was just him and Ned on
fifteen feet of boat with only the sea and the sky for
witness.

Now Kerry said impulsively, ''E's unkind to yous. I
hate 'e, 'e should be killed!'

Tristan reached over and squeezed her hand, amused
by her vehemence. 'No, 'e's not unkind. It's just 'e's
way of protectin' 'essell from love. An' pain. 'E's legs
hurts 'e all the time now.'

''E's jealous, 'cos yous everythin' 'e can never be! An' I's carn bear yous to be unhappy.'

'I's not unhappy.' He let go her hand and looked seriously into her worried eyes. 'I's not, and doan yous go round wastin' yous time thinkin' I's am.'

'Well, if yous not 'tis only 'cos yous taught youssel' not to want what yous carn have.'

Tristan said softly, 'We's all got to do that, maiden.'

The way he spoke made Kerry want to cry, to put her arms round his thin shoulders and comfort him. But he didn't want that. He didn't want anyone's pity. She could understand that.

'Yous always sound so wise,' she told him tartly. 'I's doan ever want to be wise. Pain makes people wise. I's would rather stay stupid. Stupid people keep hopin' for the best. Wise people seem to know and accept that good things never happen. No, I's doan ever want to be wise.'

'I's doan want yous to be,' said Tristan, prising open a winkle with his knife and holding it out to her. She ate it. It tasted of grit.

The rings of grey the water left on the rock were climbing towards them as the tide came in. She watched Tristan, so vibrantly alive, with his blond hair curling round his face and neck. Tall and thin, tanned like all the fishermen, his white teeth dazzled against his dark skin. Was he a boy or was he a man? She wanted to know what he thought, how he felt. They were close, and yet she was saddened by the sudden realisation that because they were separate human beings she would never really know his true feelings. Kerry could seldom read Tristan's feeling from his face. She would only know what he wanted her to know. And sometimes she felt so closed from him.

The sea was filling the gully in the rocks behind

73

them, gurgling and splashing so the level rose smoothly up its sides – a great oblong bath.

'Let's swim,' he said, bending to pull his shirt over his head.

'No,' said Kerry quickly. 'I's doan want to.' For the truth was she couldn't swim, and this seemed to prove to her what she'd been thinking before . . . because she had known Tristan all her life and yet he didn't know this fact about her. Few fisherfolk could swim. They didn't see the sea as benefit from which pleasure could be taken. For them it was a provider, both enemy and friend, above all it was something to be conquered and respected. Swimming might have been seen as a touch too familiar between them and their mighty host.

Tristan, stripped naked, shot into the air and dived confidently into the gully, bobbed up with water streaming from his head. 'Come on, Kerry,' he called. 'Come on!'

She was amazed at his courage. She'd always known he was brave, but not as brave as that.

Kerry waded in, waist-deep, forcing a smile. The sun shone, the water was cool. She would have been happy to stay like that.

Tristan lay on his back and kicked along beside her. I have to swim, she said to herself. I must swim, or he'll think me a coward.

She crouched in the water and folded her hands as if she was saying her prayers. Above her the cliffs rose cold and terrible to touch a dizzying sky. Life was too small, too timid, and the towering cliffs urged her to do what she did. She threw herself forward and sank like a stone. She rose, gasping, to the surface, choking wildly, water in ears and nose and stomach. She struggled towards where she thought it would be shallow, her drenched eyes taking in the brilliance of the day and Tristan's glistening back, before sinking again.

74

She had no breath to call, but someone called, she heard someone scream, 'Tristan!' before the water closed over her head and she knew that she was drowning . . . drowning, that terrible, black soggy word that took so long to say. Would Tristan hear Missy? Please let him! Please! The picture of those leaning gravestones swam before her eyes, bubbled before her eyes with her own breath . . . *Drowned at sea* . . . and her name would be added, a small, insubstantial stone among the others on that inhospitable patch of ground. Small, insubstantial, like she was.

She felt strong arms under her, capable arms lifting her, and then she was lying flat on the rocks, naked as a jaybird, with Tristan leaning over her and saying, 'Kerry! Kerry! Why didn't you tell me you couldn't swim?'

She lay on one elbow coughing and spitting up sea-water while his hand thumped her forcefully between her shoulder blades. Anger sparked in his icy eyes. She shivered, not from the cold but from Tristan's hostility.

'Yous could have spoilt everythin'!' he said. 'They wouldn't let yous come with me any more if they heard about this.'

She looked at the little row of cottages that appeared so small and far away from here. 'They . . .' she began, and repeated herself, 'They . . .' She was very aware of 'their' terrible power over her. With one word of impatient disapproval 'they' could destroy her leaping hopes. 'Doan show off, Kerry.' 'Kerry, hold yous tongue.' When the boys were witty they were clapped and approved of. If they were clumsy and spilled something, Mamma wiped it up. The boys could steal cake and come away unashamed. If she did so it was different, she was made to feel sly and irresponsible. With one word 'they' could stop her being with Tristan in their strangely tyrannical and incalculable way.

Crimson-faced from shock and humiliation she turned her anger on Tristan. 'I's wanted to swim,' she gasped, spitting more water. 'I's felt so small down there under the sea. Helpless like a piece of driftin' straw. Mamma makes me feel that way, so does Feyther, so do the boys and so does Rosa! Yous never tell me how hopeless I's am, but I's thought yous might if yous knew I couldn't swim. I's never want to feel that way again. I's want to be in charge of my own life!'

Tristan smiled. When he smiled like that she felt there was a bright ring of light around her. 'But youm part of it,' he said. 'That cottage of yous, and the sea and the rocks, youm woven into them. Youm strong because yous belong to those people.'

'And why not yous then? 'Tis where yous grew up. Aren't yous part of it, too?'

'No,' he said, 'I's not part of anyone or anywhere.' His slanting eyelids fell across his eyes for a moment, hiding their brightness. He stared across at the Spur rock from where he had come. The outgoing fishing fleet tossed coins in the sea when they passed it, wishing for a safe return. The ocean floor, down there in the blackness, must be spangled with coins, she thought. Then he laughed, 'Yous gone purple,' he said.

And she realised she was naked. She covered herself quickly, inadequately with both hands. 'Fetch me my dress,' she said, taking her eyes away from his unfamiliar body. They had played together naked before. But this time it was different.

Taking his time, whistling while he did so, he pulled on his breeches, and rubbed his hair with his shirt before he dressed. Eventually she struggled into her clothes, embarrassment making her clumsy. She felt she was going to cry for the loss of something.

And they sat together in silence on the sun-warmed

rocks, wondering, separately, what had happened to make them so shy of each other. Unable, for the first time, to talk about it. Below them a wave crashed into the gully and was sucked back to sea with a sigh.

TEN

Six days later and she'd started to dream. She dreamed about Tristan, about growing up and about being free. The milk jug she carried was full and heavy. Kerry walked slowly, careful not to spill any. She liked milk. She'd heard that ladies bathed in it. She thought how smooth it would feel on her body, and you could lie in the tub and drink it at the same time. *Milk* . . . the word for it was just right, thick and cool and liquid.

She felt she must drink some and looked to see if anyone was watching. There was nobody but children playing hide and seek between the cottages and old Grannie Lee sitting out in her chair wrapped in grey shawls muttering querulously to herself. And she wouldn't see.

She raised the jug to her lips.

Mamma's shout made her jerk the jug and sent a wave of milk down her dress.

'Kerry Penhale, how dare yous! An' there's enough milk for all of us, is there, to allow yous to take extra for youssef with no thought for others in the family, p'ticularly the little ones! Get inside this house!'

Grannie Lee, excited by the drama, let out a series of piercing, bird-like shrieks that brought Lizzie flying from the house opposite. Grannie was her husband Davy's mother and she waited on her hand and foot. She had to. Grannie Lee was nigh on helpless.

Mamma snatched the milk jug, wrinkling up her nose in distaste where she saw the creamy surface was broken. 'That's nice,' she said. 'That's nice for all of us!'

'I's haven't dirtied the milk,' said Kerry. 'I's only took a sip. There's nothing wrong with it! Yous looking at it as if I's spoilt it!'

Mamma didn't answer. 'Get that table laid,' she ordered.

Rosa laughed, her eyes sly, and Mamma said, 'Doan laugh. 'Tis not funny. We'm must feel sorry for anyone with such a lack of self-control.' Rosa smugly picked up a piece of carrot she was chopping and popped it into her mouth.

Kerry bridled with resentment. She was shouted at as if she were a child, and in the next breath she was told not to behave like one. If she wasn't a child then what was she?

She swallowed so hard that it hurt her and turned to Mamma to say, 'I's wish I's didn't live in this house.' She muttered on, 'I's wish I's lived somewhere else.'

Mamma came towards her, her chin raised high, rubbing her hands vigorously on her apron. 'I's'll second that, my girl.' And she flung her next words scornfully over her shoulder to Rosa, 'We'm all be better off with her gone, wouldn't we's, Rosa?'

Now Mamma often talked like that. Kerry knew she didn't mean it and that in the next minute she would be asking what would she do without her, her second pair of hands . . . She was finding the cruellest thing to think of to say because she was angry.

But Mamma's words had brought a scarlet flush to Kerry's face. She was so like her mother she understood her inside out. They had an understanding, she and Mamma, from which all others were excluded. She knew that Mamma would be pained by saying the things she said. She knew that inside she would be crying and that she stood there now waiting, hoping for Kerry to say she was sorry so that she could throw her arms around her and pretend nothing had been said.

But Kerry had a temper, too, and felt she had been pushed too far this morning. So she stood staring at Mamma, unbending, unwilling to be the first to give in, refusing to turn round and lay the table. Let somebody else lay the table. Cassy was five, Cassy was old enough now.

She watched as a mixture of emotions crossed Mamma's face. They had both gone too far to withdraw. Rosa was in the room watching, and Cassy had stopped her game on the floor in order to sit up and follow the argument with her eyes, her curly head turning from one to the other. So Mamma had her pride and dignity to protect as well as her eldest daughter to subdue.

'Are yous goin' to lay that table or are yous just goin' to stand there all day gawpin' at me with that silly look on yous face?'

There was a wheedle amongst the words. Almost a touch of humour. A way out, for Kerry, if only she would take it. It had not been an order, more of a suggestion.

She thought of how bravely she had flung herself into that gully determined to face the unknown. She might be swimming now, in some subterranean cavern; the tension rolled over her, cloying and thick as water closing over her head. 'No, Mamma. I's is not.'

And Mamma smiled and Kerry knew it was a cry of pain when she said, 'Then yous can stop yer little games wi' that one next door, youm too old now to be gallivantin' about like an urchin, rushin' yer chores and slidin' out of the work to be with 'e. 'Tis almost time yous was out of here, my girl, wi' a man of yer own to tend to, but yous can be sure, when that blessed

80

time comes, 'twill not be with the likes of 'e, a man wi' no name!'

Mamma's head seemed little and shrewish when it poked forwards on her body like that.

'Mamma! Yous carn stop me . . .'

Mamma's arm shot out and sent Kerry reeling across the room. She grabbed at the table and missed, unbalanced and fell with a mighty crash against great-grandfather's sea-chest under the window. Rosa's arm flew to her mouth and she filled it with a tense fist. Cassy began to cry. Immediately Kerry crawled across the floor, trying to put a smile on her face, to comfort the child.

She narrowed her eyes to look up at Mamma. But she had turned away and taken up her usual position of defeat, straight-backed and stiff-necked before the fire.

The silence in the room was deafening. Kerry pulled Cassy on her knee and rocked her, saying, 'There, there,' while inside she raged and fumed against her mother who had broken the pact they had established between them.

Mamma started to lay the table loudly.

Rosa said, ingratiatingly, "Tis all right, Mamma, I's'll do it.'

'There's no need, there's no need,' said Mamma in martyred tones, crossing to the cupboard and back, to the cupboard and back, an unnecessary number of times. Every item was slammed down hard. Suddenly Kerry saw Mamma as she might see herself . . . years of trivial activity piling up behind her like the snow of some endless winter. She saw Mamma's raw little hands, and Kerry knew that she did not want Mamma's life. No wonder Mamma was touchy. At the same time as she hated her Kerry loved her. The two

81

emotions mixed inside her causing a turmoil of confusion. The lump in her throat swelled so she thought it would choke her. She didn't know what was happening to her family lately, to her mother. They used to laugh a lot, yes, yes, she could remember how they used to laugh. But lately there had been a dearth of good feeling in this house. She must talk to Missy about it.

And then Mamma said icily, 'Kerry, youm in my way. Get off the floor an' go to yer bed.'

She brushed her hair, she folded her clothes, she washed her face in the basin, and then Kerry lay waiting for Mamma to come and talk to her, to make things right between them.

She planned what she was going to say. She was going to ask for a little respect and for time of her own. Time given to her on a regular basis so she didn't always have to steal it, always feel guilty when she got away from the house, away from the chores and the children. She would apologise to Mamma but she would be firm with her requests. I'm not being unreasonable, she told herself. I'm not asking for the world.

Somewhere in the dusk a nightjar called from its proper bed in the heather, touching on feelings so deep she could never express them. One by one the children came to bed, first Mabs, then Cassy, then Rosa, sullen and not speaking. Kerry lay a little longer before she realised Mamma was not coming. She felt shivery blue inside, isolated by grief.

She lay awake for what seemed hours, much later than she normally did. She heard the boys come to bed. Mamma and Feyther slept directly beneath the attic. She decided to kneel on the floor and listen, to find out exactly what Mamma told him. Maybe in this way she could gain some insight into how Mamma was feeling, would know how to approach her tomorrow. Words could be heard from the bed . . . the floor was not that thick . . . but they were muffled and indistinct and it was important that Kerry know precisely what was said.

By now the candle had burnt right away. Softly, so not to wake the others, Kerry pushed back the covers and slid out of bed. She crept across the floor to the window where there was white phosphorescence from the sea, and knelt down, crouched as if in prayer.

She heard Feyther's footsteps across his bedroom floor. Heard the heavy crump of the mattress as he lay down and made himself comfortable. Then Mamma, the footsteps lighter, quicker, and Feyther saying to her, 'Blow the candle out, Cath.'

What she heard after that made her freeze like a statue, unable to move or change her position, so rigid was she in her horror.

'Leave me be, Jake, yous stink of the drink. Turn over and go to sleep.' Mamma's voice was a broken whisper. Feyther's was a gruff growl.

'Come on now maid, yous always turnin' away.'

'I's had a bad day, what with Kerry bein' troublesome an' the widow on the borrow again.'

'An' I's had a bleedin' bugger of a day but I's doan bring it home to yous.'

'Oh, doan yous? That's the first I's heard of it! Yous bring it home nightly with yer bleary eyes an' yer stupid manner.'

'What are yous sayin' to me now? Nag, nag, nag, that's all I's bloody well hears.'

'I's sayin' to yous, Jake, that yous didn't always behave like this. I's saying that yous changed an' I's

carn love the man with the bottle in 'e's pocket and
the leer in 'e's eyes . . .'

'Yous'll love the man yous married damnit or yous'll
be goin' against yer God.'

'My God! My God! Had yous nothin' to do with the
vows we made then, Jake?'

'There's nothin' in the vows 'bout a man not takin'
a drink when he wants one.'

'Jake, I's asked yous, leave me be, for the love of
God!'

'God, God damn him! Why does 'e have to be with
us in our bed?'

'Yous brought 'e up! Yous painin' me, Jake, I's asked
yous not to . . . doan!'

And then there was a series of cries and pleadings,
the curses and grunts from her father. There was a wet
sound of fist on flesh, a cry, a stifled murmur. She
wanted to pound on the ceiling and scream, 'Feyther!
Stop! Stop!' But how could she do that? And after it
was over came the quiet sobbing, the gentle snores of
her father. Kerry pressed her hands to her ears but it
did no good. The sounds came through just the same.

It was Missy who tried to comfort her that night.

And in the morning that forced humour, that pretence
of cheerfulness. How long had this been going on?
Kerry couldn't guess.

'All done then . . . that's a nice surprise!' Mamma
nodded approval at the spotless kitchen and wiped her
hands on her apron.

'I's got up early Mamma to give yous a rest, to make
up for yesterday.' Kerry didn't care if she lost face, if
she sounded a fool before Rosa. Rosa was glum-faced,
deprived of an interesting morning.

'Did yous sleep well?' That was Gregor, innocent,

fresh-faced Gregor, filling his face with porridge. Suddenly, violently, Kerry wished to be him.

'Yes, very well. I's always do. The sleep of the just,' said Mamma.

Kerry couldn't bring herself to look at Feyther. What kind of man was he, that he could do what he did last night? And here he was, pretending to everybody, demanding respect and lording it over the house when he was nothing better than a beast, and a wild one at that. Like the great bull at Fensome's, with its fiery red eye and its wicked great horns. But that was chained with a ring through its nose. Chaining would be too good for Feyther. The bull knew no better. Feyther did.

'Kerry, yous look pale. Has yous got a headache?' This was Mamma, trying to make up in her own way for Kerry's submission. Normally she had no time for illness of any kind, and was markedly short with anyone who complained of it.

'No, no headache, just a little tired that's all.'

''Tis just as well. There's the wash to be got out this mornin'.'

Kerry smiled at Mamma. Mamma smiled back. Was that a bruise on the top of her arm? It was no good asking. She'd say she'd got it shifting beds or pulling out the mangle. Kerry felt sick. It should have been back to how it always was but there was a great pretence between them.

It was this feeling of helplessness that brought Kerry closest to panic. For if Mamma, a woman so wise and powerful, couldn't control her own life, then how, dear God, could she?

ELEVEN

They did bowsenn Maudie Carne, on a day when the sky was lapped with clouds like the scales of a giant fish. They walked in a line up the cliff-path, formal and stiff in their Sunday best as if they were going to a funeral. But the corpse that reeled at the head of the procession strapped to a mule was alive . . . too alive.

After years and years her behaviour could no longer be tolerated. Tristan was older now, a man at thirteen, and Maudie turned from him and her husband despite hours of gentle coaxing and encouragement from them, and from friends and neighbours. She neither cleaned the house nor put food on the table, and "Tis years since she's been a wife to me, proper-like,' said Ned.

So they took her to Kenack pool and ducked her as a lunatic while Ned stood by, 'real pathetic' they said, wringing his giant hands and watching, praying to a God he'd always dismissed for the return of his wife's mind.

Kerry went because Tristan went, and Tristan went because Ned made him. She felt that they trekked towards an underworld. A bald tree on a nearby hill formed a mournful signpost. They turned a corner and there was the pool, a barren place fringed by rocks and furze. Birds paddling at the water's edge fled as the group plodded nearer.

Limpid and sluggish on a blue summer day, this morning in drizzle the surface was a dead slate grey, ominous and dreary. Kenack pool, and the mournful sound of the wind in the reeds, the wavelets splashing the shore, spoke of an older lore, of evil and times past.

She whispered, 'Missy,' so no one saw her lips move. There was no answer. Missy was not here today.

To a tired old jetty that toppled into the pool was attached a ring and a rusty chain. Ned, sullen, morose and limping badly, seemed bemused, uncertain what to do and kept lifting his arm and dropping it again as if, on some level, he wanted to put a stop to the ceremony.

Kerry looked for Tristan and saw him, head bent, at the back of the little group. She went to stand beside him. She could do no more than put her hand in his, but when he took it his hand felt boneless and chilled. He acted as if she wasn't there, living and warm beside him. She looked at his face and noticed how thin it had grown, the bones of his cheeks and jaw pulled tight against the dark skin.

''Twill be over soon,' she said. ''Tis only a lot of nonsense anyhow, that's all. There's no harm meant by it . . . no bad meaning.'

'Meaning! There is no such thing as meaning! Meanings are explained by words an' look how twisted they are! I's told 'e not to. I's didn't want this! There's other ways . . . not this one . . . not this one . . .'

'Maybe it'll help. Maybe Maudie will be made better and able to enjoy life again.'

'Life is a force like the wind and the sea. 'Tis not there to be enjoyed or not enjoyed. It merely exists.' And he lifted his head and gave her a look of such withering contempt that she was silenced and could only stand by him willing it to be over for his sake as well as for Maudie's.

When they let her off the mule Maudie walked cautiously, like a top-heavy gull on ice. They had called in a charmer from Troon Head to carry out the ritual. His name was Tregony. Nausea rose and lapped bitter fluid at Kerry's throat. There was something evil about the man – and something evil was happening here. She held her breath and pressed her shawl to her mouth as Tregony caught hold of Maudie and clamped the rusty collar round her neck. A brawny, tree trunk of a man with red hairs on his arms as thick as those in his eyebrows, he hauled the sick woman to stand briefly with him on the jetty before he pushed her backwards into the water where she rose with a splutter and a startled look in her eyes.

And these, these were her people! Kerry looked about her guiltily. It was from a background of this and ceremonies like these that she came! From the little crowd there issued a moan not unlike the wind in the reeds. Tregony pulled Maudie in on the chain as if she were a dog. And when, half-hanged and heavy with slopping water, Maudie tried to find her feet Tregony slackened the chain again and again she went under.

'She cannot endure,' whispered Kerry.

'Pray God she does not,' returned Tristan.

Maudie looked weak and ill. She'd lost what strength she had. But apart from her bad colour – her swollen hand and ankles were puffy like dough – and her blotched skin she seemed to be in no particular pain and there was no look in her eyes, save for slight surprise, to show that she knew what was going on. The ritual was repeated four, five, six times. Kerry shivered and closed her eyes again but she couldn't blot out the sound of rushing water and the awful clanking of the rusty chain. Dear Lord, she thought, where is Parson Fox? If he knew of this he would shout to the Heavens for retribution.

And when it was over the women of the village wrapped

Maudie in blankets and set her on the mule and everyone retraced their footsteps across the rain-soaked countryside and back down the path to Porthclegga. Ned held back to put a sixpence in Tregony's hand, the same amount that was paid to the crow-scarers to keep jackdaws and rooks from the sapling corn.

Fury sustained Kerry as she walked home alone. She didn't stop in the kitchen but climbed the stairs to her attic room. The scent on the sheets, just washed, was of lavender. She flung herself on her bed with a pounding heart and a dry mouth.

'Missy,' she called in desperation. 'Oh Missy . . . some evil has been begun.'

Missy did not answer. But from the sea came the unearthly call of the nightjar. It wasn't dusk, and there was no clump of gorse on the Spur rock where the sound came from. No growth, no greenness in which the secretive bird could have hidden at all.

TWELVE

Later in the day Ned Carne came out of his house to shoo away cat-calling children.

'Clear off, clear off!' he shouted. His words sounded like '*Caw! Caw!*' – harsh cries of suspicion and anxiety. His face was red and sweating and his large bony nose looked curved and wicked in his anger.

Kerry stirred from her bed and watched from the window.

She was pleased to see he'd caught somebody, a black-eyed boy, one of the Pengellys, with shocked hair sticking straight up from a head as narrow as a parsnip. The boy wriggled and squirmed and then stood still, paling.

'Got 'e, miserable grubber!'

'Doan 'it I's Mister Carne, doan 'it I's!'

Ned held the boy by the thin bone in his upper arm. He gazed at him with blue-green eyes cold as water running under ice, as if to numb his captive's brain with his motionless stare of hatred.

'Well, and why not, midear? Why shouldn't I's hit 'e for comin' round caterwaulin' an' pesterin' an' being so bliddy insensitive to make mock of a man's poorly wife? That's 'xactly what yous was doin', woan it? 'Xactly!'

Ned glared round, ready to take them all on, but of the rest of the gang there was no sign.

'Or hold a minute . . . hold a minute . . . could it be yous at my door for other purposes this afternoon? Lookin' for a roof over yous head maybe, lookin' for a home . . . so yous said to youssel, "I's know what I's'll do. I's'll go to Ned Carne's for I's knows 'e'll take me in. 'E takes in waifs an' strays as if 'e's nothin' better to do with 'is time and money. 'E takes in waifs an' strays at the drop of an 'at, 'e do." That's what yous thought to youssell, didn't 'e? *Didn't 'e?*'

Ned lowered his great head into an exaggerated question. So low did he take it that he was down and looking up at the boy from underneath.

'No, Mister Carne. I's swear to 'e. I's swear! I's would rather be dead than take up lodgin's with 'e!'

'Ah!' As if that was exactly what he wanted to hear, Ned let him go, rubbing fingers and thumb together on the end of a high-held triumphant hand as if he had relinquished something nasty.

'Well, doan let me hear yous . . . any of yous . . .' he spun round crouched, nimble, looking like a wrestler ready for a second bout, and shamed but mischievous faces peeped out to watch him from behind walls and from under barrels . . . 'doan let I's hear or see any of 'e again . . . youm buggers!' He turned and shouted towards his own cottage.

'An' while I's clearin' my house of vermin there's yous to be dealt with, Mister, oh aye, yous I's talking to, carn yous hear I's in there?'

Tristan was so tall he had to stoop to get through the door now. He stepped out onto the shaly ground and put an enquiring finger to his chest.

'Me?'

'Yer cheeky varmint. There's no one else I's can see who I's might be addressin'! Yes, yous! Bad luck has haunted my house since yous came! Bad luck . . .'e's flung 'isself at the walls and lapped ' isself through the floorboards an' I's 'ad it up to 'ere, see! Up to 'ere!' Ned spat on the ground to give support to his words. With his hands he encircled his head.

Kerry came down from her bedroom and hesitated

by her own front door. Mamma frowned, but Kerry glowered back at her and raised a warning finger to her lips.

'Doan get involved,' Mamma mouthed. 'Yous'll make it worse. The man is just upset after such a morning . . . naturally.'

Kerry shook her head angrily. 'Let me be, Mamma!'

Mamma shrugged and continued to listen as, quite openly and provocatively, Ned railed on at Tristan. Relentlessly the recriminations and curses flew, with Tristan answering now and then in the flat, steady tone Kerry knew so well. His face would be full of sulky contempt.

Kerry stepped outside, holding her breath in case the door squeaked. Ned was grey-faced now; he swung his big, baleful head in remorseless accusation and tore into Tristan with a gaze so full of pure loathing he might have wanted to destroy him completely.

'If thine eye offend thee, pluck it out.' Ned was quoting Parson Fox for the first time in his life.

'What is it yous want from me, Ned?'

'Want from yous? Want from yous? What could I's ever want from yous?'

'Yous want somethin' now, or yous wouldn't be talkin' to me like this, out here, in front of anybody's gaze.'

'If thine eye offend thee . . .'

'Yous want me to leave?'

'Aye. I's wants yous to leave.'

'An' Mother?'

'Mother woan know whether yous gone or no. She'm past all that now.'

'Then there's no reason for me to stay.' Kerry felt pain like a dull blow to her heart. His voice was like a bitter wind. 'There was never a reason for me to be here, Ned.'

'That's gratitude for 'e!' Leather slithered round Ned's waist like a snake. His belt was supple and curved as he lifted it high and cracked it in the air.

Tristan stepped backwards, his face thin and wary. Ned broke into a smile, mean and cruel.

'Mother . . .' Tristan said again, his eyes moving anxiously away from Ned and up to the bedroom window.

'Yous'll not take shelter under those petticoats again. Yous'll take what's yours like a man.'

'An' youm a man are yous, Ned?'

Kerry quailed in her hiding place not twelve feet away. She willed Tristan to back down, to go away and hide somewhere until Ned was calm again. But Tristan, flushed, skipped to one side as the belt came down to cut a ribbon of spurting gravel beside him but otherwise held his ground.

'More of a man 'n yous'll ever be with yous girly ways and yous flowery words.' Ned moved towards Tristan, treading softly for so large a man, balanced and ready for the next cutting stroke. But Tristan had the speed and the arena was large; there were no confined spaces where Ned could trap his victim against a wall or swing a door closed against him.

'Out! Out!' roared Ned, swinging the belt over his head, his eyes puffy with anger.

A nervous group of onlookers had collected before the house – a mixture of wide-eyed women and curious men. The mocking children laid low in their corners. Kerry came out of the doorway to join them.

She could not be entirely on Tristan's side. Her heart felt sore for Ned who, in his uncontrolled anger, seemed more unhappy and vulnerable than she had ever seen him before, like a tormented bear. She knew this morning's terrible ritual at Kenack pool had almost destroyed him. If only he could be made to calm down and wait awhile before saying and doing something Kerry believed he would regret.

But there was no love lost between Ned and Tristan. Tristan so fair this morning that his long locks were almost white in the light. Ned, opposite him, dark and stocky, his gouty leg held straighter than the other one. Slowly Kerry realised how much Ned hated The Boy.

'If yous'll just stand aside I's'll get my things an' go. While yous standin' there before the doorway I's can do nothin' but wait an' annoy yous further.'

'Bugger yous highfalutin' reasonable ways. That's just it, isn't it? Yous always thought of me as nothin' . . . I's seen 'e . . . I's seen yer eyes when yous look at me . . . same look as is in 'em now. Who do yous think youm be, to be lookin' at I's like that? Better 'n all of us, aren't 'e?' Ned tried to include the crowd by looking round and bringing them into the fray with his arms. 'Look at 'e! Will yous look at 'e! Who do 'e think 'e is, I's ask 'e?'

'If yous just stand aside . . .'

'If yous just stand aside . . .' Ned mimicked The Boy, making his head wobble sillily. 'I's'll stand aside by God an' if yous not down here with yous bundle in five minutes I's'll be up there after 'e, yous see if I's not!'

Warily Tristan passed him and disappeared into the indoor gloom. The crowd stayed, uneasy, turning to look at each other and then back at Ned who began to look foolish standing there silent with his belt in his hand.

'I's ask 'e,' he said every now and again. But no one replied. Sometimes he looked up at the window.

Kerry, her heart in her mouth, stepped forward. 'Ned . . .' she began. He glared at her in anger, in dumb disbelief. She had not had time to rehearse what she was going to say. She searched for the right words

94

but nothing magic came. 'Tristan . . .'e doan mean to make yous feel small. 'E be grateful to yous for all yous has done for 'e. 'E looks up to yous for yous skill in the boat . . . I's knows 'e do. Doan send 'e away, I's beg yous. Give 'e another chance, please . . . for Maudie's sake!'

Ned shifted his fighting stance uneasily. He wasn't even too sure who she was. Just one of the children they'd managed to rear next door . . . one of the children he couldn't have. And what was she saying? Was he supposed to bend and listen to this mop-headed girlchild with the brilliant, tear-filled eyes? His forehead creased. He looked at the window. 'Come on, let's 'ave 'e boy!' he shouted. She heard the harsh rasp of his breath through his nostrils. She saw the sharp clench of his hand. The smell of his fury was overwhelming. Beside him Kerry felt useless and small.

'Ned!' She tried again, but this time he would have none of it.

'Get along to yous Mamma,' he deigned to say. But his eyes were hard and brimmed with words he hadn't yet spoken.

'Kerry! Have yous gone crazy? Kerry, come away!' Mamma stepped forward, put a hand on Kerry's shoulder.

'Mamma, how can I's? 'E's making Tristan go away.'

'Kerry! Yous making a fool of yousself. This is between Ned an' Tristan, midear, nothin' to do with yous.'

'It is to do with me, Mamma. Tristan carn go away.'

'Tristan must do what Ned tells 'e.' Mamma was keeping calm because the neighbours were there. If they had not been, she would have lost her patience and shaken her daughter to bring her to her senses.

'Mamma!' Was Mamma, then, not going to do anything? Were they all going to stand back and accept what was happening? Black, black, black. The world was going black . . . she felt the agony of despair as slowly Kerry realised that this was really happening. Ned Carne was not threatening, he meant every word he said. Tristan was going . . . Tristan would no longer be there. The concept was too enormous to contemplate. But where would he go? What would he do? He was thirteen years old, with no more experience of life away from Porthclegga than she had.

He was away up the cliff, gone out by the back door by the time Kerry saw him. She freed herself from Mamma's grip and fled from the dispersing crowd, scrambling and climbing up the slippery pathway.

'*Tristan! Tristan!*' Her eyes were fixed blindly on the disappearing figure with the bundle on its back. A stitch stabbed her side like a splitting knife. Frantically she scrambled, hating her body for holding her back. She remembered running like this in dreams.

She was nearly at the top. Someone was running behind her . . . crying like she was. It must be Missy. But she had no time to turn and see. She stopped. She heard a voice. It came to her over the thudding of her own heart, through the red mist that blinded her eyes.

'Kerry!'

She looked up to the top of the cliff. Tristan was standing there, his hands at his mouth, calling down, using the echoes they had played with in their games.

'Tristan! Wait!' She was not in the right place. The sound of the sea took her voice away.

'Kerry! I's comin' back!'

'Tristan!' It was no use. He wouldn't be able to hear her. 'Wait! Tristan, wait for me!' she sobbed as she clambered on, pushing herself beyond endurance, afraid of the note she heard in her voice.

'Kerry, I's comin' back!'

She paused again before carrying grimly on. He was still there, then. She still had time.

She reached the top. The smell of lavender was so thick it was sickening. She went to what they had called their bower of gorse. It was empty. But the grass inside their hidey hole was flattened from all the hours they had spent there.

Her throat was so dry she could no longer swallow. She let her arms hang forward as she bent to draw in breath. *Oh why, Tristan, why didn't you wait?* She scanned the misty countryside. Nothing moved. She breathed in and out, letting her breath shudder from her body. She shivered as the heat left her and she realised it was cold.

Missy, Missy, what shall I do without him? She sat in the bower alone. She wiped the sweat from her eyes. She stared down at her village, at her cove, at her sea. Then something happened. A tendril of mist hung on the Spur rock, a silver veil for a bridal gown . . . to Kerry it was her childhood. And as the breeze took it, it drifted across the bay and out to the open sea, vanishing slowly into the remote distance.

THIRTEEN

These days Mamma always looked tired. She didn't seem to have enough skin to pull over her mouth unless she was cross, and then her lips came over her teeth puckered like a pasty.

Kerry had to use the rags now, the same old rags they had used for nappies when the babies were small. She was glad of it because Rosa had become a woman a whole year before her and Kerry had begun to think there was something wrong.

'Shock will do it,' Lizzie Lee had proclaimed when Mamma had asked her . . . been forced to ask her by an anxious Kerry while Rosa stood with her arms folded, smiling. ''Tis probably shock over the loss of The Boy. That took her hard if I's can remember.'

'But she's only a child herself . . . children doan feel deep like that.' But Mamma paused to think of the weeks Kerry had lain in bed staring up at nothing, looking like death with her cheeks fallen in and her eyes sunk back. Mamma had put that down to exhaustion, because for a week before that the maid had not stopped working.

Lizzie Lee had rolled her eyes knowingly. 'Children are not children as long as we were, Cath,' she said. 'That maid of yours might be just twelve but she's wise for her years, midear.'

'Wise in one way, backward in another.' And Mamma looked at Kerry and tutted. Her daughter was small and slight for her age, and growing pretty in a pixyish sort of way. Her eyes were so dark they were opal, which went well with her jet black hair. But she

98

was quick and sprightly, sexless as a leaf, the opposite to her sister's soft, slow voluptuousness. They had always been different like this, right from the time they were tiny. And Cassy, poor Cassy took after Feyther in her stolid ten-year-old way; it was early days to see which way Mabs, at seven, would grow.

Three of her sons were now at sea with Feyther with only Jody, aged nine, to follow. Will Trelliss had mentioned about an apprentice, and Cath would have liked . . . well, wide-eyed Jody, the cuddly one, was rather special . . .

For a long time after Tristan's banishment Kerry had spent her time looking for him . . . thinking he would come back and just be there again as he always had been. She couldn't accustom herself to life without him.

She even went to the tavern in her desperation, that curious man-place that smelt of smoke and to which no woman ever went. It was the only place where she hadn't looked.

She pushed open the door and went inside. She saw the colour leave her father's face as he recognised his daughter, her loose hair falling round her shoulders and down her back like a rippling black shawl, peering anxiously from man to man. He'd been staring into his mug, twiddling the handle, and on his face had been that cold, closed look he sometimes wore at home.

Jessop, looking as if he couldn't be bothered to stand up straight so busy was he, came bowing across the floor with a jug in his hand. But Feyther was already on his feet . . . 'What's this then, maid? Has something happened at home?'

'No, Feyther. I's just lookin' for Tristan!'

'What?'

'I's lookin' for Tristan.'

Jessop's eyes twinkled as he turned back to Feyther. 'Yous maid 'ere be lovesick, Jake midear.'

By now all eyes were on her. Some of the men started to cheer. She pulled her shawl across her chest and tugged her skirts around her bare legs, blushing. Her clothes seemed inadequate for modesty.

Kerry sobbed under her breath as she turned to leave but a soft voice stopped her. 'No, maiden. Doan go! Now youm here yous must have a drink wi' John Yelland. I's remember 'e. Yous refused me once before, yous'll not refuse me again now, surely?'

'Get home!' Feyther's voice boomed across the room and Kerry automatically twirled round to escape but not quickly enough.

John Yelland's body was between her and the door. He stood with his arms against the frame, his long legs crossed, looking down at her with speculative interest and amusement.

Feyther was up and moving unsteadily towards them. 'She'm only a little maid, John, let her go.'

'She'm old enough that she can come searchin' in here for some man.'

'No man, no,' said Feyther, wiping his face with his hand. 'The Boy. She'm lookin' for her playmate. Wait until her mamma gets hold of her.'

'Well, maybe we woan tell Mamma, Jake, eh?' Yelland brought his mug down to Kerry's lips, pushing her back into the room as she retreated from the nauseous smell of it. 'Take it, maid, take it, and then yous woan care what yer Mamma says to 'e later.'

There was a roar of laughter from the corners of the room. Kerry lifted her eyes in dismay and stared at the revellers. Her eyes picked them out from the corners as slowly she recognised them. Men fathers like her own father was, fathers to her neighbours, to Hannah and Jeanie and Mary and Kate. Then why were they

laughing at her like this? Why did they have that look
in their eyes?

John Yelland had her trapped at the bar, twisting
between the wet wooden surface and his own lowered
chest. He came with his finger towards her, he pushed
it between her lips. 'That's it, that's it, open yous
mouth for Dadda. I's got some ripe milk for 'e here.'
Kerry, wincing, closed her eyes as she tasted and felt
the hot rumfire on his finger.

'Leave her be, John.'

Feyther was not a small man. He might have grown
smaller lately, might seem to take less space at the
table but in here, planted as he was in the middle of
the room, his grizzled head low and challenging, he
was big, every bit as big as Yelland and twice as broad.
The force behind his voice had silenced the titterers.
All that could be heard now was the washing of the
waves in the cellars beneath, and the tapping of John
Yelland's boot on the leg he had forced between Kerry's
to pin her there.

John Yelland did not back down but he changed his
tactics. 'Jake! Jake! Calm down, mister! I's only funnin'
wi 'er. I's not yet reduced to takin' my fun with babes!
Now who be yous looking for, maiden? Perhaps I's can
help 'e. I's know everyone in these parts.'

The laughter rose again uneasily from the corners.
The tension had gone from the air. But they were never
quite sure of Yelland, and when Jake Penhale's temper
as roused . . . The moment could have been nasty.

She didn't want to say Tristan's name. She didn't
want this man's ears to hear it. She shrank timidly into
herself, trying to prevent the tears from coming to her
eyes. She stayed silent, forced to stare foolishly straight
in his face.

'Speak up maid! Speak up! Tell me the swain's name!'

If she wanted to get away she had no option. 'Tristan Carne, Sir.'

John Yelland slapped his thighs. His flaxen hair curled round and stuck to the sweat on his face. His teeth when he smiled were sharp and even. Kerry noticed that his skin was flawless. This man had neither wrinkle nor scar, no laughlines, no marks of grief, either. His face was smooth, fluid like the body he thrust so cruelly against her. 'Tristan Carne, the madwoman's boy? 'E left months ago, didn't 'e?' He asked his companions with a pretence of seriousness which did nothing but mock her.

''Tis no good yous trailin' around after a young boy like that with nothin' but his wits to keep him alive.' He let her go in order to turn and smile at the company. He let her go on purpose, Kerry knew that, for his parting words sent all colour from her cheeks, choked her with humiliation. They were not the words he turned and said for everyone to hear. No, they were the words she wrapped up in shame and took home with her.

His words to the crowd were, 'Yous feyther wouldn't want that, would 'e, Jake? No! Youm must look for a man to take care of 'e. Someone who knows how to handle the sort of contrary young maid who would come to a tavern in her eagerness to find a man!'

At this he slapped his thighs again and roared with laughter. His eyes, she saw, were alight and almost silver in their colourlessness. She moved to see if she could without his noticing. She could, for he was too taken up now with his own bawdy humour and the reactions he was getting from his audience. He had said what he wanted to say, in private, to her.

102

Holding her breath, wishing for invisibility, Kerry slunk from the room, slipping on the straw underfoot. The brightness and the sharpness of the air outside that dark place blinded and almost winded her.

But it winded her nothing like the beating she got from Feyther when he got home that night . . . a beating even Mamma pleaded with him to stop. 'For yous'll hurt her Jake . . . yous'll hurt the maid.'

'Nothin' like 'e will if 'e gets his hands on her,' said Feyther, bringing the belt across her back once again.

Kerry didn't hear her cries, or the lash of the belt as it came down again and again. No, all she heard were the words of John Yelland, the words he had said under his breath before he let her go. '*I's shall be the first to have 'e maid, the first to ave 'e. Now yous remember what Yelland has told 'e!*'

FOURTEEN

The years went by and gradually she found herself searching no longer. When she went to sit in the bower of gorse she went alone, or with Missy, not expecting Tristan to be there.

But not a day went by when she didn't think of him. When she didn't remember something they had done together or something he had said.

'I's want to go and find him, Missy,' she said. Hot tears started to her eyes. She turned and stared at the sea, at a seagull that swooped and vanished and swooped again.

'I know, sweetheart, I know.'

'I's have the courage, Missy, it isn't that. 'Tis just that I's knows I's could search all my life and never come near.'

'Kerry,' Missy took her hand and put it into her own cold one. 'You have to wait for him here. He'll come back. He said he'd come back!'

'But how do we know that, Missy? How do we know for sure?'

Missy hooked her pale hair behind her ears. 'Use your reason, sweetheart. This is where he belongs.'

''E told me he didn't. 'E told me 'e didn't belong anywhere.'

'But when he is a man he'll know different.'

Kerry moved her hand. Cold ice crept through her veins. She could not smile although she knew that Missy was waiting for her to do so. ''E couldn't even wait to say goodbye.'

'He knew how cruel that would be.'

'Crueller not to say it!'

'You must have hope.'

'I's carn!' And she was angry with Missy for expecting too much from her.

Feyther came home and flung a paper down on the table.

'What's that?' asked Mamma, always anxious now to see what mood Feyther would be in when he finally reached home.

'Plans,' said Feyther. 'Drawings!'

'Well, get them out of the way if yous want yous food,' scolded Mamma. 'Drawings and plans are of no use to me.'

'They will be of use to yer sons yous small-minded old cow.' And no one took any notice because this was how Feyther and Mamma had taken to talking these days.

'Move them away, Jake. I's need room for the halibut stew.'

'Halibut stew! Halibut stew! Yous whole life is taken with halibut stew!' And Feyther made a song of it, and the family fell silent and let him sing it in his drunken way because afterwards he might agree to be quiet.

He made a point of laying out the papers on the table in such a way that there was no room for anyone's trencher. Mamma put on her patient voice, wiped her hands and walked over. 'An' whose drawings are these?' she said, in the way she might speak to Jody.

'Will Trelliss did them proper for me. I's paid 'e.'

'Huh! Yous paid 'e! You's paid 'e, big man! An' wi' what money did yous pay 'e?'

Feyther screwed up his red eyes and stared hard at Mamma. 'Wi' the money I's earn! Wi' my own hard-earned money . . . that's how I's paid 'e.'

Mamma gave her pasty-look and said, 'Well, Will

Trelliss 'e should know better. An' did yous ask 'e about Jody?'

Feyther had forgotten about Jody. Guiltily he shouted louder as he said, 'I's could have called it men's business. I's need not have included yous!'

'But yous have now, Jake, because the papers are there before yous on the table.'

Feyther bowed his head over them, swept his hands across them and flattened them out for Mamma to see.

'It looks like a boat,' said Mamma, humouring him while she moved the spoons from underneath.

'Leave fidgeting woman and look! That's no ordinary boat! That's a specially designed boat that me and Sam and Rory are going to build together.'

'Get away mister . . . when have yous time to build a boat? An' where is the money for that kind of thing? We's can only just eat as it is!'

'Will yous listen to me!' Feyther's face was beetroot red. 'This is the result of a whole month's work . . . an' plannin' an' schemin' . . .'

'Oh aye, down at Jessop's. That's a fine, upright place for plannin' an' schemin' . . .'

'Will yous shut up woman and listen!' Feyther passed wind, long and loud and noxiously. Mamma turned away and walked back to the fire.

'Yous tell me about yous boat, Jake, in the mornin', when the roar of the devil has passed out of yous!'

'The roar of the devil yous mazed bitch! The roar of the devil! That is the roar of an empty stomach and there'll be more empty stomachs offendin' yous dainty senses with their stinkin' gases if we's doan think on and get ourselves organised for the boys to come on . . .'

'The boys are doin' real fine as they are. If Jody gets wi' Will that'll be a steady income not dependent on the fishin' . . .'

'Hold yous tongue and listen to me!'

Feyther farted again, and Mamma, almost in tears, said, 'How can I's listen when above the words comes the likes of that! I's never thought to see the day when in my kitchen . . .'

'Bring on the halibut stew!' Father shouted drunkenly. ''Tis all been decided, anyway.'

For the first time Feyther had Mamma's attention. 'Decided? How can a thing like that be decided?'

'I's have worked it out . . . me an' Yelland has worked it out.'

'Yelland?' Mamma stiffened.

''E'll loan me the money for ten seasons an' after that . . .'

Mamma was pale. 'There'll be no after that, mister! 'Tis money yous talkin' about, not fresh air. Money? Since when did we's have money to pay people back?'

'But we's will have, Cath, we's will have.'

'Well, yous go back to Yelland.' Mamma picked up the papers and walked purposefully towards the fire, crumpling them as she went. 'Yous go back to Yelland an' yous tell 'e from I that we's don't need any of 'e's filthy money!'

'Stop!' Feyther flung himself on Mamma in his eagerness to retrieve the papers, knocking her to the floor with the weight of himself on top of her. The oak settle which had stood so long in that place in that kitchen swayed and toppled. It creaked as it fell and came down heavily on top of them, Feyther cursing and swearing underneath as if the devil had him by the tail.

It rocked. Rory and Samuel rushed to right it. Gregor turned away, ashamed and embarrassed. Feyther, the papers in his hand, retreated to the table. Mamma pulled herself to her feet and turned to Kerry with tears in her eyes. Kerry ran towards her, 'Is yous all right, Mamma? Is yous all right?'

Having made her silent appeal. Cath pushed her

daughter away. She was herself again. Mamma dusted herself down and scowled round the room at everybody. 'None of us will be all right if someone doan stop yer feyther in his drunken foolishness,' she said, taking a duster to a cobweb exposed by the movement of the settle. 'None of us, I's promise 'e.'

FIFTEEN

Winter was coming. The wind stormed in from the sea whipping up the white horses. It was cold in Porthclegga and damp, damp which brought a penetrating cold that the thickest cottage walls could not keep out.

But in daylight, no matter what the weather, the cottage doors stayed open. The timber for Feyther's boat came in mule carts right past Mamma's door. She watched it, then with pursed lips said, without looking at Kerry, 'Kerry, push it to.'

But Kerry saw her watching tersely from the window, wrapped in fierce curiosity as if she hoped one of the beasts might slip and go over the edge.

''Tis the wood for Feyther's boat! 'Tis comin' on mules, must be at least ten of 'em! The children are all followin' . . . there's a great crowd out there.' Rosa rushed in, pink-cheeked, calling in a high, excited voice, bunching her hair behind her neck with her hands in the way she had. When she saw Mamma's reaction she stopped smiling and began to puff, drawing out her tongue and almost licking the tip of her cold nose. 'This'll mean we's'll see more of Yelland, woan it. Now that 'e an' Feyther are nigh on partners?'

'Yer feyther is an embarrassin' fool!' Mamma snorted and paced back and forward in front of the window pretending not to look outside while Rosa watched her with a smirk on her face. But Mamma didn't tell Rosa off because if she did she would sulk and lock herself in the pantry and refuse to eat, making little shrieking noises now and then to scare off the mice. But Kerry knew she hoarded bread in the bedroom for just these times, and wondered how Mamma could be so stupid as to believe in her.

Mamma never talked to Feyther about the new boat – she considered that Yelland had the devil's power over him – and the silence was something that settled in the kitchen as intrusive as a most unsuitable piece of furniture. Cassy and Mabs helped with the chores now so Mamma sat more. Her chair was no longer left empty. And this was such a change in the life of the cottage that every time she heard the rocking Kerry felt anxious.

But Mamma's attitude – 'we's are so deep in debt we's'll never struggle clear,' – far from dissuading Feyther, seemed to increase his determination. For Feyther was in a good humour these days, and nothing Mamma said could nettle him now he had, as he called them, his plans. But the wood sat on the jetty and it continued to sit on the jetty because, as Mamma had said, Feyther had no time to work on it.

Rosa made herself a dress in red, dyeing it herself with lichens and hanging it outside the cottage to dry. She took great trouble over it. From the puddle beneath slithered red ribbons of juice that meandered to sink in a pothole, an ugly orange.

Kerry watched her do it, gratified that she would never be allowed to wear it, for red was the colour bad women wore, and Rosa wasn't even a woman yet.

Although to watch her you'd think she was.

Cassy went to stroke it. 'Doan maul me!' said Rosa.

'Please, Feyther, let me keep it.' She put her arms behind her back and went coy.

Feyther ignored her. Then Rosa stamped and said, 'If yous doan let me keep it I's'll tear it up and then I's woan have a dress to wear.'

110

'Then yous'll have to go naked!' said Feyther.

But he was just joking. Everyone knew he would let Rosa wear it in the end. Because, as Feyther said, 'She'll wear it anyway whether I's says so or no.'

Rosa went to the cave with the boys. Moodier with each year that went by, she was man mad. Kerry didn't know how she could! She'd hear her sister laughing with her friends, 'Yous got to watch that one . . .'e'll get the better of 'e if youm not careful!' and 'When I's said there was somebody comin' 'e let me go!' They giggled and whispered and sniggered behind their hands when Kerry walked by. Rosa's behaviour left her feeling lonely and afraid but she didn't know why. Kerry didn't want to grow up. Rosa let herself down from the window at night, and when she came creeping back the pupils of her eyes were big and black. Once she was caught coming in the door by Mamma who was waiting up for Feyther.

'Where have yous been, Rosa?'

Rosa bent over double and put an expression of beautiful agony on her face. Even in this she managed to look sensible. Her soft, pink mouth began to tremble as she said, 'Oh, Mamma, I's such a pain I's doan know what to do with myself. 'Twas such a pain, Mamma, that I's was cryin' wi' it. I's didn't want to bother anyone. I's didn't want to be a nuisance an' keep yous all awake. I's couldn't sleep, so I's went for a walk to see if I's could ease it.' And Rosa actually managed to weep.

'Poor child,' said Mamma. Kerry heard her skirts hurrying across the floor. 'Poor child! Doan I's knows the feeling well myself. Let me mix yous a possett. An' I's thinks yous should stop a'bed tomorrow.' Mamma – who had such little time for ailments!

Kerry was back in bed when Rosa came up looking

smug and self-satisfied. 'Yous'll get yousself caught one day,' she told her defiant sister, yet hurting inside by her own sense of meanness. 'An' then there'll be all hell to pay!'

'Dear dear, that's 'xactly what yous would really like to see, isn't it Kerry? 'Tis not my fault yous so miserable, is it? Yous never liked me . . . yous jealous of me, always has been since I's was small! Well, there woan be all hell to pay as yous so hopefully puts it 'cos I's has 'em all eatin' from the palm of my hand! I's can get away with anythin' I's like. At least I's is normal, unlike yous. Youm sixteen years old now . . . everyone is talkin' about it . . . where is Kerry, they say . . . when is Kerry goin' to start goin' with boys. An' I's doan know what to answer 'cos they's all think yous peculiar an' I's has to agree, they's right! They talk about yous Kerry . . . they talk about yous an' calls yous behind your back! Joe Pengelly told me the other day 'e thought yous was mazed in the head, always moonin' about for Tristan an' talkin' to that pretend friend of yous!'

Rosa got into bed and Kerry moved aside so she didn't have to touch her. Mamma had even given her a candle and supper . . . a pilchard on a chunk of bread. She sat up in bed and ate it, pushing back her heavy curls and eyeing Kerry now and then with a look of total satisfaction.

Dismayed by the outburst, Kerry was hurt because most of it was true. She was jealous of Rosa. And she didn't like the snot-nosed boys Rosa went about with. She couldn't imagine being kissed by one of them, just the thought of it repulsed her. But she knew she was different, so perhaps she was mad? Her friends of her own age were all coupled with somebody by now. There was obviously something very wrong with her.

'Anyway,' Rosa went on moodily, 'I's was wonderin'

whether or no I's should, an' now I's definitely decided not to tell 'e my secret.'

''Tis probably not worth knowin' anyway.' If she feigned disinterest Rosa would tell.

Pettishly Rosa lay down. Kerry hoped she wouldn't fall straight to sleep. She didn't. Both sisters lay side by side staring at the ceiling while they waited for Rosa to take a decision. Finally she said, ''Tis about Maudie Carne.'

Kerry, wide awake, propped on her arm and said, 'What?'

'She's dead!'

'Never! Mamma would know.'

'No she wouldn't, 'cos they's only just found her.'

'Found her . . . where?'

Their eyes met for a moment before Rosa carried on. 'Halfway up the path. Tonight. John Trelliss found her. They's reckons . . .' and she looked up at Kerry's impatient face. 'Yous want to know now, doan 'e?'

'Doan be silly, Rosa! What do they's reckon?'

Rosa's voice took on a tone of respect. 'They's reckons she took her own life. They's reckons she swallowed belladonna.'

Kerry gasped. 'But she never went out!'

'She went out tonight . . .'cos they found her there.'

'But Ned's out with the men.'

'Exactly. She picked her night an' she went an' did it!'

'Ned'll be sorry!' She despised Ned Carne almost as much as she despised John Yelland.

'No 'e woan. 'E'll be glad to get her off his back, silly old crow.'

Rosa's attitude towards the dead shocked Kerry. Tristan! If he heard about it he would come home for the funeral! But how would he hear? Who would tell him? Who would know outside Porthclegga? The village was a world unto itself.

Rosa smiled cynically to herself, knowing her sister's thoughts. 'Miss Goody Goody,' she said in a voice just above a whisper. 'An' thinkin' of nobody but youssself now I's'll wager!'

It was true. But over the faint hope she felt bitterness mixed with sorrow . . . bitterness because nothing had been done to help poor Maudie, and sorrow because she had known the woman all her life and would miss her. But she remembered that Mother Carrivick had spoken of pain being too hard to bear, so she supposed that, for Maudie's sake, she ought to feel glad.

'They'll be bringing' her home. Yous'll hear it all in a minute,' said Rosa, 'if yous stop awake an' listen.'

And they did.

SIXTEEN

It was Rosa the coquette who brought John Yelland to the house, batting her eyes and flirting. And Feyther could do nothing about it.

Mamma's voice was high. 'How can yous let 'e into this house, Jake Penhale? In all decency how can yous let 'e in 'ere? What have we's come to? We's are the laughin' stock of the village. Why that man wants to leave that palatial place to come an' slum it down here wi' the likes of us God only knows. Why, 'e's got everythin' at home a man could dream of – servants to do his biddin', silk sheets to sleep in, tables piled high wi' meat and fruit. 'E ought to be mixin' wi' gentry, the likes of 'isself. What is 'e doin', Jake, spendin' 'is time in that filthy tavern conversin' wi' the likes o' 'e? It doan make sense.'

"E's a right to spend 'is time where 'e likes. There's no law against that, Cath. An' e's livelihood's involved down here. 'E's invested a fair deal in t'other business.' Feyther turned his face away and was guiltily loud in his protestations.

'Aye, t'other business. I's wonder any of 'e follow him the little yous gets out of it.'

'We'd be starvin' wi'out it, Cath.'

'Starvin' be damned! We's nigh on starvin' wi' it, Jake, now youm the interest to pay!' Mamma's face was red, her whole attitude showing such anger that Kerry cringed at the sight.

'Shut thy mouth about that now! Yous for ever naggin'. We's been through all that!' And Feyther clamped his hand over his ears. During the silence that

115

followed the younger children, wide-eyed and open-mouthed, stared at their mother waiting for a response.

Mamma jerked her chin. Her mouth puckered. But not as badly as it did on the nights Yelland called on his way back from the tavern for a nightcap with Feyther. That was his excuse, but by late evening Feyther was not a good companion, so Yelland sat and talked to Rosa instead.

Once, Trewen had been a byword, never mentioned without disapproval. Once, Yelland's name had been forbidden in this house. But now things had changed so much that this 'monster of depravity', Satan's son, was given food and drink and a place at the Penhales' table.

Kerry watched Rosa's behaviour and felt enraged and humiliated.

Mamma asked Rosa, 'Have yous no shame at all, girl? What are 'e on, flirtin' an' carryin' on wi' a man like that? A man old enough to be yous feyther?'

Rosa sulked, secretly pleased with herself. 'I's doan mean to flirt with 'e, Mamma. 'Tis just my way. I's sure 'e doan think I's flirtin'. An' if I's didn't talk nobody else would. Samuel and Rory just sit like a couple o' hard-done eggs. Gregor is to sleep on the settle. Yous turn yous back and Kerry goes to bed. Some hospitality we's show to visitors in this house! Shamin' it is.'

'Huh! An' 'e should be 'shamed of hisself. 'Tis time 'e took a wife. Maybe that'd keep 'e to his home like any decent man!'

Rosa hesitated. 'I's think 'e misses home life, poor man. 'E likes to come here . . . to feel hisself part of a family.'

'Rubbish,' retorted Mamma, raw anger on her face.

116

'That man is no more lookin' for a family than I's is. An' I's lookin' to get rid of mine!'

'Well, yous'll not get rid of Kerry the way she's goin' on. She hasn't made eyes at any boy yet an' she's older 'n me! Even little Cassy is courtin'.'

'Youm a hussy an' without shame . . . always were!' said Mamma, turning to poke the fire and raise the embers to blaze. 'Dizzy as a jackdaw!' But now there was no real cut to her voice. Rosa was able to laugh.

Yes, when Yelland came Kerry went to bed, because wherever she went in the drink-soured kitchen he followed her with his eyes . . . cold, emotionless eyes that made her shiver inside. John Yelland's face was evil. She hated his visits. She dreaded them. She'd never forget the awful threat he had made to her in the tavern.

He always sat in the same place, at the end of the table on Feyther's right hand. And from there, with his back to the window he had a view of the whole room. He stretched his legs lazily under the table as if he sat in his own house, and leaned back with one arm dangling over the back of his chair while, with his other hand, his fingers drummed the table.

He endeavoured to bring her into the conversation but Kerry would not be drawn. And when she could keep from rudeness no longer, she yawned and told Mamma she was tired and wanted an early night.

Missy left the house when Yelland came into it, and on these nights Kerry missed her dreadfully. Missy refused to talk to her about Yelland. Tightened up. Went all sulky and silent. And Kerry knew better than to push her. If she did that Missy would disappear and not come back for weeks.

Yelland knew very well the effect he had on her. His eyes met hers and she saw the shameless humour there.

Wasn't Rosa enough? He could see that she adored him! Why wasn't he satisfied with the conquest he had already made in this family without forcing the unwilling to fuss about him?

November. The wind whistled under the door and whisked out the candle by the window and John Yelland spoke of love.

As Feyther flopped and Mamma dozed Rosa scolded Yelland, teasing him about his reputation. 'Man is an animal,' he said, his hand held loosely round his mug and a relaxed smile on his face. ''Tis expected that young men should sow their wild oats.'

'An' what of women?' Rosa wore her red dress and Kerry was sure her lips looked pinker tonight.

'Women are made to be virtuous. To cleave to one man only.'

'I's doan think there's any difference between the feelings of men an' the feelings of women,' said Rosa, goading him on.

'Men an' women are different as well yous know,' said Yelland, his voice softly slurred, his cold eyes narrowing. 'A woman cannot look at a stranger an' feel lusty as a man does.'

'Oh, aye she can . . . it only takes a glance.'

Mamma would put a stop to this conversation if she had stayed awake. But she sat dozing in her chair, and when she woke she would deny she had dropped to sleep.

'Oh aye,' Rosa went on with all the experience of her fifteen years. ''Tis that easy for a woman to fall in love.'

'Yous call that love? The games yous play wi' little boys?' Yelland's laugh was cold and tinged with malice.

''Tis a start, maybe.'

'Well, maiden, if yous knows so much yous tell me

118

what love is!' His glance moved to Kerry. She forced herself to hold the stare of his yellow eyes. 'Yous tell me,' he repeated, 'because Kerry is too afraid to even talk to me.'

'Why should I's be afraid of yous?' She heard his threat. She remembered his smell. She saw the evil in his eyes.

'Love is that feeling between men and women,' started Rosa, guilelessly. 'An' it makes them want to stay together for always.'

'Lust,' spat Yelland. 'It lasts for a few moments . . . at best ten minutes.'

'Then what keeps folks like Feyther and Mamma together?' asked Rosa. 'They must have started with lust, an' it went on to love.'

'Doan yous believe that, maid,' said Yelland. ''Tis habit and necessity that keeps folks together, an' often they hate each other as a result of it.'

Kerry thought of Feyther's nightly violence. She knew that Yelland was right in one way, but talk like this bewildered her. All men weren't like Feyther. All men weren't like Yelland. Thinking of Tristan she was forced to say, 'Love is a mixture of small things between two people an' they grow and grow like flowers in sweetness until finally they express themselves in full bloom in one another's arms.'

'Ah! Now that's a lovely speech! An' they say that out of the mouths of babes . . .'

Kerry, stung by his sarcasm, retorted, 'An' what do yous know of love? Yous, who has never found it!' It was strange that he had not married. Many a woman would like to be mistress of Trewen, and in spite of the fact that he disgusted Kerry he was not ugly. Could he help it that his face was too thin, his teeth too china-white against lips too narrow, his skin too peachy and his voice too feline? Rosa, for one, didn't seem to mind.

Far from it. Rosa's face, as she watched him, was washed with adoration, alive with excitement.

'An' how do yous knows I's never found it?'

Kerry hesitated. 'Yous had a loveless childhood . . . everyone knows that yer mother . . .'

'An' my feyther detested women!' he laughed at her, but with bitterness. ''E called them daughters of Eve, the instigators of all sin. But even 'e, at his end, succumbed to their charms.'

''E never remarried?'

Yelland raised his thin gold eyebrows. He held out his mug to be refilled. Kerry crossed the room with the wine jug. When she was within reach he caught her wrist. The jug slopped on the table. 'Lust!' he whispered, and the word was wet in his mouth. 'That's all there is maiden, for old men an' young, is lust!'

He let her go and only then did she feel how vice-like had been the grip of his fingers.

Tristan did not return for Maudie's funeral. It was a sad little affair, conducted in mist and drizzle high above a grey, sluggish sea. This dismal place smelled dank and of death. The almost silent rain put a sheen on the plain wooden coffin and polished the stones of Maudie's dead children. There was no sound of weeping, and Kerry's grief, real as it was, was over the absence of Tristan.

They had come, like they came when they bowsenned her, a cortège of black-garbed men and women, to take her solemnly up the path to the church perched on top of the cliffs. The tin bell rang so thinly, with so forlorn a knell that Kerry thought of the clanging sound of a lost ewe on a storm-beleaguered hillside. Parson Fox moved forward to bless the mourners, his cloak swirling like the black wing of a blue-black crow.

Rumours ran like rats in Porthclegga, and rumour

120

had it that Ned had gone to the tavern last night and left the body lying alone in the cottage. Kerry watched him covertly from under her lashes. He would be quite alone now. He would be sorry he had sent Tristan away. He might take himself a second wife . . . but who would have him? The stubble on his face was uneven and grey, and the scowl-lines beneath were deeply etched. He could not even stand still in respect, but shuffled from foot to foot as if eager to be off to console himself at Jessop's.

There was no pleasure to be taken from Ned's suffering. Kerry tried to pray. *'Ashes to ashes, dust to dust . . .'* Parson Fox had refused to accept a verdict of suicide. He would not have Maudie buried in unhallowed ground beside the drowned bones of strangers. He was determined to bury her beside her eight children.

Kerry thought that no one was sorry to see Maudie die. The one person who had cared for her was not here, and she wondered if her children would be there to welcome her to Heaven. There would be nothing Maudie would like better than to be surrounded by a family of fine, strong children . . . it was all she had ever wanted. Life was cruel that a woman could want something so simple so badly and yet be denied it.

Like Mamma did.

Like she did.

SEVENTEEN

An icy fog, colder than she had ever felt before, swathed Porthclegga on the night that Feyther was drowned.

Two years on and Maudie Carne was almost forgotten. As if she had never lived next door . . . or been the mother of Tristan.

The news came to the tavern first and Jim Lee, a skinny lad of eleven dashed up the track from the jetty to the cottages, eager to be the one to pass it on.

'They'm drownded,' he shouted at the top of his voice while banging on the door. 'They'm drownded.'

Mamma opened the door, grabbed him and pulled him inside. 'What, boy? What is 'e sayin'?'

''E went over, sozzled as usual, an' then the boys went in to save 'e. None of 'em came back. The current must have sucked 'em out.'

Mamma struck the cringing boy across the face. 'Now hold youssell, an' tell me again!'

'They'm gone, missus. Yous men am gone to the sea. Drownded . . .' his voice trailed away as he tried to free himself from her clutches, sorry now, that he had come. 'Drownded.' He dripped the word into the room.

Mamma threw a shawl over her shoulders and without another word ran down the track to the jetty where returning fishermen moved ominously slowly, eyes to the ground, as they made fast their boats and dealt with the catch.

Kerry caught her lip with her teeth and followed her, ice in her heart.

The air buzzed alive with desperate questions. 'An' did 'e search?'

"Tis bad, Cath.' Davy Lee shook his head and was careful not to look at anyone. A crowd formed round him, awed and inquisitive. 'Cath, we'm searched everywhere. We'm searched an' we'm called an' we'm swept the place careful as if we'm was lookin' for a needle. We'd not have come home, Cath, if we'd thought there was a chance. An' Gabby Ross an' his boys are still out there now . . .' Davy's voice trailed off, telling her not to hold out any hope. ''E was bad before 'e left this mornin', yous know how I's mean, Cath. Some of us told 'e not to go . . . it's been that thick out there you couldn't see yous hand in front of yous face at times . . . I's sorry, Cath.' Davy shook his head. 'I's sorry.'

'But how do yous know 'e fell?'

'We'm was passin' when the boy Rory shouted to us what had happened. 'E said 'e was goin' in after 'im so we'm hove to alongside 'em to wait until them came back. We'm waited for two hours, Cath. We'm called and we'm waited. Death cold out there 'twas. The sea was calm . . . just a slight swell on 'e. An' then the others came . . . there's been twenty boats spent this afternoon to-in' an' fro-in' an' searchin' . . .'

'Yous knew there was men overboard an' yous let Rory go to help them?'

Davy sighed. 'We'm was half a mile away when 'e shouted us. Cath, we'm could do nothing.'

Was this it then? Was this how disasters happened? And was it normal to feel nothing? Absolutely nothing? In fact, Kerry felt a wicked impulse to laugh, to shout something obscene into the horrified crowd . . . to shout, or to remove all her clothes and dance before them.

Don't let me laugh! Please God don't let me laugh! And if she laughed and danced as she wanted to she knew the sound would echo hysterically from this side of the cliff right across the narrow bay to the other, hidden completely in mist. Come away quickly, Mamma, before I laugh and you'll never forgive me and never love me again! Kerry felt the cold as if for the first time and her clenched teeth started to chatter, her limbs began to jerk. Come away, Mamma, oh, please come away!

Mamma's voice sounded mysterious like the mist. 'We's'll have to live with the corpses upstairs for we's cannot afford to bury 'em.'

The cliff reared up behind them and disappeared in the mists. Kerry smelled woodsmoke. They were down at the bottom of a huge ravine . . . up there somewhere was reality . . . this was surely the dream.

'I's'll go and tell the children now, an' explain it.'

'I's'll come with 'e and get Lizzie, midear.'

'Aye. Bring her. I's'll explain. 'Tis very late. 'E was all right you know. Quite all right. How strange these people look. Who are they all then, Davy?'

'Go wi' yer Mamma, maid. She's badly dazed.'

Kerry knew she should touch Mamma but she didn't know how to. So she gave her a kind of little push to put her in the right direction, and, like a sheepdog with its nose to an unruly ewe, she prodded and poked her home. It was the sound of Mamma's anguish which stopped her wanting to laugh, not the knowledge of the deaths. Inside the house the misted windows seemed to weep with Mamma, a cold, grey, pervasive kind of white-weeping. Slow. Exhausted.

Forlorn and small Mamma allowed Kerry to put her in the chair, to cover her with rugs and to stoke up the fire.

The children gathered round with their fingers in their mouths, Jody, Mabs, Cassy, Gregor, Rosa.

'Aren't yous goin' to tell 'em, Mamma?' Kerry wanted to tug at her mother's clothing and make her

124

stop. Lizzie Lee came in, tall, lean, efficiently big, ducking under the door frame, her surprised eyes swivelling round to take in the scene.

'Doan just stand there gawkin' . . . your feyther is daid,' she said as she bustled through. 'Fetch me the laudanum, Kerry!'

'An' Samuel. An' Rory,' Kerry added, because it was not something that could be said with care. Lizzie Lee was right. There was no way you could tell it gently.

The children didn't appear to have heard because when Kerry came back with the bottle they still stood there staring just the same, unused to seeing Mamma like this . . . never having seen her cry before.

'Tell them to light the fire,' moaned Mamma. ''Tis very cold in here, midear.'

'The fire's lit, darlin',' said Lizzie, chattering on in a way that Kerry found very soothing. But she wanted to do something, to stop feeling like an onlooker. These were their deaths, and Kerry felt herself both mentally and physically excluded. She felt nothing.

So she moved forward and reached up to the mantelpiece and felt with her hands what she searched for. She lifted down the wooden Madonna and went to put it in Mamma's hands. Mamma took her cold hands from under her shawl and automatically stroked it.

So God had cheated on her at last. All that staying awake, all those prayers, all those sleepless nights when Mamma had waited for Feyther and the boys to come home. She might as well not have bothered because it had happened, behind her back so to speak, at the end of the day, after all.

Time went slowly. They waited for it to pass, huddled in misery, waited in a stillness broken every now and then by a cough, a change of stance, a movement

125

of eyes, Mamma's sobs and Lizzie's comfortings. It was with relief that they heard footsteps coming to the door, a knock, a voice, and Parson Fox in his huge winter coat came softly in.

He seemed to start time up again. He sat, unasked, in Feyther's chair and beckoned to the little ones. They gathered round him while he talked in hushed tones telling them gently but exactly what had happened. Rosa was at his shoulder, Mabs was on his knee. Gregor, guilty for being alive, sat in the chair beside him and the others fitted round him. Only Kerry felt out of place, not child, not adult, not welcome at either of the two little groups now so separately defined in the room.

She felt a dull anguish wash over her. Her loose hair hid her face as she lifted her head slightly to look at the darkness beyond the window. What would happen, what would happen to them now? She wanted to run in the sun again, clinging to Tristan's shirt-tails. She wanted the dark shadows to go away and let the warmth come back. She wanted to lie low in the gorse and watch a tawny pheasant lead out its young. She wanted to run through the brush and break the silver cobwebs, to count the time with pollen balls, to answer back the cuckoo and deck herself with daisy chains. She wanted to feel Tristan's hand round her own, squeezing it, saying, 'Shush . . .' as they watched a velvet-footed fox passing by.

'Tis not fair . . .'tis not fair, she cried silently.

She heard as Lizzie Lee tossed a faggot into the fire and it blazed suddenly and defiantly, briefly lighting the room. It was as if it searched in childlike anticipation . . . perhaps . . . perhaps . . . and finding nothing, fizzled sadly for a moment before going out.

EIGHTEEN

You could go to too many funerals. You could say
goodbye to too many people. In the end you came to
expect it and then you weren't shocked any more. You
just began to wonder if it was anything to do with you.
And went round feeling sad all the time.

Kerry sometimes wondered if Mamma was glad Feyther was dead what with his drunkenness and bullying.
Kerry looked closely for signs but there were none.

When they found the bodies they were black.

After Feyther's funeral, and Sam's, and Rory's, the
mourning time was quickly over. Life, said Lizzie Lee,
must go on. People must pull themselves together and
get back to normal. But how could they, when nothing
was normal any more? When there was no money
coming in and Mamma was getting chary about having
to ask the neighbours.

Mamma tried to sell the timber back to the merchant
but the fleshy-faced man told her that times were hard
and there was no call for it at the moment and what
was he to do, get himself in a debtors' jail on account
of a fisherwife and her family?

'I's begged 'e, Lizzie.' And Mamma flushed as she
recounted it. ''Twas no good. 'E's a hard-hearted man
an' a scoundrel. I's'd never have bought a pack of nails
from 'e let alone half a forest,' she said. ''E was the
sort of man who has that look in 'e's eye.'

Kerry speculated.

Talk to me, Mamma. Talk to me! Yous doan need

Lizzie now, she's not family! Kerry thought it but didn't say it.

Yelland, in his self-imposed role as friend of the family, said that he would take Kerry, Rosa and Cassy into the house to work. 'An' that'll be some of 'e off yous plate, an' the eldest boy 'e can work with the horses, the youngest in the kitchens.'

There was shame attached to working at Trewen. No self-respecting servant took a place there now. The house's reputation spread far and wide. Most of the servants were dullards and drunkards, women without morals and men without pride, who had graduated to service at Trewen down a spiral of misfortune and degradation.

'Jody is taken, Sir,' said Mamma defensively. 'Will Trellis as 'e as an apprentice at the carpentry. An' Gregor is to the boat. We's still has a boat workin' yous knows!'

'Mamma,' Gregor interrupted. 'I's need Jody with I's now.'

And that was that.

But that didn't last long. To pay off the loan the boat had to go, and it was Gregor who went first, proud Gregor, with his cap on his head and his trunk in his arms, away from home and up the path to Trewen.

The girls followed, although they went daily, came back in the dark and left before daylight in the mornings. Mamma and Jody and Mabs were left at home. Mamma cast sad eyes next door. 'An' to think,' she said, 'that I's thought they accursed!'

Accursed? There was worse to come.

The second instalment came due and Mamma could not pay. Nor could she pay Yelland his rent.

'I's carn do no more for 'e Mrs Penhale,' said Yelland when he came round after the bailiff.

'Wi' the money yous pays yer workers 'tis no wonder we carn pay 'e,' said Mamma, flushed and uneasy.

It hurt to see Mamma try to keep control in a situation she didn't understand . . . Mamma, who had been so able and efficient in that former, sweet world. Kerry thought of a spider trying to spin a fragile web in a gale. No sooner had she got another strand safely hooked than the first one came away in a gust and she had to scuttle back to see to it. You could see there was no way that the threatened web could hold. But nor could the spider stop trying.

The house was enormous – a medieval manor extensively enlarged over the years. Kerry, who had only ever seen it from a distance, was overcome by its fabulous splendour. It stood, solid and solemn, half a mile back from the sea with scrubland and a few tortured copses between it and the clifftop. The gardens were terraced and here and there impressive bronze urns sprouted from lawns swept by purples, pinks and blues . . . azaleas, camellias and hydrangeas. Its leaded window eyes seemed to be watching and waiting for something. Inside, Kerry didn't see the worn tapestries, the unpolished pewter and brass, the neglected suits of armour and the unhappy furniture with its sprouting protestations of horsehair, the frayed rugs and the rot in the staircase.

She was enthralled by its sad magnificence.

She saw that the cook was a bully and the housekeeper was a drunkard. The housemaids were poor, scared creatures who went in fear of Yelland and his friends and were afforded no protection from the hierarchy. All except for one, and that was a kitchenmaid called Daisy, a nondescript, greasy-skinned creature of middle years who ran the kitchen single-handed and whom Yelland left well alone.

'Where does Daisy come from?' Kerry had asked Mrs Gibson. 'Oh, Daisy,' said the cook as if suddenly remembering someone from the past whom she hadn't thought of for years. 'Oh, Daisy's always been here.' Yelland recruited from the grubber, taking slaveys who had nowhere to fall back on. There were cockroaches in the kitchen and fleas in the walls.

'It wern like this in 'e's feyther's day,' Mrs Gibson the cook told Kerry when she saw her looking critically at the rat-infested pantry. ''E ran a proper household, 'e did, where everyone knew where they'm was an' went in fear of a rollickin' from the Lord 'esself. Rod of iron, oh yes, a rod of iron. Things is gone downhill fast, aye, since 'e passed on, bless 'e's miserable soul. Now 'tis no more than a bawdy house an' a brothel. 'Tis impossible to keep any discipline when one minute a maid be servin' 'e and the next be rompin' with 'e in 'e's bed.'

'Then why do yous stay?'

'Mr Jardine, the old butler went. Several of the younger girls followed 'e. But at my age where could I's go?' The cook had gone to fat which hung round her eyes and made them small and pig-like. There were no lines at all on her pasty face, just cracks, and Kerry thought of dough left to rise until it acquired that yellow, toughened skin. Her ankles were so huge she had to heave herself around the enormous kitchen, and her dresses wouldn't do up properly so she exposed an immodest amount of blue-veined breast which she never seemed to notice but liked to rest on the table.

'An' Mrs King? Why does she stay?'

The white-haired cook rolled her sleeves higher as though to wade into a fight. 'She's allus had a problem that one,' she said darkly. 'The porter,' she sniffed.

'She's allus had a weakness. An' I's 'spect it all just got the better of 'er. By, she used to be a fierce one in the old days. A right tartar! People went afeared of 'er, with her hoity-toity ways an' her strict Methody ideas. If there was anything of her left,' and Cook tapped her forehead with a floury finger, 'if there was anything there she'd go barmy wi' the goings on 'ere now. But she doan know, poor soul. She just doan know.'

Mrs King had the peculiar untidiness of a once-fastidious woman – and you could almost see how strict she used to be because her face was still hard, albeit grey and shrunken now. And most of her unkempt hair escaped from her bun, harsh as tendrils of burnishing wire. Her straight, thin lips hung open but often tried to go the way they went before . . . straight like a gash across her face. Most of the time she stayed in the room labelled *Mrs King, Housekeeper. Please knock.*

It was safer to keep yourself downstairs because if you went up, vulnerable with a bucket or brushes in your arms, you were likely to be tormented by Yelland's obnoxious visitors. They were a debauched lot . . . mostly very red-faced men . . . tied up with Yelland's nefarious business interests in France and Spain and Portugal. They came and they stayed, 'Roisterin' the nights away,' complained Mrs Gibson, after sending a tearful girl no more than a child upstairs without supper for some mild misdemeanour. It seemed that the more Mrs Gibson was hurt the more she felt she had to hurt others.

Poor Rosa.

For a while Rosa submitted, humiliated though she was to be doing such menial work. She always kept herself looking nice, but rouges and paints eventually spoiled her skin and she stopped looking like fresh, ripe fruit and became more like a sun-burst windfall, got at, Kerry thought unkindly, here and there by the wasps.

'Yelland wants me to work nights,' she told Mamma coyly one evening after spending the day upstairs having been summoned by the Master and his guests.

'Well, good heavens, what work is there to be done by any self-respectin' girl in that house at night?' Mamma was disgusted by the very suggestion!

'There's the boots to be cleaned an' the lamps to be kept burnin'. Early breakfasts to be served. They's keep late hours, Mamma. Gentry do!' said Rosa haughtily. 'They's not like us, in bed an' asleep before midnight.'

'I's never heard such nonsense.'

But the next day Rosa stayed in bed in spite of Mamma's protestations, and after Kerry and Cassy came home, weary and ready for their beds at ten, Tom Geary the bailiff came to collect Rosa on his horse.

'Oh no, madam.' Mamma stood before the door preventing Rosa from leaving. 'I's havin' none o' this, my lass. We's might be poor but I's rather we's all go to the grubber 'n have yous sellin' youssself to the likes of 'e.'

'Yous just envy me 'cos I's havin' a life an' yous is over! Mamma, move aside!'

'Is'll not move anywhere.'

'Mamma, I's quite old enough to leave home. Youm has no authority over me!'

'Hear her!' Mamma turned round with a sneer on her face, and in that instant Rosa was by her, out of the door and hauled up onto the broad haunches of Geary's mount.

'Is'll see yous in the morning,' called Rosa happily, her black hair streaming like glossy seaweed behind her.

'She looks like a mermaid with a glittery tail, Mamma,' said Cassy, wearily removing her boots.

'She be no mermaid, midear,' said Mamma with pursed lips. 'An' that be the devil's tail yous saw. She be no maid of mine either!'

And Kerry saw Mamma's despair.

NINETEEN

'Sit down, Kerry!'

'I's carn, Mister Yelland, Sir. I's got my work to do.'

'Youm answer to me an' me only in this house. An' I's says sit down!'

She had been sent by Mrs Gibson to clear the dining room table. It was not her job but Daisy was ill again. Kerry was tired. The threat of snow was in the air. The sky was laden and the sea had taken on that grey look. She would be late getting home and Mamma would worry. She had not expected to find John Yelland sitting there smoking, alone and morose, while his guests played cards in the anteroom.

Trying to ignore him she picked up the tray and set about filling it as quickly as she could. He banged down his tankard. 'Woman! I's told 'e to sit down.'

He was drunk, she was certain. Remembering Feyther in his drunken moods, Kerry sat to humour him.

She chose the chair at the opposite end of the table. 'No, here,' he said quietly, tapping the seat beside him.

His open shirt was frothed at the neck with snow-white lace. His waistcoat was unbuttoned and hung beneath his arms. In the dying firelight she thought his leanness skeletal. His smile was certainly so. His hair looked silver-white, like Missy's, in the light. It curled down over his forehead and was taken into a loose pigtail tied with a black velvet bow behind. His long fingers fiddled with the silver salt cellar. She watched as he carelessly tipped it up and made tiny white mounds on the oak.

She thought of the snow, of a treacherous journey home.

'Yous sister is a most obliging woman,' he started, staring at her under lidded eyes.

'She's still a child, Sir,' she said.

'Old enough to be married an' with children of her own.'

'She is childish inside,' said Kerry. 'She dreams like a child. She has the naivity of a child.'

Yelland swept the salt from the table. 'Why are we's talkin' of her?' He raised his voice. 'When we's ought to be talkin' of yous!'

'There is nothing to say about me.'

He leaned forward and with an appreciative finger held up her chin. 'There's a great deal to be said about yous.' And he closed his eyes.

The talk from the other room grew louder. Someone accused of cheating was vehemently denying it. Kerry was afraid they might come in here and decide to play some different games, games she had heard about from the other maids. Had he dropped to sleep? She didn't know. He didn't move but his breathing was soft and regular. She moved back cautiously on her chair, but he leaned forward keeping his finger in place. He opened his eyes a fraction. Raised thin eyebrows. She remained still.

'Yous realise of course,' he spoke in a whisper. It was a threat. 'Yous realise what must now become of yer family?'

'Times be hard, Sir. We's'll pull out of it. My mother is convinced of it.'

'Oh?' And a wide smile sharpened his face. 'Is that so?'

'Yes, Sir. That is so.'

'The rent, Tom Geary tells me, is two months overdue. An' that's without accountin' for the interest on the loan.'

'If yous demands full payment then we'm must leave the house.' She sounded more confident than she felt. 'There's work for us all, Mamma says, in the new factories in town.'

'An' do 'e know the conditions in those places? Do 'e know the squalid conditions in which these people live?'

'There is no alternative for us, Sir. If yous demand payment then we'm shall go.'

'An' how long do yous think yer mother will last in those conditions? How long the youngest children . . . what are their names now . . . ?'

He didn't want her to tell him. He wanted to make her think of them. And she did. With a sinking heart.

'They are used to fresh air an' full bellies . . . a good life I's thinks, compared to the poor idiots who live on the floor at the mills an' choke theyselves to death on the dust.'

'There is no alternative for us,' she said again.

'But what about the loan?' Yelland persisted, still in that same quiet voice but with his harsh breath moving the candle-flame.

'The loan?'

'Yes. The loan.' He made the word sound sweet as he brought his tongue out around it. 'Mill wages will not cover the loan. Yous lives would be sacrificed for nought. An' the gaols are already full of people who cannot pay their debts.'

'Gaol! But the debt was not Mamma's in the first place!' Kerry brought her hand to her mouth, glanced at the open door, tried to stop her voice from rising.

Yelland followed her glance. He let his finger fall and brought it down to her bare arm. This girl was extraordinarily beautiful, with an inner fire that flickered through her eyes . . . tantalising. He took his finger up to her short sleeve and down again, leaving a trail of ice on the flesh behind him. She shivered and turned her head away.

'Yous wouldn't see Mamma in gaol. We's always been good tenants until now . . .'

'Until now . . . until now . . .' and his voice stroked her like his finger had.

'Aha! Yelland! There you are!' A red-faced buffoon, bored with the cards, came with a bottle in his hand and smashed the sinister quiet of the room.

Kerry stood up to go. 'Surely youm not plannin' to leave . . . so early?' shouted the boisterous man so his cronies could hear.

'I's must get on. My sister is waiting.'

'The more the merrier,' the blusterer joked, as hastily Kerry picked up the tray and made for the door. But she was ten seconds too late. A second man crept up behind her, circled her and clamped his hands on her breasts, squeezing so hard that she cried out.

She dropped the tray. She whirled round to face him, her cheeks aflame and her arm raised to strike. Yelland's friend caught it just as it reached his florid face. 'A little blazer!' he boomed, catching her other wrist so she could not move. She kicked for his crutch and he spun her round, bringing her arms up so hard behind her back that her bones cracked. She was helpless before the ribald company.

'Now, now, now,' said her captor. 'I's thought this evening was provin' pretty dull. Perhaps 'twill liven up now we'm have a wench who needs to be taught good manners.'

She struggled to raise her head enough to see Yelland. He remained in his chair. He sat back now, with his legs, his buckled breeches up on the table in the clear space she had made. The five men who made up the party stood round the walls of the wood-panelled room while the man who held her and was called Harry, hoisted her painfully onto the table. If she tried to climb off they pushed her back until at last she gave up and stood there still as a stone, her chin held high and her arms behind her back. She hoped they couldn't see her ankles wobbling. She hoped the tears would stay at the back of her eyes.

'Name?' The man called Harry put a doily on his head and took on the learned ponderousness of a judge.

Kerry stayed silent.

'Name?' he asked again, bringing titters from the crowd.

'Every time she refuses to answer she must be punished,' called a brutish-looking man with a head of carrot-coloured hair. 'Who agrees to that?'

'Aye!' they called loutishly, refilling their glasses. But Yelland stayed silent and watched.

'Name?' called Harry. And Kerry stood stock-still and refused to answer.

The red-haired man strode forward and purposefully moved a chair into position beside the table. He stepped up beside her and she whirled to face him. Her heart hammered so hard it threatened to deafen her. Shame suffused her cheeks so they seemed to puff under her eyes. He reached out a hand and ripped her bodice from neck to waist, taking the thin material of her petticoat with it. A cheer went up as the man climbed down. Kerry covered her nakedness and hung her head.

'Name?' Harry called again. And she heard her own voice softly answer, 'Kerry Penhale . . .'

'Milord!'

And Kerry obediently repeated, 'Milord.'

They played the game until she became giddy with

138

horror. She answered her age, her address, the names of her family, and then they started asking her questions she could not answer. 'The name of the third Duke of Buckingham. The third Duke, I say! Speak up, girl. What has happened to your tongue?'

Kerry shook her head.

''Tis no good. We's carn hear her, can we, Harry? Or is it me? Is it me whose ears are all bunged up?' And he thrust his little fingers into his ears and wiggled them until the fat on his face wobbled.

The red-haired man again climbed onto the table. And this time Kerry didn't fight him. She wasn't there. She was out on the cliffs with Tristan, watching the gulls, making pictures in the sand, playing down on the jetty making mud-pies that baked hard on the big, flat stones. So that when they stripped her naked and she stood there before them, she heard none of their lewd jests. And when John Yelland, silent until then, prevented them from taking her in turn there and then on the great dining table, she didn't see the look in his eye, nor hear the anger in his voice as he bade them leave the room.

He lifted her down. She let him. She was rigid like a statue with her head held high and a small smile on her lips. He thought he had never before seen a woman so beautiful, nor one he so badly wanted to bed. He resented her strength, her unreachable innocence. He wanted to break her . . . as he always broke delicate things. But he knew that just to take her as she was, with no commitment from her, would bring him no satisfaction.

No. Let time pass. He had sowed the seed tonight. He must be patient . . . let it grow.

He wanted her and she knew it. That, for now, was enough.

TWENTY

Rosa refused to speak to Kerry. The truth of it was that after a fortnight Yelland and his cronies grew tired of her. Tom Geary's horse no longer came to collect her and Mrs Gibson had a down on her because of her wanton ways.

She was given the heaviest, dirtiest work, and was scorned by the servants because of her obvious adoration for their detested master. Kerry felt sorry for her because, as Mamma always said, she was childlike with her ridiculous posturings, her great hopes and her dreams. And the worst of it was that she still adored Yelland and now blamed Kerry for turning him against her.

"Tis yous! 'Tis yous! Yous lead 'e on wi' yous smoulderin' eyes and then yous tosses yous head and leaves e' danglin'. Any man'd be tormented by that! He doan love yous . . . not like 'e does me! 'Tis me 'e wants only e' just carn see it. Yous bewitched 'e with yous sly ways! The man's enamoured of 'e.'

'But Rosa, how can yous say that? If 'e wanted me 'e'd have me like he do all the others . . . an' I's always said I's loathed him an' that is true!' She had told no one about the night they stripped her. About the time in the tavern when he whispered those ominous warnings through drunken eyes and lips. She couldn't even bring herself to think about that night herself. After it was over and Yelland let her go she had run to Daisy for a set of clothes. Sad-eyed Daisy, who had not even asked what had happened, but had comforted her and petted her just the same. She had walked home alone in the snow. Had sat in the gorse bower before climbing down the path, had sat there to think while she watched the white flakes fluttering and twirling, resting light as thistledown on her hand before melting softly into herself.

But she had cried when finally she got into bed, and told Missy. Missy had let her own tears fall on Kerry's hair, pale, cool tears like weeping stars. Had said, 'Shush, sweetheart, he carn hurt you. Bide. Tristan will come!'

But Rosa brought messages down to the kitchen and gave them to Kerry with hard eyes. "E wants 'e up there, Kerry, an' 'e says yous to jump to it.'

'I's not goin' anywhere near 'e. 'E can sack me if 'e likes. I's stayin' this side of that door an' that's that!'

Even Mrs Gibson gave up trying to make her. And the cadaverous, secretive Mrs King had nothing to do with the running of the household anyway.

And Rosa, between the silences, moaned on, "E's allus askin' about 'e. Callin' for 'e when 'e's drunk. Yous taken 'e from me. An' all my plans are come to nothin'.'

And then came the day Tom Geary arrived with the summons. Mamma was to pay what she owed or answer to the courts for it.

'I's carn pay, that's all there is to it. I's carn pay.' And Mamma sank defeated into her chair and wept.

Kerry went to comfort her. 'I's always wanted to keep yous from the world,' Mamma sobbed. 'I's always wanted to keep yous all safe here in Porthclegga wi' the fishin' an' the sea an' the good neighbourliness of all of it. An' now it's all gone wrong an' look at 'e all. There's Sam an' Rory, my two strong boys . . . lost to the sea. There's Gregor hatin' his life . . . bowed down

141

by work under a stable-master that's no better than a beast. There's my little Cassy who ought to be playing games here on the step, peelin' great bathfuls of potatoes so that her hands are all sore an' weepin'. There's Jody who missed 'e's chance to go wi' Will an' now cleans shit from under horses so 'is legs are too tired to bring him home nights. There's Rosa wi' her dreams who's let herself down so much that her feyther would turn in 'is grave to see her all bitter and wound up . . . an' there's you, little Kerry, wi' yer mass of black hair an' that wild life inside yous . . . I's nursed you once, in fever, the year that little Nelly Carne died . . . yous woan remember yous was too little. I's wonders now was it worth it . . .'

'Mamma, of course . . .'

'The only one as is kept her innocence as I's dreamed is Mabs. An' what will her life be now? Tell me, what will it be for Mabs? Truly we's would be better dead. I's carn see any way out 'o this. God help me I's carn, Kerry, I's carn.'

'Shall I's fetch Lizzie Lee to yous, Mamma?'

'No, no, Kerry. Yous'll do.'

'An' I's want yous to take back the summons.'

'Ah?' John Yelland sat in his chair by the fire at Jessop's, his tankard with his own initials on it overflowing frothily on the table beside him.

She would show him up before his friends. If the men in the village saw how he had treated Mamma maybe they wouldn't work for him. Maybe they would band together and bring pressure to bear. Maybe . . . maybe . . . there was nothing else Kerry could think of to do.

The last time she had come here she had been looking for Tristan. And Feyther had been there to protect her. Now there was no one between her and Yelland, and Kerry was no longer a wide-eyed child.

'Ah! Now how can I's do that? If I's do I's'll have the whole of the country owin' me money an' refusin' to pay it back. I's'll look a right fool.'

'I's has a bargain to make with 'e, John Yelland.'

Yelland's hand moved slowly over the table to his cup. He kept his eyes upon her. Truly she was the most beautiful woman he had ever seen. With each year she took on more beauty . . . a wild kind of beauty born from the sea and the wind but yet with a softness that came from inside. He'd often tried to define it but couldn't. She was pretty . . . with her jet black hair and her wide black eyes, white teeth against dark gypsy skin. Her smile was like the sun breaking through the clouds, and yet with all the cold, white mystery of the moon, something always hidden from him. A spirit of fire. He was tantalised. He was obsessed with this fishergirl who made it so clear she despised him.

'What bargain?'

A crowd gathered round them. Tristan had once said she was one of them and she was! She might be a woman among men but she was one of them. She was a Penhale . . . from a long, proud family line going back to her great-grandfather the pirate and beyond. Feyther had fought with these same men shoulder to shoulder against the French. Many of their fellows had not returned from those wars. Mamma had fought shoulder to shoulder in just the same way against illness and poverty with their women . . . had battled alongside them for the lives of each and every one of her children. No, Kerry did not feel alone this time as she made her proposition to Yelland. She made it with dignity, knowing that none of her people would see her brought down. If he wanted her, he would have to take her properly, with decency and respect.

143

'Yous needs a wife . . . yer house needs a housekeeper an' 'tis time yous had children of yer own to work for. Yer house is a disgrace . . . the food that's put on yer table is disgustin'.' She looked round for reaction. 'Nowt but muck! None of these men here would stomach it! 'Tis maggoty, 'tis badly cooked an' there's no taste in it.

'An I's here to offer mysself for the job, providin' . . . providin' that yous wavers the loan on Feyther's wood, wavers the rent on Mamma's house, an' makes sure my family be well looked after! An' I's declare here an' now that no man 'as 'ad me an' that I's come to yous pure an' that's on my honour!'

'Well!'

He might smile like that! He might look round for support from his cronies. But she knew he wanted her. Surprised, she realised she'd always known it. Even when he was teasing her all those years ago here at Jessop's there had been an underlying truth behind his vile words. And now she knew it as a woman knows it. And she had made it clear that there was only one way he was going to have her. And that was through marriage.

'Well! An' I's had some offers in my time but none as bold as that!'

But nobody laughed with him. They watched Kerry Penhale. They watched her set face, they watched her fiery eyes and the straightness of the little body as it stood there, upright, staunch, demanding respect from a man notorious for his revilement of women. They watched and they held their breath, waiting for his answer. And he gave it. Loud and clear so that all could hear.

'On the day of the twenty-fourth of June, Midsummer's Day, after the big run, we's'll be married.'

'In church, properly?'

'Aye.'

'An' yous'll honour the rest of the bargain?'

'Aye. I's'll honour it.'

No feelings . . . like being dead . . . like being a snow-flake giving up magic to melt to nothing.

She left the tavern and walked up the path to the house. A nightjar called from the gorse in the cliff-top, a long, lonely cry from high above. She stopped and stared at the sea for she thought she saw blue flames out by the Spur. But it must have been a figment of her imagination, for corpse lights shone only on her birthday. And nightjars only sing at dusk.

BOOK TWO

MERCY

ONE

At six o'clock the great studded gates of the prison opened.

On either side of it the walls of Newgate rose, swelling from the stench of the city, towering grey as the forbidden cliffs of a lost world.

It was a strange and pitiful assembly which came up from the bowels of hell that day, defensively shading eyes that watered against the light. They had come from where three hundred women and their children, ragged and half-naked, convicted and unconvicted, wicked and innocent together cooked and lived in four squalid rooms littered with filthy straw.

Three open wagons waited to take the female convicts sentenced to transportation along the road to Deptford.

An early morning crowd gathered, spoiling for a fight. Chained to their sisters, depraved by the coarse brutality of gaol treatment, the prisoners acted like furies, caterwauling, spitting and throwing stones and curses. Doomed to a fate worse then death, their crimes . . . passing forged Bank of England notes, coining, shoplifting and prostitution seemed insignificant now.

Four months ago, on Midsummer's Day 1806, a boy child had been born into this little purgatory. His birth had not been entered in any ledgers, had not been attended by any midwife and he had not been received into any church. So his name, when it was given, could well have been given thoughtlessly like a number for identification . . . a handle to hold him by . . . something to single him out from the others. Certainly it could not have been given with love, for that was beyond his mother's experience.

But he was given his name by the distracted wretch who bore him with as near to love as could be got in such a place. It was a name Mercy Geary had once seen and liked – Tristan – and that was the only thing other than life itself and a piteously small amount of gin-tainted milk she was ever able to give her baby son.

The light hurt Mercy's eyes although it was the palest pearl this September morning. The damp and cold and the unfamiliar use being made of her limbs caused them to ache intolerably.

The stone walls of the surrounding houses were layered with decaying notices that told of another life: of steamship departures, of artistes currently appearing at the Opera House, the Adelphi Theatre and St James', of livestock auctions and travelling shows. There was a picture of Ham Shoo who would eat a hogshead of burning pitch, and Simon Paap the celebrated dwarf. The lower half of the notices was totally obscured by mud and slops thrown off the streets by passing carriage wheels. Mercy could read none of them from this distance, but they formed a pattern for her on the walls.

She saw a waif in the crowd pull a string between the legs of a small cardboard figure which jerked and jumped like a man on a gibbet until, to bawdy applause, his legs got stuck round his head.

'Give us your children! In the name of God let your children be saved!'

The sixteen-year-old whore clutched her baby. It could not have been for love, you understand – just a primeval urge to protect, cruelly programmed from some far distant, happier time through a wavy line of women into Mercy.

She wiped spittle from her dress and snarled at the jibes and lewd insults levelled at the cartload of humanity by the baying crowd. Scowling sideways through matted hair she searched for the speaker with the quieter voice.

Only the most wretched were out at dawn on this chill London morning . . . the bleary drinkers waking up to demand more of the black ale that addled their wits, tattered urchins with no homes to go to, sleepers from under the dry arches of Waterloo Bridge . . . and none more pitiless to the scum in the wagons than those who could truly say, 'There but for the grace of God go I'.

Through streamers of white breath blown by the horses the Methodist women in their raven black silks, bonnets screwed to their heads, appeared as though through a mist – ghosts, thought Mercy, fresh out of the graveyard, and their faces pale as death masks.

She pulled Tristan closer. The puny child was wrapped tight from head to toe in scraps of grey blanket. Even his hands were mittened in this way.

'Let me take the mite, for the love of God!' The woman who stank of mothballed death drew near and sniffed into a dainty handkerchief. She came to Mercy's side of the cart and the way she was forced to look up put appeal into the stony face. 'The baby's name?' she cried. 'Tell me his name?'

'Tristan,' whispered Mercy. To give his name wouldn't harm.

'Speak louder, child!'

'Tristan!'

And the woman filled in a tag which she handed to Mercy to hang round his neck. Despite the tightly-fitted coat which was buttoned from neck to hem, Mercy saw that the woman was cold, but driven to stand there by some inner fire the light of which scorched her iron-grey eyes. She held out her arms for Tristan. Her severe bonnet, without frills, was pulled forward and shadowed the top half of her aquiline nose.

'Hand me the child! Let him be saved from a life of infamy and destruction!' The woman came nearer to Mercy. 'Help us to uproot him from the poisonous weeds of crime and sow the seed instead on healthy ground where flowers of love and faith will blossom!'

Two screaming children were dangled from their arms down the side of the cart, their faces crusted with mucous, their hair moving with lice. They struggled against their rescuers with stick-thin limbs, bruised and scarred, and kicked helplessly with rag-wrapped feet.

It wasn't until, with a lurch, the cart started and stopped on the uneven cobbles prior to settling into a rhythm, that the woman realised that Mercy was not going to give her the child. The wagon lurched and set off on its way into Cheapside towards King William Street, and the woman was startled into a screech of sanctimonious abuse.

'You selfish whore!' she raved from the constrictions of her tight-corseted morality. 'Love, you call it! And is it love to deprive your son of his one chance of decency, of respectability, of repentance!'

Repentance? Mercy pulled back the blanket and stared at her baby's face. The wagon rolled out of sight, and Mercy pulled him closer to her. Dull-eyed, empty and bleak inside she was afraid of the future she had doomed him to share.

But nothing on earth would have made her give him up to those women. Methodists and their cold brand of love had done little for her. She knew, oh, yes she knew what life would be like for him with them, and anything, even the journey to the end of the earth must be better than the childhood those women had given to her.

TWO

Up until the day Mrs Theresa Geary walked, feathers in her hat and cocky as a songbird, into the quiet of Mrs Mountebank's baby house, declaring herself to be Mercy's mother, Mercy hadn't imagined she had such a thing.

Unthinkably, Mercy Geary's mother arrived to fetch her on a Sunday. It was extraordinary for anything to happen on a Sunday, let alone anything as revolutionary as this. Mercy was embarrassed, everyone was embarrassed, except Mother, who was furious and insulted.

But Mercy could stand it. Mercy was strong, whereas her best friend Annie Clegg, being soft, would have been broken by it.

How Mercy detested Sundays.

'If You're there, God, give me a sign and blow out that candle!'

Didn't everyone know she was cheating? When she prayed Mercy looked out from conveniently long lashes. No one else appeared to be cheating, only her.

Yes, she loathed Sundays. They were long and dreary and boring. Diversions . . . she only had to catch Annie's eye and mouth, 'Sexton Foster,' and 'May bug!' to achieve total hysteria. And once Mercy saw Annie's shoulders shaking it was too much, she laughed until her jaws ached from clamping them. She didn't know why she did it . . . the punishment for being caught laughing in church would have left her hungry for a week. But she couldn't help it. The temptation, the urge to flirt with danger was too great.

Sexton Foster and his reaction to the may bug that had got in behind the choir stalls was the only good thing she could ever remember happening in church.

The orphans sang. The wail of the lost was in their voices. With no idea what the words meant, they took the hymn to the vaulted rafters. Mrs Mountebank, wearing a careful look of good-fellowship, disliked the nasal tones she heard and thought that the starting of the verses was straggly.

Mercy was a mixture of opposites inside and out. Her straight, silver hair framed a pale complexion. She looked like a scrap of nothing but was tough as old boots. She dreamed of being ill so that everyone would be sorry but she never was and they never were. Sometimes at night she cried quietly, not knowing why, but by morning things were always better. She realised she ought to be living in the 'rude hut in the distant land' they sang about in the hymn. She identified with that rude hut much more than the 'Where stately cities rise in pride, where hamlets dot the countryside', for she was constantly being told she was a nasty, ungrateful child, but didn't know how to be otherwise.

She secretly sided and sympathised with every single native from Madagascar to Mexico, knowing that if they did not fight hard their Sundays would become like hers. But the brown sketches of the missionaries who stalked those floppy-treed lands showed them to be fiercely determined people with jutting chins and walking sticks, and in her own experience resistance was not only impossible but unthinkable.

And when the fourth verse went on to say, 'No day for thoughtless rest and ease, no day to seek ourselves to please,' she felt an overpowering surge of hatred

towards God Who condemned you to sin the moment
you started enjoying yourself.

Mrs Theresa Geary not only walked in on a Sunday,
she also broke a window in defiance.

'To what tribe did the prophet Jeremiah belong?'
    They were back from chapel and every girl who was
old enough to walk was lined up against the dining
room wall, stiff in starched calico and serge petticoats,
clean pinafores and boots that dug into soft flesh
unroughened by the once-weekly-worn, tightly-laced
encumbrances. It was a gloomy cavern of a house,
riddled with passages, fuzzy with creeper and painted
green and brown. It stared out from its unlit windows,
from its own square of haughty poplars across a little-
used road to its twin where the big girls lived.
    When someone answered they could eat, and to her
shame Mercy Geary prayed selfishly to God that someone would know the answer. This was a test to find
out how well they'd been listening in chapel, but it was
hard enough to sit still during the long sermon, let
alone take it in. The minister didn't preach in the
language of children, and Mercy, her head of long hair
drooped demurely so that it looked too large for her
slender frame, found it impossible to follow one complete sentence.
    'What was it that made the widow's two mites so
much more acceptable in God's sight than all the gold
and silver which was cast into the treasury?'
    Mercy remembered this story. She considered the
widow mad to give it, and Jesus wicked to take it. But
it was hopeless. She knew that no one would know the
answer. The food would be cold before they got to it
and Sunday was the best day for food.

156

To the worthy guardians of the Mrs Mountebank Home for the Daughters of Fallen Women, love and understanding, and to some extent, change, led down the surest road to the ruin from whence their charges had been plucked in the first place. It cost thirteen pounds a year to keep a girl here in moral safety so it wasn't cheap. And these children, whose mothers had made such foul blots on the pages of Christian England, would be more likely to be harbouring the Devil in them than most. And the best way to keep the Devil at bay lay in hard work, a spartan life, and much prayer.

Mrs Miriam Mountebank, dedicated, wealthy widow, secretary and founder, considered the 'babies' now as she sat squat in a high-backed chair facing the fidgeting row of tots. She was a large-boned person with a massive square face and a mole at the end of her chin from which sprouted a single hair of great length. They only saw her on Sundays.

She was a powerful woman of regular habits, deep prejudices and high principles, and had been called on by God to do this work. She was intolerant of dissent in the belief that she was always right and whoever challenged her, no matter how small or in how minute a way, was either stupid or wilfully bad. Mrs Mountebank could spot the Devil a mile away.

Mercy sniffed, bringing a grubby hand across an ever-wet nose and shuffled closer to Annie, a wispy girl with a habit of scratching so that her flesh was broken in many places under purpling rings of scabs that were never allowed to heal. Annie's hair was an unruly black mop, cut short to prevent infection.

'Annie,' whispered Mercy. 'Think up an answer!'

Annie was eight, like herself, and due to go across the road with the big ones very soon. Age wasn't judged by birthdays here because few girls had the luxury of knowing the day they'd been born. No, it was judged by weight, and when you reached eight pounds it was judged to be your first birthday.

The thought of meat and jacket taters going dry burnt a hole in Mercy's hungry mind. And there might be rice milk. The well-scrubbed table was set. It had been set before they left for church. Mercy ached to be sitting at it, to be spooning the food she could smell into her mouth.

'How should I know?' Annie, Mercy knew, was every bit as desperate as she. She would have answered if she could have done.

'Try something,' implored Mercy. 'Think of the tribes you know.'

'You think!'

Mercy couldn't think. They ought to have known the answers. They'd had them drummed in often enough. A thought, unattached to anything else, flashed into Mercy's mind. If she'd searched for it it wouldn't have come, but it hung there brightly in the surrounding darkness quite on its own and so Mercy said, 'The tribe of Levi, Ma'am.' And then, remembering how she must say it she repeated correctly, 'The prophet Jeremiah belonged to the tribe of Levi, Ma'am.'

Mrs Mountebank raised her eyeglass and shifted her great buttocks with a silken rustle to propel herself further forward so that she could look more closely at the unlikely child who had spoken. The last thing she'd expected were answers to her questions. They were set primarily to make the girls understand, before being fed, that something one day would be expected in return . . . that nothing was free . . . and until she knew they were exhausted with the standing she would keep them here away from the table with two simple questions taken from the morning's text.

Mercy Geary . . . the waif-like one with the extraordinary silver hair . . . a sign of the Devil if ever Mrs Mountebank had seen one. Mercy, with eyes as old as time . . . a strange child, and the friend who stood next to her, Annie Clegg, still wide-eyed, guileless and naive as a baby.

'And the second question, child?' She squinted down to check what she had written in her little black book before she doggedly repeated, 'What made the widow's two mites so much more acceptable in God's sight than all the gold and silver which was cast into the treasury?'

She peered at the child over her glass so it was easier to hear the nasal reply. Mercy raised her serious, grey eyes towards the illuminated text on the otherwise bare walls before she answered, 'They were all she had, Ma'am. The widow's mites were more acceptable because they were all she had.'

She almost laughed because she was thinking that mites sounded more like bugs than pennies.

Heaven had long ago been closed to Mercy Geary, she'd been told so. She would have liked to go there. She imagined exactly how it would be. But she saw the gates shut hard against her and caught only a distant glimpse of gold from behind. Sometimes she lay in bed and listened to hoofbeats outside on the road, and then she hid her head under the covers thinking the Devil had come for her. But so far he had merely paused on the road before moving on.

'Quite!' said Mrs Mountebank disapprovingly, and a sigh of relief went up round the hall and hovered on the ceiling where it mixed itself with the stale smell of watery food and polish.

'Very well,' the woman stood up reluctantly. 'Take your places for Grace.'

Never in her life had Mercy been more popular and she revelled in the feeling, squeezing pleased hands tight behind her back. She had saved them all a good ten minutes of standing. She had managed the impossible because she had wanted it so badly to happen. Could she always do this? Had that genius been there, unnoticed, until now?

Sundays made her want to bury herself in bedclothes. It was a hunched-up kind of day with lots of staring and lots of silence.

She'd made a mess of her sampler. Every Sunday it got grubbier, and now she'd pricked her finger and the more she tried to dilute the brown, bloody mark with spit, the worse she seemed to make it. She wished she'd been put to darn stockings with the little ones.

> *Just as a tree cut down, that fell*
> *To north or southward, there it lies*
> *So man departs for Heaven or Hell*
> *Fixed in the state wherein he dies.*

Fixed in the state . . . that was what was written on Annie Clegg's work. A great black tree lay like an ugly smudge across the material, splintered and torn as if by storm. Mercy envisaged God's face as her friend arrived in Heaven for sorting, before they realised who she really was, with her bloomers down, or picking her nose, or scratching her bottom which itched her to near-distraction at night.

'You've made a right mess of that!'

Mercy quietened Annie with a withering look before glancing towards the top of the schoolroom where, in front of the four cracked and antiquated maps, one of Mother's helpers, a big girl from across the road who was not yet old enough for service, sat on a tall stool

160

and kept strict watch over the bent rows of industrious paupers.

'I'll go over it in brown,' Mercy whispered, seeing that it was safe. 'Nobody'll notice till next week.'

Sitting sewing silently made Sunday afternoons long. The windows were too high to look out of and the girls were certainly not allowed to do nothing. Sometimes Mercy opted for punishment rather than boredom. She was sent to stand on a chair in the wind-blown courtyard with her hands on her head until teatime. At least she could move, could make noises in her throat, could convince herself she was alive! She never passed out from the cold like some children. She never had to be warmed up with hot broth and stone bottles. She never had that sort of luck.

'Mercy! Your mother, a Roman Catholic person from Ireland, is here.'

Into the roaring silence came Mother's quiet, controlled voice. Her tiny bird-like head was covered in a down of light red fuzz. She had a tread like a cat's and demanded from her charges the title of Mother. Her neck, unlike Mrs Mountebank who didn't have one at all because her head came straight from the frill at its base, was long and thin and moved like a chicken's. Tight-lipped, with a faceful of bones, Mother only ever became expansive when Mrs Mountebank was present.

But Mother possessed an astonishing knack . . . that of keeping children alive despite all odds; no matter how frail her latest intake, no matter how pathetically starved or cruelly treated, Mother managed to maintain life and keep the numbers in the books at an almost unheard-of fifty per cent. These staggering statistics helped the money-raising efforts of the Prison Mission ladies, towards whom the daughters of the wayward were prodded into an almost perpetual round of ceaseless gratitude. Hence the wording on Mercy's sampler this Sunday afternoon; *I was homeless and Ye took me in* and on Queenie's, to which it would be attached when finished, *I was hungry and Ye fed me.*

When Mother entered the room there was a scraping back of chairs as her charges respectfully stood.

She made her stunning announcement in a sinister, confidential sort of way, and added, 'Come with me, Mercy Geary.' Her long neck stretched, exposing the chickeny skin at her throat.

All the little girls lifted their eyes but not their heads, pretending they hadn't heard. Annie, beside her, had started to scratch but now she stopped, and to Mercy who sat near enough to feel her warmth, she seemed frozen solid, all movement gone. It wasn't good to be singled out even if you were, like Mercy, one of Mother's favourites.

Annie was more frightened than Mercy was. 'I'll be all right, Annie. Don't worry, I'll be all right.'

Mercy left her friend with a thin line of blood dripping from the latest scab on her calf, which finished as it soaked into the tight band of leather at her ankle. She laid a comforting hand on Annie's shoulder as numbly she stood and then walked, head bent, towards Mother.

The thrill and the dread that something was happening! But she felt such concern for Annie that her heart was splitting like an overcooked tater. Annie was a softie, she couldn't help but be one. Mercy knew that Annie was wondering, right now, that if Mercy's mother *had* come to claim her – and from the sounds that came from the red confines of Mother's parlour it would seem that she had – then how would she live without her. Who would she talk to? What would she do?

162

Mercy was all she had. Mercy was the only soft bit in Annie's world. Mercy Geary bit her lip as she walked behind Mother. She loved Annie, yes she did, more than any other person alive. But Mercy had her dreams, too. And now she was going to find them out.

THREE

'Theresa Geary, your mother, Mercy!' Mother made the introduction, over-pronouncing the words and managing to get the taste of infidel into the back of her throat. The name Theresa was a heathen name if she'd ever heard one, and Mercy, who knew Mother's every inflexion, swallowed twice in quick succession.

The woman who stood back in the shadows of the room which Mercy had never before been allowed to enter was only a girl, with sharp, bright eyes and wavy hair. Mercy knew about the Irish infidels, but she'd somehow never imagined that her mother could be one.

When Theresa Geary shyly said, 'Mercy?' that was the first Irish lilt the confused child had ever heard.

'Well, don't just stand there, girl. Come and meet your mother and use the proper manners you have been taught!'

It was clear that Theresa Geary had only just regained control because her mass of heavy brown hair was ruffled and her bonnet clung to it at a precarious angle. Her pale cheeks had rosy dabs on each centre. It was also clear that she was not prepared for what she saw, a pale, undergrown child with frightened eyes, and hair as silver as moonlit gossamer.

But Mother was enjoying herself. 'Your mother wants to take you away to live with her, don't you, Mrs Geary?' She had to go to the door to pull the reluctant Mercy into the room. 'She's come back for you! I advised her against it but she insisted, even managing to become hysterical and break a window in her determination to force herself back into the house!'

164

It was hard for Mercy to look at her mother without catching hold of the eyes that stared at her so hard. This was not how she had dreamed it would be. Her mother was nothing like the one in her dreams. At once she felt let down and a little cheated.

'Well, Mercy, and what have you got to say about this?'

Mercy would have liked Mother to be quiet so she could hear Theresa Geary's voice again. She stared hard at the ground and when she started to rub her arms because she felt suddenly cold, Mother slapped her hand and she let it fall limp by her body with the other one.

Theresa's lips were tight together. She kept staring at her daughter, and then out of the window, and all the while she made sweeping patterns on the carpet with one foot.

'Well? What do you say? What do you say? Speak up, child!'

'I want to stay here!'

Mercy's word spilled messily into the silence. She had wanted to say, 'How can I go with someone I don't even know?' But she didn't know how to. She might have asked, 'How will I know she won't leave me again?' Or 'What would happen to Annie?' But she couldn't.

She should have said, 'I know that you've already changed your mind, Mrs Geary,' because Mercy knew that to be the truth.

Theresa Geary didn't try persuasion, she just gave her daughter the saddest look Mercy had ever seen on a person's face before.

'So you see, Mrs Geary, if you had accepted my summing-up of the situation in the first place, we would all have been spared a great deal of inconvenience *and* a broken window, which I'm afraid you'll have to pay for, and the disruption of the girl's Sunday studies. As I explained to you before, I don't really think you're in any position to provide Mercy with the opportunities and the necessities of life that we are able to offer her here at Mrs Mountebank's, do you?'

Mother went on dominating Theresa Geary with her quiet reasonableness, adding bricks to her natural feelings of inferiority. As she spoke, Mercy watched the white patches of skin glistening through Mother's sparse red hair and marvelled at the contrasting thickness of her mother's. She raised a hand to her own hair in order to feel it, wondering why it was silver when her mother's was brown like that, but Mother, thinking she was fidgeting, knocked it down.

'Of course you are quite welcome to visit, Mrs Geary. It's understandable that you'll want to keep an eye on your daughter's progress now that you're in a position to do so.' Mother's eyebrows dangled like red catkins as if pained that such a creature should be allowed out of prison in the first place.

But Mercy knew she wouldn't visit. Mother had squeezed a woman easily-squeezed right out of the house.

Mercy tore up the handkerchief Theresa Geary gave her, ashamed by it, disgusted with it, with its *G* for Geary embroidered on the corner. It was the wrong present . . . it would make the others laugh at her.' She must have known about your snotty nose, then!'

She tore it into tiny strips and forced herself to swallow them before going to find Annie. Swallowing the soggy little pieces made her throat and her tummy hurt. That was good. Because emotionally she was too small to take on, with each little bite, her own betrayal and her mother's pain. It rent her.

166

'Fancy you being Irish! You'll be able to go back to your own country one day when you're grown.' Annie sighed, making out there was a great deal now, for Mercy to look forward to. She was riddled with guilt that her own selfish prayers had been answered. 'You might have a family . . . people who might take you in. Everyone isn't poor in Ireland, you know. Did she kiss you goodbye?'

Mercy frowned as she tried to remember. 'No, she just played with the ends of my hair, sort of lifted it in her hands like this.' Mercy tried to do it with Annie's but it wasn't long enough. 'Annie, why is my hair so peculiar?'

But she was Irish! Irish! She wasn't just a pauper, she belonged to a whole different country, to a whole breed of people, and to Mercy that made all the difference.

Mother always warned she had too much spirit, 'Dangerous in a person of your position,' and now Mercy knew why. The Irish were a spirited race.

Both of them knew that Mercy had lost her dream. Both of them knew how heavily the betrayal of her mother weighed on her heart. And both of them knew why she'd done it, too, but neither of them ever spoke of that. But from that time on Mercy would practise her 'perfect Irish', sitting for hours with daft Mary Ludd, the only other Irish girl at Mrs Mountebank's, repeating her words until even in bed at night the lilt of the language obsessed her and she rocked to sleep in it . . . dreamed in it.

'Mercy, I heard someone say there'd be jam for tea tomorrow,' said Annie, hopefully.

FOUR

'So long ago. Yes, I realise that this was a long time ago but it's *most important* I should know. I wouldn't be here, otherwise.'

Tristan Carne was angry. So angry he could hardly bear to be civil. He was tired and cold, and uncomfortable. There was not one comfortable chair in this room, not a single cosy, homely stick of furniture anywhere in the house as far as he could see. It was oppressive and repressive – and deliberately designed to be so. And if it was like this now, what had it been like twenty-seven years ago? No better, that was certain. A home . . . a home for children. An unkind smile moved on his lips. He sat across from the desk and regarded this desolate old woman with hate engrained on her face and distaste on her breath. She didn't approve of the way he sat, with one casual leg curled over his knee, and one arm hooked over the back of the chair. But Tristan was in no mood to pander to this . . . to this Mrs Bowls.

'You are telling me that Mercy Geary chose, she *chose* to stay *here*?' He looked around him, not bothering to disguise the revulsion he felt, the contempt that rang clear in his voice as he went on, 'And I suppose you considered that to be a right decision.'

'I did, at the time, most certainly, yes.'

'You didn't approve then, of Mrs Geary?'

'There was little of the Mrs about her, if I may say.'

'You may say what you like, Mrs Bowls, but it's not your opinion I'm interested in.'

Mother was not used to entertaining young men, not

168

ungodly young men like this one. Every so often the vicar sent the young curates round to tea, but they were not like this man. They were softly-spoken and shy and knew their places. They handed round the bread and butter and said, 'Thank you, Ma'am,' when she poured the strong brown mixture into their dainty cups. She had offered tea to this young man. He had declined.

So Mother, in her parlour without a teapot between her and her antagonist, for that is what he was turning out to be, was nervous and defensive. He was lucky to find her still here. She could have left years ago, and then there would have been no one to provide him with the information he was seeking.

Tristan's five-year exile had changed him more on the inside than on the outside. Taller, broader, there was sadness, now, in his gentle eyes but that same astuteness had always been there and missed nothing. His wrists were fringed with expensive lace, his hands seemed poised and calm, but his long fingers signified impatience where they tapped the chair top. His hair, paler than in his childhood, shone and curled in a lazy fashion, framing his angular features and dropping back at his shoulders into a loose velvet knot. Mother knew that his high-collared frockcoat was of the best fabric, even if she disapproved of the flagrant way he wore such a strong shade of blue. And then, as if he read her thoughts the young man leaned forward and said, 'I'm surprised you still remember. Twenty-seven years is a very long time and you must have had many children pass through your hands since then.'

Mother clamped her face, and out of tight lips she said, 'Some you remember, others you don't.'

'But you remember Mercy Geary?' said Tristan.

'She came to a bad end.'

'She came to a bad beginning,' said Tristan.

'I am not prepared to sit here and be insulted.'

'It is hard for me to take any other attitude.' But Tristan felt surprise, because she did sit there, and she did listen, and she did answer his questions, albeit sulkily, reluctantly even, but she answered. And yet the woman was hiding behind a mask so that when he came away, when he was sent across the road to follow in Mercy's footsteps later that afternoon he felt he had learned very little, very little at all.

Yes, Mother had sat there and answered, for Tristan Carne was not a young man you wanted to cross. Richly dressed and with confident bearing, he was not from the usual mould and Mother sensed his lack of respect for the accepted conventions. He would say anything if pushed far enough. She was not going to push him. She'd never even have agreed to talk to him if she'd known who he was. But all that silly girl Tilly had said was, 'A young man to see yous, missus, a nice young man, well spoke.'

Well, Mother wanted him out of here, out of her parlour and cleanly away so that she could wipe her hands of it all and say 'That's that!' – much as she had done with Theresa and Mercy Geary. Guilt was a feeling she rarely experienced, so that when it came it was sharper, more debilitating to her than to most other folk. Of course she remembered. It had been 1798 – two years before the turn of the century. Everyone was hopeful then . . . the vicar's sermons had even vibrated with hope. Of what? No one was sure. But Mother remembered, not because of the date or the time or the hope in the air but because, of all the children she had dealt with, Mercy Geary was the one of whom Mother had been most fond.

That, of course, had changed. Naturally. You can't

170

have feelings in this job, said Mother to herself, ignoring the reasons why. Making up excuses.

For how could she tell Tristan Carne how it really had been. How could Mother, honestly, admit that even to herself?

It was all Mercy's fault . . . and that terrible mother of hers. Coping with the children was bad enough, but dealing with parents of that sort was intolerable. Mother sniffed as she remembered. The women were lice-ridden, some of them, diseased. Who knows what foul contagion they carried? What they needed, like their children, was a good scrubbing in disinfectant.

Mother had started her little campaign at teatime on the day of Theresa Geary's unfortunate visit. Mercy wasn't chosen to fetch Mother's lemon barley water – Hattie Cawdle went instead . . .

Mother sat at the end of the table on the only chair, the one Mrs Mountebank had used before lunch. She sat there because she could position herself in front of the only fire in the house other than the kitchen range.

The children stood before their benches while she sat to say Grace. They stood and waited until she nodded, until her barley water arrived.

'Your barley water, Mother,' said Hattie Cawdle, smirking at Mercy from the sharp little sides of her eyes. The beads on the linen jug-cover winked in the firelight.

Meals were usually taken in silence. Sometimes Mother talked, expecting answers only when she asked for them, sometimes she didn't. Today she did.

'We had a visitor today, girls.' Her first nod allowed them to sit, the second to help themselves to a slice of bread. So carefully had they been watching for this signal that few of them heard her opening sentence. After they had started to eat, she repeated it.

171

'We had a visitor today who came straight from prison where she had been sent for stealing. Her name,' and now Mother smiled and the little bones in her face showed rigid under the skin like the hackly back of a snarling dog, 'her name was Theresa Geary, and she was a Roman Catholic from Ireland!'

There was no response. Everyone knew that Mercy's mother had come to fetch her away but had left her behind, instead. Unconsciously, Cathy Pratt, who sat on one side of Mercy, inched herself away. It was the mental distance she required, but her body insisted it be moved from danger, too. Annie, on the other side, moved closer, her hair stiffening on the top of her head as she sensed the charge of hatred in the room. Mercy, nervous, hooked a tress of hair behind her ears.

'We all know about Roman Catholics, don't we?' This was not an attitude approved of by the Mission, but Mother wasn't looking for approval. 'And what are Roman Catholics?'

'Mere animals, Mother.' The response was dispassionate, in perfect time, and chanted on one note like a psalm in church.

Mother sniffed approval and nodded again to release more bread onto the crumbless plates.

At the bottom of the social pile, Mother's only power lay in this company of abandoned children sitting on benches before her down the sides of the long table. Herself the product of a cruel and vicious childhood, and a marriage whose violent end had come as a relief, her world had shrunk so that it was encapsulated only in the Home. Her passionate religious fervour was, for her, an unconscious sexual release. The perverted demands it made upon her sadistic nature suited her down to the ground. There was nothing she liked better than a cause, and she eyed today's as she would a steaming game-pie, eager to taste the tender flesh she could already smell. Her mouth watered. She swallowed.

'There is a Roman Catholic sitting here amongst us today, children. A reformed Roman Catholic, but a Roman Catholic nevertheless.'

Obligingly the children looked around, playing the game correctly, pretending not to know who it was until Mother told them.

'The Roman Catholic sitting here disguising herself to look like everyone else has a mother who is not only violent but also a thief!'

The cold room sighed with the obligatory gasp.

'Mercy Geary!' Mother drew herself up to a terrible height in order to drop the noose-like accusation over Mercy's head. 'What are you doing at this tea table?'

Mercy's hands were very small, curled on the edge of the table. She knew she wasn't required to speak although Mother pretended that she wanted her to.

'What? I asked what?'

Mercy hung her head in shame. She felt Annie's thin frame tremble and, trying not to betray her friend by staring like everyone else, Annie's eyes were focused hard on the back of one of Mercy's tight fists. Mercy could feel them there, a hot little buzzing on the back of her hand.

'Get into the corner! We don't want to sit with you! We don't want to look at you! Turn your back to the wall so that we don't all have to sit here looking at the daughter of a thief!'

In her mad scramble, in her eagerness to comply, Mercy scraped her shins against the table and normally, would have winced. Annie felt the pain for her. Because by now Mercy felt nothing.

The meal continued as if nothing had happened. To kill the love! To kill the love! To kill the love, she put the thorns round Mother's head. They said that Mercy

173

was Mother's favourite. The pure, almost sweet hatred she invented for Mother made Mercy surprisingly calm. And when it was time to line up behind the benches and file out of the room in turn, she heard that Annie's voice, too, was polite and natural, saying 'Goodnight, Mother', as she passed the chair. But Mercy turned to watch. She stared at Mother's head because what she saw looked like a halo round it and her hair looked as if it was made of thorns, neat plaited thorns, not one of them out of place.

Deliver us from evil . . . evil . . . evil . . . The words vibrated in Mercy's brain as she waited to be released from her place of disgrace.

Much later, when she finally got to her bed she heard the sounds of little night mutters from twenty other girls in the long dormitory. But Annie was waiting for her. Annie wouldn't sleep until Mercy came.

She didn't like Annie's sallow skin. She had never liked it, never. She was always just pretending. What would Annie say if she knew the awful truth, that Mercy would rather be in Mother's bed, safe and wrapped in the arms of the person who had reared her from babyhood? The two girls cuddled down together. Mercy didn't sleep until Annie went off, and then she crept back to her own bed.

Mercy found it hard to sleep that night. She stayed awake and laid her plans. She was going to deliver Annie from evil because God certainly wouldn't. God was one of them, they were all in this together. They wore the same crowns and the same haloes.

Mother had stopped loving her. Perhaps she never had.

Mercy wasn't going to stay at the Home any longer. She was going to tell Annie about her plans in the morning. Her heart hammered at the daring in the very thought of it. No one had been known to do it before. She and Annie were going to run away. Mercy didn't care about Mother. Serve Mother right.

That night . . . that dream . . . that cruellest caress.

The mattress cradled her in the pool of warmth that creeps. While she woke it cooled until, fully aware of what she had done, she was wet and cold down to her knees and up to her tummy. She had to peel herself out of the bed.

Then it was down long corridors in the dark with the wet sheet flapping and her bare feet slapping on scrubbed grey stones. All the way, passing the dark, blistered banisters, down the back stairs to the wash-room where the long-legged spiders lurked around flagged floor and stone basins.

She was very awake now because she was frightened, frightened that Mother might wake and find her soaking her sheet in soda again. And while she smacked her she would say, 'Mercy! Goodness, you are eight years old!'

Where was her bravery now? Where was the spirit with which she had gone to sleep?

Not a soul in the world, not even Mercy herself, knew what this loveless childhood was doing to her.

But when she returned to her bed there was Annie, worried, awake and waiting, and she, the strong one, let herself cry in Annie's arms for dreams that always came to nothing.

FIVE

Tristan was not in a place he wanted to be. No one could want to be *here*. But he'd soon be away, leaving this crone to her memories, back in Porthclegga ... Sometimes it pulled so hard at his heart, sometimes he dreamed he had never left. He could hear the soft lap of the water, caressing the jetty-side. Wherever he went, if he closed his eyes he could smell the salt tang of the sea, the tar, the fish, the aura that came from the closeness of the houses ... the way the air seemed to share and delight in the rich pungency of the cooking pots.

Porthclegga – Kerry – they could not be split. They were one in Tristan's heart. Never, in his five-year absence from Porthclegga, never had Kerry Penhale been far from his mind. He carried her with him, and if, in the daytime, he sometimes forgot her, if an hour or two went by, he made up for the lapse at night, taking out his memories as he rested his head on his pillow, smiling, always smiling as he thought of her and her sweet wildness. She would be angry with him for leaving without saying goodbye. But she would forgive him again when she saw him, with a coy half-smile and the slant of a softly lashed eye.

Mostly he remembered how she looked with the wind in her black hair, perched on the clifftop looking out over the sea. Oh yes, and that smile, half-smile, half-scowl, and her eyes challenging him, dark eyes, opal eyes that sent rushes of emotion right through him. Even here. Even now, in this dark place.

Not long now. Not long. If only he could tell her he

was near. But he couldn't go back until he had completed this, a task Mother Carrivick had set him on the night he had left. He'd been a child then, just thirteen, wary and suspicious of the witch who said, 'You owe it, Tristan. You owe it to yourself to discover the truth'. Can five years then turn a child into a man? Yes, when they're lived as he had lived them, aching with the loss of the girl who meant more to him than life itself.

Mother Carrivick had given him his task, and his direction. He had been taken in by people who cared, cosseted for the first time in his young life, taught a skill and the ways of the world and lost the narrow beliefs he had acquired in the confines of Porthclegga. Almost eighteen now, Tristan was a wise young man for his years. Wise enough, and knowing enough around people, to learn when to believe them and when not. When to feel good among them, and when to feel bad. And here, in this room, with this hard-faced, righteous guardian of the young, it was not possible to feel good.

Love? It had never visited this place. When he'd arrived at the Home he'd tried to blot out the faces of the children, for he'd seen hardship in his travels, oh yes, and desperate poverty, neglect – misery in so very many forms – but never before had he been surrounded by such utter despair.

The faded woman who sat in the opposite chair, so erect and unbending, now asked him, 'I should like to know why you're making these enquiries, Mr Carne. What is your interest in the matter? An intelligent, prosperous young fellow like yourself can have no connection with the girl, Mercy Geary, of whom we speak. She was a pauper, an orphan, of dubious stock. There is never much hope, Mr Carne, for girls like that. They come from bad seed, contaminated, sadly, like so many of my charges. We do what we can, of course, with

God's help, but naturally bad blood will always out.'
Mother could have been speaking of a particularly
vicious kind of dog, a dog she would, if she'd had her
way, put down.

'You did what you could. Of course you did. You
gave her food and succour, warmth, shelter and
religion, too, no doubt. But what about love?'

Mother drew herself up. 'You must try to understand, Mr Carne, that given an inch these children
would take a mile. They are like animals. They need
the security of firm discipline and a steady hand. There
has often been far too much "love" as you call it,
already in the seamy worlds from which many of them
come from before they are rescued . . .'

'Oh yes, of course, I understand what you say. When
did Mercy Geary leave here, Mrs Bowls, and how long
was she with you?'

Questions, questions, questions. When would he go
and be done with his questions? How did he expect her
to remember exactly what had happened all those years
ago? 'She left in the year we speak of, when she was
eight years old. She was brought to us as a baby, one
of the many we rescue direct from the prison gates.
These mothers breed like rabbits, so they are relieved
to hand their babies over when approached and offered
help from the hand of Jesus.'

The young man nodded. 'Well, we can both be sure
that your rewards will undoubtedly be waiting for you
in Heaven.'

And Mother bowed her head. She often told herself
the same thing, but coming from this young man, well,
she felt uneasy. She couldn't quite place his tone.

Was that, then how it had been?
'Why are you doing this? Why? Why?'
There was more than a little madness in Mother's

vendetta, and as time went on and it grew into out-and-out persecution, Mercy's difficulties increased.

If Mother had known the answer herself perhaps she could have replied to Mercy's silent question. She would have explained that there was something about keeping children who had no choice that appealed to her – but what about Mercy *who had chosen to stay*? The shrill voice that had innocently said, 'I want to stay here', had nudged Mother's conscience. If she was honest she might have said it had something to do with failure, too, and that when Mercy's own mother turned her daughter down, Mother had been forced to regard the child in a starkly realistic light. When she stared at Mercy she stared face to face at failure, for the child was suddenly real, trailing around with that dratted snotrag as a more attractive child would clutch a teddy bear . . . and oh, that feeble, repetitive cough. Mercy didn't seem to notice it herself but it irritated Mother beyond endurance. Something about the child's help-lessness drove Mother wild – that injured look in those wistful, slanted eyes . . . as if she was asking for something else! And the child never seemed to grow! It sometimes seemed as if she wilfully refused to respond, in spite of Mother's earlier attempts at kindness. The worst of it was that Mercy had been her favourite.

So the persecution continued, until a broken cup presented Mercy with her first opportunity to push forward with her plans.

Mercy didn't break it, Annie did. And it happened on yet another morning when Mercy couldn't find her clothes.

'What am I going to do? What am I going to do?' Mercy wailed over and over again as she frantically searched and searched again in the same places.

'You're going to be late for prayers.' What else could

Annie say? It didn't help matters and Mercy was sobbing with dismay by the time they found the clothes, which had been strewn, meanly, piece by piece, down the stairs. By the time Annie retrieved them they'd been trampled over by a hundred feet.

And they had found her secret bag of lavender. Mercy showed it to Annie. 'Look, they've ripped it to shreds and tipped it over my bed.'

'Take no notice of them,' Annie said. 'They're worse than savages.'

'They're frightened,' said Mercy, 'like I am.'

When Annie was kind Mercy felt guilty, guilty about not sharing. She would sometimes creep out and steal cabbages from Mrs Potter's garden plot down the road, bring them back in her apron and eat them raw and greedily, sharing with no one. Then she used to pretend to be off her food.

On kitchen duties, Mercy found pans deliberately burnt. Days went by and in the scullery pots were piled high, messed up unnecessarily with food rubbed in. 'There's so many here it looks as if the Board has been to dinner,' moaned Mercy. Annie, busy herself, could only commiserate. There was no alternative but to clear the sink and draining board . . . that porous, shallow grey sink that stank of years of foul water, with the soda stinging her chapped hands.

And children asking in cruel sing-song shouts. 'Why didn't you go with your mother, Mercy? Didn't she want you? Didn't she want you?'

And, 'Mercy, don't you think it's time to go to Confession?'

She was just so glad it was happening to her and not to Annie. So why was she making it worse? She didn't know. She wouldn't have dreamed of criticising the behaviour of the children, many of whom were her friends and Annie's, too. They were a family. They had grown up together. But in this insecure world there was nothing safer than to gang up with the leader against a helpless one. Mercy knew this. She understood it only too well. If the tables had been turned she and Annie would have sided with Mother, too.

But Annie still didn't want to hear about Mercy's plans to run away. Always frightened, she lived in dread of most things. The very thought of it made her scared stiff, she said. 'You're too impulsive, Mercy Geary. You never stop to think things out. We'd starve to death. We'd be brought back and then what?' And those were just two of a hundred of Annie's arguments.

Their ideas were coloured by the view they'd been given of the world outside. There, people lurked, according to Mother, like a subhuman horde, seething rebelliously in the darkness and just waiting to catch little girls. It was a dangerous place out there. It was often compared to a sea, and here in the Home they were in a safe vessel, sheltered from the storms of temptation and the sandbanks of immorality that would otherwise beset them. And because they were girls, so the Sunday sermons went, they would drown under the first wave of corruption to hit them.

Mercy brought her idea up again and again, but the worse life became the more vehemently Annie would argue, 'I can't, Mercy. I can't. I can bear this, but I don't know if I could bear that! We wouldn't know where to go. We wouldn't have anywhere to sleep! Anything could happen to us!'

Mercy was relieved that Annie hadn't immediately jumped at the plan. Mercy didn't really want to run away. Very often she scared herself with her wild ideas and her violent changes of mood. She needed more time to dream. The dreaming and the planning were the best part.

But even when, days later, Annie broke the cup

and Mercy, coming up from the boothole raised her eyebrows as if to say, 'Now will you come with me?', Annie, miserable, stood on the chair and shook her head, tears of despair sliding mechanically down cheeks that had long since lost any baby chubbiness.

She'd been cleaning the white wood dresser. To do it properly she had to remove every piece of crockery while balanced on a high chair to reach the top shelves. The crockery, a mass of it, all plain white, was only used by the adults, but there were enough pieces to set before an army. And once a week, it was hard to see why, but it had to be taken down and the shelves it sat on scrubbed before it was replaced, every piece in the exact same position it had come from, all handles turned to face the right.

The cup opened like a white rose on the flagstones, exposing its treacherous heart. Everyone stopped what they were doing and turned to look at Annie's face. Everyone wanted to see what would happen next. They were weak with relief that this hadn't happened to them. Because this was serious.

Mercy heard the crash. Garbed in an old sack apron, her legs aching from kneeling, she ran into the kitchen suspecting the worst. She was greeted by a shocked silence.

Annie's fingers pulled her lips into a pout as she gazed down with brimming eyes upon her friend. Now was not the time to remind her of running away . . . this was reality, hard and hot, while the other was soft and far away like a cloud.

'I suppose I'll have to go and tell Mother.' Annie absentmindedly numbed herself as much as she could against the awful situation that was weaving itself around her.

'No!' Mercy was even more certain now that God, Who alone could have prevented this, was working against them. 'No, Annie.' Hope rose in her heart as she said it. 'I'll go.'

Mercy had been thinking hard for days. She had seen Mother sitting there in her big chair at the end of the tea table with a look on her face that resembled the one so often worn by the youngest child. 'There's something wrong with her,' she had confided to Annie. 'Mother hasn't grown, and all the bad things that happen are because of that.'

Annie had remained unpersuaded.

'Why isn't it obvious to you as it is to me?' Mercy persevered. 'All this fear comes down and down like hailstones on our heads and it makes the hunger and the cold and the dark feel worse . . . it stops us caring about each other. Instead of that, what do we do? We shake and scatter the hailstones off ourselves and onto other people. And all because of Mother.'

She wanted Annie to hate Mother with a pure hatred that was impossible for Annie to feel. But Annie did dislike her . . . it was Mercy who still loved her. And if this wasn't a prime example of what she was trying to say, if Annie, standing there forlornly holding the broken cup, couldn't see what she meant and come to detest Mother with furious vehemence, then Mercy couldn't imagine what *would* make her understand.

Even now when she'd broken the cup Annie was busy saying, 'No, no, Mercy, I'll go,' when it was clear she was much too terrified to go and even more terrified of letting Mercy go for her. Why? In case Mercy stopped loving her?

'I'm going, Annie, because I'm braver than you. She can't hurt me in the same way she hurts you.' Where had this foolish feeling of invincibility come from? Was it just because she'd once got Mrs Mountebank's questions right? On the strength of that could she, Mercy

Geary, eight years old, ride along in the slipstream of that success and conquer the world, conquer Mother?

Whatever she felt she scooped up the bits of cup and put them in her pinafore pocket along with her fear. She would stand up to Mother, stand up and defy her, show her she didn't care! The others stood in a ring around her, making a polite hole, a sacred opening for the sacrifice to pass through.

Mercy knocked on Mother's door and was straight away answered with a 'Yes?'

'It's Mercy Geary, please Mother,' she called, with her mouth almost touching the wood.

Mother was not in the habit of being disturbed in her inner sanctum, and Mercy could imagine the sigh of annoyance she'd be giving as she got up from her chair and came, in her quiet way, to the door.

The light underneath sneered like a widening mouth as it opened. With eyes held down where they were required to be, Mercy dipped her hand into her pocket and brought out the pieces of white china.

'I'm sorry, Mother,' she said with her voice on the floor as well as her heart and her eyes, 'but I've broken a cup. It was an accident, please Mother.' Even as she said them she thought how unnecessary those words were. No one in their right mind would break a cup on purpose.

There was a long silence. Mercy studied the tips of Mother's boots and let her eyes wander fractionally up to the hem of her dress. Because of the mud spots, Mercy knew that Mother had been out to oversee the feeding of the fowls. Because of the specks of sawdust, she knew she had been out prodding the meat delivered by the butcher, carefully choosing, no doubt, the cheapest pieces of scrag-end she could find for general use while picking out a juicy mutton chop for herself.

Although of course it didn't show, Mercy coloured as she realised that Mother was sniffing out her difference in attitude. How, she didn't know, for she was looking as wretchedly dejected as possible. She wasn't so stupid as to ask for trouble. *I don't love you any more. I don't love you any more.* She was out to prove to herself and to Annie that Mother could no longer touch her.

'With every month that goes by you grow more clumsy, Mercy.' Mother started off carefully, looking hard at the miscreant before her. 'You are clumsy and careless in every way – in the way you talk, move and act.'

As she spoke Mercy lifted her eyes past the waist-high bunch of keys and on, up, until they were staring straight at Mother's hard, flat chest where the shawl crossed over and tied. What lay beneath those clothes? What lay under that skin that had never held a child's head against it?

Relent! Hold me! Hold me! Love me! I gave up my own mother in order to stay with you!

Uncomfortable there, Mercy lifted her eyes up until she felt her hair move down her back. Face to face with Mother she felt like a mouse confronted by a buzzard: it was like being tethered flat out on the grass and seeing the bird's head right up there, its beady eyes blazing as it sized up its prize . . . missing nothing! The neck was slightly arched, just like that of a bird of prey, and the lips were blown out into the shocked sharp shape of a savage beak.

'Yes, Mercy Geary.' Horrified by the brazenness of the girl before her, seeing in the child's eyes a challenge that was intolerable, Mother finally found words to speak. 'You might well stare at me straight in the face like that. But God is seeing you through my eyes now, and no punishment I could give you will be like that meted out to you on Judgement Day. You are the most evil girl I have ever had pass through my hands. You are a hussy, Mercy Geary, daughter of Jezebel, and no amount of prayer will save your soul, God help you. I see defiance. I see a total lack of humility. These sins, girl, are a thousand times more ominous than the breaking of a cup.'

Mercy stared at Mother, not meaning to be insolent but merely fascinated by the intensity of hatred she saw there. She was unaware that her own face looked as if it was smiling. Her teeth were clenched and her fists were tight. And suddenly she said, in a voice full of mysterious grief, mysterious because it was so full of rage, 'The greatest of these is love. The greatest of these is love. The greatest of these is love . . .'

This was intolerable! The hand that came and knocked her down was determined to wipe off that smile. It knocked Mercy back against the wall. She hit her head against the ledge that changed the wall from wood to plaster, that changed the shiny brown into moss green.

Mother's voice was just above a whisper. 'Dirt!' she said. 'Dirt, just like your mother. I did you a kindness, girl, when I told you she was in prison for thieving. She was no thief, but a whore and oh, how it shows.' Mother shuddered and hunched her shoulders.

With her mouth wide open, as much in reaction to her own daring as to the blow, Mercy, who had often heard the word, listened as her own small voice asked what it meant.

'A fallen woman! A woman of the night! A woman who sells her body for money, Mercy. And I see the same trends in you. You will sell your soul to the Devil one day . . . for you want too much . . . and mark my words, girl, because I am never, ever wrong!' At no time was Mother's voice raised above a whisper.

'You're lying!' Mercy reeled from the knowledge as

she had reeled from the blow. Behind Mother's figure
the room lay dark like a womb, solid with virtue with
its heavy mahogany furniture, velvet curtains and
carpet of patterned maroon. Mercy wanted to creep
inside it and curl up. Leafy plants obscured what light
might have come through the windows. And Mother
was the monster who lived in this den, as cluttered as
their own accommodation was spartan and bare.

Mercy saw everything in sharp definition; the great
glass dome of fruit wax, the blue and white china knick-
knacks and the ornaments of coloured glass. And
amidst all this she saw the pathetic, framed embroider-
ings of girls who had left the baby house – religious,
grateful and pure, carefully-worked words that meant
nothing hanging in rows, souvenirs on a monster's wall.

'You're just saying these things to hurt me. You
don't know!' And still she pleaded.

'Oh, I know! I know all right, Mercy Geary! Your
bitch mother gave you away because you had become
a "nuisance" to her when she went to ply her trade.
She said so!' lied Mother. 'There was never a doubt
about it! She begged that we take you in. She compared
you to a crippled hamstring, if I remember rightly.'
Mother paused to think, to allow her warped imagination to take the strain, 'That's what she said, but
I don't think it was a hamstring to which she was
referring . . . So it's no wonder you are as you are, is
it?'

Mercy gripped the broken cup so hard it cut her
skin. She crouched on the floor in front of Mother,
defeated, whimpering like a beaten dog.

And the final disclaimer came with a dull thud to
her heart . . . 'Go and get your friend, Mercy, the one
who broke the cup, and tell her to collect her things.
Today I am taking you both across the road.' And

187

Mother rasped her hands together as if freeing them of muck.

One more day and Mother might never have told her. Mercy might never have found out the truth about the lady in the cocky hat with the rouged cheeks.

Blinded by tears of frustration and despair Mercy went to find Annie to tell her the news. Energised by the drama, back in the kitchen the scrubbers were busy on the floor and clanking pails of water were being brought into the house from the yard and poured noisily into stone sinks. Always the work went on . . . the work went on . . .

She told no one about her mother, not even Annie. She forced a smile to her face and made her eyes twinkle as they always did before she said, 'We've got to fetch our mattresses. We're going across the road.'

Together they went upstairs to take a last look at the place that for eight years they had called home. The babies rolled about on the floor unattended most of the time. The remainder of the day they spent sleeping. Inadvertently Mother had stumbled across the key to survival . . . and it was not love, it was cleanliness. Mother's brand of cleanliness had to do with purity and hard work and the fact that a good child is a useful child.

'I'm scared, Mercy.' Annie was kneeling on her bed, her scruffy hair standing straight from her face as she concentrated on tying her flock mattress with string. Her tongue curled out and touched her nose. 'I'm scared. I don't want to grow up.'

'You're already growed, Annie,' Mercy answered seriously under a broken heart. 'Completely growed like I am. Else they wouldn't be sending us, would they?'

SIX

'The Lord Mayor's Parade,' said the vicar of Chelston. 'That's when I first remember that business with Mercy Geary. How could I forget it? The experience, for me, was a singularly bad one, my son. Sad and bad. A nasty little episode.'

The vicar had lived a long life and was proud of it. He told everyone his age as soon as he could. He expected amazed admiration – his wide, round face demanded the same. So Tristan, to pacify him, gave it. He had walked the short distance across the small road which separated the two tall, dark houses, the baby house from the home of the older girls, leaving his horse outside by the railings. Nobody here seemed to know Mercy, but Tristan had not given up. He had come this far, he would not be defeated, not at the end of his quest. Then someone mentioned the vicar, 'Retired now, of course, but here at the time. I remember because it was that special year, the turn of the century, and he was here for the Lord Mayor's procession.'

'I'll call on him,' said Tristan, thanking the shawled old woman who showed him to the door. 'I'm sure he'll remember something. Mercy Geary was not one to melt in a crowd.'

He freed his horse from the flaky green railings, mounted, and rode away with his back to the place. Relieved to put it behind him, he didn't turn round for a last look. There was a bad atmosphere in both those houses. He'd spent long enough in one, he wasn't much interested in pausing for any time in the other. The sun shone hard on the road, the hedgerows were tired and dull with too much dust and a scorching spring. The village was only a mile away; it was not much of a place – a few fowls pecked in the dirt and washing flapped from the lines. When he heard children's laughter Tristan's face turned hard. He had come from two houses full of children, and yet not heard this sound.

The vicar, who lived in a careful cottage neatly thatched with a tidy garden, seemed pleased to have someone to talk to. The Reverend Ernest Ainsworth said, 'I don't get about much now. I am seventy-five, you know.'

'You look well on it,' said Tristan, hoping the man was as proud of his memory as he was of his florid, healthy looks.

It was the mention of the year that jarred the old man's memory. He sank deep in his chair with a port in his hand and reflected, slapping his stomach in a comfortable way. 'So many children,' he said. 'It is hard to separate one from another. But I particularly remember this child because of the scandal . . . because of the numerous scandals that seemed to surround her. I wonder what became of her in the end.'

'I know what became of her in the end,' said Tristan quickly. 'It's what became of her at the beginning that interests me now.'

'She had to leave, of course,' said the Reverend Ainsworth, and his lips came over the top of the glass and sucked the golden liquid up between them. 'It was I who took her away . . . she was lucky, in the circumstances. Every chance, some of these children, you give them chances, and I ask you . . . what do they do?'

'You're going to tell me what they do,' said Tristan, deliberately contained.

'They ruin them,' said the fat man, settling down more happily in his chair. 'They don't know how to make the most of God-given opportunities, you see. They are not,' he confided to Tristan, 'like you or I.'

'No,' said Tristan.

'There's some devil inside,' said the vicar, warming to his subject, 'and given time, this devil will come out.'

'And Mercy Geary had a devil inside her?'

'Oh, yes, she most certainly did. Most certainly. We discovered that, of course, in the summer you mentioned, young man. She and that other unfortunate child . . . I can't remember her name . . . all those names, all those faces. But strangely enough I *do* remember Mercy Geary.' He heaved himself out of his chair with great effort and crossed the room, breathing gustily. 'Are you sure you won't join me?'

'I'm sure,' said Tristan, trying to keep the impatience out of his voice.

'It was her hair, of course. There was something not right about that, and she had the most unusual face – a mysterious face, one might call it. Sly, now I come to think about it. And then she was a thief and a whore – and how can anyone forget a girl as wilful as that?'

'After all that had been done for her,' said Tristan.

'Quite,' said the vicar, settling down again. 'And you, young man? What is your interest in such a miserable person?'

'Call it a fascination with the Devil,' he said. 'Call it a macabre, peculiar trait that I have. I like to find out such things. I am interested,' said Tristan, with a half-smile on his face, 'in the Devil and all his works.'

'Oh, yes?' responded the vicar, regarding his visitor with slightly more interest. 'Funny,' he told Tristan, confidentiality puckering his face, 'there is something almost more appealing about the Devil than there is . . .' The vicar stopped. 'But I digress. This girl, the one you ask about, she was certainly the Devil's daughter. You could see it – in her bearing, in her eyes, in the very insolence of her manner. Oh yes, after a lifetime of trying to bring sinners safe to the fold, I can spot a black sheep when I see one. Let me see . . . as I say, it began one September, on a day such as this. It was hot, I was hot, we were all hot as we waited, outside on the road for the procession to go by.'

'I will have that glass,' said Tristan. 'I'll join you if I may.'

They were forced out in the end, by Annie and her stupid lie. It was not at all as Mercy had planned it. She was beginning to learn that things never went to plan.

The intensity had gone from her dream of freedom. She could no longer punish Mother, for Mother didn't love her. So the dreams had settled, like sleep, somewhere deep in her mind, and there they rested, enjoyable and refreshing whenever she wanted them.

The year was 1800. Two years later and taller by a good five inches they stood on the road and waited. Two years after the time when they left the baby house with their brown paper bundles and mattresses, behind a silent Mother, who strutted like a duck ahead of her charges – two more for Jesus saved by Mother's successful child-rearing recipe; fresh air, firm handling, hard work and a little bit of laudanum.

Now they waved their flags as they waited for the Lord Mayor to pass in procession on his way to Truro.

Mercy cherished her flag. She'd never been given such a lovely thing before. The colours were vivid, the patterns of the Union Jack so bold, and they were all part of England, all part of this great country! She'd never realised it quite this way before. She swallowed back the tears. She felt so proud! The Lord Mayor was there for them! They were lined up on the road to see him pass, the babies on their side, the big girls on theirs, on this Indian summer day at the beginning of one long, hot dusty September.

They waved but discovered they couldn't cheer, no matter how hard the vicar exhorted them as he wielded his little practice baton.

They were much too self-conscious. They had never been allowed to let their feelings surface before, let alone voice them.

And they'd been given a holiday! All that morning they had laboured to get themselves ready and put the finishing touches to the house and garden. For a month they had worked on the garden, the thin strip that met the road. They had hoed and dug and pruned so that if the Lord Mayor should look out of his carriage window at the moment he went by, the garden would look a real picture. Some of the girls were carrying posies of mignonette and heartsease, 'To make you look a little more cheerful,' Sister Henry said.

But Mercy preferred her flag.

'What'd you give to be the Lord Mayor?' Annie asked, licking her lips in anticipation of a colourful answer. Mercy did not reply. Once upon a time she would have dreamed. Not now. But she managed to get her imagination to show her the inn where the procession would spend the night, the soft feather mattress that would be waiting to iron out the aches and pains of the road, the hotpot that would be steaming already on the inn fire, and the wine that would be settling in jugs in the kitchens. She sniffed and almost tasted the warm bread that would be rising in the ovens.

'Gawd! In't he little? I imagined he'd be . . .' There were not enough words in the excited Violet's vocabulary to cope with the size of the Lord Mayor so she stretched her arms instead and stood on tiptoe to reach every inch of description she could.

'They look just like we do!' said a breathless Annie.

It couldn't just last for that fleeting moment, could it? All those preparations, all those days of anticipation, waiting for that? Mercy swam in sensations of sound and smell as the Lord Mayor's retinue jingled past, splendid in cords and velvets, the harness on the muscled horses winking gold as it caught the sun. No . . . let it go on . . . don't let it end! She hadn't even had time to wave her flag!

'Gawdblessim!' There'd never been so many people. There was a line of them all the way up from the village which the Mayor would miss as he turned off before reaching the crossroads. The children had never been allowed to mix so freely. Not that there was anywhere much to go. They were only wandering up and down the road while they waited, not crossing it, because that was against the rules. But Mercy could hear people talking and they were louder and a great deal more expressive than they were when they came out of church.

The Cornish wore their Cornishness like an outfit of well-worn clothes. They were comfortable in it. They had their own way of gesturing and talking, quite different from the Mission children who could have been brought up anywhere, so insulated was their lifestyle. Mercy watched them and listened, totally fascinated by the colours and sounds of ordinary people.

''E's gone!' It was over! Someone said it out loud for her. 'That's it then. E's gone.' The words seemed empty, like the hollow rumblings of a stomach after an insufficient meal. And Mercy knew all about those. But surely things were different now. Their eyes had not been considered so low that they could not see greatness when it passed, or their minds acknowledge it when

194

they saw it. What must it be like to pass by and hear people cheer, 'Gawdblessim!' and know they were saying it about you?

She could smell the dust and oh, it was rich today, thick with a pungency of harvest home and summer dying. She picked a hairy-stemmed poppy and rubbed the scarlet petals between finger and thumb, marvelling at their velvety, royal smoothness.

Things could never revert back to how they'd been before the grand visit. Oh, yes they could and they were, and the familiar voice of Mother, a stranger now, across the road gathering her babies around her, and the strident tones of Sister Henry, the matron, on this side, could not be ignored.

'Back inside now girls. Back to work!' They traipsed indoors, leaving the sunshine and the holiday excitement out on the road behind them.

Then Annie showed her the half-crown. It had sat in her hand so long it was wet and slippery. It had made an imprint of itself on Annie's skin.

SEVEN

'Where did you get it?'

Annie turned at the door and gestured as if to show her. 'She's gone. She was standing just there! An old woman gave it to me!'

'Annie!' The story was too unlikely. Mercy didn't believe a word of it. Annie's small face was wearing its lying look again. 'Annie! Put it back!'

'I can't!'

'Throw it away then!'

'I won't! I was given it!'

'Stop talking, girls, and come inside.'

'One thing about the Lord Mayor,' Annie changed the subject, 'he certainly wasn't handsome. I think that's sad, to have all that money and not be handsome. Don't you, Mercy?' Annie became braver and set her face against contradiction. 'In fact, in my opinion, to tell you the truth, I thought he was ugly! Didn't you, Mercy?'

Mercy didn't answer. She wasn't going to tell anyone but the fact of it was the Lord Mayor had gone by so fast that she'd missed him. Tears sprung to her eyes . . . she who rarely cried could blub over a little thing like that. Even in this she had failed! She must be the only one . . . the only one after all that . . . who hadn't even seen him! The silly insignificance grew out of all proportion, so she didn't take as much notice of Annie and her half-crown as she should have done.

Here in the big house they worked mainly in the laundry. They not only washed for the baby house and for

196

themselves, but also for the nursing institution connected with the village. They washed for the inmates of the institution, they prayed for them, too. Oh, how they prayed, until their knees were like their hands, chapped, wrinkled and sore.

Whatever the weather the day started in the open air of the collecting shed, where they sorted out the laundry from the heaps of clothes into good, bad or filthy. All doubtful articles were passed through tanks and stirred with long wooden poles through a flow of continuously running water. Then they would wash and scrub the linen, turning the wringing machine, superintending the drying closets, arranging the clothes on the mangling tables, folding them, and all the time feeding the fires.

Those who were good at needlework darned and mended in the workroom beyond. They made garments, under-linen, children's clothes and patchwork quilts, and sold them in the entrance hall on a Saturday evening. All proceeds went to the Mission. They made all the clothes for the Mission homes, too, dresses, pinafores and petticoats, as well as doing the everyday mending of the garments.

Annie had cried for a month after leaving the baby house, cried even while she worked until ten o'clock some nights on the old stocking machine, unable, by then, to keep her tired eyes open. Then the handle of the stocking machine would fly and hit her in the chest because she wasn't concentrating, but the doctor, when they sent for him because the pain got so bad, said it was nothing.

Mercy, stronger than Annie, worked in the washhouse all day. Real, hard backbreaking work it was. Packed off to bed at night straight from the washhouse, often she would be wringing, dripping wet, hardly able to drag one foot behind the other. And she never got a bite to eat for supper afterwards. They never saw milk, or the eggs they used to pick up so casually from the nests in the yard at the baby house. Those days were gone. Their childhood was officially over.

And all the time they were hungry. Food? All Mercy could think about was stone, stone, stone that had to be scoured. Stone, coal fires and oil lamps.

For dinner on a Monday it was pea soup and a round of dry bread. Tuesday it was meat, black as the ace of spades and taters in their skins. Wednesday they got suet pudding and treacle, and you could kick it about like a ball. Thursday tater hash and rice milk without sugar. Breakfast was the same every day – bread, butter and tea. For tea there was porridge and bread and butter and on Sunday nights bread and cheese. There were no cups here. You had to drink your tea from a basin.

Washing, or on her knees scouring floors, Mercy's clothes, Mercy's legs, Mercy's arms never seemed to be dry.

Beautiful. What *was* beautiful?

Three times now Mercy had been called beautiful, and on the day the Lord Mayor passed the door she looked at herself in the mirror and wondered vaguely what it meant. She had nothing to compare herself with. The lilies of the fields were beautiful in a pure sort of way, but deprived of all literature other than the Bible she hadn't known that women could be beautiful, especially women like herself – ten-year-olds with wracking coughs and lumpy knees. As far as she knew, women were rather disgusting creatures – look at Eve – to be watched and avoided, for they could lead men into temptation. Men . . . she wasn't sure what they were, either.

For it was thought that those who did not know could not be sullied.

She closed the closet door and took off her bloomers. She held the mirror down and looked at the place between her legs that she wasn't supposed to know was there, and if Sister caught her she'd be hanged. Let God watch! She would be pleased to hurt Him. The thing she looked at had no name. She touched it. It had a smell. It smelled of rain gone old and green in buckets. It was her smell.

On this special day she wore a new dress and apron . . . black and white of course, the same as the others, but luxurious with newness. In return for the gift they had prayed for the donor, a Miss Gibbard of Stratford-upon-Avon, who had presented the material so they might look their best for the Lord Mayor's passing.

So today when Mercy looked in the mirror she was wearing something new for the first time she could remember.

Three different people had told her that she was beautiful. Annie . . . who didn't really count . . . Mother, three years ago, with a vague warning that she would have to watch herself, and a village woman today.

'Unusual, isn't it,' she heard the stranger tell Sister Henry. 'Unusual to find such a rose among thorns. Her hair, the slant of her eyes, the girl is quite extraordinary. She could be really lovely.'

Mercy had looked round and wondered who they were talking about, but seeing four contemplative eyes looking at nobody else she had accepted that they must have been referring to her.

She pulled up her bloomers and stood before the mirror, pushing her hair back from her high forehead. It left a V, a pronounced widow's peak, and from it the hair fell loose and fine, beginning to curl at her shoulders.

She opened her eyes wide. She had always thought they were oddly unnatural. They ought to have been blue, but they were grey eyes, shaped like the stag's eyes in the picture on Mother's wall, the stag that had been captured in oils as it fell, pursued by men and dogs, into the ravine. Curved eyes that after widening fell into slits at the edges.

But it was hard to compare herself to others. She knew them all so well that she didn't see the outsides of her friends any longer, just the way they were inside. If asked to describe them she would have said moody, or helpful, or funny, or contrary. She wouldn't have thought of describing them in any other way except, perhaps, to give the colour of their hair or say whether they were big or small.

She would probably have called Annie the most beautiful of all, because she loved her, although, to look at, Mercy supposed that with her scabs and sores and cross little face Annie was probably not beautiful at all.

'I've been looking all over for you! Where have you been?'

'I was looking in the mirror.'

Why was she standing here talking of ordinary things when Annie paraded before her with that half-crown still in her hand? Mercy had forgotten all about it.

'Why didn't you throw it down like I told you to?'

'Why should I when it was given to me?'

'Annie, sweetheart!' Mercy's frustration sharpened her voice. 'You can't expect anyone to believe that! Where did you find it? It doesn't matter . . . just go outside and drop it and get rid of it. It can only bring trouble. What do you want with a half-a-crown anyway?'

But it was too late. 'I want everyone assembled in the hall . . . now!' Sister Henry, her metal grey hair pulled back into a severe bun, was merely walking through to spread the message, but Mercy felt her guilty heart beat against her ribs making it hard to breathe. And was that the vicar's domed head hovering in the porch, glistening like a poisonous puffball, bidding a final goodbye to the lingering congregation of cheerful villagers, just as he would on an ordinary Sunday? It was the vicar, and he was coming in, mopping his brow with a handkerchief he had bought from the Home. Mercy, at this most perilous time, still had the wit to recognise it as one she'd hemmed.

And she knew, she just knew, that this was to do with Annie's half-crown.

Annie seemed to know nothing of the sort and so Mercy hissed, 'Hide it, and whatever happens Annie, say nothing!'

If she'd glanced in the mirror now Mercy wouldn't have seen herself as beautiful. Her skin had gone blotchy and her eyes stared warily, huge in her face. Warm September scents washed the room through the open door, carrying from across the road the voices of children. Everything was normal, and yet Mercy stood there palpitating like a caged bird. Something dreadful was about to happen. She could feel it. And she still had the smell of herself on her finger.

'Oh God oh God oh God,' she chanted under her breath as they assembled, the proof of Annie's wickedness still sticking to her hand. They curtseyed to the vicar on trembling legs and Mercy prayed he could not read the fear on their faces.

And in his pulpit voice, which made his words sound hollow as if they echoed off some distant rock, the vicar said, 'My flesh is clothed with worms and clods of dust;

201

my skin is broken and become loathesome.' And Mercy knew that her fears were justified.

To herself she quoted a passage from *Proverbs* that she had learnt by heart the previous Sunday, instructed to do so by the vicar himself. 'Whoso keepeth his mouth and his tongue keepeth his soul from troubles.' She hoped Annie would remember that, too, no matter what pressures were brought to bear.

They wiped their hands on their aprons, they puffed their hair from their faces, they looked round enquiringly to find what this was all about . . . girls of all shapes and sizes lined up in the echoing hall as if this was a Sunday. Luckily, as far as Mercy knew, Annie had told no one else about her 'gift'. So if the two of them kept their mouths shut all would be well. Organising themselves into respectful silence, gradually the flusterings ceased and the audience was a quiet one by the time the vicar came to his point.

He began on a low note that was hard to hear but throughout his discourse he grew louder. Round as a paper ball he stood with his stout legs wide apart as if to brace himself to take the rigours of his grandiloquent voice.

'If sin had not entered the world, do you think we should need to have shutters for our windows, bolts and bars for our doors, policemen for our streets and soldiers to defend us from our enemies?' There was no answer from the dumbfounded congregation.

'Of course not! If there had been no sin all men would have loved one another and lived happily together as brethren. No one would have thought about injuring a neighbour or robbing him . . .' The pause was dreadful, and Mercy felt her face turn from white to pink to red before finally reaching purple. She hitched her hair behind her ears. Her heart hammered so hard it drowned out some of the vicar's words.

'We could have left our property around and no one would have taken it. We could have walked with money in our pockets without the fear of being robbed.' He continued in this vein for twenty minutes. For those who didn't know what was happening the time dragged. For Mercy it ceased to exist. He came to his point with an alarming boom which startled everyone into terrified attention.

'But there is sin, isn't there? There is sin wherever we look! There is sin amongst us here . . . terrible sin!' He changed his tone and became suddenly confidential. He used a strange but sinister form of politeness.

'I was standing out there with all of you, feeling joyous as the occasion merited, glad to be taking part in the celebration. Nothing was further from my mind than the protection of my property. Now I am a man of the church, not a rich man. It was not given to me to be rich and so the money I have is important to me. I did not keep my hand on my pocket because I felt safe . . . ah, Sister Henry . . .' he turned and beamed sorrowfully into her watchful face, 'was I so wrong as to have assumed that on this sunny afternoon there was no sin among us?'

Sister Henry shook an unhappy head.

Mercy felt excitement rise. It started in her secret place and rushed up on hot pins and needles through her body. What had possessed Annie to do such a thing? To steal money . . . to steal money from the vicar, and to tell Mercy such a stupid lie. Mercy's knees went weak with tension. She couldn't swallow. She tried but she couldn't. Her mouth was blotting-paper dry.

The vicar laughed then, suddenly and uproariously, as if he had made a joke, and nobody knew whether to join in or not. They followed Sister Henry's po-faced example and did not. There had been something ominous about the vicar's laugh.

As he resumed his speech, Mercy had visions of the coin falling out of Annie's paralysed hand and rolling across the floor ending up under the eagle's head on the lectern where the vicar stood. She'd be glad if it did! She wanted Annie to be caught! She loved her, yes, yet she wanted to see this most awful thing happen. She half-turned, taking Annie in with the furthest corner of her eye. She was standing to attention, arms straight by her sides, showing no sign, so far, of weakness or collapse. She wasn't even scratching.

Mercy desperately needed to visit the privy. She wanted to cross her legs but didn't dare do anything that might single her out from the rest and thus bring attention to Annie. The hands behind her back were hanging on to each other, nails biting into flesh, tiny veins standing out in purple strings.

'But we all know the perpetrator of this dreadful crime. What we're waiting for is to hear it from her own lips.' What? They knew, then, that Annie had done it? Mercy knew now that if Annie was called to the front and faced with the charge she would, believing they already knew, admit it. And then what? Prison? Mercy closed her eyes, knowing that she would never see her friend again.

'Oh, foul weakness!' cried the vicar. 'Oh, coward of cowards! Face up to thy sin, daughter of Eve, the Father will forgive!'

Mercy dared not look round. She saw a sea of baffled faces doing just that but she didn't dare move. *'Don't, Annie, don't.'* She willed her friend to keep quiet. They couldn't know. It was a ruse to force a confession. But Annie, Mercy knew, was not only not the most beautiful of people, but not the most intelligent either, and she would be quite likely to . . .

She was seized with a frantic compulsion to confess to the crime herself. She grew hot with the desire of it . . . to feel . . . to waken . . . to come alive to such pain . . . saint-like, to fling herself down in place of her friend. A broken cup was one thing, the theft of a half-crown quite another. The thought of it was full of ecstasy. She stopped herself. Mercy's sense of self-preservation would not allow her to confess to this, but not so, it would seem, the bed-wetting, smelly, buck-toothed Mary Ludd. Because this girl stepped forward now with her arm half-raised, and was immediately seized by the vicar's eye and he said, 'Praise be to God,' as she walked, like a sleepwalker, to the front.

'Mary Ludd!' said the vicar, Sister Henry having whispered the despised name into his whiskery ear. 'Was it you who stole my half-crown from my pocket this morning?'

'Yes, vicar.' Like a sacrifice she went, mesmerised, as if, having been a victim of both girls and staff for the whole of her life, suddenly she was willing, even eager to bend to the part. Had she been fooled by talk of the Father's forgiveness? Had she perhaps, extraordinary though it might seem to Mercy's by now tortured mind, felt like Mercy felt, seen a chance to fill a role that would take the world with marvellous disgust?

Mercy stung with jealousy for the stupid Mary Ludd.

'Where is the money, child?' The vicar spoke to her as if she was retarded, which was quite right because she was.

'I lost it, Vicar. I put it in the grass and then I couldn't find it.' She gave him a fat, vacant look, but swelled in a particularly proud sort of way as she stood up there at the front, as if at last she had become a star. But not an inch of sympathy was extended to her hapless condition. Stupid or bright the law was the law and it didn't require a complicated mind to understand it or obey it.

The inquisition over, the girls were dismissed. Because nobody liked Mary Ludd they could be as damning as they liked . . . and as self-righteous. And they were, disclaiming her as if she'd come from another world and had never shared their misery.

'Fancy!' said the straight-backed Hattie Cawdle, as if she had never sinned.

'Don't speak bad about her! She is Irish, like me!' said Mercy.

It wasn't until late that night that Mercy and Annie were able to talk without fear of being overheard. Annie, on Mercy's instructions, had put the half-crown in her drawers. It would never escape from under that tight elastic. Mercy imagined it would be burning her flesh wherever it rested and that served Annie right!

'We can't let Mary take the blame. They have informed the sheriff. They are coming to fetch her in the morning!'

Mercy was astounded by Annie's indifference. 'She doesn't mind, Mercy. She's different from us. Let it stay as it is. Mary won't notice what is happening to her.'

'Of course she'll notice!' Mercy was angry. 'There are worse places than this you know, and if we don't tell them you took it then Mary Ludd is going to find herself in one. No, Annie, you've got to tell them and we've got to go.'

'Leave Mrs Mountebank's?'

'Yes, Annie, leave! We can't stay here now. You must see that.'

Annie still looked blank so Mercy gripped her by the shoulders and shook her.

'Mercy, I'll do what you say . . . I'll throw the money away.'

'It's too late, Annie. Mary Ludd has taken the blame . . . your blame.'

'Why should we suffer because Mary Ludd is cracked in the head? Since when did you care about Mary Ludd anyway?'

'I don't care.' But that was the trouble. She did care. No matter how hard she tried she could not get the pathetic sight of that false confession out of her mind. She knew why Mary Ludd had done it. She knew the awful things that would happen to Mary Ludd because of it.

Mercy had been deprived of her big moment. She felt dead inside. Now there was nothing else for it. The time had come. It was the only thing she had left. They were going to have to run away.

EIGHT

Mrs Mountebank used to say, 'Girls! There are two things in this world that are yours by right – a place to be born and a place to die. Everything else is charity for which you must be grateful!'

This freedom showed no charity. This dark night was too big to care. They were outside the confines of Mercy's understanding. Mercy was terrified. How would they eat? How would they keep warm? Oh no, she and Annie hadn't thought of this!

Mercy and Annie crept along the road. Were they following the crow or was the crow following them? Either way it was unnerving. So was the way it looked at them with that calculated malevolence. It put Mercy in mind of Mother in one of her pensive moods and she shivered.

The day had been hot. The night was cold. Their brown paper parcels bumped against their legs. 'Listen!' Mercy wished Annie wouldn't make her jump like that. She was still angry with her, couldn't help it after all they'd been through.

It was music Annie heard. Someone was playing a mouth organ. They stared through narrowed eyes, clutching at each other, and saw a hatless man sitting in the road. He wore a stained grey coat which still retained some of its original shape, thin, ragged trousers and broken shoes with pointed toes.

'Quick! In the hedge! We'll have to go round him.'

They only moved to the sounds of the mouth organ. It was a bizarre dance they did. When he stopped playing the silence was terrible and they crouched down apprehensively, terrified of being discovered. And in this way, starting and stopping, they made slow progress.

It might have been better if they hadn't left in the dark.

Once they smelled food and crawled towards an eating house, a small room with oblong tables and high-backed settles on either side. Every time the door opened the food smell came out and Mercy heard Annie's tummy rumble.

They heard somebody order, 'Drip an' tea.' The customer was a young man but he looked old, pinched and drawn, blue with cold. His hands, Mercy noticed, shone blue with dirt and bloodlessness. Through the rips in his collarless shirt they saw he didn't wear underclothes. Poor as they were, Mercy and Annie had never dressed like that! They were shocked by the poverty they saw.

'Penny ha'penny,' said the blowzy woman who served behind the tiny counter, and Mercy saw, through smears wiped by sleeves in the steamed-up window, that he got three slices of bread and dripping and a cup of hot, strong tea. The customer added vast quantities of salt to the dripping and almost filled his cup with sugar.

'We should have kept the half-crown. I told you it was stupid to give it back,' moaned Annie.

Mercy didn't see why Annie should have the half-crown when she hadn't owned up to it. And Annie was the sort of person who might have held it over her. Why was she being constantly thrust into the role of Annie's keeper? They were out in the world now and Annie was going to have to start thinking for herself.

Being free was a peculiar thing, like going out without a hat on. Mercy felt relief from the tight band, but was worried, no, worse than that, she was petrified that she would catch cold from the foolishness of the whole venture . . . and die. She kept trying to reassure herself by saying to Annie, 'We had to do this. We had no other choice.'

Annie was not prepared to play the game. 'Yes we did,' she answered. 'We could have stayed. We could be warm in our beds by now.'

'Warm? Warm? Mercy was scornful. 'Since when were you warm in your bed?'

Annie sniffed and wiped her nose on her sleeve. She could never win an argument with Mercy. But she was right, she knew she was. No good could come of this. 'Somethin' awful bad'll happen to you one day, Mercy Geary.'

It was men they were instinctively afraid of, although they knew nothing of men. From the last remnant of cloud the moon sailed clear, bright and full, and turned the dusty track they followed into a shimmering silver highway. Mercy's spirits rose. She saw this as a good sign, until once again she saw the crow sitting on a gate further along the road, waiting for them.

Eventually the landscape gave way to fields. The girls jumped back as a rat fled a wurzel heap. And in the next village, heavy-footed, muddy labourers were congregated in the tavern, the dogs at their heels – spaniels, lurchers and greyhounds curled up against the cold, asleep. The men, they noticed, did not taste their cider or beer after they had bought it. They carried it back to their tables and made it last all evening.

'Poverty,' said Annie. 'What they told us was right about the poverty.'

The girls backed into the shadows to watch the men come out, both of them staunching their coughs. Deep-voiced, the men sang together, and when they left the safety of their friends they stamped their feet and blew on cold fingers.

'I envy them,' said Annie bluntly. 'They're going home.'

Mercy looked hard at Annie for a moment, wondering if she knew what would have happened to her if she'd stayed. She refused to admit, even to herself, that Annie's theft had nothing to do with why they were here. But even she had visions of a neat row of beds: bleak and comfortless though they were, at least they were under a roof. But they had well and truly burnt their bridges now. There was no going back.

NINE

They had written the letter in the simple language they had been taught, with Annie protesting all the while.

'Be quiet! There's somebody coming!'

There wasn't. But there might have been. And it was the only way to keep Annie quiet.

Mercy, white-faced and on tenterhooks, had slipped it under Sister Henry's door. Then, with Annie still indignantly protesting, silenced by a furious Mercy, they had made for the coal-hole where they could climb out through the shoot. It wouldn't be clean, but it would be easy.

'*Dear Sister Henry,*' Mercy had put. '*Please don't blame Mary Ludd for the money. We took it. Signed in greatest repentance,*' and then they had taken it in turns to write their names.

There had been a brief argument as to whether or not they should return the half-crown. Annie was all for keeping it because she said, 'We'll get into trouble now whether we've got it or not.'

Mercy wanted to take it, too, but she felt she had to say no to punish Annie. 'That's not the point, Annie. If we give it back we halve the wickedness of the crime, and then, if we're caught, they might not send us away.'

They had lain in bed listening to the jangling of the keys as Sister Henry made her last rounds, praying that tonight of all nights everyone would fall quickly to sleep. They were lucky. And there was no response from the mounds in the beds to their first tentative movements. They had packed their bundles earlier and hidden them under the covers, but brown paper makes a horrendous rustle at night.

The getting out, then, had been easy, probably because it was something that no one expected. Paupers had been known to break into charitable institutions – rarely to break out.

Without a candle they discovered how dark darkness really was, especially down in the coal cellar. Mercy Geary experienced real fear as they blundered about in their efforts to leave the house undetected: that palpitating fear sharpened every sense in her body and made everything exhilarating. She breathed quickly. She half-hoped they would be caught.

For Mercy Geary came alive only when she feared. Fear was bigger than she was. It caught her up and held her in its arms. It made her feel helpless like a little child.

It loved her.

TEN

They spent their first night of freedom under a hedge
with Annie sulking, but Mercy was not going to chivy
her out of it. Let her deal with this one herself. Mercy
did not believe her story about the money, and she
wasn't going to tell her she did.

Annie had grown very crotchety lately. She said she
wasn't well.

As they walked, the dew that had drenched them
from head to foot dried on them. Every now and then
they had to stop to cough and scratch. 'We make a fine
pair, you and me,' said Mercy. Everybody at Mrs
Mountebank's coughed. So much so that nobody took
any notice of it, but Annie's cough racked her whole
body. And sometimes there was blood. But she had
seen the doctor so she must be all right.

'I'm tired, let's stop.' It was annoying how many
times Annie held them back.

Hand in hand together they crossed stepping stones,
they walked up lanes baked hard with weeks of sunshine. Mercy began to cry and Annie pretended not to
see and didn't look at her.

'I am crying because I can't say things,' Mercy said,
and Annie ran on ahead and waited for her, scowling.

'You know when my clothes went missing, and we
found them over the stairs? Well, I did it,' said Mercy.
'I did it lots of times.' It wasn't fair that Annie didn't
know. Annie's world was black and white and Mercy
was always wanting to destroy it.

'Why would you do that?'

'I don't know. I don't know why I do things.'

214

'I knew you cut your lavender bag because I saw you.'

'But you made me another one.'

'Yes, I did.'

'Do you know why I do things?'

'No. I don't know. But it doesn't matter now.'

The further into the countryside they went the safer they felt. When they passed anyone, on horse, cart or foot, they smiled pleasantly and replied to the polite 'Mornun' they were invariably given. But something was wrong. They looked different.

'People are staring at us from behind . . . like this.' Annie gave a good imitation of barely concealed surprise.

Mercy stopped and stared at Annie, considering her with a frown. 'It's our clothes,' she concluded. It wasn't that their garb was tattier than anyone else's. They were, if anything, more darned and patched. But it was the sombre colours and a kind of institutional drabness about them that made them stand out. Mercy was frightened. She couldn't get that dark shadow of pursuit from her mind. It hovered, it touched her with terrible fingers. She couldn't stop herself from turning to look behind.

Annie's feet hurt and they stopped to rest while she took off her boots and spat on red-hot, shiny toes.

'One day,' she said, with her bent leg waving in the air as she surveyed the damage, 'I'll be married and have a house of my own and it'll be somewhere in the country like this, not near anyone else's house. And I won't have visitors, just my husband . . .'

'What about me?' She would not allow life to be simple for Annie when it was so confusing for her.

Annie paused while she coughed up blood-speckled

phlegm. 'Oh, I might let you come occasionally . . . if I'm feeling bored.'

'What about children? It was hard work to think of little Annie as a woman. 'Are you going to have children?' Mercy lay on her back in the grass and watched, hypnotised, as the clouds floated past. They had never talked like this before. The sensations of freedom were airy and wild. Freedom smelt sappy, of grass and stones.

'No.' Annie was adamant. 'No children. I'm not going to share anything with anyone. Not even children.'

Mercy could understand that. If you found somebody to love you, why would you break their love into sections . . . one for a boy and one for a girl until there wasn't enough left for yourself?

'Now that I'm free I'm going to learn to dance.' Mercy got up and started to point her toes. 'How do I look? Will I make a dancer?'

Annie laughed and tried to join her but had to sit down again, white and exhausted. For the first time it looked as if they were enjoying their first day of freedom. But Mercy was pretending. She was jealous of Annie's ability genuinely to enjoy herself. Wasn't she worried? Didn't she realise the danger they were in? Someone could come and take this away. It wasn't fair the way Annie was so easily pleased.

Mercy danced harder to try and make herself happy.

The shepherd watched Mercy's performance from the top of the knoll. He watched her dance, and yes, she did move like a dancer.

Rooks rose and fluttered in the air light as paper from an autumn bonfire. A great hooded crow detached itself from the cloud and harangued him from the air, its ragged pinions rustling like rags in the breeze. 'Get

216

on . . .' The shepherd flapped back at the strangely behaved bird. And from the rolling waves of red soil that followed a ploughman in the distance, he heard the seagulls scream as they topped the ridge like foam.

Mercy stretched out her arm and pointed. 'If we follow the valley up through the hills it won't hurt our feet so much and nobody would see us. We could even leave our boots off.' She bit her lips as she spoke. Never had she walked barefoot over fields before.

Mercy's excitement was contagious. They exchanged wide smiles and felt a sudden mutual love for each other, for life, as they scrambled over the wall and started climbing towards the shepherd.

ELEVEN

Annie's chin was mauve with blackberry juice. Striped like a savage she stopped in her tracks and ceased her chewing to stare open-mouthed at the gamekeeper's gibbet. Heavy with death it swung in the wind giving its trophies an eerie appearance of life. The stoat and the weasel snarled with needle-sharp teeth even in death. A sadly tattered sparrowhawk hung by its feet side by side with its old companions of the sky, magpie, jay and carrion crow.

Ants of horror crawled along Mercy's arms but she said nothing.

They had reached the wood by the time the hunt came by. All morning they had heard it in the distance. It followed a fox found earlier in the day, across the moorland behind the valley, hounds in full cry. Here in the wood the sounds were muffled, but the soulful, unearthly call of the hunting horn slid down to the children on thin shafts of sunlight.

The wood was dark, and to Mercy and Annie huge in its mystery. Underneath the giant trees of ash, oak and chestnut, briars and thorns tumbled in prickly rolls, grabbing greedy handfuls of wild clematis, old man's beard and honeysuckle.

Sticking to the more open ride they were surprised by a stray hound which ignored them totally, cocked its leg against a sapling and, nose down, loped by with flapping ears.

Mercy felt better. In that one moment of time she was perfectly happy and not pretending. The world was hers and there was no one to spoil it. The elusive feeling settled with a comfortable warmth in the pit of her stomach and she wished she could hold and carry it with her always. They should stay away from people. They should stick to the hidden places. They could keep their freedom if they were sensible. She watched Annie exploring. Wise for her ten years, she recognised the growing wonder in her friend's large brown eyes, the excited, quick turn of the head, the lips so ready for laughter, and felt not jealousy now, but an over-whelming surge of protective warmth, and pride that she had brought her here.

'We're going to be all right!' Mercy shouted sud-denly, stretching her arms out and tensing her hands with glee. 'Annie, I know it, we are going to be all right!'

As if in answer the whole earth growled. The sound of the baying hounds swelled like a towering wave that curled towards them before it sluiced down on top of them. The ground shook with the pounding of hooves before the mudded huntsmen came into view. There was only just time for the children to fight the tangled briars and find a hiding place beside the ride.

Speechless with fear they could taste the bestial viol-ence of the chase. It tasted of ink. Annie's hand was pushed, trembling, into Mercy's own, and her face was fixed, rigid, into a grin of terror.

There she was, the vixen, tongue lolling, plastered with mud, her tail dragging behind her like a saturated floor mop. Her yellow slit eyes saw them and perhaps that's what killed her . . . that she could not turn off the track where she planned because of the human children. Annie's hand gripped Mercy's like a vice. Mercy spared her a quick glance . . . there was no message . . . Mercy was the vixen . . . *she wanted to be the vixen* . . .

*

219

The master, not much of his pink showing above the dirt, gave a triumphant blast on his horn as he rode his lathering mare thunderously past the hiding place, pulling her up with a flurry of spume just yards to their right. It seemed that hundreds followed him. They could see nothing now but horses and legs and dogs' tails waving, red dust that choked like steam from a pot boiling over.

This new silence pricked with horror.

'A vixen!' The man's voice was gruff with disappointment.

'No matter!' The answer was high-pitched, in a young girl's voice but harsher, and it rang with piercing authority. 'Let 'em at her, Master, filthy vermin!' There was no sign of breathlessness in this almost sweet voice as there had been in the man's tone. It cut the air with a freezing coldness and caused a thin icicle of silence before the ensuing uproar.

The hounds broke into a scream that defied all other sound. Mercy could only see the steam rising from the flanks of the panting horses as they pulled back from the kill to allow the hounds to finish their work.

In desultory pockets the huntsmen rode back past them, and Mercy had a clear view of the young speaker whose influence had ended in the broken vixen. While his companions had florid cheeks caused by wind, exertion and years of drinking, his were white, pale as clean sheets and his wavy hair was flaxen fair. His hands were long and slender, tightening and easing on the reins. His slight figure was mounted on a horse as large as any of the others. He might have chosen it for contrast because it was a wild, black creature, as significant to life as its white rider was to death.

A thrill moved down her backbone. A thrill of horror and of exhilaration.

*

Mercy stared from her bramble curtain and shivered as the boy went by. Someone was walking on her grave. But her eyes were bright.

There was little left of the vixen. Mercy wanted to stay and look but Annie pulled her away. A short time later when, on shaking legs, they hurriedly made their way out of the wood, Mercy and Annie found the cubs in a shallow hollow under a fallen tree. Their mewing sounds attracted Mercy's attention. Blind, and likely now to starve to death, their tiny legs moved about like fuzzy stalks.

Annie's voice was shaky. 'Mercy, they're so small!'

Mercy checked anxiously over her shoulder. Her feeling of wellbeing had long since gone. She was afraid the hunt might return and catch them unawares. Still, she bent to touch the mewing creatures. 'They can only just be born . . . so furry and so light!' But wild! Wild! Mercy remembered Heaven, that vast, solitary place just beyond her that she was always touching with her fingerends but could never really grasp . . . because, she thought, she had been banned from there. Now she understood that you had to be wild to grasp it . . . not good, not obedient, not afraid of punishment, afraid to sleep for fear of wetting the bed, but wild. She thought that perhaps only uncaged animals really knew about Heaven.

'Look Mercy, I've got one in my hand!' Annie raised the newborn cub to her lips and rubbed the soft fur against them. It was the first time she had held an animal and yet she had a instinctive way of doing it. She had always had a special way with babies, too. Mercy watched her with narrowed eyes. Annie was essentially a good person . . . sweet and kind and loving. The three remaining cubs whined and mewed as they stumbled about on top of each other in their rooty home, waiting for the milk which they still expected.

'What are we going to do?' All the bright hopefulness was gone from Annie's face. For her friend's sake Mercy felt a sudden fierce hatred towards the boy. But it was mixed, it was mixed. What made her think of Mother now?

'Do foxes have souls?' asked Mercy.

'No, of course they don't. They're animals,' said Annie.

Mercy said, 'What can we do? We can't take on a family of fox cubs. For a start we don't have any milk, and . . . oh, Annie, don't be silly, it's impossible for us to do anything.'

'You's found 'em then!'

They whirled round to a pair of legs bound with sacking strips. They looked up to a homespun smock. They stopped at the twisted, badly-disfigured face under a rimless hat green with overwear. They stared, trapped, helpless, for there was nowhere to go. Annie with the cub balanced in her hand and the feel of velvet on her lips.

TWELVE

The shepherd was used to such tactlessness. He'd lived with his disfigurement from birth. In a deep but kindly voice he said, 'They's had it, poor varmints. There's nothing for it now but to end the sufferin'.'

Gently removing the cub from Annie's hand he picked up a stone and firmly finished off all four cubs before the children had time to stop him.

His accent was hard to follow. Mercy was sure she was in the presence of one of Mrs Mountebank's devils and this one hadn't bothered to disguise himself. He looked and acted like one.

''Tis kinder.' He rose to full height and smiling at their horrified expressions, went on to say, 'You's wouldn't have liked to think of 'e starvin' to death, now would 'e?'

Anger replaced Annie's fear. 'We could have fed them! We could have nursed them until they were old enough to fend for themselves . . .'

Mercy couldn't help but like his smile. It cracked his face so the corners of his mouth and eyes crinkled. 'Oh, yes, midear, and with what? Have 'e got spare milk that 'e can give it away to such as these? If you'm has, then I's knows of a few who could do with a visit from 'e, folks as doan know how they's goin' to feed their own babies this winter . . .'

He didn't speak like a devil, and his twisted expression did not worsen. Mercy liked him because she thought him from the earth, and was excited by the rank smell of animal he had about him. The sunlight caught his hair and tangled in his eyes. His voice

223

was gentle, and the fox cubs hadn't suffered. And even Annie had to ask herself what she could have done to help them.

'They be wild things. Vermin . . . they's takes folks' chickens.' He touched the fur of one of the dead cubs irreverently with his boot. 'They's wouldn't thank 'e for yer pity. What would yous've made of 'e, pets to amuse 'e?'

'No. I would have set them free. And they're not bad. They've been made bad like Mercy's been made bad. People expect you to be a certain way, so you are . . . look, they made Mercy a sinner! All I would have done was set them free.'

'Oh, would 'e now? An' in two months we's shall be in the middle of winter. With no knowledge of the wild, what do 'e think they'd have made o' that?'

Annie sulked. She never used to sulk. This was a new thing that freedom seemed to have given her. 'I would have found a way.'

The shepherd sighed. ''Tis hard for us to see that Nature has her own way of doing things.'

'That wasn't Nature.' Mercy spoke, strangely un-afraid of the man who looked down with such amuse-ment in his grey-green eyes. 'This was the work of men.'

'And aren't men part of Nature then, maiden?'

'Yes, you're right, they are. They are the wildest of all, in spite of the fact they know better.' She was quoting from a sermon.

'Ah, I's'll not argue wi' that.' He whistled his dog, and prior to leaving them he asked, 'An' where are you'm two bound?' There wasn't much interest in the answer or the question. His manner of asking threw them offguard.

'Walking,' said Mercy, not caring that it sounded

224

foolish. She was enchanted by his leanness, his strength. So this . . . so this was a man!

'If you's was from the village I'd know 'e. An' you's wouldn't be sittin' there cool as yous likes exchangin' the time of day wi' Seth.' But there was no criticism in his words. They were put there as facts to be taken or left at face value. Mercy was not used to hearing words spoken like that.

The over-hot, moist September day was becoming drenched in a yellow afternoon mist that smelled of peeled apples. So as he left Seth said, 'E's goin' to rain, carn you smell 'e?' I's'll be out till late but if you's needs shelter there's nothin' to stop you's takin' it in my house.'

He gave simple directions before disappearing through the trees, leaving the two girls staring at each other uncertainly.

'Shall we go to the shepherd's house?'

'I think we should maybe stay away,' said Annie.

The decision made, they covered the cubs with stones and soil, unable to bear the thought that their bodies might be taken by wild animals in the night. They found it hard to leave the rough grave, feeling there was something else they ought to have done and could still do.

'What about a prayer?' said Annie, wiping her eyes and staring hard at Mercy to prove she had not been crying. She yawned instead so that Mercy would think that had caused her watery eyes.

'No, not a prayer,' Mercy was insistent. 'I think it's best that God doesn't know they're dead, safer for them.'

'You're blasphemous you are, probably 'cos you're Catholic,' said Annie, flattening down the soil with the palm of her hand. 'You shouldn't speak about God like that. He'll strike you down one day if you're not careful.

One day, Mercy Geary, something terrible bad is going to happen to you!'

Annie made a pattern with tiny stones while Mercy watched in silence. It was a far better memorial than some old prayer, and would last longer, too.

They brushed their knees clean and headed out of the wood. By the time they reached the fields huge raindrops spattered the dry earth which, like an overpowdered lady, her pores filled with dust, was unable to absorb it, so it streaked away in silver rivulets seeking re-entry.

They doubled back to the edge of the wood for shelter, their shoulders hunched in the way of people not used to the outdoors.

'We'll wait until it stops and then go on.' Mercy squatted down with her back to a comfortably solid oak tree.

They could choose what they did . . . and there was no strict sense of time. All she could remember now when she looked back was buckets and water, cold and pain, and over all of it the fear of Sister Henry. If only they could stay out here, live in freedom on their own, needing no one but each other. She looked up into the thick, dripping branches and childishly dreamed of a treehouse.

THIRTEEN

The rain didn't stop. The hours passed and they were still there, trapped, staring out at the downpour which had settled into a steady rhythm. They didn't talk about what they should do because it was a subject neither of them could truly enjoy. The future they had brought upon themselves was a frightening thing, not to be looked at too closely.

It was as Annie put it. 'Something'll happen. It always does if you do nothing.'

Dusk came early to the wood. 'I don't want to stay here after it's dark,' wailed Annie. 'I'd rather get wet than stay here.' She shivered and coughed. Her face was blue.

'We're going to have to go to the cottage, aren't we?' Funny how fate so often worked to get her what she wanted. 'He said he worked late. Come on, there's no danger in doing that.'

They followed the shepherd's instructions and went up a steep pasture through an avenue of giant beech trees, then through a gap in a tangled hedge at the southernmost corner of a five-acre field. A roof of thatched hurdles covered an empty square wicker pen protected by straw. This had been built for last year's lambs, but the shepherd's house was no better.

It had a low, sloping roof which leaned against a wall of timber and wattle daub. Underneath the thatched overhang was a neat pile of firewood and a rainbutt which filled so quickly that its hollow sides sung.

'D'you think this is it?' Annie leaned against the wall, puffing and out of breath.

Mercy nodded slowly. 'Let's look inside.'

The one room was sparsely furnished with a table and a couple of green wooden chairs. There was a rug before the fire over which hung a none too clean black pot. Mercy went across and sniffed it. 'Stew,' she said, 'of a sort I don't recognise.'

The remains of the shepherd's breakfast were on the table . . . a cup of fresh milk three-quarters gone, and a bowl scraped clean of porridge.

Mercy climbed up a stout homemade ladder of lashed saplings and stuck her head through a hole in the ceiling. This was where the shepherd slept, on this mattress of straw with a blanket thrown across.

'Come down! Let me see!'

Annie went up and exclaimed, 'This is the sort of house I want to live in when I'm married.'

'Annie . . . this isn't a proper house. It's a hovel.'

'Well, I like it. It's cosy and there's nothing here that needn't be. Think of all that cleaning and all that stone at Mrs Mountebank's. Here it wouldn't take five minutes to make the whole place shine. I think it'd be warm when it's cold outside, if you got a good blaze up on that fire. And it's out of the way . . . I like it.'

The gulp Mercy made in her throat was audible. She turned to Annie and asked, 'Why were we never born to a place like this? We never . . . we never . . .'

Annie let her ragged curls fall forward to hide her expression.

They lit the lamp when it grew too dark to see, and built up a fire when the air turned chill. Mercy mixed some rough ground flour she found in a bin into a loaf and put it to rise beside the chimney. They washed the simple dishes and laid them out fresh on the table for the shepherd's return, pointedly not adding bowls for themselves for they hadn't been asked, although their stomachs grumbled now and warm water filled their mouths, triggered by the smell of the sparse vegetable stew.

No adult had ever treated them this way before. No man had looked at her in quite this way, either.

The big man's hair was too long to be acceptable, and now that he was home they saw that he was younger than the impression he gave with his hat on. His wide, pleasant mouth opened into a smile, and you could ignore the disfigurement which pulled his features out of shape when you saw the sadness in his eyes.

He was bending, cutting up potatoes to add, with stock, to the hotpot. The smell of sheep, of grass and earth and rain was embedded in the thick material of his clothes.

He lifted the pot and sniffed, stirring the contents with a wooden stick. 'You's two can sleep in the loft while I's makes a bed for myself down here.' His green eyes shifted in the lantern light. He turned them on Mercy the dancer. His face was leaner than it had looked in the day. Mercy thought of the hunters and the hunted.

She bumped into him as she crossed the room and he opened his arms in time to catch her, blond hair falling over his eyes. For a fleeting second she was close to his chest, wrapped in his arms, warmed by the body and breath of a men ten years older. He didn't feel anything like Annie felt. He felt strong . . . substantial. She heard and felt his heartbeat.

Suddenly Mercy knew she wasn't hollow inside.

He held her back and gently cuffed her ear like she'd seen him cuff Moss, the dog who slept outside the door. He couldn't keep his eyes off the silver-haired Mercy. The child was so radiantly alive . . . so excited, so thrilled with every little thing. No, he could do nothing but watch her. In Seth's life there had been few moments of gold.

He sat in his chair and told them about 'Satan's Child' . . . the boy on the horse this morning. 'They's owns all the land round about here. 'Twas young John Yelland,' he said, 'Roger Yelland's son. An' 'e's feyther so keen to force out the Devil 'e's taken up residence in his own child!'

'We've seen him at work,' said Annie, still shivering, her face softened by the firelight as she stared up at Seth with a look of fondness already on her face. He was that sort of man.

The shepherd told stories about Roger Yelland, so fanatical a man he cared for no one but his God. Mercy wanted to stroke Seth's hair just to see what it felt like. She watched him run his fingers through it as he talked and wanted to push them out of the way and put hers there instead. He saw her staring. After a moment he turned away. He looked tired.

'Get e'selves to bed.' His voice was gruff and short. 'I's a long day ahead of me in the morning.'

And his orders weren't the orders of Sister Henry.

The rain beating on the roof kept them awake. 'He likes you,' said Annie, flattering her. 'I can tell. He likes you in a special way.' And then, 'You're very quiet. Are you bad or something?'

Mercy wanted Annie to be quiet. She wanted to think about the shepherd. She frowned and stiffened slightly under the blanket. He was strong, strong enough to save her. When she had fallen against him tonight he had wrapped his arms round such brittle vulnerability . . . and Mercy had felt it.

'I'm going to marry him,' she whispered suddenly

230

to Annie, and then wished she hadn't because Annie just laughed.

'You've got to make him kiss you first.'

'And I will. Then we can stay here always.'

'And you'll have to let him touch you in special places.'

'How do you know?'

Annie sighed, 'I just know.'

Mercy was furious that Annie knew something she did not. 'What special places then, Annie?' She issued the challenge.

Annie turned away, and no amount of persuasion would turn her round again. Mercy heard her fall to sleep and the sound of rasping breathing went with the wind-puffs that sighed round the rag curtains.

When she climbed down the ladder she saw that the shepherd was awake by the fire.

She felt she was confessing to the missing half-crown. She was holding the cup before Mother. She was frightened. She was excited.

In the ten-year-old's mind the equation was simple – oppression equals caring equals love. She longed to be crushed and conquered, to be possessed by sheer strength and power. This man who had looked at her so strangely, this man could somehow do that.

Maybe all men could . . .

'I'm cold,' she said timidly, wrapping her arms about her.

'Sit then,' he said.

He knew, then! He knew why she was here! His eyes promised her that something would happen. She saw the promise in them before he turned away to watch the fire again.

She sat in the chair beside him. She closed her eyes and willed him to kiss her. She felt powerful, magic tonight, a ten-year-old woman, because she had beauty, she could weave spells. She willed it . . . she willed it . . . it must be.

They sat in silence for almost an hour before the shepherd moved towards her. His arm rested, at first, across her slight shoulders and she shivered as she felt his warmth. She responded by moving into his body and then she felt his mouth touch her cheek, gentle as a butterfly. She teetered on the edge of a tall mountain . . . a cavernous drop with nothing below. Like the stag in Mother's room . . . like the stag! She could go with her spell or she could fight against it, crawl away painfully back the ladder upstairs to her cold, lonely place beside Annie. That was the hard way. She decided to go with her feelings completely, to let herself go with the wind, down, down and down with the stag, to swoop and follow the madness.

Later, she would come to believe she gave her heart easily, never asking why she was so eager to give herself away.

He drew her closer. Now he lifted her down and laid her on the rug. He carried the chairs away before lying beside her. Now he covered her face with kisses, removed her clothes one by one and stroked her childish body. He touched her where she dare not touch herself. But with awe. With tenderness.

Then he pushed her from him with a violence that startled them both. He ran distraught fingers through his hair as he stood. His face was rigid as a mask, drawn and terrible. His voice croaked as he said, detesting her, 'Child! Get away from me! Get up to yer bed!'

'Seth?' Never had Mercy felt more abandoned or humiliated. What had she done? Why had the spell gone wrong?

'Seth?'

But he pretended not to hear. His hand came to his cheek as though he had been hurt. He ripped his coat from the peg and went out of the door, leaving her naked and ashamed on the floor.

She drew on her clothes and spent the night by the fire, waiting for him.

But Seth did not return. And Mercy didn't weep for fear Annie would see her red eyes in the morning. Because why should Annie know that her offer had been rejected?

Annie would never understand.

Mercy felt an unreasoning burst of anger towards her friend. Fierce and unexpected, it verged on hatred. She didn't want Annie's love. She hated to see it in her eyes. She would never love Annie who was good and kind and innocent. In Mercy's experience the good were weak, and Mercy abhorred weakness.

FOURTEEN

The constables came on horseback. Seth led them in, in the morning.

There were two, inscrutable men with moustaches and tall black hats on their heads.

Mercy's heart fell. She couldn't believe it! And the law! He had no need to call the law! They would have gone if he'd told them to go. There was no need for this! What on earth did she do last night to make him react so aggressively? She turned to ask him but he would not meet her eyes. 'What could I's do? I's couldn't keep 'e 'ere.'

'Yous did the right thing if I's may say so, young man,' said the tallest of the constables, looking critically round the room Annie had thought so wonderful. 'In the circumstances . . . what with the village girl still missin' an' you's background an' all . . . 'Twould have been terrible speculation.'

Mercy didn't understand. She saw that everything Mrs Mountebank told them about the outside world was true. It was all here – poverty, cruelty, violence, betrayal. The only thing about it was that otherwise it was so beautiful, and if circumstances could have been different . . .

Annie kicked and screamed. She rammed her booted foot against the constable's shin and he brought up his hand and cracked her across the back of her head with his fist. Her head snapped forward and she fell.

'Don't, Annie!'

'We can't go back!'

'We've seen it now, Annie . . . we know . . .'

'We can't go back!'

On all fours on the floor, Annie's nose was dripping and saliva dribbling from her mouth. Quick and small she moved like a whiplash, her black hair ragged from lack of attention and her face smudged with tears. She swayed and bared her teeth, and when the man who had hit her moved his hand towards her – concerned perhaps – she bit it, possessed.

'Don't, Annie!'

She glared at Mercy, too. 'I wish we hadn't done it! I wish, I wish, I wish,' and she moaned, her eyes rolling.

'It's Nature,' said Mercy, looking behind her at Seth. 'Isn't that what you said?'

'You's better back . . .'

'How do you know?'

'Yous'd never survive . . .'

'You said that about the cubs!'

'Well, you's couldn't have. Two young girls . . .'

'I'd rather you'd given us the chance! Annie! Annie, don't! What'll they think of you? What'll they tell Sister Henry?'

But Annie didn't seem to hear and they had to bundle her up in her coat and bind her arms together with rope, tie her to the horse that would carry her home. 'We're going a-travelling . . .' yelled Annie. 'Come on, Mercy! Isn't that what you sang when we left? When we were walking through that village in the middle of the night. We're going a-travelling. . . . travelling . . . travelling . . .'

Mercy was ashamed. She couldn't bear to watch. This was her fault. She had forced Annie to come with her, used the half-crown incident for blackmail. And now, because of her behaviour with Seth last night, this was happening. Yes, this was the worst thing she had ever done. For this she could not forgive herself. And she knew God never would.

She played with people's feelings – that's what she did – arrogantly thinking she could make them dance to her tune just because she willed it. Well, Seth hadn't danced. Seth had been disgusted . . . with her body? With her manipulative behaviour? She had wanted Seth to love her, to give her and Annie a home and protection. She had used her body as barter, happy to trade it for security and love, the things she desired most in the world.

She had only succeeded in making Seth revolted with himself and her . . . and apparently in driving Annie mad.

On the way home across the country, when they were stared at by everyone they saw, Mercy made herself think of Sister Henry. If you faced the thing you most feared it ceased to be terrifying and became, instead, something within your control. Or that's what she told herself.

Annie was asleep. She drooped like a doll behind the constable, swaying to the motion of the horse, mercifully, at this terrible time, dead to the world. Exhausted.

Sister Henry was loved by nobody – not secretly, not openly and not in any other way. She was loveless and unlovable. Satisfaction with that fact showed in her face. She was a woman but she looked like a man. She had the strength of a man but the neat, petite wrists of a woman.

While Mother was small and tight and hen-like and pecked her way about, Sister Henry had the brutal face of a successful forty-year-old prize-fighter and strode about her domain.

Her job gave her kudos. She mixed with the higher

echelons of the local church community and with the butlers and housekeepers of the big houses she visited, high, but not as high as she would have liked. She ran her house with a rod of iron. It would be foolhardy to flaunt her. She spoke in an affected accent which resembled cockney and it was interesting to see how this overpowered her visitors. Early on they would be saying, 'Reely?' or 'Mah deah, thet is remarkable!' just as she did.

She wore one item of jewellery on a chain around her neck: a tiny crucifix with red jewels alive in the Christ's eyes. She would never get a pin and poke them out . . . never allow Him to die.

Her hair was a thin wire-grey, every wisp independently visible and clamped fiercely to the back of her head in a square pill-box bun.

No one had ever run away from her establishment before.

It was pathetic to see what little ground they had covered on their journey. Mercy expected to travel for at least one full day . . . maybe more.

But by lunchtime she recognised the village. They were within minutes of arrival. She debated whether or not to wake Annie up. She should be prepared. She could not face Sister Henry bemused and straight from sleep.

The constables were polite but aloof. Throughout the uncomfortable morning they had chatted to each other but not to the girls. These were men, but they did not look at her in the way the shepherd had done. She asked the man she rode behind, 'Can we stop, just for a moment, to prepare ourselves?'

But Annie's custodian turned round and said, 'Yous do what you likes. I's not waking this fiend up.' His hand was still bandaged from her bite.

So they ambled down the road, that awful, familiar road, with Mercy calling from the horse behind, 'Annie! Annie! Wake up now! We're there!' But Annie, from some inbuilt self-protection, was so deeply asleep they had to poke and prod her from the horse, lift her down and stand her on the step. And even then she looked as if she might fall over. Her face was blue and pinched, but she was quiet. She had stopped her terrible screaming.

FIFTEEN

Mercy squeezed the lavender bag in her pocket to take away the smell in the room. She hitched her hair behind her ears. Her legs had not yet ceased trembling. She lay next to Annie on a palliasse in the attic. Annie was shivering from head to toe. Her eyes were surrounded by black shadows, as if someone had thumbed them there. The one blanket they shared was thin and torn and smelled of vomit.

If they had passed their companions on their way up, it was certain no one had seen them, for all eyes turned away and conversation stopped. Mercy heard the whispers, knew they would, for ever, be shunned, but she was too weary to care.

Sister Henry had not spoken. She had talked to the constables, passed the time of day with them, offered them a glass of port . . . but they had refused, saying they must get back they had work to do, and Sister Henry had said, 'Quite so.'

Then she had called to an older girl, Martha. 'Take Mercy Geary and Annie Clegg upstairs,' and Martha hadn't needed to ask where.

This was the room Mary Ludd had been taken to, waiting for the law to come and fetch her. This was the room Violet had been carried to when she collapsed in the washhouse and wouldn't get up. This was the room Jessie Tarrant had lived in for almost a year before she had taken her own life by hanging herself from one of the beams . . . they said.'

Which beam?

This was a silent room. The noise of the house did

not carry up here. This was a draughty room. There were gaps in the roof where the rain came through and every gust of wind moved the cobwebs.

Mercy moved forward to reach the pitcher of water which Martha had been instructed to place at their disposal. A jug but no bowls. Mercy tipped it and wet the front of her dress.

'Are you thirsty?'

'No, it's just something to do.'

'What is going to happen to us now?'

'I don't know, Annie.'

'She didn't say anything, did she?'

'No, she didn't have to.'

'I'm glad we gave the money back.'

Mercy gave a wry smile. 'It doesn't seem to matter much now.'

'At least we've got out of the work.'

Mercy looked around their dingy home. 'I dunno. I think I'd rather work than be here.'

'Did you get the shepherd to kiss you?'

'No,' Mercy lied. 'No, nothing like that.'

'Well, you were gone for a long time.'

'I sat on my own. He wasn't there.'

'If you'd got him to kiss you he'd have let us stay, maybe. That would have been good, wouldn't it, Mercy?'

'Have some water. Your mouth is all bloody again.'

'It comes with the coughing.'

At night the attic felt bitter as winter. The draughts came like silver knives through the blanket. They were given no candle. Mercy wrapped her arms round Annie, tried to keep her warm, tried to doze, but she could not.

Breakfast was brought to them and the pot they had used to relieve themselves in was removed. There was fresh water, and as Annie was too weak to hold her spoon Mercy fed her small amounts of watery pease porridge.

'Bread?' she'd asked Martha.

'Not today. No bread.' And the girl had left them without another word.

Throughout that day Annie seemed only dimly to understand what was happening. When she slept she shouted in her dreams, 'Stop the horse . . . we're going too fast . . .' and 'This is my room and nobody else is to have it or ever come in.'

'Shush, Annie, shush! Wake up, you're having a nightmare.' But when Annie woke she seemed as bemused as she'd been in her sleep.

The time passed slowly. Mercy paced the room and tried to haul herself up to see out of the high window, but couldn't. She could only see the sky, and that little patch seemed higher and further away than usual, nothing like the sky she had seen on her back in the grass during their day of freedom. All things had seemed vast and possible then. Now the world had shrunk to its proper size, and she cocooned herself in self-pity and fear.

She wanted to shake Annie better. Instead she took her hand and held it gently, looking down at the bitten nails and the scarred fingers. Chapped and roughened by work, picked and bitten as they were, they might have been beautiful hands for they were shaped long and fine. Annie's fingers closed round her own, and Mercy shook them free.

Annie opened her eyes. 'It'll come right,' she said. And Mercy thought she must still be dreaming. For things never came right.

Another sleepless night and in the morning Mercy said

241

to Martha, 'Annie's ill. She needs warmth and food and looking after.'

Martha took up the pot and the empty pitcher and said, 'I'll tell Sister.'

When she came back bearing more gruel, she sent Mercy a pitying look. 'Sister says Annie's no more ill than you or I and she's playing for attention. You're to ignore her.'

It rained today. The rain ran in strips down the slanted glass, changing colour, white, yellow and silver. Annie said she couldn't feel her legs so Mercy rubbed them, not liking the feel of the moistness of flesh, the pitted skin which flaked in her hands. But Annie's plight was her fault and for punishment she rubbed and she rubbed until her arms ached.

She got up and walked restlessly round the room, counting her steps and trying to remember long passages of biblical text. 'Moon's out, Annie,'

'Wax flowers under glass,' said Annie.

And Mercy thought, 'She's lost her mind.'

'Let's go home now,' said Annie. And Mercy watched the moon until it sailed out of sight. But it was still there. Just because she couldn't see it . . . it was still there. And that's what she thought about life. It was happening to other people all around her, but so far she had only been allowed a glimpse.

The days merged, turned into one long night. 'Annie, I'm sorry.' Mercy met the long gaze of the sunken eyes without flinching. With every sharp intake of breath they held an agonised appeal. Annie was not beautiful. The muscles of her mouth and eyes sagged. The young skin that covered the small boned face was loose and yellow at the throat. Annie was growing old as she lay beside her. And all Mercy could say was, 'I'm sorry! I'm sorry!'

'I heard you,' said Annie suddenly in a voice that came from a distance.

'I didn't want this to happen. Annie, sweetheart, please don't die. Don't die, for don't you know I'm goin' to need you.' She couldn't help her feelings of exasperated impatience. Why was Annie making her feel like this? Why was she being ill? She tried to will life and health back into Annie.

Mercy was asleep when Annie died. She woke to find her stiff and cold as the pool of blood on the mattress, an awful halo round her head.

She tried to clean the blood from Annie's hair, certain she would want it to shine now as it never had in life. She spat on it, she licked it. She ripped open the lavender bag with her teeth and scattered the tiny mauve flakes on Annie's hair. She raged in her pain while she waited for someone to come. Her heart broke because it had all been pretence. She thought she had never loved Annie, and if she hadn't, then no one had.

No one, she thought, should die without ever knowing love.

She raised dry eyes to the patch of sky above her. She raged and she cried out loud, 'If You're there, God, leave her alone! Leave her quiet where they put her under the grass . . . she doesn't want to be with You, God, can't you see that!'

Slowly she shook her head over the body, rocking herself backwards and forwards with Annie's head in her arms, trying to staunch this unbearable sadness.

'Oh God, oh God!' she cried. 'How I hate You!'

SIXTEEN

'Oh yes, it was all a very bad business, most unfortunate indeed,' said the Reverend Ainsworth, the sweat giving his face a waxen sheen.

His recollections of the girl in question were given to Tristan between thunderous bursts of learned morality, to which he reverted when floundering or at a loss for anything else to say. His high voice quivered when he said, 'She brought a great deal of trouble to the worthy Mission Homes, and Mrs Mountebank, at one time, was quite ill over it. Never had a child run away before, and never had we had to deal with a theft of that nature. It was because of Mercy Geary's wilful actions that the child Annie sadly passed on, in spite of all the good efforts of the ladies of the Mission, and in particular the strivings of dear Sister Henry. I don't think the poor woman ever quite got over it. But luckily, as is His wont, the Good Lord intervened and we were able to move the distressing child on to a better place – Trewen. There was a vacancy, if I remember . . .'

The word 'Trewen' brought Tristan to attention. For a long time now his mind had been wandering. The vicar's voice was boring, and too readily slipped into sermon-style. He loved the sound of his own voice. The heady scents of honeysuckle streamed in from the tiny windows, travelling on bars of sunshine that landed on the vicar's empty hearth and played on the brasses there like firelight. Tristan heard the swishing sound of his horse's tail as it dealt with the blood-sucking flies, the impatient beat of a hoof on the ground. The tight heat of the day made him frown; concentrating on the vicar's exuberant vocabulary also made him frown and trying to cut through and find some shred of truth behind the bland words made him frown hardest of all.

And always, Tristan was aware that he was being drawn nearer to Porthclegga. His investigations had never veered from this direction, and now that he was so close to Kerry, so near to seeing her again . . . when his thoughts took him this way the miserable stories he heard were lifted, swept away like a sea mist, leaving everything clear and sharp and blue and sunny behind them.

Tristan felt impatience rise and nearly throttle him in the claustrophobic atmosphere of this musty little room, where the old books, old papers, even the ivories on the piano were yellow. The vicar's nails were yellow, too, and so were the smoke-marks that streaked the chimney wall and moved up over the low beamed ceiling: musty and yellow with years of age. Years ago . . . all this had happened such a very long time ago, and he was growing tired of his own questions. He wanted to go to Kerry *now*. He wanted to leave this room, fling himself on his horse and ride until he could smell the sea, until he could bury his face in her hair and feel her tight in his arms. He was growing weary of battering himself against these various walls of deception that beset him at every turn. Were they put there deliberately, or were these people honestly describing the events as they interpreted them? That Mercy Geary had been evil they seemed to have no doubt. That she had little alternative, that she might have been desperately seeking for some other way, had never seemed to cross their blinkered minds.

Mother Carrivick had said: 'Whatever yous do, do

not return until yous has found out the truth. Yous owes it, Tristan, and I's owes it, God help me I's does.'

Do I care, Tristan asked himself as the sweat from his back soaked his doublet. Do I care what I owe, or what that half-baked old woman thinks she owes? What is it to me? I only want one person in my life, I'll soon be eighteen and a man by law. I have money of my own and skills at my fingertips. I can give her the sort of life she deserves, and no one can stop me from returning to claim her.

But Tristan, so in love, was haunted by his need to know, was haunted by the picture he had formed of the slant-eyed, silver-haired child with the mysterious face and a past that seemed so fraught with misfortune. No, he had to know for himself now, not because of Mother Carrivick. And he would continue to ask his questions until he satisfied himself that he had eventually discovered the truth . . . whatever that might be.

Tristan forced himself to listen to what the Reverend Ainsworth was saying. 'She should have been grateful, young man. But do you know . . . by God she wasn't!'

She was clean and washed and pale-faced downstairs in the parlour. She didn't know where Annie was. She didn't know where they'd put her.

'Now then, now then, it's not as bad as that!' The vicar's voice was firm but kindly. He wiped his perspiring face with a large handkerchief. This was a difficult business, and the girl who sat so straight on the chair before him looked as if she might become hysterical.

'You have been lucky enough to have been offered a post as kitchenmaid at Trewen – a God-fearing Methodist household very highly thought of by Sister Henry and a place she normally reserves for her best girls. For you the good woman has made an exception. I have come to escort you there.'

246

'Now?'

'There is no time like the present.'

'But what about Annie?' The vicar didn't answer. The child was in shock. Hard work and a change of circumstances would help her get over it.

He had expected gratitude. Without his intervention this girl would be in the hands of the court by now. He knew of several girls, particularly in the poorer villages of Porthclegga and Collenew, who would give their right arms for a post at The House. The few shillings they sent home would help their families stave off starvation. And this girl, Sister informed him, had just turned eleven years old. It was best to start them at eight or nine but Sister liked to train her girls to a high standard before she let them go.

No one said goodbye. Faces flickered like reflections at the windows as the vicar's bay mare highstepped away from Mrs Mountebank's towards the village, taking the route the Lord Mayor had taken. The windows of the baby house where Mercy had grown up were blank, expressionless. For the big girls' house behind her Mercy felt nothing. She did not look back as they entered the village with its neat gardens and rows of fresh washing, past Mrs Potter's garden where Mercy had stolen her cabbages, scattering a few listless fowl as the dogcart turned out and on to the road that led to Trewen.

The vicar tickled the mare's rump with the end of a whip that dangled like a fishing rod. They took the road that she and Annie had taken not one week before, passing a few ill-disposed looking vagrants with bundles on their backs.

The summer had stayed long that year and the banks were masses of wild flowers. Once they sighted the sea, but it was far away and shrouded in mist. Chimneys and engine houses stood naked against the distance, while men worked in golden fields to bring the harvest home. Far behind them the moor rose high like a granite cut-out, purple on a Wedgwood skyline.

They road beside a high stone wall, impossible to see over. They clopped down a central avenue, flanked now and then by an ancient oak, beech or elm. In the distance dappled deer grazed on pasture smooth as lawn. Before the house was a lake, a lake so still and wide it looked like a mirror, reflecting the waterfowl which waddled nervously among the stately swans. Even the deer seemed to take on the quiet dignity of the place, staring into the distance like philosophers, munching.

'Trewen,' muttered the vicar, touching the horse lightly to keep up the spanking pace.

The house rose high above the gardens keeping watch over the lawns and terraces, its mullioned window-eyes finding their way down the shaded yew-hedged borders, dovecotes and broad, rhododendron-lined walks. It brooded over the fountains and basins, appearing to sneer at their frivolity.

It was a manor house built of stone, and as they passed across the front of it Mercy's eyes widened because it went on and on.

A tall, thin man dressed in black was coming down the steps with a cane in his hand. 'Squire Yelland,' said the vicar in tones of respect. 'Take a long look, child, for that is your employer. You'll not be likely to see him again for you'll not normally be round the front.'

'But he's mad, isn't he?'

'What?' The vicar was appalled. 'He's a fervent, religious man. Don't you ever speak of him in that way again. To you he is gentry. To you, gentry are above criticism.'

But Mercy remembered what Seth had said and Mercy, in spite of his terrible betrayal, believed Seth.

The vicar took the cart round the house to the back. They went under an arch and pulled into a stone-walled courtyard made up on two sides by stables, the other two by storerooms and kitchens. The vicar would normally have used the front door, but he was here on domestic business and to be truthful he felt more at home here at the back of the house. Here he was treated with the respect due to his cloth and could throw his weight about. The master of this house listened to no man . . . tolerated no moderate belief. Would have no truck with the incumbent of this Parish, the notorious Parson Fox.

A stout man, the Reverend Ainsworth dismounted with difficulty and was followed by a bewildered Mercy. She had never seen so much action. Two young girls in print cotton uniforms were beating a carpet over a line. Boys scurried everywhere, carrying baskets of bread and vegetables, brooms, saddles, and one wrestled with a wheelbarrow larger than himself. Horses stamped and whinnied in various stages of grooming. A man in long boots carried an enormous pike on a stick over his shoulder, and a mangy dog had followed the cart round from the front and was sniffing around everything it passed.

'Come on girl, we haven't got all day.'

No one was taking the slightest notice of her. Once Mercy realised this she felt better.

In a dream she followed the vicar down passageways so narrow he filled them with his bulk and Mercy could not see past him. She liked the clicking sounds her boots made on the flagstones. Maids they met backed into walls and flattened themselves to make way, unable even to curtsy. The vicar led on, ignoring them all, until he came to a door with a yellowing label, *Mrs King, Housekeeper. Please knock*.

He turned and inspected the child, straightening her lapels and sighing with resignation. 'You'll do,' he said as he knocked. Whatever he did to her he could not make her plain as she ought to be, could not brush that alluring beauty from her eyes as he would an eyelash. Those almond-shaped eyes gave her face a shade of secrecy which at her tender age, he thought, should not be there. There was something not quite as innocent as there should be about this girl.

'Ah, Vicar! About your good works as usual, I see!'

'Indeed, Mrs King. But without good people like yourself to help me it would be impossible to carry out the Lord's work, as you know.'

'Sit down, Vicar, and join me in a glass of port while we talk.' If anything he sat with rather too much haste. Mercy was left standing. So far they had not directly referred to her. The housekeeper asked about Mrs Mountebank and Sister Henry. He told her. She asked about the new curate and his wife. He told her.

It was hard to keep from fidgeting. They were taking so long over their port. The room looked like a man's and smelled of stale biscuits. No flowers. No pictures. The shiny cream walls were covered with lists on hooks. The only other furniture in the room apart from the desk and the two occupied high-backed chairs was a tall cupboard meant for a bedroom with a wardrobe at the top and drawers at the bottom. Mrs King had taken the port from one of the drawers. Later Mercy would learn that the top half was stashed with delicacies from the kitchens, a flowery thin tea set, an assortment of decent glasses and a linen table cloth with which, on important occasions, Mrs King covered the scarred table. There were packets of expensive tea meant for upstairs, boxes of sweetmeats, sugared fruits and lots more, all accepted as housekeeper's perks.

Finally Mrs King brought the interview to a halt by stepping outside the door and calling, 'Daisy Wyatt, please!'

The vicar stood up and picked up his hat, downing the dregs in his glass while Mrs King's head was briefly out of the room. There was a sound of running footsteps and a grey-complexioned creature with nondescript mousy hair appeared anxiously in the corridor.

'Daisy – take the new maid to her quarters, please.'

Mercy didn't know whether to say goodbye to the vicar or not. The two adults had resumed their conversation and it would have meant butting in. So she meekly left the room and followed the beckoning girl, her bundle banging against her legs as she climbed staircase after staircase.

'Please wait a minute!' Mercy was breathless and gasping. She was not long recovered from her starvation diet. 'Is it much further?'

'Come on!' The girl looked agitated. 'We'm not allowed to loiter on the stairs. 'Tis against the rules.'

The stairs were wooden and the walls were green, growing dingier and darker the higher they climbed. Along a narrow landing, the only light there was having to fight its way through a high, multi-cobwebbed skylight, and Daisy Wyatt stopped outside an unprepossessing, paint-peeled door. Mercy could smell her now. Stale body odour combined with cooking grease wafted from her, pungent as the scent of an unfolding rose.

Mercy followed the girl into the room. 'Yous to share with me,' said Daisy. 'I's laid out yer uniform on yer bed this morning when they told me you's be coming.'

251

She crossed the rugless floor to Mercy's iron bed and fingered the serge material reverently. 'Yous put this on and yous one of us,' she said proudly. 'There's lots of girls would love to wear this uniform.'

Mercy knew Daisy. There'd been girls like her at Mrs Mountebank's, girls who were so absurdly grateful for their board and keep they were pitiful. Brainwashed and down-trodden by birth, they were the ones who hadn't rebelled, the ones, Mercy thought, who'd probably had the worst of it all. Daisy Wyatt would rather die than break a rule, would have her tongue cut out rather than answer back. And what was worse, when put to the test, would come out on the side of authority against her own kind. Yes, Mercy understood Daisy and knew how it was. So, of course, did They. Daisy Wyatt would probably remain a kitchenmaid all her life. There was no reward, in this earthly life, for this sort of abject humility. Annie had it . . . and look what had happened to Annie.

Downstairs, Mrs King was seeing the vicar out.

'I think I have a clear picture,' she sniffed as they went outside into the yard. There were some things that shouldn't be discussed with men, even men of the church. A boy stood by respectfully, holding the vicar's mare. 'Don't worry, Vicar, I will personally keep an eye on the girl. I swear to you that in one year from now you won't recognise her. You won't be able to pick her out from the rest. Hard work will see to that.'

'Well, I'm grateful, Mrs King,' the vicar replied, doubting her but unwilling to argue. Mercy Geary could never look like all the others. 'Who knows what happened between her and that wild man . . . a ten-year-old girl and a man with a reputation like that. Most unfortunate, I'm sure. I know she'll learn her lessons well once she settles.'

252

'Oh, she'll settle,' said Mrs King. 'She'll settle, of that I have no doubt. She'll soon forget about everything other than her daily responsibilities.' Her face set, and Mrs King rubbed her hard, long hands together. It was a habit she had. It made, thought the vicar, rather an unpleasant rasping sound.

His duty done, the Reverend Ainsworth's ride back to the village was a pleasant one. He waved and chatted and doffed his hat to those he passed on the way.

What a piece of luck it had been that only yesterday he'd been called to Trewen to discuss discreet arrangements for the burial of a hapless kitchenmaid who'd died giving birth to a stillborn child round the back of the stables. The morals of these people! They were no better than animals! He'd had the ideal opportunity to recommend Mercy to Mrs King who needed a quick replacement with no fuss. The Lord certainly works, he thought to himself with a rueful smile, in mysterious ways.

It would have been difficult keeping the child at Mrs Mountebank's when they were explaining to the Board the circumstances of Annie Clegg's death. 'Consumption' went down on the certificate. She had died, poor thing, despite all the administrations of Sister Henry who had done everything in her power to help her. These things can't be helped. But Mercy was better away, where she would be forced to keep her pretty little mouth shut.

Mercy, meanwhile, to Daisy's whining disapproval, was balanced on the bedstead trying to get a better view from the window in the roof.

'We's'll be late! We's'll be late!' cried the wretched Daisy, pulling her lip with frustration.

Mercy could see a church spire in the distance, a

string-straight segment of road, and then a dip that disappeared into a basin of silver. 'It's the sea!' she called, with all the excitement of a little child. 'I can see the sea!'

She caught sight of the vicar speeding home, and from where she looked the large, night-black crow that flapped across his path and almost caused the mare to bolt, seemed to be outrageously out of proportion.

Like the Spur rock, whose head she saw, an outline of black like a canine tooth, in the distant bay.

SEVENTEEN

'The responsibility of running this great house, it was all on me, it all rested on my shoulders. Everything. And the master, then, was a forbidding man, wouldn't take excuses, wouldn't listen to reason. I ran it like a ship, nothing went on there that got past me. But I had to deal with everything . . . and then the master died and things began to change. Everything sunk, and we sank with it. We older ones, you see, we who were used to the discipline, well, we found it hard to cope.'

Her voice trailed thinly into the air and Tristan felt sympathy for this woman who sat in front of him, stains on her dress and wisps of hair escaping from the fierce bun at her neck. Her face was pinched and tired, her shoulders sagged, and she sat in the room marked *Housekeeper*, which smelled of stale drink. Ancient, yellowing notices hung on pegs on the walls, stuffing came out of the chair he was invited to sit in.

The whole house appeared to be in a slow, ageing process of decay, as she was. Fuddled by drink, and yet trying to hold herself together for just long enough to talk to him, Mrs King the housekeeper said, 'And I don't take much part in anything any more.' Her eyes slid slyly round the room, then over his person, as if in search of a bottle.

'But there were good days, Mrs King?'

She brought her thin lips into a smile that wasn't a smile. Her eyes softened. 'Do all days seem good days when you look back?' she asked him, and he noticed that her head nodded all the time. 'Or do we soften them to make our memories bearable?'

'I don't think Mercy Geary had many bearable memories by the time she arrived here, do you?'

'Lazy good-for-nothing.' Mrs King seemed to come alive all of a sudden, to find some of the energy that had made her the efficient, bustling person she once had been. 'Most of them were, you understand. They came to me with references from this place or that, but when I got them started what did I find? All the same . . . sluts most of them. Never done a good day's work in their lives. It took me the best part of a year, Mr Carne, to bring them up to anything worth their salt. Yes,' the pale-faced woman sank again, deflated again and drooped, 'the best part of a year. If I was lucky.' And she seemed to lose the thread, her eyes started scuttling off round the room again.

'And Mercy was one of those?'

Mrs King wrinkled her thin nose and sniffed. 'No better, no worse. But of course, that one eventually went right off the rails. It was her looks of course, she was unfortunate to be born looking like that. There's one rule that has to be obeyed above all others for the efficient running of a household, Mr Carne, and that is, that servants and family do not mix. How can they?' Tristan noticed that her hands were never still, that they ranged the table top between them clutching at nothing, tightening and loosening. Without touching them he knew that they were cold hands, that they would rasp, like reptile skin, that they were dry from lack of toil, lack of anything. The sharp-faced woman went on, 'It's like mixing two breeds of animals together. It's not Nature. But Mercy was wild, she came to me with an unhappy reputation and left here with a worse one I may say. No better than she was worth, that one, and a good many others besides.' Mrs King shrugged her shoulders before adding, 'She went the way of so many.'

256

If Tristan went to the window and looked out over the heathland he could see where the cliffs dropped away. Below them, down below them was the bower of gorse: it would be in flower now, a wreath of golden, summer sunshine, and below that was Porthclegga. So near now. So very near to achieving the one aim in his life that had kept him going for these five lonely years. The energy in the air fizzed like champagne, the colours were almost impossibly rich and beautiful. In all his travels he had not seen colours to compare with these. He'd begun to believe he'd only imagined that the sky, that the grass, the trees and the moors had looked like this. But now, now he knew, and he knew that Kerry would be as beautiful as he remembered her also.

'I did my best with all of them,' continued Mrs King. 'Lord knows, I've always done my best, all my life I've done my best. And it's come to this.'. She bit her lip hard, screwed up her face as though trying to work out the most difficult sum. She raised puzzled eyes to Tristan who, with so much in his life to hope for, could feel sorry for her once again. Why should he hurry away? Why not stop and listen? He was waiting for someone called Daisy, he could not leave without speaking to Daisy, they all told him that. So why shouldn't he wait here in the housekeeper's room and let her talk of the good old days. They were all she had left.

Good days? No wonder Daisy Wyatt stank. The full-length black serge dresses they were forced to wear on the master's instructions, for modesty's sake, were warm enough in winter, but in spring and summer, with the heavy work they had to do, they were sweltering. And there was little free time to spare for such luxuries as personal hygiene.

At night the garret room they shared held any linger-

ing heat from the day, sealing it tight like the lid of a
can. Flies knew it and it was a popular haunt for
armies of buzzing bluebottles . . . but in winter, Mercy
discovered, the cold slid off the great expanse of roof
above.

Mercy had been at Trewen for three days before Mrs
King deigned to speak to her. In this short time she
existed in a state of unreality. She saw her new world
through a barrier of misery, as if in a trance. Was it
her this was happening to? Was she still Mercy Geary?
And was Annie really not here?

After a brief introduction to the cook, Mrs Gibson,
a monstrously large woman with arms like great pink
sausages and a voice like a spoon-clang in a cauldron,
she was asked what she was doing standing there and
sent to the scullery. That's where she went first thing
in the morning and that's where, worn out, she finished
last thing at night.

She was used to hard work, but the Mission had
been nothing like this. Here it was lonely. She began
to learn her place. She spent her time being shouted
out for being under people's feet. She seemed incapable
of moving fast enough. She tried to talk to Daisy about
'the family' when they were in bed, for she knew that
the pale boy lived upstairs, but Daisy was not forth-
coming. 'Now go to sleep and stop askin' impertinent
questions or yous woan be ready to get up in the
morning.'

Mercy, pretending to be asleep, watched Daisy hide
a blood-soaked rag under the mattress. She'd known
the smell in the room was heavier than sweat and
cooking, and now she recognised it. It was meat gone
off. Where was she getting the rags from and why
was she putting them so furtively there? This must be

258

another rule of the House which Mercy hadn't been told about.

Mercy was haunted by Annie. She tried to tell Daisy about her and Daisy said, 'Bessy died, too. She used to sleep in yous bed. She was a dreamer like you . . . she lived in cloud cuckoo land.' Daisy didn't care about Bessy. Daisy said she didn't even miss her. 'She was no better than she should have been, that one. As ye sow, so shall ye reap.'

That Bessy had done something shocking before she died was apparent from the prudish tone in Daisy's voice. Mercy frowned, and wondered if it had anything to do with rags and blood.

The sleeves of her dress were grimy and never dry. When she took it off to hang it on the bedframe at night she remembered Mrs Mountebank's, and in the morning she winced as the rough, cold edges rubbed her wrists again. No matter how high she pushed up her sleeves, the greasy water got to them, soaked in and stayed.

Because she was junior to Daisy, Mercy was the one who had to trot down four flights of stairs with the wash jug to fetch cold water from the yard minutes after waking, always making quite sure she wasn't seen by the master. ''E carn stand women . . . particularly 'e carn stand to see 'em upstairs,' was the warning she had been given. Up the stairs again, strip wash to the waist in the cracked basin, and when she had brushed her hair and dressed, when Daisy had finished, carry the slop pail down to be emptied outside. When she arrived in the scullery ten minutes later, the pots and pans were waiting, burnt or slippery with grease, because Cook began getting the breakfasts ready early.

There were two staff dining rooms, one large and rough for the outside men, the other smaller and more civilised, boasting a threadbare carpet. The outside men had breakfast first – the grooms, the gardeners, the hall boys, the lamp boy and the steel boy.

After they'd worked for an hour the indoor servants went in to the other, slightly better dining room. There were housemaids, sewing-maids, stillroom maids, laundry-maids, kitchenmaids, vegetable-maids and scullery-maids. How would Mercy ever get to learn all this?

And why were so many servants necessary to serve the stern-looking gentleman dressed all in black whom she had seen on the steps when she arrived? The upper ranks of servants, the butler, Mrs King, and the cook would congregate round the vast kitchen table to eat theirs in leisure later.

Only after this was over and out of the way would Cook start preparing the third breakfast, the one for the family. Pile after pile of pans and dishes flowed in an almighty tide to the scullery. Breakfast was a lavish meal, of cold game-pie or devilled kidneys, ham, oysters, eggs, bread and rolls. And it had to be served on time, for the master was a stickler for time.

On the first day Mercy hadn't believed she must do all the work alone. Where were the other scullery-maids? Looking round, her arms steeped in greasy, grey water, she had quailed to see the over-balancing heaps collecting on the floor behind her. She realised she would not get to bed until the room was completely clear, wiped and swilled down . . . and this was only the beginning, the first meal of the day.

'The other one is polishin' pots and pans, stackin' the dishes an' crocks an' putting 'em all back,' Daisy explained impatiently.

She'd noticed the silent, downcast girl who came in now and then pushing a trolley and sighing.

'I don't see why she can't help me and polish the pots when it's over.'

'Bessy managed,' sniffed Daisy. 'The pans have to be perfect before Cook will consider using them a second time.' She was disgusted by Mercy's slap-dash attitude. 'Things have always been done this way. Yous carn come 'ere with yous slovenly manners an' expect to change things. Yous has to learn to work the proper way. That's why youm here, to learn, after all.'

'Why?'

'Yous doan ask why, Mercy, yous just do as yous is told an' be grateful.'

Ah yes, that was a message that Mercy could understand. She pulled a face at Daisy's back as the other girl left to answer Cook's call. Daisy was a kitchen-maid and proud of it.

'I thought that's what I was going to be,' said Mercy later.

'Yous have to learn to earn respect and promotion,' said Daisy haughtily, 'like I's had to.'

Soon Mercy's hair, like Daisy's, took on the steamy grease that rose from everywhere. Her long locks separated and fell dankly straight past her shoulders and over her face. But if she complained Daisy was always there with her arguments. 'It should be hidden right under yer cap like mine. At least yous not in the poor-house. At least yous eatin', unlike some others. Youm not hungry, is yous?'

No, Mercy was not hungry. But she ached all over from bending and scouring and lugging. She ached inside, too, with a kind of desolate loneliness. From what she had seen it appeared that the women and girls suffered most from the heaviest drudgery. Even the lamp boy had help when he fell behind with his work. But the housemaids struggling upstairs in the late afternoons with heavy hip baths, hiding from the master, there was no help for them.

And all this, Mercy kept thinking, all this for one man and a boy.

Daisy's first job was to clean and light the kitchen fire around which the whole house revolved. It ate up timber and heated the water cauldrons and it was Daisy's privilege to lug the heavy baskets of wood in from the yard, and at all times throughout the day to make sure the temperature of the brick oven was right for Cook. But instead of loathing the dirty, back-breaking job, Daisy seemed proud of the responsibility and treated the fire like a revered human being, talking of it as if it were alive.

"'E's not as hungry as 'e were yesterday,' she would say. 'But 'e was a bit lazy this morning. Didn't want to make a start. I's'll have to watch 'e around teatime. That's when 'e tends to get awkward.' And Mercy wouldn't have been surprised if she'd added, 'Bless him!'

And Daisy's last job of the day was worse than that. She had to empty the spittoon that the tobacco chewers among the servants used so frequently during the day. But again, Daisy didn't seem to mind.

How did they all accept this life? Mercy had accepted Mrs Mountebank's, but never without a fuss.

On the day Mrs King spoke to her, Mercy hadn't even noticed there was anyone else in the room with her. She had gone into a storeroom to fetch a fresh cloth and the next thing she heard was, 'Mercy Geary! I would like a word with you!'

She looked up, cowed by the steely voice, and as she followed Mrs King she noticed that Jethro the houseman was searching for something on one of the high shelves by the window.

'Follow me, please, Mercy.'

Ignorant of what she had done, and concerned that she would get behind with her work, Mercy had to trot to keep up with the housekeeper's purposeful strides.

At the door of her room the tall, thin shape whirled round, stopping Mercy in her tracks. 'How dare you!'

'Sorry, M'um?'

'Surely you are aware of the rule that no female servant should be alone in a room with a male servant under any circumstances at all. The master is absolutely adamant about that!'

'I didn't see him there, M'um.'

Mrs King shot her a look which accused her of lying. 'Ignorance is no excuse! I am sure Jethro must have felt extremely embarrassed . . .'

'I don't think he knew I was there either, M'um. If he did, he could have waited until I came out.'

The look Mrs King gave her then would have dampened the most raging fire. Tiny material buttons were hooked together in a perfect line down the front of her austere black dress. Her thin, white hands she held in front of her, clasped together an inch from her body as if it would be immoral to let them come too close. Mrs King's hair was drawn back in a bun as severe as Sister Henry's, exaggerating features that clustered too closely on the narrow face. Whatever she did with those features she would look disapproving. Now she looked shocked, and Mercy was startled.

'Your impertinence astounds me! Don't ever come back at me with answers again or there will be trouble! Do you understand?'

'Yes, M'um. I'm sorry, M'um.'

Mrs King nodded dismissal and Mercy fled to her scullery, cheeks aflame with injustice. She hadn't known she'd been doing wrong And why had nothing been said to Jethro? Surely he had been more at fault, knowing as he must have done about the rule?

Tears of unhappiness and anger fell into the scummy water. No one bothered to speak to her except to reprimand her. No one noticed her. It was as if she didn't exist. She clenched her teeth and screwed up her face. It wasn't fair! Life just wasn't fair!

She was jolted from her misery later in the day by a housemaid called Doris who appeared to have lost her mind. She jumped around the kitchen, flapping and swinging at her bottom in a grotesque dance of pain. Her eyes nearly popped from their sockets as she issued a series of discordant shrieks. Behind her ran the cook with a bucket of water, trying to catch her but failing. Doris moved astonishingly quickly.

'Youm on fire, Doris, let me get at 'e with the water! For Lord's sake, girl, stand still!'

Everyone else was reduced to gawping, the hands at their mouths covering smiles.

Cook flung the water, missed Doris and hurried back shouting to a blank-looking Daisy, 'Fill me another bucket. Quick! The girl's on fire! There's smoke coming from 'er backside!'

Cravenly Daisy obliged. But it was almost too late. Doris was making, like something possessed, for the door.

'Hold 'er, Will,' screamed the cook, and one of the onlookers moved to grab the demented Doris. 'Bring 'er 'ere! Bring 'er to me!'

Despite her struggles they bent Doris over the kitchen table while Cook dowsed the fire with a bucketful of water.

'Now then,' said Mrs Gibson, her great arms akimbo as she rose to her mighty full height. 'What's all this about?'

The weeping Doris remained slumped. Cook investigated the source of the fire. Every time Doris felt a hand on her sore spot she screamed.

'Doris! Be quiet! We's has to know what happened to 'e! Yous clothes was on fire, child. Hold still! Hold still! Let me see!'

Between finger and thumb Cook drew out a dead coal and held it aloft in dismay. She exclaimed, 'How in God's name did yous get this in youm pocket?'

Doris, a fresh-faced, well-scrubbed girl full of freckles, glanced round, afraid that, if she moved, the pain would come back.

She shook her head in bewilderment. 'I's doan know, Mrs Gibson. I's really, truly doan know. I's had just fixed the fire in the morning room an' I's had gone back with my bucket to sweep the hearth and tidy 'e. I's was on my way downstairs when I's felt the burnin'.' She continued to shake her head stupidly. 'I's must have . . . I's must have . . .'

'Must have nothing,' shouted the cook. 'Someone must have put it there.'

Mercy quaked as the terrible accusation hung, unanswered, in the air.

'Why would they do that?' Doris was allowing Mrs Gibson to apply salve to the spot.

'As a nasty, cruel joke,' said Mrs Gibson, sticking a large finger once more into the jar to make sure she covered the blister. 'Now Doris, think hard.' It was clear that poor Doris did not merit a high intellectual rating in the servants' hall. 'Was there anyone in the mornin' room when yous went back with yer bucket to clean the hearth?'

'Only Master John,' stuttered Doris, overcome by the attention now the drama was over.

Cook's great lips smacked together into a bulldog frown. She raised knowing eyebrows towards Mr Jardine the butler.

That dignified man managed both to nod and shake his head at the same time.

'Get on with yer work.' This was not the business of the rest of the servants, but it was too late. They had all heard.

Mercy went back to her work considering what sort of person would decide, for a joke, to put a live coal in the back pocket of a kneeling servant girl and think it funny. Then she remembered John Yelland's face at the hunt, his voice when he had urged the hunters to kill the vixen, and she knew.

All day the servants tittle-tattled with the drama. At least it made the day stand out from the rest.

In bed that night she asked Daisy, 'What will happen to him?'

'Nothing will happen to 'e. No one will say anythin' 'cos of 'e's feyther. 'E's like a great black cloud over this house. What that poor boy's 'ad to put up wi' in 'e's life doan bear thinkin' about.'

'But Mrs Gibson, the cook, she was angry.'

'Yous got to remember, Mercy, that the family is different from us downstairs. Master John will grow out of his mischievous ways eventually, an' the world 'e has grown up in an' has to face is more difficult than ours. He'm be our future master. We will depend on 'e, one day, for our well-bein'. An' wi' what 'e has to put up with 'tis no wonder 'e has to find odd ways to express 'isself.'

'I was told off by Mrs King this morning for being in the same room as Jethro.'

'Mercy!' Daisy was shocked.

'I didn't know it was against the rules. You never told me.'

'I's carn be expected to remember every little thing.

266

Surely there are some things yous knows instinctively without bein' told?'

'I don't see there's anything wrong with a female servant being in a storeroom with a male one.'

'Mercy, that's enough!'

'What do you mean? I don't understand why you're so cross. What harm is there in it? Now if I had put a hot coal in Doris' pocket I could have understood Mrs King being angry. I know that's wrong . . . but what I did . . .'

'Surely yous know what can happen if men and women spend time alone without anyone else bein' there?'

'No, what can happen?'

Mercy heard the bedsprings creak as Daisy turned over. She heard her sigh of annoyance. 'They would be rude, that's what would happen, an' then they would get pregnant.'

'Just by being alone together?'

'Yes. It happens. It happened to Bessy an' now she's dead. Punished by God for bein' rude.'

Mercy felt raging disgust for a God Who could punish the helpless so readily yet turn blind eyes on the actions of the gentry.

'Who did Bessy go in a room with?'

'Nobody knows. Probably Jethro. It doan matter who 'twas. Yous just has to obey the rules, that's all, an' know they are there for yer own good.'

The silence was a long one. Mercy thought of the bloodied rags but didn't like to mention them. She didn't want to know any more about poor Bessy. But she thought she knew what you had to do to make a baby. Seth the shepherd had nearly made a baby with her . . . but had pushed her away in time. If he hadn't done that then maybe she would have died, like Annie,

267

like Bessy. Clearly there were worse crimes than putting coals in housemaids' pockets.

Daisy was silent. She had stopped being able to be happy because she was ill and suspected that if she didn't stop bleeding soon she would die. She had no one to tell. If they knew she was ill they would turn her out and she would have no choice but to throw herself on the mercy of the poorhouse. Three times it had happened to her now, and each time was worse than before. But all that blood! And from such a disgusting place! And sometimes it made her feel nauseous and she had such pains in her tummy. She vowed to keep her condition a secret for as long as she was able.

'I still think it was a bad thing for Master John to have done.' It was nice talking, tucked up in bed, knowing that they had the whole night to go before they got up again. Mercy fought against sleep to prolong the feeling.

'Well, my girl, yous knows what Thought did,' said Daisy, quoting what had often been said to her, and sounding far older than her thirteen years. 'If yous disapprove of that, yous'd be shocked by some of the other escapades John Yelland has been involved in during 'e's time, I's sure.'

But no matter how hard Mercy persisted, Daisy wouldn't explain.

'Go to sleep,' she said, turning over so that her deaf ear was uppermost. 'I's carn hear 'e,' she kept saying, 'So yous might as well be quiet.'

Mercy was too disturbed to sleep. After she heard Daisy's snuffly breathing settle into a rhythm she hitched up her calico nightdress, got up and balanced on the end of her bed, steadying herself by resting one hand on the sloping roof so she could look out of the window at the night sky.

She felt like a prisoner staring out through bars. She remembered the attic room at Mrs Mountebank's. She remembered Annie. She longed to lie down flat on the grass again feeling the warmth of the sun on her face. She longed to sit in a firelit room and listen to the voice of the shepherd as he told his tales. Mercy felt sick with misery. Was it all over? Was it her brief time of freedom that fostered her discontent? And would she ever experience any of those beautiful things again?

A young moon hung sharp as a sickle in the sky. She thought she could smell the scents of haymaking and roses. She could hear the sea, soft, as if the night was breathing, away over there in the distance. She was sure she could see it . . . where the landscape dropped away and the shades were paler. She could see a rock, dark, right out in the water . . . she was sure it was a rock but the waves kept obscuring it and from here she couldn't be certain.

She uncurled her toes from the cold metal. The springs creaked as she stepped down and fitted herself neatly into the hollow in the mattress, the body shape made by a girl called Bessy and hundreds before her. But Bessy was dead. Annie was dead. And Mercy Geary was alive with her whole life in front of her.

It didn't feel as if she was alive. She buried her head in her pillow and wept.

EIGHTEEN

She'd been told all about the Sunday prayer meetings.
She'd been told all about the master. He was feared
and revered by all his servants. He ran a puritanical
household . . . no flamboyant livery for the male
servants . . . no drink was supposed to find its wicked
way into the house . . . and no work was allowed to be
done – by those upstairs – on a Sunday. If you met
him on the stairs you must avert your eyes meekly.

Trewen was a house where few visitors were welcome. There were no balls and hunting parties as there
had been in the past. And apart from the lavishness of
the food and the army of servants he kept below stairs,
Squire Roger Yelland considered himself a frugal man
and of the highest moral integrity.

The highlight of the week for the servants was the
Sunday meeting.

Mercy went dishevelled to Sunday prayers because
Mrs Gibson found bugs in the kitchen.

She spotted two of the nasty red things crawling
across her newly-washed floor, and she roved around
the kitchen like a frantic white whirlwind slapping her
forehead and shouting, 'By Jove I's carn 'ave it! I's
carn 'ave they buggers goin' round the food! We's got
to stamp 'em out. Everything out! Everything out!' Mrs
Gibson, delirious in her fury, had gone a fearful red.

Out of the silence came a nervous titter. Mrs Gibson
looked up suspiciously as if the noise could have come
from a bug. Everything stopped. A determined woman,

270

she would not give up until she found the source of the infestation.

Mercy threw herself into the search with vigour. Everyone did. No one would have dreamed of being late for the service. Sunday morning was an event! Something different happened. Something to break the monotony of the work-long days at Trewen.

Mercy had flown round to get her work finished, even managing to give Daisy a hand polishing the fenders and grates with emery paper and a burnisher. She helped to get the kitchen floor scrubbed before the bell went for breakfast. She helped her sulky counterpart, Ada, get through peeling a bathful of potatoes. She scrubbed the scullery table and tidied the room, leaving her workdress and apron to soak in the starch and soap she was told would be deducted from her five pounds a year wages. She knew nothing of wages, of money. The only money she'd seen in her life was Annie Clegg's half-crown.

She was ready, and waited impatiently for the door to open that would let her through to the house 'upstairs'.

And then Mrs Gibson spotted the bugs.

'Look, Mrs Gibson, look! They've eaten the underneath of the chair clean away!'

And it was true. 'Abominations!' cried the cook, appalled. 'They'm bin livin' on the stuffin'!' She sounded insulted they had preferred this to her food. She lifted the heavy chair as if it was made of paper and heaved it out into the yard where she set a man to burning it immediately. It was the only comfortable chair in the room. Only Mrs Gibson and Mr Jardine were allowed to sit in it, but there had been something good about seeing someone sitting there even if Mercy couldn't. Sometimes Mr Jardine smoked a pipe while he read the newspaper. Mr Jardine didn't look at her like Seth had looked at her, even though she'd tried to make him with her eyes.

The excitement over, Mr Jardine led them, in order of seniority, up the stairs that had seemed unreachable to Mercy before. Daisy went in front of her, and Mercy waited obediently for Ada. Mercy didn't need telling that she'd be the last.

Up the stairs and they were straight into the hall. A stone floor, an ornately carved, vaulted ceiling, and Old Testament stories carved in the plaster over the massive fireplace. Priceless Brussels tapestries hung on the panelled walls, and on every niche and podium stood suits of armour, breastplates, halberds and chain-mail. Curtains of red damask were drawn across an altar that took up the graceful base of the stairs. The scale of the hall at Trewen was staggering. The double doors to the gardens were open which made it seem, to Mercy's astonished eyes, immeasurably huge.

The servants took their places at wooden benches brought in by gardeners for the weekly occasion, the females segregated from the males by a high, linen screen.

'That's there so's yous doan think dirty thoughts about the men,' commented Ada.

'Yous cap!' whispered Daisy, prodding painfully with her finger. 'Yous cap's all untidy. Straighten it up before they come! Or 'e'll single yous out, 'e will!'

Candlesticks came out of the floor. Their flames wagged solemnly, and they burned down slowly. The altar was almost obscured by a white, marble pillar, but Mercy peered round, determined to miss nothing.

She knew He was there because, at his approach they coughed and then stood. She stood with them, unable, now, to see. But when they sat down she saw

Roger Yelland. She sat, and her mouth hung open as she absorbed the power of the man.

On the steps, before his great house, he might have looked small but now, in his high white collar and black frockcoat, standing above them and glowering down, it seemed as if the grandeur of the room had been built around him. His eyes were narrow points of fire. His head was abnormally large, his forehead marbled as the podium on which he stood. The hair that started back from his dome sprouted in wild bursts of silver.

Extraordinary! Mercy tried to move her eyes away. She could not. He held them. He held every eye in the room. She waited with bated breath to hear his voice. She needed to hear his voice! She trembled to hear it. But he stayed silent, staring at each and every one, tearing, Mercy felt, the thoughts from their heads, the feelings from their hearts.

In her line of vision was a chair, set before the servants' pews. A fine, carved chair it was covered in royal blue satin. In the chair sat Yelland's son, facing his father, five paces away. Mercy could not see him, but she knew he was there. She saw his hands resting on the wolf's-head arms, saw fingers curl into fists then slowly ease . . . fine, smooth, long-fingered hands. She had seen those hands grip the reins of a horse. They were the hands of a boy in turmoil.

But it was the man who fascinated Mercy. His voice started softly, rustling like the leaves outside. The eyes bored, fanatical, relentless. She was drawn and repelled by the intensity of those eyes.

'I's has one message,' said Roger Yelland. 'One message for every one of 'e.' Mercy had to strain to hear him.

Silence again. There was no birdsong, just the

273

unearthly silence, created in this room by the man who stood before them. He repeated himself gently, 'Yes, just one message.'

So magnetic was the man that Mercy felt her mind was not her own. Lulled, sleepy, so hypnotised was she that when he screamed, '*REPENT!*' it was more than she could bear and she clutched at the woman beside her. Her instinct was to run, to flee through the great open doors behind her and run away as far as she could . . . run to the shepherd, run to the hills, run for somewhere safe . . . for this man was powerful. This man was dangerous.

She clenched her fists. Her arms and legs were trembling. This was nothing like the vicar's sermons at Mrs Mountebank's. This was not a sermon. This was a series of silences interrupted with violent exhortations the like of which she had never heard before. She felt tears sting her eyes. She did not know why they were there.

'*OBEDIENCE!*'

'*STRUGGLE!*'

'*FORTITUDE!*'

'*WICKEDNESS!*'

'*REPENTANCE!*'

'*THOU MUST NOT! THOU MUST NOT!*'

'*DAMNED! DAMNED! DAMNED!*'

He was a preacher. . . . an old man. But these were the words Mercy heard. She had wanted to throw herself down in front of him, to beg forgiveness, to beg protection. He knew what she had thought of God. He knew how she had condemned Him. He knew about her love for Mother and her betrayal of Annie. He knew of her temptation of the shepherd. He knew every single thing about her. Mercy was terrified.

He had the eyes of the shepherd. But there was no shame in them.

*

Mercy was afraid. She felt she had stared destiny in the face. She was intoxicated by her fear. It was all too big for her, too hard to understand. Back in the kitchen she crept from the house. She knew that she was not allowed to leave, but she went all the same. She had to get away, to clear her mind, to retrieve her soul.

She ran. He seemed silently to call her back. Breathless with sorrow, afraid of something so dark she couldn't name, she ran through a murky drizzle. She ran towards the sea.

NINETEEN

Sultry, windless, the murky Sunday morning was charged with storm as Mercy ran blindly on to where she thought the sea would be.

Condemned to Hell! Condemned to Hell! Sin – she was steeped in it! She had betrayed her own mother to buy a monster's love. She had offered her body to the shepherd for his! Neither had given it . . . they saw her for what she was!

Poor Annie! She would have treated her differently if she had known she was going to die. She would have loved her! Daydreams of living alone, building a treehouse, existing on nuts and berries swarmed like bees over the hive of her mind. She dropped down into a copse, where the trees were lichened by winters of rain and formed strange shapes. She wasn't afraid. Nothing could be worse than the reality of her life at the moment. No ghost or demon could hurt her more than her thoughts, no spook or ghoul could spring from the undergrowth and threaten her with anything worse than her future at Trewen.

Breathless, her throat sore, she stopped running. Now she wandered in the vague direction of Porthclegga, following the undulating sheep-walks that covered the patchy ground. Sometimes she saw the sea over a bluff. She could see this wide, open place from her window.

"Ware yer bugger, 'ware!'

Mercy stopped in her tracks. She hadn't seen the old woman, hadn't noticed the odd little house, draped as it was in creeper, folding into a background of moss so it was hard to distinguish from the sloping land around it.

It was set back from the path. She wasn't trespassing – she was only walking by, but from the attitude of the old crone who crouched in its narrow black shadow waving a spindly hazel stick, you would think she was trying to oust her from her home. Mercy's heart hammered hard.

"Ware! 'Ware!' She hissed and stretched out her neck like an angry goose, her small, black-garbed body paddling around behind it.

Mercy tried to walk by, pretending to take no notice and doubling the rate of her footsteps. Trewen, with all its horrors, seemed like a sanctuary now.

She was nearly past, about to breathe again, when the crow that had perched camouflaged on the hummock ahead of her started to take a bath in the dirt. There was something about the peculiarly vindictive way it looked at her that made her unhappy to pass. 'It's only a bird,' she told herself, willing her legs to walk. They wouldn't. She was rooted to the spot, standing there, staring at it in horrible fascination, wishing for it to move so she could leave this place.

While she stood with her skin crawling the old woman came up behind her.

'I'm going,' she said hastily. 'I'm only waiting until the bird has gone.'

'She doan want to hurt 'e.' The old woman stared from her to the bird and back. She was watching its performance, too. 'Yous have to learn to be kinder to yous friends than this, Mercy.'

'How do you know my name?' It was awful that this old hag should know it. Horribly, Mercy imagined the crow had told her. The old woman seemed to be communicating with the dreadful bird.

"Tis right that yous should come to me today, little bride. An' fancy old Mother Carrivick nearly lettin' 'e go an' not recognisin' 'e . . . thinkin' 'e was just another passer-by. Tut! This old biddy is losin' her wits. Yes, yes,' she circled Mercy, sucking the one tooth in her mouth and making the sign of the Cross over her chest. 'She's right for 'e, oh yes darlin', she's right for 'e.'

Should she make a run for it? She flashed a quick glance at the basking crow. No! She could not cross its path, it was impossible. Should she retrace her footsteps and go back the way she'd come? But then she would have to pass the old woman and she was weaving about on the path like a coiled snake, her skin as scaly and as unappealing. The thought of passing close, of accidentally touching her, made Mercy shudder.

'Have yous met the bridegroom yet, I's wonder?' She didn't look up for the answer but scuffed at the ground making frantic movements in the dirt with her stick as if, from her weird markings, she would read the answer. Seemingly satisfied with what she saw, she sniffed and spat, wiping her face with a bony hand.

Quite unexpectedly, and with deliberate violence, she threw the stick at the crow and that bold creature curled back its head, recognised its mistress and hopped off down the path, looking back over its thin shoulder now and again with a knowing eye. For balance, it uncurled its wing and trailed it in the dust, at the same time issuing a hoarse, ugly cry.

The old hag left the path. Mercy's way was clear. 'Yous no need to be frightened here,' she said, conveniently forgetting her threatening attitude. 'There's nothin' can hurt 'e here, my lovely.'

There was kindness now in the rusty voice, a kindness Mercy wasn't used to. She responded. She hesitated and that was enough. The threat she had felt such a short while ago had vanished.

'No, there's nothin' goin' to hurt 'e here.' And after muttering these quiet words of reassurance, Mother Carrivick appeared to lose interest and hobbled back to the three-legged stool that was set before the creepered door of the house.

For a while Mercy watched as the hag plaited bunches of herbs that would join the others hanging in the wooden porch. The bony feet of tiny creatures were tacked with nails to the half-opened door and formed a gruesome pattern there.

It was quiet here, and peaceful, and although they didn't speak the old woman and the child in the quiet glade were communicating in some deeper way. The house – squat and wide enough for one room only, tapered off into a chimney shape which decayed into ruin before it reached its full height.

'Yous woan come in this time, Mercy Geary, but yous will the next and that's enough.' And Mercy knew she would come again because she needed a place to run to and she sensed that Mother Carrivick would let her hide here.

But for now Mercy told herself that the ancient crone was senseless and that this was probably the way she talked to everyone who was unfortunate enough to take the unworn track and stumble onto her territory. But still, she might go inside, next time she came . . .

TWENTY

That same Sunday night, at suppertime, Daisy Wyatt was stuck by such excruciating pains as she sat at the table over Cook's special kipper tartlets that she had to be carried upstairs.

'Somethin' she's ate,' mused Ada into the silence after she'd gone. She looked carefully at the rock cake she'd just tasted. Talking was allowed at the table on Sunday evenings.

'I's doubts that,' snapped Mrs Gibson. 'Unless the foolish girl went an' stuffed her mouth with berries while she was fetching water.' She turned self-righteously to Mr Jardine. 'I's worn out wi' telling 'em, I's really am. Yous'd think they was starvin'!'

The pain, coming as it did so soon after the first bloody discharge, convinced the girl that she was dying. She'd heard of the bloody flux. She lay with her knees pulled up to her chest, moaning, on the narrow bed. Every now and then a big, fat tear of self-pity swelled from a pain-bleared eye and slid down a pale cheek.

She was glad when Mercy arrived, because Daisy Wyatt was frightened.

Abandoned at birth by a mother too young to know what was happening, responsibility for Daisy had been taken by the authorities in Truro. She was put out to nurse and Daisy could just remember a warm room that always smelled of mint, and a rocking chair occupied by a smiling fat woman with gentle arms. Along with this memory was a woollen blanket of knitted squares, the greasy feel of a rag rug to her knees, and the clacking, loose-fitting wheels of a wooden horse. Of this happy time in her life Daisy had no souvenirs, so she took the memories out to polish them often, in case, over time, they should fade and she might think they had never happened.

Old enough to walk and be dextrous with her hands she was given to a local man thought of as a harmless rogue by those who didn't know him. An oyster catcher and a shellfish seller, he needed someone to open and cut the fish from their shells and sit by his stall on the quay serving his customers. On other days, with frozen hands, Daisy would gather winkles on the rocks when the tide was out. It was hard, cold work and unfortunately for Daisy the man, Charlie Moore, had no liking for children. Half the time he slept, drunk, on the shingle, wrapped in the warmth of an excess of alcohol. Daisy used to cuddle up beside him, or wander off to find somewhere warmer, under the tavern steps or in the stable straw. Occasionally, when it was very cold, Charlie would pay for a room for the night in some garret. This, to Daisy, was absolute luxury.

When business was bad and more efficient, sober competition threatened, Charlie took to wandering the roads, begging. Here Daisy was useful because she was small and pathetic, particularly when he dressed her in his huge greatcoat which was almost too heavy for her to stand up in. But when she grew to the spindly, unattractive-looking girl she was at ten years old she was no further use to him. For one thing she cost too much to keep. For a second time she was abandoned, and this time the City Fathers took her back to the poorhouse, equipped her for service and bound her to Trewen.

After the insecurity of her gypsy life, the world at Trewen was all Daisy could wish for. She liked the discipline. She knew what was required of her and that in return she would be well-fed and safe. She was used to hard work, but not to associating with other people. She had no idea of cleanliness or manners and it had taken Mrs King time to train what she called 'this uncouth, disreputable creature'. The proudest moment of Daisy's life was when she was elevated from scullery to kitchenmaid just over a year ago. She'd known, then, that she'd finally come home.

Now Mercy, concerned and remembering Annie, begged to do something to help. 'Let me get you something. I'll wrap a fire brick. I'll go down and get water. What about another blanket for your bed? Are you sure you're warm enough?' She wasn't overfond of Daisy but there was no one else.

''Tis no good. Yous carn do nothin'.'

'They say it's something you've eaten. You're going to be all right, Daisy, really you are!'

'I's not! I's knows I's not!'

The stench coming from underneath Daisy's mattress was overpowering. Mercy held her breath as she wiped the mousy hair back from Daisy's damp forehead. Her face was waxen.

'I's goin' to be sick!'

Mercy rushed for the basin and knelt beside the bed holding it in place. Daisy reached over and retched, her goldfish eyes starting from her head. She lay on the pillow exhausted.

Mercy felt useless. If only she could do something. If only she could clear some of the bloody mess under the mattress, perhaps that would make Daisy feel better. The terrible smell couldn't help but add to Daisy's discomfort.

'I could move some of those rags,' she ventured.

'What rags?' Daisy didn't care much about anything any more.

'The ones I've seen you stuffing under the mattress before you get into bed.'

Daisy might as well tell her. She was going to die anyway. 'It flows from me,' she confessed, too ill to feel humiliated. 'It comes from deep inside me. It started about three months ago . . .'

Mercy was aghast. 'Why didn't you tell someone?'

'Because if yous ill they doan want yous. I's'd have to leave here an' then what would happen to me? Yous carn understand . . . yous been coddled all yous life, looked after, kept warm.'

The idea that she had led a privileged life was a new concept for Mercy. She considered Daisy's problem. 'But they might be able to cure it.'

''Tis too bad to be cured.' Daisy was adamant.

'I'll ask someone,' said Mercy, thinking of Mother Carrivick. She was a witch. She could cure people.

'Yous carn talk about things like that! Places like that!'

'No.' Sometimes Mercy could be over-hasty with her promises. It was just that she wanted to help so much. 'But we could take the rags out. We could take them down first thing in the morning. You could burn them on the fire without anybody knowing. At least if you did that nobody would find out . . . and you might get better.'

'We could do that, if I's ever well enough to get up again,' groaned the sick girl, rubbing her sore stomach gently. She was feeling a little better, but dare not admit it even to herself, in case the pain came back with a vengeance.

Finally, after an hour had gone by, she dared to declare it. 'I's think I's feelin' easier.'

'I knew you would. And first thing in the morning we'll start getting rid of those rags. They stink the

283

place out, Daisy, they really do. Someone would have discovered them sooner or later.'

Daisy looked a better colour and Mercy felt she could go back to her own bed. She had grown cold and stiff kneeling on the bare boards. Her strange meeting with Mother Carrivick already seemed like a dream.

But now, for Daisy's sake, she had a reason for going back. And she might have made herself a friend.

Of all nights, John Yelland, heir to Trewen, chose this one to make one of his nocturnal sorties. Because they were both still awake they heard him. It was a frightening sound, and if Daisy hadn't been there to explain it Mercy would have thought there was a monster rampaging through the corridors.

It started with a series of high-pitched, devilish cackles. The two girls lay in silence and listened. Never in her life had Mercy heard such lewd words of devilish curses. ''E's trying to frighten us,' said Daisy. 'This is how 'e starts. Cover yer ears, 'tis best 'e doan hear such things.'

'What is it?' Mercy had no intention of covering her ears. If there was a mad devil out there she needed her wits about her. 'What's he doing?'

In the darkness she saw Daisy shake her head. ''Tis 'e's game. 'E only ever plays it on a Sunday . . . to spite 'e's feyther.'

'But what is he doing?'

''E's tryin' to get somebody out there. But nobody goes. 'E's harmless if yous keeps to yous bed. Yous'll get used to it.'

Mercy doubted that. 'Does Mrs King know?'

'She doan listen to tales about the family.'

The cackling turned to a grunting, and from that to a deep-throated growling. Mercy's teeth started to chatter.

'But what's he doing?'

'Bessy looked out once. 'Twas soon after she came an' s'e had a room of her own. She was so frightened she told us she'd rather know what it was than just lie there and let it come for her.'

'What did she see?'

'Just the lad, havin' a game, she said, outside her door.'

'What did she do then?'

'I's didn't ask her what she did then. Close the door, I should think, an' wedge a chair under the handle.'

'Can't we do that now?'

'We haven't got a chair. 'Tis all right, Mercy, 'e woan come in. They say 'e does it because 'e's feyther woan allow 'e any fun on a Sunday so 'e comes up here an' takes it out on us.'

'But why is he using such terrible words?'

''Tis the drink. 'Tis loosened 'e's tongue.'

'But he's only a boy.'

'Hardly a boy . . .'e's sixteen now.'

'I don't know how I'll ever look at him if I meet him face to face. This is all I'll be able to think about.'

Daisy laughed softly. 'Doan worry. Youm never likely to meet 'e. An' if yous does yous drops yer eyes all the more meekly.'

Mercy couldn't understand how Daisy could react so placidly to such a terrible thing. The boy must be mad! Something made her ask, 'Did Bessy often sleep in a room alone?'

Daisy thought about this. 'She moved out of here when she had scarlet fever . . . that's the only time. Why, yous doan think John Yelland . . . ?'

It was far too great an assumption to make. Not even in her mind could Mercy make it. 'No, I don't think anything at all. I only wondered if he did ever go into rooms.'

There was a pause while they both thought their own thoughts. Outside the door the horrible noise went on unabated. Mercy knew that sleep was impossible until he'd gone.

'How long does it go on?' Mercy asked Daisy. Suddenly the fear and the extraordinariness of the whole situation met inside her with a thump and Mercy started giggling. She tried to stifle it by pushing the sheet in her mouth but she couldn't. Daisy caught her mood. Tears of laughter were pouring down her face. It was a new experience for Daisy, and Mercy hadn't laughed like this since Annie had been alive.

'Shush!' they kept telling each other during pauses for breath. 'He'll hear us! He'll come in!'

Each time Mercy heard Daisy's muffled gasp she was set off laughing again. She realised what was missing from her life and it was this . . . laughter. If she could somehow live the dreary days seeing the funny side of things perhaps she could get through. Perhaps . . .

She had a friend! Happier than she'd felt since Annie died she eventually went to sleep convinced she had found an answer to her misery.

For the first time since she'd arrived at Trewen Mercy felt hope.

And the crow at the window took its piercing eye from Mercy Geary, flapped off into the night and let her sleep without pain.

TWENTY-ONE

The gardener looked discomfited when Mrs Gibson picked an imperfect carrot from his basket and held it close to his face.

Behind her in the kitchen Doris and Ada struggled to hook a haunch of lamb onto the great spit.

The years had passed and this life, so strange at first, was natural to Mercy now. She was neither happy nor unhappy, she merely accepted. She had friends . . . Daisy and Mother Carrivick. The latter had sorted out Daisy's problem. Mercy had learned the times and days she could slip out to see the old woman without being missed. In this Daisy helped her, although she said, 'I's doan know how 'e dare go consortin' wi' a witch! Doan go tonight, Mercy, whatever yous do.'

'Why not tonight?'

''Tis the last day in April . . . Walpurgis Night!'

'I don't believe in superstition.' And she thought to herself, I don't believe in anything.

'Satan's birthday,' muttered Daisy, rolling her eyes. 'Yous be foolish to go today.'

Daisy wasn't so stupid that she didn't believe in witchcraft. Hadn't a mob stormed the poorhouse the year they'd taken her in and fetched out the little old man and the little old woman to be ducked in Grimm's pond? They'd tied their thumbs and big toes together crosswise in the traditional manner and when the old man floated hadn't they pushed him under with a pole so that he'd eventually choked to death? They'd let the old woman go then, but Daisy had watched her die from shock and a broken heart three weeks later.

And hadn't Jennie Martin died from her wounds after being scoured by a nail for bewitching the farrier's daughter? Oh yes, there were penalties for witchcraft. She was afraid for Mercy. Mercy ran straight into things without thinking. Mercy was strange in other ways, too.

Mercy ignored the warning and she did go. She was fifteen years old now and well able to make decisions for herself. This time she saw Mother Carrivick first. Her back was bent and she was gathering some of the wild herbs that grew round her peculiar home. Mercy stood watching, resting her back against the lone tree trunk.

They were used to each other. The old woman didn't look up but said, 'I's made 'e some tea. I's was expectin' 'e earlier. 'Tis probably overstewed b' now.'

She stood up and pushed her fists into her back before banging the roots free of soil and putting them in the basket.

Mercy followed her inside, ducking in the doorway to avoid the bunches and knots of dried greenery that hung there. She was quite unafraid. Mother Carrivick had told her, 'They's calls me all names under the sun, oh yes I's knows they's do! But when their children fall ill an' their cows woan milk an' their grain woan grow . . . where would they be without me?'

'But that's witchcraft!'

The woman had adjusted her shawl and given Mercy a long look out of crow-bright eyes.

'Witchcraft . . . call it what yous likes. There's some calls it magic, some the Devil's work.' Her voice was surprisingly high and smooth. 'I's doan care what 'tis so long as it works.'

Mercy sipped her tea. It was strangely comforting. The cottage was familiar to her now. The one window was boarded up. Underneath was a rickety table with

288

no space on it. A stick fire crackled in the chimney and a hook hung over the flames. It was in that fire-blackened pot that the tea had been brewed. There was a bright red rug on the floor and two, three-legged stools but as the old woman chose to stand, so did Mercy.

She stared at the tooth that hung on a leather thong round the old woman's neck. 'A dog tooth,' she explained as she fingered the amulet. 'Against madness, my darlin' . . . the only condition, you's'll find, that is beyond my powers.'

'They told me not to come today. They said it was Walpurgis Night!'

Mother Carrivick cackled. 'They's might have been right.' Then she turned away and looked into the fire. 'But nothin' can change yous destiny, Mercy Geary, Walpurgis Night or no. Yous were right to come to see yer old mother. But listen! Listen to the weather! 'Twill hail in a minute. The signs have come right. 'Tis today yous will meet the manikin.'

'Today? What manikin?'

'Go, child . . . before the weather changes,' was all she said. And she turned back grumbling to the knot of herbs she'd been tying.

She'd thought it was the rustling of the leaves, but it was the hail Mother Carrivick had predicted. It started finely at first, but as Mercy approached the copse beside Trewen the stones came thick and round as pearls and she had to take shelter just until it calmed. So noisy was the sound of the frozen rain that it battered and crashed on her flimsy shelter, assaulting her ears. And Mercy hunched against it and wrapped her arms round her chest for comfort.

When hands came from behind and covered her eyes and mouth she thought she would die from shock.

289

Suddenly she was a prisoner, blind and dumb, held in a grip of steel. Every instinct told her to fight and she did, kicking and scratching to no avail. She froze, only wanting the cold hands to leave her skin, only wanting to run away from here. She froze again as she heard the words, 'Well, what have we's here? Be still yous little vixen. Yous can fight as hard as yous likes but you's'll not get free until yous has shown yousself to me. *BE STILL I'S SAYS!*'

Trembling with fright she obeyed the speaker and hung limp, no fight left. Coolly he turned her round to face him. Her eyes widened. For if she was to believe in fairy tales then this was the prince of her childhood – the one who had always been coming to take her away. He was beautiful and white as a marble statue. His pale skin was flawless, like a girl's. His golden hair curled towards his face and his amber eyes were flecked with violet. His mouth was an amused line and his hands, when he held them out to bestow freedom, were soft and white and unroughened by work.

And he? He saw a fairy-like creature, fragile as a fawn, with honey, deep doe-eyes, her silver hair as velvety-soft as thistledown. He thought of the rabbits and hares he caught in his spring-traps. He thought of the white moths he crushed under his fists. She was poised for flight. Her heart would be fluttering inside . . . like wings.

'Let me introduce myself an' then, perhaps, be honoured by a proper introduction to yous, maiden!' His voice was smooth and silky when he said, 'I's John Yelland, an' to whom do I's has the honour of speaking?'

'I must go! I must go! Mrs Gibson will be missing me!'

Mercy knew who he was. The mixture of terrible fascination and revulsion took her prisoner as surely as his arms had done. She was powerless to move. There was something unreal about this boy/man who smelt of violets.

She remembered Mother Carrivick's words, "Tis today you's'll meet the manikin,' and Mercy knew that John Yelland, Satan's Child, would have a hold on her for as long as she lived.

As his father would.

TWENTY-TWO

'They think you wicked. And I understand why. It's because of the cruel things you do and the strange jokes you play . . . wandering along the corridors at night terrifying the servants!'

They sat by the lake in the grounds of Trewen, on the steps of the boathouse where they always met. Tonight the water was pewter with moonglow. 'I's gets pleasure from hurting people,' he said. 'Yous should know that about me. Most people get pleasure from being hurt . . . why else do they believe in God? Why else do they allow bad things to happen to them?'

'Most people don't have a choice. Things happen to them whether they like it or not. But what about your father? Which sort of person is he? He believes in God and yet I can't believe he'd be the victim, or he'd enjoy being hurt.'

John Yelland threw back his head and laughed. 'Oh aye, 'e believes in God . . . but at the same time 'e deceives hisself into thinkin' 'e *is* God! Oh yes, my father is like me! We's both enjoy inflicting pain. An' there are those who accept that, who think 'tis to do wi' the natural order of life. The Church, for instance, instructs people like yous, Mercy Geary, to accept things as they are. A mill-child lost 'e's fingers last week an' was put back to the machine after 'e's hand was bound.'

'But people are rebelling against all that!' Mercy argued. 'They have marched . . . Wesley himself preached of love . . .'

'Hah!' John laughed again. 'The natural processes

of Nature are designed to strengthen the powerful against the weak,' he told her. 'No, little Mercy . . . I's afraid in this world the meek will never inherit the earth. They's is too busy playin' at martyrs. An' yous know it! Yous youssell is attracted to the strong . . .'

'I'm attracted to self-preservation,' she said. 'That's all.' But she knew, with a wave of self-disgust, that that was not true. She accused him, 'You say . . . you admit terrible things about yourself.'

'I's choose to be honest, that's all. An' does my honesty make yous afraid of me?'

'I am not afraid of you because I know that what you say is not true. There is nothing real about you. You have no real feelings about anything.' She forced herself to hold his stare, to prove her convictions to herself.

The white knuckles of dawn crept stealthily over the horizon . . . gripping. Mercy jumped up and adjusted her dress. 'It can't be this late! I must get in! I must get to bed!'

He moved slowly. 'Daisy will have left the stillroom window open for yous. What's the hurry?'

'If I don't sleep I shan't be able to work and Mrs King will dismiss me!'

This spoilt, petulant boy had no idea what life was like on the other side of the kitchen door.

'Listen to yous!' he sneered. 'Yous lets the misery in! Yous likes it! Yous makes it happen when yous fear it so! Resist, like me, it is easy!'

'When will I see you again, John Yelland?'

Mercy touched his face. He had brought her over the wet grass to the side door, the back way into the kitchens beside the stillroom. Their footsteps were clear in the night-dew. By morning they would be gone. She stood by the open window and exhaustion overtook her. It was all right for him. He could spend the day in bed if he wanted . . . if his father was preoccupied with other things which he most often was. But Mercy, she still had her work to do.

He took her hand and squeezed it. 'I's'll wait for yous the day after tomorrow,' he said. 'Same place . . . down there by the lake. Doan let me down!'

'I won't.' But she was only concerned with getting in undetected . . . with mounting the stairs without causing them to creak, with creeping along the corridors without causing doors to open.

Daisy would be asleep. But in the morning, she would chastise her again for being what she called such a fool!

''E's using yous!' she always said. 'When 'e's had enough 'e'll drop 'e like a pancake on the griddle . . . an' then yous'll fry, believe me!'

She knew he was using her, even as she lay, aching with tenderness for his tall, golden body as he stood in a flood of moonlight. She loved every fold and angle of him. She had never dreamed a man's body could be so beautiful. His full mouth was quick to smile, and his eyes were silver in the light.

Help me, she often begged alone in her bed at night. Help me. But there was no answer. Only a scorching flood of yearning and a longing to lie with him again. Oh yes, she knew she was foolish but Mercy couldn't stop herself. She believed it was love. John Yelland filled her life with excitement and fascination. She craved the daring of the stolen nights they spent in the boathouse by the lake. She loved his conversation, the way he looked at her . . . touched her . . . parted her shawl and kissed the soft skin at the edge of her bodice . . . undressed her . . . stroked her . . . tormented her . . . mocked her . . .

She felt like a ghost moth dazzled by the moon.

She often asked him, 'Why? Why me?'

'Yous was the one I's bumped into. It could have been any of 'em. I's not particular!'

When it stopped – and she wouldn't let herself think about that – her life would go back to the wretched round of work, sleep, work, sleep, that she hated so much. She wanted to make it a fairy tale. She made him say he loved her, 'Lovers should speak of love and I want to hear it from your lips . . .' but even while he spoke she knew he was lying.

'I love you.'

'How much do you love me?'

'Very much . . .'

'You may kiss me again, but gently.'

'I's'll kiss you as I's likes, my little nymphette!' But to have those words said in a lie was better than not having them said at all. And it was she who pulled him down on her, urgently, wantonly, with no thought for any tomorrow when she might find herself humiliated, abandoned and disgraced – as Daisy said she would.

She flirted with danger. She courted it. She taunted it. For she knew as sure as night was night that the old man knew. And was watching.

TWENTY-THREE

A summer, an autumn of loving, and then it was winter. Trewen lay naked in bare gardens under a cold, grey sky.

'Snow's on the way,' said Mrs Gibson.

'Too cold for snow,' said Mr Jardine, going to wipe the misted window.

'When the end of my nose goes white,' said Mrs Gibson firmly, 'then 'twill snow. An' I's is rarely wrong.'

They had been having this same argument every morning since the end of November. Mercy didn't hear either of them. As soon as she was finished with the breakfast things she was going out.

Mercy had never really believed that she would bleed like Daisy. In the same way she believed she wouldn't die. Nor did she believe she would ever get pregnant. Why she thought she was the only woman in the world to be so unique was hard to explain.

If she was pregnant and, incredibly, she thought she probably was, then as far as she was concerned the world might as well end.

If she was pregnant . . . then death was possible, too.

Oh no, oh no, oh no! She would not die, as Bessy did, like a spurned bitch whelping behind the stables.

She would go to Mother Carrivick now that she was sure. Mercy was certain the crone could take this infliction away . . . with a potion, with one of her foul-smelling brews, with a rabbit's foot or a toad's eye . . . it was well-known that she could do it . . .

It was early evening before she finally managed to get away.

The ground was cold and hard. In her haste she turned her ankle and had to stop to rub it. An icy wind cracked across the scrubland like a whip and the air behind Kergilliak, the old crone's cottage, whispered of snow. It was different being out at twilight on her own, without John. And her limbs were stiff, wouldn't move. A wavering candle showed at the witch's window and looked like a glow-worm trapped on the sill.

She pulled her cloak around her tight with one hand while she rapped on the door with the other. 'I think I am with child. I think I bear John Yelland's child.'

The door was very closed. Tight. She repeated her words over and over as she continued to knock. They made her feel dizzy . . . the simplicity of saying such a huge thing confused her.

'Come out! Come out and listen to me!' Mercy was sobbing, long, slow tears of self-pity, of desperation.

Finally she came. The old woman gazed at Mercy, a piercing scrutiny of her face and her body. 'So . . .'tis done! A plague on 'e's head! Yous lays an impossible weight on me, Mercy Geary.' Mother Carrivick spat on the ground. 'I's can do nothin' to help 'e. Yous and yer offspring is beyond my powers, doan yer understand? Yous must leave here at once.' Mother Carrivick was neither friendly nor helpful. She seemed embarrassed by her powerlessness. Her door was only half-open. She might well be embarrassed: for black magic there must always be a sacrifice, but she had grown fond of this little foundling over the years, the foundling picked with such care by her avian familiar, the foundling who had always been so willing for sacrifice. Mother Carrivick had done nothing but take what was already there and direct it . . . for the eventual good . . . always she worked for the eventual good.

'Yous must get yousself to Exeter and from there take a ride on a wagon goin' as far from here as possible. The journey alone will be dangerous. There are thieves on the roads and beggars roam the hills, but yous must go.' The old woman looked weary.

'But first yous must see Roger Yelland, tell 'e yer plight, maid, throw yousself on 'e's mercy. An' then, when that's all over an' done, yous must go to London and never come back till the time is right. Only far from here will yous be safe, hidden from the manipulations of evildoers who be out to harm 'e and the boy.'

'Do as I ask and take it away,' begged Mercy, 'or make John Yelland love me! I love him, I need him and I cannot bear this.' The sound of her own voice flung into the wind in desperation like that made Mercy cry, and she stood forlornly listening to the old woman's reply.

'Yelland will have to know, Mercy, 'tis the only way from here. An' I's cannot take this child from you. 'E will be born. I's cannot help yous, Mercy Geary.'

Mercy didn't believe her. It was the mood she was in. Her ague was plaguing her. Surely she would help her tomorrow. But as if, once again, she read her thoughts Mother Carrivick said, 'No, no I's carn,' and shook her head and went indoors, muttering to herself words that Mercy could not understand. She shut the cottage door behind her.

Hurt and indignant, Mercy called, 'Don't leave me to face this alone! I trusted you! I thought you were my friend. You *knew* this would happen, didn't you? You've always known! Then why didn't you warn me?'

The door stayed closed.

As if the old witch had communicated her dark premonitions, Mercy was drawn towards the sea.

It was evening. She would be missed in the kitchen

if she delayed any longer, but she couldn't go back . . .
not yet. She walked along the path, through the dusk,
to the edge of the cliff where she stood, letting her body
go against the wind. For a moment she considered
letting herself go completely with it, right over the edge
into the blackness below. The sea was a dark, oily
black, churning. She found a bower of gorse where she
would be sheltered, and there she sat considering her
plight while the sky grew darker.

The lights in the little village below started to flicker
and glow. All those tiny houses and the people in
them . . . warm, secure, safe, each with its own lantern
in its own window like a beacon to guide them home.
She had never had a home . . . and now she was being
cast out from the only refuge she had . . . one she had
hated until John Yelland came along to love her.

A lonely wind tugged at the gorse. A nightjar called
from the heather behind her. It was the call of life as
opposed to the dark deathly sighs of the sea. She sat
with tight-clasped hands to see if she could hear the
bird again, her heart hammering. For one short
moment she felt she touched Heaven, and realised that
desolation could take her there as well as joy.

Snow fell as she sat, feather-light flakes that circled
and hesitated before lighting on her hand. And then,
try as hard as they could, they were flattened and
forced to melt into her . . . and when, finally, she made
her body move to take her back, she saw the frenzied
circles made by rabbits in the snow, the tiny cross-
prints of the birds, looping and circling as if they were
headed for no particular place for no particular reason,
and she felt that her tracks should look like that, for
she was lost and confused in this white world as they
were.

The house stared at her with a look of angry
impatience as if it had finished with her now. She

watched the windows and wondered which one he sat at . . . her lover and her master. She was afraid to tell John Yelland that she was with child . . . in case . . . in case he stopped playing his love games. But she was due to meet him tonight after supper was served and cleared. And she would go. She would have to go.

Daisy had wept when she told her. 'I's knew it, oh I's knew it. What will happen to 'e now? What will happen to me, alone again without a friend? I's loved you, Mercy Geary. Yous was the only person in my life I's knowed I's could trust. Now I's feel yous has betrayed me with yer wilful ways . . .'

Mercy thought of Annie when she saw the love in Daisy's eyes, but pushed her anger away.

'It was a spell I was under,' Mercy cried with her. 'And I'm still under it. I love him, Daisy, I love him more than my life!'

'An' how can yous love a man like that? Yous always knowed 'e was playing with 'e . . . tormentin' 'e as his feyther tormented him. 'E's evil, that one, everybody knows it. Doan say yous wasn't warned. 'E's had women an' brought 'em to disgrace more times than 'e's had hot dinners.'

'Don't speak like that, Daisy. I can't bear to think of him loving anyone else . . .'

'Well youm a right fool, Mercy Geary. An' the worst of it is yous knows it an' carn do nothing about it. I's feel sorry for 'e now . . . I's really, really do!'

'I am going to tell him. I am going to tell him tonight.'

'I's'll wait for 'e no matter how late 'tis. I's'll wait for 'e an' we's can cuddle up and think of what's to do.'

And Mercy remembered how Annie used to wait in that desolate dormitory at Mrs Mountebank's. And how it wasn't Annie's comfort she craved but Mother's . . . a woman who could never give it. And now it was the same. She had a friend again but it was not her she needed. It was John Yelland – who was no more capable of loving than Mother was.

TWENTY-FOUR

White wrappings of snow covered Trewen. Everywhere was frozen and silent. The snowflakes fell in dizzy circles, putting a white veil around her and Mercy shivered as she approached the boathouse. The passion had gone, and the cold grip of fear replaced it, pinching her face and taking some of her beauty away. The snow leaked into her boots where the soles were coming free. She winced at the icy bite of it.

She removed her shoes and rubbed her stockinged feet, putting the feeling painfully back. She lit the candle and settled down to wait. John Yelland used to arrive first . . . that should have given her some clue to his flagging desires but Mercy was in love. She would not see what she did not want to see. Tonight she missed the slap-slap sound of the punt on the ripples, for the flat-bottomed boat was locked in a vice of iced water. She lay on the pallet and covered herself with the blankets that Yelland had brought. They reeked of damp and tonight there was no warmth in them. Even the candle flame burned silver instead of gold, and looked frozen as the water, stiff and unflickering.

She heard him arrive. She held her breath to hear for it was so soft a sound. No footsteps, but the creaking of his leather coat and the squeaking of his kneeboots. And from this she could tell how he walked, swaggering purposefully across the lawns, not caring that he was found out in his wenching or not. It was easy for him . . . so easy!

She held out her arms. He sat with his back to her

against the pallet, removing his boots without one word of greeting.

'Oh John, I missed you,' she said. Knowing, oh yes she knew.

'Why, 'tis only been two days. Yous can hardly miss a man in that short time.'

'Why, then – didn't you miss me?' What did she want him to say? Did she really want to hear the truth, or was it the strength of his lies she was testing?

Still shivering, she drew off her clothes to be ready for him. Without performance, he climbed on top of her, 'By God it's cold . . . enough to freeze yer balls off . . .'

'I'll warm you, John. Let me warm you.'

But he didn't hear her as he thrust his way to quick relief. And under him she lay cold as stone, listening to the creaking of the ice as it gripped and clawed and took the flotsam, tree litter, punt, boathouse, took it all for its own in its brief moment of cruel mastery.

She wanted to lie in his arms like she used to do but he sat straight up beside her when he had finished and turned his back when she said, 'You see, John. You see how much I love you?'

'Why? Because yous lets me pleasure 'e?'

He hadn't loved her right. Her arms still ached for the roughness of his hands, for his force and for her surrender. She taunted him to get it. She loved his utter mastery of her body and soul. 'But it works both ways.'

'It doan matter to me who's underneath me. As long as she doan have a pocked face or crabs in her crotch.'

'But you care about me? You must do. Or you wouldn't come.'

'I's cares about the food I's eat and the horse I's ride, but only while they tempt me. When I's finished with them then I's cease to care, like all men do.'

303

'You never mean what you say!'

He looked at her then. Turned his face towards her with something like interest and said, 'Yous know that I's mean it. For what are yous needlin' me tonight?'

'Your father would not be pleased if he heard you!'

'Doan 'e threaten me with my feyther!' His face turned dark and brooding and she knew she should not have said it. He prepared himself to leave.

'Are you not taking me back?'

'Aye, I's'll take 'e back. But hurry. 'Tis too damn cold in here. Not fit for a humpin' cats let alone a man.'

And then she told him. She gathered her courage from where it massed like a rock in her chest and she said, 'John. I am having your child.'

He didn't interrupt his preparations. He pulled on his second boot and stood to buckle his belt. He flung his coat around his shoulders and slapped his hand with his glove. 'Is yous comin' or no?' he said. 'I's told 'e to hurry.'

'John? You heard what I said?' Her voice was timid and quavering. She choked back a sob. Now was not the time for his cruel games.

'Aye. I's heard 'e.'

Dazed, she said, 'And what then? What is to be done?'

'Yous can rid yourself of the brat or yous can have it. 'Tis all the same to me!' His voice was hard and impatient.

Mercy stood up, half-dressed, uncomfortable and chilled to the marrow of her bones. 'That's all you are going to say?'

He stared at her incredulously. 'What did you expect me to say? I's has never pretended to you, Mercy Geary. I's has never made out to be more or less than I's am. Yous took me for what I's was, not what yous

304

would have liked me to be. An' yous are the victim. Yous an' the likes will always be victims. I's told yous that, too. An' now I's is goin'.'

Bewildered with pain she called, 'Wait, John! Wait for me!' Somehow the thought of that cold walk back to the house, desolate and alone, was too much for Mercy to bear. She needed to be near him, even if there was no comfort to be had from him. She wished she could have screamed, shouted, told him what he was! She wished she could have squeezed some pride from the sponge of desolation inside her. But there was none to be had.

Different ways, oh yes, there are so many different ways of dealing with desolation. Children learn ways early on of dealing with that, they learn to protect themselves, from experience. John Yelland walked ahead of the girl, walked out across the cold and squeezed his heart against her. A child . . . his child . . . *again*. He could not face it again.

Needing warmth, needing the comfort that sweet Bessy gave him, they had made promises together, plans. She would bear the child and they would go, together, far away from this place he so detested. 'No, not in the house John, they's'll find me in the house, they's'll take the child away, they's'll take over from us, doan yous see? 'Tis warm in the stables an' I's feels safe wi' yous, as long as yous keep yous arms round me. I's is young an' strong, I's knows that nothing'll go wrong. Trust me John, we's must trust each other.'

He'd sworn to take care of her, for he loved her, against all the odds he loved her more than his own life. John Yelland smiled grimly as he felt the pain of the cold in his chest. He had stayed with her, he'd held Bessy in his arms all night and into the pale chill of the morning. The child he'd wrapped and put to one side . . . no good . . . it was Bessy he cared about now. After the birth she had started to look better, the colour came back to her face, she'd managed to smile, she'd said, 'Hold me John. Doan leave me.'

He'd rubbed her hands, her feet, he'd stroked her forehead and pulled the wet hair back from her face, smoothing it out around her. ''Twill be all right, Bessy, 'twill be all right.' And he had held her, with all his strength and with all his might he held her. But it couldn't have been tight enough. He could only have fallen asleep for just a small moment because when he woke up she was colder . . . too cold . . . she wasn't with him any more.

It was God's punishment, for then he remembered his father coming into his room when he was a very small child. A dark man who stood so still, so sternly, with that terrible tolerance in his voice, not rushing, not impatient, just knowing that obedience would come if he waited long enough.

'What is your name?'

And John raised his chin and squeezed his fists, defiant, he would not obey.

'What is your name?' His father's face was immobile, without emotion.

John Yelland crossed his fingers behind his back because he was going to tell a lie. He would never believe the words his father forced him to say – no, never, *never*.

'What is your name?'

Sunday after Sunday after Sunday. His breath shuddered inside him like the end of a long, long cry, but the voice he replied in was clear and sweet. 'Nobody, Father.'

'And you must always remember that, John. To God Who made the winds and waves, the sun and the moon, to that great power that created the firmament, the

306

birds of the air and the flowers on the earth you are nobody. You are but a grain of sand, a speck of dust, and not worthy even of a name. His is the power, yours is to worship. Your body is dirt, boy, and all the passions that come from your body, dirt, filth – foul. And always remember that. Now tell me again: what is your name?'

'Nobody, Father. Can I come down now?'

'When you have recited the psalm of the day to me perfectly, then you may come downstairs.'

Oh yes, he had wanted his father's love, had been prepared to call himself Nobody for it, and if you repeat the same words for long enough, over the days and over the years you come to believe them in the end. Even with your fingers crossed.

Punishment – terrible punishment. He hadn't felt Nobody with Bessy and he had gloried in it, had felt himself huge, and special, and precious somewhere deep inside. So Bessy's child had been a Nobody boy, and hadn't lived. Love never lived. And this silver-haired girl, no needy beside him now, well, he might have loved her once, he would have liked to have loved her still, but what she asked from him now he no longer had to give. He was empty, quite empty inside.

They weren't so dissimilar, after all.

She sobbed as she trotted along at his side and, all pride gone, took a deep, shuddering breath to say, 'Just to be near you, I want nothing more. I would cook and wash for you. I would keep house for you . . . make your clothes for you, look after your children. Spurn me, scorn me, I wouldn't care. Just let me have a cottage on the land where I can bring up my babe and have some of your time and I'll be your slave for ever.'

Then, 'Don't look at me like that! You treat me like a whore!' And for the first time in years she thought about her mother. She felt like a whore now, scorned and nothing, and she wondered if Mother had been right – that her pathetic behaviour was inherited, if, somehow, all this had been decreed years and years ago and that, whatever she had done, there had never, really been any way out.

He stopped walking and spun round to face her. A savage look came to his face. 'God damn 'e for the fool yous have turned out to be!' he told her callously. 'An' now yous whinin' round my legs like a poor starved bitch.'

They walked on in silence. Mercy's throat was raw, her body ached and shivered as if in fever. Hope would not let her believe he was not jesting. This was her last chance. She could not let him go. He had to help her . . . he had to . . . he had to love her . . . he had told her he did so, once.

They arrived at the stillroom window. Silver-cone icicles spiked sharp under the sill. She held her breath. What to say? What to say? His eyes told her they hated her, and yet . . . and yet?

John Yelland was the handsomest man Mercy Geary had ever seen. Fine-featured . . . delicate even, and powerful in anger with the smile of a wolf and eyes of brilliant fire. She would have flung herself at his feet if she thought that would work. She longed to raise her arm and stroke his soft curls. She longed to trace the pattern of his face once more, take it down to his stiff frockcoat collar, to his foamy white-shirted chest. To lay her head on his chest and feel his heart beneath her. Never – was that a word she must use now – *never* – was it possible that none of these wonders would ever come again?

When she turned her face towards him she begged the question, foolishly, like a child. And he answered in his own way. 'Leave yer boot by the fire tonight,' he sneered at her, his words ringing in her brain. 'An' in the morning yous'll find a sixpence inside. An' that's my payment for a half-penny whore. An' that's the most generous vail yous ever goin' t' see!'

'Yous lost all yous pride an' yous begged him like that?'

Mercy could see Daisy cringe but she had to tell the truth to try and halve the pain she could not bear on her own. The telling didn't help after all.

'An' did yer leave yer boot out?'

'Yes, I did. It's before the fire. I wanted to see if he really would . . .'

'Oh Mercy! Oh Mercy!' And Daisy rocked her friend in her arms but there was no comfort in it.

'Yous still carn believe it, can 'e?'

'No, Daisy! No, Daisy I can't.'

'Not even if I's tell 'e 'bout Bessy.'

Mercy didn't want to hear about Bessy . . . about any of the others that Daisy had drawn herself up to reveal. Just the thought of John Yelland in the arms of another woman caused such a stab of agony it was unendurable. Even now, when it was quite apparent that he didn't want her, the thought of him with someone else made her sick with jealousy.

There were few options, they decided between themselves. Mercy couldn't put her mind to practical things so she let Daisy talk while she listened. Mercy could remain here until her condition began to show and then Mrs King would dismiss her . . . turn her out without a reference and let fate take her into its arms. 'No messin',' as Daisy put it.

She could try beseeching John Yelland again, but that was going to prove next to useless.

She could leave of her own accord and try to get

work in the town . . . or go up-country and try for work in the mills.

'Or,' whispered Daisy, 'Yous could do what the witch said. Yous nothin' to lose so it might be worth a try. After all, 'e's supposed to be a religious man an' religious men are meant to be charitable . . .'

Mercy had known that Daisy would favour this. How had she known? It seemed the only conclusion to reach. 'The squire? Take Mother Carrivick's advice?'

'Aye.'

'But whatever for? He'd curse me to Hell for being a wanton.'

'Maybe, maybe not. 'E hates 'e's own son. 'E's up to 'ere wi' 'is whorin'. 'E might take pity on yous an' punish 'im for 'is wicked treatment of 'e.'

'Or he might not.'

'Either way, yous would've tried! Yous couldn't be worse off than yous are right now. We'll try an' sleep on it.'

So many feelings. They rose and tore and rent like the wind. There was no sleep for Mercy that night.

The wind got up from the north. Mercy lay and listened. It tore at the windows and shrieked under the door, rolling away with a roar into the distance before returning again with a mightier fervour. By morning the snow had drifted along hedges and walls; the pump in the yard was frozen up and stood hunched with disapproval like an old, old man.

The wind and the cold were part of Mercy's nightmare. She was going to do what Daisy had suggested, and see the squire. But she had to pick her moment . . . had to catch him when he went outside to the trap because Mrs King would catch her if she went upstairs and there was no such thing as an appointment between Master and scullery-maid.

The morning seemed to stretch interminably on and on. Daisy, pretending to be busy in the warm kitchen, mixing a cake in the bowl for Mrs Gibson, saw him first. She was keeping watch at the basement grill.

'Get on . . .' she called when she saw the trap pulling round. 'Go now while yous got the chance.'

Flustered, almost before she could think what she was doing, Mercy ran from the back door and round through the yard to the front of the house where men were clearing snow from the massive front steps. She reached the trap just as Roger Yelland was about to step into it. They were holding a warm blue blanket out to him. Mercy could hardly catch her breath to speak. She expected to be knocked to the ground by a groom, to be hit by the squire's gold-topped cane. But when she whispered her request she was so close to his ear she could see the whiskers, so grey they could have been got at by hoarfrost. But he didn't strike her. He paused. His eyes burnt her as he listened. He set his terrible countenance. And he said, 'Hold the horses, Foster, I's woan be a long while.'

Up the front steps to the house she went, timidly following her ponderous master, looking to right and left, terrified that John would see her.

Sacrifice . . . she had found the ultimate way at last. From the moment she first saw him she had known that somehow it would come to this. She didn't know what to expect from this man, a personage so awe-inspiring she had never been able to meet his eye until now. A man with a reputation so cruel that she was sure he would think nothing of eating a baby alive.

This was how it had always been meant to be.

And now, here she was, watched by all the servants, accompanying him up the front steps into Trewen!

TWENTY-FIVE

All day Daisy worried. In the broad light of day she didn't know what had possessed her to suggest going to Roger Yelland! It was quite unlike her . . . and now she wished she hadn't.

She couldn't keep her mind on her work. Mrs Gibson and Mrs King kept pressing to find out what was going on but Daisy kept quiet. 'It's unprecedented,' said Mrs King in disgust. 'Lord knows what the repercussions of this will be. I always knew she was an impudent hussy but this takes the candle! Mercy Geary's gone too far this time!'

Daisy kept glancing to the stairs and then back to the grille in the ceiling, expecting to see Mercy's tear-stained face after a beating from the master and an order to get out of his house instantly.

Mercy did not return that day. Nor that night. There was no sign of her in the house or in the gardens or anywhere that Daisy went to search.

But the next night, when Daisy was sleeping Mercy nudged her awake and whispered, 'Daisy! Daisy!'

'Oh Mercy!' Daisy cried. 'Where've yous bin? I's bin out of my mind . . !'

'I can't tell you, sweetheart. I can't tell you.' Mercy was sobbing. She looked different. Daisy thought she looked defeated like a colt that had been broken. Dead-eyed with resignation . . . all fight gone.

'What did 'e say, for Godsake?' Daisy was instantly wide awake. 'Yous carn not tell me now!'

'Believe me, I want to tell you – but I can't. I swore!'

Mercy's face was white and pinched. Exhaustion brought tears to her eyes. 'I took an oath!'

'But yous back?'

'Only for my bundle. And then I must go.'

'At night?' In the dark like this? No! Yous carn go, Mercy! It'd be too cruel!'

'Daisy, I have no choice.'

Mercy was beaten. But her voice sounded satisfied . . . satisfied and relieved as if some great burden had been lifted from her. Daisy sat up, bewildered, and rubbed her eyes for clarity. 'But where will yous go?'

'I don't know yet. But I'll find somewhere. I have to.'

'Something's happened!'

'Aye, something's happened.'

'Well . . . was it good or was it bad?'

Mercy wearily shook her head. 'It was the only way out for me,' she whispered into the darkness. 'And I don't know if it is good or bad.'

'Yous comin' back?'

'Not for a long time, Daisy.'

Daisy shook her head. 'I doan understand any of this! I just doan understand what's goin' on.' She felt crushed, robbed. It had been her idea!

Finished with her work, for there wasn't much to collect, Mercy straightened the covers of her bed. She called softly from the door, 'I'm going now.'

'Oh no! Oh no, yous doan go like that. I's comin' with 'e.'

'Daisy, you can't.'

'I'm comin' with 'e to bid 'e goodbye. An yous carn stop me!'

She followed Mercy down the stairs. They crossed by the fire. Mercy reached down for her outdoor boots. She bit her lip as she felt inside, gasped with the pain of ultimate humiliation. There was a sixpence in the toe. It glinted in the dying firelight. She held it in her hand and showed it to Daisy who clucked in disgust.

Mercy lifted the latch. The heavy kitchen door creaked open and both girls were hit by a blast of frozen air. Daisy had her wrap, but was bare-footed. She could only walk to the far side of the yard.

'I's want 'e to tell me what happened!' Daisy wanted to shake her friend and stop her, wake Mercy from this hypnotised state of terrible resignation and defeat. She knew it would be no use. Mercy was determined and certain, as if she was setting out on a journey she had always known she must take.

'I can't! I will one day, God willing. But just now I can't.'

And Daisy tried to hold her back but couldn't prevent her from leaving. Mercy was walking away into the night.

'Goodbye.' Mercy's voice was whispering, somewhere in the darkness.

'Good luck,' Daisy cried softly from the other side of the gate. And, turning back, she looked enquiringly up at the dark windows of the house to see if anyone was watching.

The house stared back at her with half-lidded eyes.

TWENTY-SIX

''Twere sheer bliddy 'ell, all of it. I's'll never forget it, an' I's'll never forget 'er – well, why would I's when 'er were the only friend I's ever 'ad?'

Daisy Wyatt bustled from one corner of the kitchen to the other, her mouth tight with concentration as though it was full of sharp pins. What with the wedding tomorrow, she told Tristan, what with that and the lack of competent help, she didn't know if she could cope with all the work. Was anyone upstairs getting the dining room ready? Would the fish delivery come on time, for the oysters would have to be soaked for the recipe . . .

'We's never imagined,' she managed to say while passing, while stooping and bending over the table where Tristan sat to push her finger into a thickly pink mixture and taste it. 'More salt . . . no, we's never thought we's'd see the day when Master John got 'isself wedded. We's all hopin' things might change for the better wi' a woman in the house. Well, as we's tells each other so often, it carn get worse. Can it?'

And Tristan looked at the turmoil around him in this great stone kitchen and imagined it couldn't.

Finally Daisy came to rest beside him, rolled up her sleeves and started folding pastry cases into complicated patterns, licking the dough with none too clean fingers in order to hold it together. The cook, nervous, agitated, was shouting at everyone who came by, but she ignored Daisy who appeared to be in a higher position than the rest, a position of trust, someone to let alone to get on with things.

Gardeners brought bundles of decorations round to the back door and were cursed by the cook and told to take them to the front. A little, pale-faced maid wept at the sink as she peeled onions. A man with one leg was stoking the range and on a separate table was a grand wedding cake, glistening sweetly all pink and white with a silver ribbon round it.

'Who's the lucky lady?'

'A girl from the village. She used to work here. 'Er's done well for 'erself, if 'er can stand 'e, wi' is wenchin' and boozin' and up all hours o' the day an' night.'

'A big occasion then, for all of you?'

'Oh yes sir, 'tis certainly that.'

'You don't know then, Daisy, what happened to Mercy that night? The night she went missing, the night before she left?'

'I's told 'e in all honesty all I's knows. If'n I's knews more I's'd tell 'e. I's explained how it was wi' er, how 'er were besotted by the young master an' how 'e let her down in 'er hour of need. How the old woman she used to call a friend let 'er down. An' I's feels *I* let 'er down by not going wi' 'er.' Daisy left her pastry for a moment and stared, her eyes lost in distance. 'I's was different in them days, younger,' and she turned to give Tristan a defensive look. 'I's was scared, to tell 'e the truth. Here at Trewan I's was safe, as safe as I's'd ever been, an' the thought of takin' off into all that cold, out into nowhere, no plans, no family to go to, well, to be honest wi' 'e I's couldn't bear to think o' it. An' I's still feel 'er shouldn't have gone! Something must have happened to make 'er take off like that an' wi' a child inside 'er. They's would have taken 'er in at the poorhouse, I's knows, but 'er wouldn't have that. Oh no, 'er had to go an' there was no arguin' wi' 'er on that point.' Daisy stared into Tristan's eyes. 'Oh, I's missed that maid. We managed to have some laughs together when she were 'ere, really we's did. 'Er had such a sweet way wi' her if'n yous ignore that wilful streak, that foolish streak that seemed to take 'er over so that 'er were never, really, quite in control o' 'erself.'

'I'm grateful for all you've told me,' said Tristan, strangely comfortable sitting here amid the frenzied preparations with this damp, nondescript, middle-aged woman fiddling with the flour beside him. 'You've told me more than anyone else has told me. I feel I am closer now than I have been before.'

'I's's only passed on what 'er told me,' said Daisy, uncomfortable with the compliment, not sure what to do with the feeling it gave her. 'We 'ad lots o' time for talkin' once we's was upstairs in bed wi' the candle out. An' 'er always had a lot to say. 'Twas no easy ride workin' here in the old days wi' that harridan King in charge. 'Twas no life, not really, not for us, so young, yous knows. An' Mercy, 'er used to long for somethin' else. 'Er were never satisfied. I's told her at times, I's said, "Yous court disaster, yous," an' then she told me that Annie, a girl 'er once knew, used to tell 'er the same. Yous doan change really, do yous? No,' and Daisy smiled wistfully, looked sweetly at Tristan for a moment, 'No, nobody ever really changes.'

'I must let you go.'

'I's feels I's not been much help, not able to tell yous about that last night. I's would, yous knows . . .'

'Yes, I know. What would Mercy have done without you, Daisy? It sounds as if you were always a real friend.'

Daisy was desperate to help him. She was overcome by his manners, his ways, by his gentleness. He looked at her as she always imagined a man might look at a woman, and his voice was full of respect. 'An' I's wish I's could have told yous what happened to 'er when 'er left 'ere,' she said. She badly wanted to give him

317

something in exchange. She wished she was not so busy with the preparations, but she could not stop. If she stopped they would never get done.

'I know what happened to her when she left here,' said Tristan quietly. 'I found that out before I came away. It was only her early life that was missing and I have a good impression of all that now, of the people she lived with and of the life she led. There's just one missing link, and I think I know who can provide me with an answer to that.'

'I's should like to know,' said Daisy timidly. 'I's should very much like to know what happened to 'er an' where 'er is now.'

Tristan looked at her with such sorrow on his face that Daisy turned away uneasily. 'And I'll tell you,' he said, 'when we've longer to talk. I'll come back, Daisy, for there is more I want to say to you but not when you're busy like this. I'll wait until after the wedding, and then I'll come back. One more visit to make, and after that . . .' And mixed with his sadness came thoughts of Kerry to light up his face. So near now, oh, so near to all that he longed for, to the end of five years of desolate loneliness without her.

Yes, he had found out so much before he left. He knew precisely what had happened to Mercy after she left Trewen that cold winter's night.

The journey to London took Mercy Geary a full month. And on the way her eyes were opened to a different world . . . not a better one in any way . . . but a different one.

Her companions varied along the way. She paid for rides on six wagons and two pack mules. Every day they saw hunger and violence. Every day they passed poverty and neglect. The Cornwall she left behind was a black and white faraway land with vast and rugged landscapes, mine chimneys, glimpses of the sea, stunted blackthorns and soaring sparrowhawks. Now she came to the red and the grey, houses of brick, countryside that was flat as far as the eye could see. The grey wood of the gibbets at the crossroads, the bloated red of the corpses with their eyes half-pecked away by birds and the swollen greyness of their legs.

As the wagon approached London she covered her nose with her hand against the stench. Smoke was rising on the rank, raw February air. Here, colours had no meaning. Green turned yellow and red turned orange. Even the children looked pinched-faced and old. The women wore hard-faced looks, like men. And the beggars . . . 'It's all so shabby and smelly,' she said to the driver. 'Don't the people object to smelling themselves?'

'Nah, they're used to it b'now,' said the kindly man. 'An' you will be in time.'

'Never.' But Mercy said it to herself. This was certainly the den of iniquity that Mother had warned her about. Men turned to look in her direction as she rode into the city. A country lass, in spite of her terrible journey there was a fresh sweetness about her that was missing from the women of the capital. And Mercy Geary was beautiful.

Down the alleys behind the finer houses tenements had sprung up to accommodate the workers of the new industries. Now and then came the sights of a dingy stairway, rotting rubbish, scabby, three-legged dogs and pitifully dressed children playing aimlessly in the dirt. They tried to sell their wares in the street but Mercy had never seen such poor cabbages, such listless fish. She felt sick.

They had left the smell of the countryside behind them. She thought of Cornwall and in spite of the unhappiness in her life tears sprang to her eyes. There had been happy times, too. People she had come to love. There had been Annie and Daisy and even Mother Carrivick before she went and let her down by refusing to help her. And even when things were bad, she had always been able to look out and see the beauty of the country all around her. It was free . . . you needn't be moneyed or gentrified to enjoy it. She was sure they would take it away and keep it for themselves if they could, but it was too big, they couldn't. Here, they had.

Here, if you were low, you had nothing but misery to look out on.

The friendly waggoner dropped her at Covent Garden market and wished her luck then turned his back and greeted his friends. Mercy, walking away, felt cold as never before – cold, sick and exhausted, and aching with despair. Now she must find her way to Wigmore Street: Yelland had written to inform them. They were expecting her . . .

As she walked through the unfamiliar streets, asking every now and then for directions, men turned to admire her dainty loveliness. Her cheekbones were high and finely-moulded, and her cloud of silver hair gave her pale face an angelic appeal that was rare and striking.

Darkness was falling, the streets were ill-lit. Strangers came to walk beside her and whispered lewd suggestions. They offered her money – a great deal of money. Others spat and laughed, nudging each other as she passed by. Mercy walked faster, terrified now and then by the savage-looking dogs that lunged at her from dark doorways.

She was defeated by exhaustion and terror by the time she reached the house. She stood on the pavement and looked up at it. Thick, velvet curtains covered the upstairs windows but she saw lights glowing from the basement and climbed wearily down the steps, burning her hand on the cold of the iron railings as she went.

When the face came to the door Mercy sighed and felt her tiredness deepen. She had seen so many faces like this before, for on it was written distaste, mockery, resignation and bitterness. Mercy could have spoken the woman's welcoming words. 'Well?'

She shifted her tired feet and lowered her eyes as expected. 'I'm Mercy Geary. Someone is expecting me.'

The eyebrows rose as she'd known they would. The tight mouth hardened. 'You'd better come in, then.'

Round and round went the circles of her life. Round and round and round. When would someone see her as the person that she was? When would someone realise that all she wanted was to be treated with kindness . . . she had plenty of it to give in return . . . and love . . . but nobody wanted that. She was treated like dirt, less than dirt, because at least somebody bent to pick that up before throwing it away. Mercy was tired of it . . . tired of it all.

She followed the neatly-dressed maid into the kitchen. It was the kitchen of the Mission baby house, of the big girls' house, of Trewen, all rolled into one. And the way everybody turned to look at her, with not a word of welcome, just that same cold, appraising stare that said, well here she is, one more skivvy to sink our teeth into and make sure her life's not worth living. She's of no importance . . . we'll just get on with what we are doing . . .

'They'll want to see you upstairs. Better smarten yourself up a bit or you'll be out before you know it.'

Mercy tried to react like a human being. 'I've been

321

travelling for twenty-eight days. All the way from Cornwall . . .'

The woman, who must be one of the kitchenmaids said, 'Well, hear 'er! Most impressive I'm sure!'

And Mercy tried to smile but could not.

'We don't eat hot food on a Sunday.'

'We don't allow followers.'

'We like our servants to wear black at all times.'

'You'll get your board and nothing else . . . *under the circumstances*.'

'Not everyone would take in a girl with such low moral standards.'

'You'll be expected to work right up to the birth.'

'When you're working upstairs we don't expect you to be seen . . . especially by visitors.'

'Sunday morning and evening both, we expect you all to go to chapel.'

And eventually, 'Pay attention, girl! Have you listened to a word I have been saying?'

Mercy shook her head, bewildered. The sharp voice made her start. The mistress of the house was an austere woman with yellow skin that stretched tightly over sharp cheekbones. Her little hands were folded neatly in her lap. The fire that burned beside her in the grate looked neat, cold and unwelcoming as she was, while the burnished firedogs shone brightly. Mercy saw them through the rainbow colours of tears.

She raised her head high and drew herself to attention. 'I'm not staying here, Ma'am. I've seen all I want to see of this household and I'm leaving tonight.'

'What?' The woman's face turned sharply towards her. The blanched skin even seemed to pale.

'I said I'm not stopping, Ma'am, thank you very much. I'd rather take my chance on the streets than stop here.'

Even after a lifetime of subservience rebellion was extraordinarily easy. And pleasurable . . . oh yes . . . most pleasurable. She watched the woman's jaw fall open, saw the cheeks draw in to form some more venom. The prim little mouth, together again, salivated with it. Spittle bubbled at its affronted corners. Mercy did not wait to hear. She simply turned and left the room, marched straight across the hall and out of the forbidden front door. She went unhesitatingly down the steps and out into the cold, dark street.

High in the sky the stars were fierce with frost. There was a strange, green moonlight which made the buildings seem unreal and weirdly illuminated. Mercy Geary breathed the air of a cold, hostile world and made her decision.

She had managed her life quite successfully on her own for a month, without the protection of these 'good', religious people. She had survived: she was used to nothing greater than survival. That was all she had known and all she could hope to expect. She would never put herself into their evil hands again.

She didn't know it then, but Mercy had discovered pride.

TWENTY-SEVEN

The fact that she was pregnant put none of her clients off. Indeed, some of them seemed to prefer it.

A child of Satan . . . the Devil's daughter . . . she laughed when she thought how easy it had been . . . just a slower way of walking and an oblique slant of an eye. She laughed at all the lies she had been told. There was nothing wrong with her life now. In fact, rarely had she felt happier. She'd always been pitifully willing to put herself up for exchange . . . right from the time, a lifetime ago, when she had betrayed her own mother for some kind of hopeless love. But now, for the first time in her life she was exchanging herself for something positive . . . something she could see and feel and expect.

She happily gave her body. She gratefully took the shilling in return, but her clients gave her more than that. They gave her a brief moment of warmth, of communication – sometimes they shared a confidence.

She worked from a room above a hostelry popular with waggoners putting up for the night. It was simple but clean, with a hearth, a pallet and a chest that did for a table. Behind were the stables, and the smell of fresh manure that came wafting up in the mornings was the only firm reminder she had of the country.

She was often knifed by bitter memories of John Yelland. She believed she still loved him and thoughts of his cruel behaviour wounded her deeply. None of her customers came anywhere near to him, not his beauty, performance or arrogance. But she could pretend . . . and on many occasions she turned the heaving, grunting brute on top of her into the sensually powerful, smooth body of the squire's son to whom she had foolishly given all of her love. And coarse, matted hair could be transformed in the blink of an eyelid into silken, sweet-smelling locks.

She tried hard to save, knowing she would have to stop work for a while after the child was born. She talked to the landlady, Mrs Briggsworthy, once in a while when they met in the yard fetching water. She watched the landlady playing with her little daughter, Flossy. Once the landlord flung her up in the air and opened his great arms to catch her. Flossy screamed and went pink with delight. Her father held her tight against his leather apron and stroked her hair. Mercy felt a sadness so deep she could not have expressed it had she had the opportunity to do so.

She started exchanging odd words because Mrs Briggsworthy did not look away as she passed by as so many of the good wives did. The landlady had no axe to grind . . . Mercy paid her rent, she was quiet and clean and she attracted extra customers to the hostel.

The landlady was a picturesque person who wore brightly striped skirts and a blue serge gown. She kept apples in her ample pockets and took them out to give to the toddler. Eventually Mercy took to going downstairs at a time when the woman was there, for she was lonely. Grunts and whisperings do not make for good conversation. She missed the gossip of life in a big house. Slowly and gradually she began to tell Mrs Briggsworthy her story. The placid, round woman, who was pudding-faced as a farmer's wife and looked as if she had been dumped and stranded in the middle of a city, was a listener . . . it was her trade. And she listened and tutted and exclaimed and thought to herself that given better luck this girl could have done quite well for herself instead of ending up in the gutter.

'And how do you feel about the baby? It won't be long now, you know.'

'Sometimes I hate it. I resent having to have it. I would have got rid of it, you know, if the old Cornish woman had helped me.'

Mrs Briggsworthy shook her head. She flapped at herself with a cooling hand. 'You might have died . . .'

'I wouldn't have cared – then.'

'It must be meant.' Mrs Briggsworthy sat down to take the weight off her legs. It was hot, and the spring sun beamed down into the centre courtyard. She looked around her on the floor as if searching for an example. Finding none she looked at Mercy blankly and said, 'Some things are meant.'

'I don't agree,' said Mercy thoughtfully. 'I think that you allow everything that happens to happen.'

'You can't mean that! What about that poor old fellow with the twisted face who comes to you on a Monday. He couldn't help being born like that. It must have affected the whole of his life. Terrible! Awful! He puts me in mind of Satan!'

'Oh, he's not Satan,' Mercy said, suddenly thinking of Roger Yelland. 'I've met Satan and He looks nothing like that.'

Sometimes her lodger said some peculiar things. Mrs Briggsworthy shrugged. Her brown hair was rolled up so it looked like a hat. A greasy smell of boiling mutton came from the kitchens. She was concerned that the girl wasn't eating properly. She would have asked her down for tea but she knew that Mr Briggsworthy wouldn't like it.

'You never go out,' she said, pulling herself up. 'You should get out more. Properly out, I mean – make some friends of your own age . . . enjoy life while you can.'

'I don't like to be with people,' said Mercy. 'I'm all right on my own.'

And Mrs Briggsworthy thought she was a poor little thing who was probably lacking the confidence to try. But then she remembered what she did for a living, shook her head and said, 'Well, that's enough philosophising for one day. I'm off.'

But she liked Mercy enough to stand up for her in court. It did no good, of course, but in the end she was the only person in the world who was prepared to try.

Mercy *had* to steal from Janus Paul. She had to steal because he had spent the night and refused to pay.

'Tomorrow,' he said drunkenly, pushing her off like a fly.

'Tomorrow is no good, Janus, sweetheart. 'Tis today that I need that money for I promised to buy myself some boots.'

'I promised to buy myself some boots . . .' Janus mimicked her, his big, corduroyed backside swaying from side to side as he leaned across the bed for his jerkin.

She went to stand in front of the door. 'You've never done this to me before,' she accused him, arms crossed. 'You're always a good payer.'

'Yes, I am.' Janus was in one of his belligerent moods. He stuck out his bristly chin. 'So don't push me, gel. I've said tomorrow and tomorrow you shall have it.'

'That's not fair.'

Drink had sozzled Janus' great ox brain. He smelled like a stale beer keg. He would never remember that he owed her if she let him leave it until tomorrow. More often than not he forgot where he lived and had to be taken home like a great, lost baby. 'Anyway,' he said, confronting her. She could see his brain trying to work. He had to squeeze up his eyes very tight to make this happen. 'Anyway, we didn't do it!'

'That's not the point,' she argued. 'You were here. I was with you when I could have been with somebody else.' Now was not the time to remind him that he could rarely 'do it' these days, but that most of the time he snored like a great horse on the bed after demanding that his swollen feet be stroked.

'You're a nag!' He flung the accusation at her so that his jowls wobbled. 'Like all women!'

He pushed her side and went out into the street. She followed. His pocketbook was dangling from his back pocket. If she hadn't taken it the daft bugger would have dropped it. She was going to take what he owed and put it back. She didn't have to tiptoe. Janus lurched from one side of the narrow street to the other, his eyes spiralling, his breeches at half-mast. She leaned forward. She flipped his purse from his pocket.

'Thief!'

A beady-eyed woman on the other side of the road had been busily picking her way between the filthy puddles. In her hand was a chain with a hook on the end which prevented her skirts from trailing in the dirt.

She had looked up for a moment to see where she was going and there, right in front of her, in broad daylight, cheeky as you please, she had seen this woman . . . 'Well . . .' she drew herself up primly in court, 'well, I don't know what you could call her, really.' She sniffed, and brought to her pointed nose the pierced gold lid of her vinaigrette. The stench from the cells below the courtroom was enough to make anyone feel faint and the sweet herbs that were strewn on floor and benches were nowhere near enough to combat it.

'But I stopped,' Mercy interrupted. The judge looked

328

down his nose and drew in his breath tò speak. 'But I stopped to explain! I didn't run away, now, did I?'

The beady-eyed woman turned her head away. The judge said, 'Quiet!' The flies started buzzing again and Mercy watched the dust motes dance on the shard of sunlight coming in through the courthouse window.

Fear of things unknown is realised in glimpses like fork lightning. The flash comes without warning: the blackness lifts for a second, revealing the violent scene . . . rods of rain, weeping trees, blood-red flowers . . . and then darkness snaps down until the next flash illuminates it all again. And this was what was happening to Mercy now. The blackness of disbelief was comforting, but every now and again she saw only too clearly the awfulness of what might happen to her now if nobody believed her. People had been hanged for less than this.

Mrs Briggsworthy was speaking. She was saying only good things, but then they asked her her trade. They asked her if she condoned Mercy's profession by letting rooms in her house to women of the night and when Mrs Briggsworthy innocently replied that yes she did, then in their minds they dismissed her. You could watch how they did it!

And then she was asked, 'Mrs Briggsworthy, is it true that you came here today deliberately against your husband's expressed wishes?'

She replied, 'Yes, M'lord. I had to! I had to come and see that proper justice was done. This gel has nobody else, Sir, nobody else to stand up for her . . .'

'She's no innocent! It looks to me as if she can stand up for herself very well,' said the judge, leaning over the bench and eyeing Mercy's bulging stomach.

They read out a reference from the employer she had shunned in Wigmore Street. The outraged woman had put into words all she had failed to say on the night Mercy so ungratefully fled the sanctuary of her godly house.

'She doesn't know me,' Mercy stammered. 'I wasn't there for half an hour!'

'She knows your type,' said the judge sternly. And implied that they all did. 'I know this lady very well. She would say nothing mean or unfair.'

Sister Henry, up in London for the annual Mission meeting, heard about the court case and told them that Mercy had always been promiscuous. Round her full, white throat hung the crucifix with the bright red eyes. She told them all in a formidable voice that the Mission had been advised to send Mercy away to Trewen after a particularly scandalous episode in which she had spent a night with a shepherd who had a reputation for interfering with young girls. 'We were worried about the moral character of her companion, a backward child called Annie Clegg.'

'You were not worried,' Mercy shouted. 'Annie Clegg died! You let her die!'

'Promiscuous, and a thief to boot.' Sister Henry steamrollered on, determined to crush this impertinent obstacle, and thoroughly enjoying every moment of her court appearance. She told about Mary Ludd's half-crown. She told them Mercy had stolen it from the vicar on the day of the Lord Mayor's Parade.

'I never did! I never!'

'I have a letter before me that says you did,' said Sister, letting the one eye Mercy could see roll terribly, accusingly, in its socket.

'You have sworn to tell the truth in this courtroom.' The judge bent forward and looked concerned. 'And

330

now it seems, young lady, that you have chosen to perjure yourself. I think you underestimate the seriousness of your situation.'

Janus Paul was too drunk to take the stand but they took a verbal statement down, and when they had finished with it it made some sense.

She hoped they would not return her to the place beneath the courts where she had waited for trial. She hoped she would be able to convince them to set her free.

She didn't even know what 'transportation' meant. She looked round the court for clarification but bewigged men were standing up, moving around, arguing and talking, people were coming and going in the public gallery, and the whole place had suddenly turned into a busy thoroughfare, almost with the bustle of a market-place. She had been forgotten.

The warders who had stood behind her throughout the proceedings caught her arms and took her down the steps behind the defendant's bench. Her trial was over! It had all happened so quickly. She had been expecting an opportunity to defend herself, a chance to tell them what had really happened. A man dressed in black had spoken for her but he had not spoken well or with any conviction. She had been denied her chance. It had all suddenly ended with a man coming in at the end of the break, standing up to face her and saying the one word, '*Guilty*'.

She could remember the judge saying, 'transportation', and quite a bit more besides, but that was all cloudy now. She was left with the one word she could not understand.

She asked. She kept asking, but nobody listened. Nobody would enlighten her.

They were leading her down deep into the black heart of the earth. They followed a lantern light. She retched. She thought she would suffocate. No one would ever find her here – who was there to look? They were burying her. They were burying her alive!

Maybe that, she thought in a brief, black panic before she fainted, maybe that is what 'transportation' means.

TWENTY-EIGHT

Tristan was born on Midsummer's Day. But summer in all its stages had abandoned the creatures of this dark, dark underworld just one hundred and ninety yards in area, divided into four rooms and inhabited by over three hundred women and their children.

Here these ragged prisoners ate, lived, dressed and slept, not on palliasses but on filthy straw, using raised boards for pillows. So wretched, so brutalised were the dwellers of this gloomy, satanic world, that even the governor would not visit unless under military protection.

In the first week after the child's birth a particularly vicious bout of gaol distemper caused a regular twelve deaths a day among the total of eight hundred inmates.

John Yelland. He was the monster who had caused her to come here . . . and yet . . .

In the beginning, unable to believe where she was, Mercy crouched in a corner while her eyes acclimatised themselves in constant semi-darkness. Gradually the shadows that moved and spoke turned into human beings who, after callously searching her for scraps of food or money that she might have brought with her, ignored her completely.

She was glad of this. She didn't want to be one of them. She prayed for sleep, for this was the only bearable way to pass the time. But sleep was followed by wakefulness, and every time she opened her eyes and realised where she was she sank into a misery so deep it was physical. She found it hard to move her limbs, even to turn her head. She heard her own heartbeat and felt surprise. She had thought that she might have died and come to Hell.

She was so terrified of the impending birth she couldn't bring herself to think of it. Many of her companions spent the time rocking, humming with their eyes closed, and soon Mercy found herself sighing to the same lament. It was comforting. It was important to try and cut herself off from the actuality of her situation. For the worst part was not knowing how long it would last.

John Yelland!

Two weeks later, when the first pains came, she said nothing but, like an animal making a nest, cleared for herself a place in the straw by the wall which would not be trampled on by passing feet. With blank eyes she watched the scrawny children play, making toys from anything they could find . . . dolls from scraps of torn linen . . . boats from discarded wooden bowls . . . and animals plaited from strands of straw. Her child, too, would be one of these.

Over the space of a night and Mercy was wracked with pain. A giant hand was grinding her backbone. No position she took would ease it.

'Poor mite. She's only a child herself.'

'Best thing for both of 'em if it be born dead.'

'More'n likely that'll 'appen. Come on, pet, stop your strugglin'. Try to relax . . .'

She recoiled from their ministrations. She feared their witchy-haired heads, their long, broken nails, she believed their very presence would make the pain worse. But they would not leave her: Jenny Mead, Maggie Donnovan and Nancy Garner were made of sterner stuff. Weren't they all mothers themselves?

Hadn't they been through it? Didn't they know just how she felt?

Mercy writhed and struggled and didn't believe them.

'They didn't ought to allow it,' said Jenny Mead. 'They ought to give a birthin' woman the dignity of a bit of privacy.'

'Aye, thee's right.' Nancy Garner took another look at her surroundings and spat. 'There's no dignity to be 'ad in 'ere, an' those bliddy warders peerin' in all hours of day an' night . . .'

Why were they talking about dignity? It was impossible to believe that these scarecrow people knew the meaning of the word! But in spite of the squalor, the horror, their meaningless lives, the three women stayed with Mercy, held her hand, talked to her, stroked her back, consoled her and calmed her for the twenty-four hours it took for her son to be born.

And, most extraordinary of all, they were exultant, joyous, triumphant at the thought of another life come into this place of wretchedness.

All the dark feelings Mercy had felt about her baby were replaced when she saw it. Gone was the resentment, the anger. Instead came an intense, burning desire to protect him. And this in its turn led to despair, the knowledge that he would probably die never having felt the sun or seen the sky.

Sodden with the sweat of her efforts and feeling more defeated than she had ever felt in her life, she wept. She pushed the baby from her and wept inconsolably. The women seemed to understand. They didn't force her. Maggie Donnovan took him, washed him clean and wrapped him in a blanket of her own.

Nancy Garner stayed with Mercy through the day, stroking her hair and urging her to sleep when she could while Jenny Mead persuaded another nursing mother to give the child his first suck. 'Just till 'is own comes up from the doldrums.'

So Mercy slept and wept and slept, alternately hating her rejected baby and loving him, knowing the two extremes of pain.

'Seven years?' declared Maggie Donovan through her sharp, yellow teeth. She put them to good use on the hard prison bread, chewing it up into balls to make it palatable for her three small children. 'Well now then, darlin', an' that's nothing'! The chance of a new life for both of yer and if yer don't like it, when the seven years is up, yer can bring 'im 'ome and start again in England! What's to be so sad about? Maybe it's the best possible thing can 'appen . . . eh?' she appealed to her friends.

Jenny Mead cackled impatiently while she heaved a small boy with weeping eyes onto her knee. 'I wouldn't mind a spell in bleedin' New South Wales. Certainly better'n seven years stuck in 'ere.' She gave a lick to the hem of her skirt and wiped the mucous away.

'I've heard there's folks that like it there! I wouldn't be surprised if people don't start payin' to go there before long.'

From grotesque shadows – to humans – to friends. She knew they were humouring her. Mercy was no fool. She might have kept herself to herself but she had heard the word 'transportation' spoken in tones of dread since her arrival at Newgate. But hope is a funny thing often born of desperation – magical, it can feed off itself and be created out of nothing. If she didn't have hope then she had nothing, her baby had nothing, and that simply could not be endured.

Newgate murdered fantasy and illusion. Gradually, in its stark confines, the truth about John Yelland and how he had used her dawned upon Mercy, and the durability of the love she had for him made her breathless with humiliation. It was Yelland who had brought her to this, Yelland who had used her so abominably and cast her off like a worn-out shoe. And yet . . . and yet . . .

After all I have endured you will love me, John Yelland, if it is the last thing you ever do! For without your love, without your presence near me I cannot live.

There was hope, after all. Seven years, no matter how terrible, would pass. An idea dawned.

She asked for her son. They brought him, trying to make him nice by spitting on his hair and pulling the threads of gold that cobwebbed his head. Mercy took him hesitantly into her arms, searching for a likeness to Yelland. There was none, save for the colour of his hair. She searched his small face again for some illusive sign of the ominous strain. She lifted wide eyes to question her new acquaintances. Maybe they could see it while she could not?

Maggie Donnovan nodded brightly. 'That's it,' she said. 'Take a look at 'im. 'E's a lovely bairn, you must give 'im that!'

'Give 'im a name,' suggested Jenny. 'You'll feel differently about 'im when 'e's got a name.'

Mercy regarded them intently. She knew that by naming him she gave him a future and all that that would bring with it. If she gave him a name she must love him. She sat on straw in the corner of the cell, her back propped up against the weeping stone wall.

'Poor mite,' Maggie whispered and Mercy didn't hear her.

'I'm calling him Tristan.'

'Well, then!' Maggie beamed down upon her. 'Now that's a nice, unusual name, isn't it?' She had carefully

337

inspected the child from head to foot. Incredibly, he was a fine, strong baby with a good chance of life if he was soon got from here. However, it was important that this pathetic mother give her tiny son her protection. Without that essential factor he would survive the bowels of Newgate but a matter of days.

But Mercy Geary was not interested in her little son's survival for mere survival's sake. She was interested in the bargaining power she realised he provided.

Gin! Miraculously, benefactors supplied it, warders were bribed for it and prisoners passed it down in exchange for dubious promissory notes. Gin deadened anything if you could get enough of it, even Hell itself.

And it aided sleep . . . a sweaty sleep full of clammy dreams . . . but sleep nonetheless. And there was sometimes singing . . . London songs which Mercy did not know but soon picked up. They played cards. They told stories. They fought each other for food and a wider space to lie in.

When Mercy was shown Hannah Gant and her family of little ones, and was told that Hannah Gant was to be taken out and hanged the day after next her sorrow was such that she could not weep. She covered her ears when the bell tolled the hour and the little Gants played in the straw. Later that day they were taken out, but she didn't ask where they were going.

When Mercy was shown Lilly Gaymore, who was sentenced to spend the rest of her life in this place and yet still sang with the others, then she wept. Because she thought that she could never be so strong as that, and she hated the world for its mindless cruelty.

They woke her up roughly before dawn. She roused to

bright lights and a jangling of keys. They picked her out with thirty others who moaned and complained and were cursed by those they disturbed.

She hadn't time to say goodbye to Jenny, Maggie or Nancy. And anyway, in her four months of living in this place she had never seen anyone bother with goodbyes. Pleasantries such as that were reserved for the higher world where they might have meaning.

She held Tristan tight in her arms. Her future was his and she would face it with hope and determination for his sake. Her legs were trembling when she reached the top of the steps. She was dizzy and weak but the prisoners were forced to stand in a square, stone room just large enough to hold them while they waited for the wagons to arrive.

There was no room to sit down. They stood, scratched, cursed and they waited. Bewildered, the children cried. Mercy saw the dawn coming through a high, barred window. Tristan stirred. She moved the blanket from his face so that his waking eyes might see the sky for the first time. A woman next to her said, 'Whatever happens to us now cannot be worse than what has gone before. At least we shall breathe clean air again.'

And Mercy agreed.

TWENTY-NINE

Nothing could induce her to give her child away to those withered crones who crowded the wagons with their do-goody ways and meaningless promises. She needed him for her own ends.

She fingered the tag they had tied round his neck. He could wear it, as a protest, for yes, surely he had been saved. By God? Charity? Kindness? Compared to these scavengers in black she had left angels behind her in the dark dungeons of Newgate.

By the time they reached the transport vessel *Seagull*, Mercy's brain was crowded with images and sounds which, after so long in incarceration, sent her almost crazy with their vivid intensity. She clung on to her child, wrapping herself like a shield around him.

Selected prisoners from gaols and prison hulks all over the country were being brought to Deptford. They were manacled to coaches, chained to wagons, or rode in heavily guarded, especially designed horse-drawn 'vans'. Many had spent months already waiting in prison hulks where they worked under the lash by day and slept in filthy, cramped quarters at night. On arrival the convicts, men, women and children, weakened and half-naked, were chained beneath the decks where the headroom permitted was four foot five inches exactly. The hatches were well secured by cross-bars and bolts, the atmosphere quickly grew fetid, and armed guards kept position on the quarter decks at all times.

*

On 5 September the *Seagull* with its pitiful human cargo of one hundred and forty-five convicts sailed to join the fleet at Portsmouth. There they waited for the Admiralty to provide such necessities as legal papers, clothing, medication, fresh food and additional liquor supplies for the crew.

Finally, on 22 September, eight ships laden with convicts imprisoned for such crimes as sheep-stealing, breaking and entering, extracting monies deceitfully and minor assault, set off for their first port of call, Tenerife, where, weather permitting, they would take on fresh water and vegetables.

The *Seagull* never made her destination.

It was a foul night for sailing. As soon as they rounded St Catherine's Point they hit gale-force winds from the south-west. The sea dashed against the sides of the boat: the *Seagull* rolled and lurched and Mercy retched again and again, falling back on her bunk space, the size of a coffin. Women wailed. Tristan slept. She inched herself into a crouching position and tried to steady her head against the rough planking.

'Open the scuttle-hole . . . give us some air, for pity's sake!'

Mercy opened the air-hole cut into the side of the ship. Wind and grey light rushed through the evil-smelling darkness. She clenched her teeth as she looked at the fearful sight of the sea. She could just make out land in the distance – her last sight of England forever, perhaps, jagged and stark against a laden sky.

It must get better, she said to herself. This can't last. And, to her shame, she prayed, not for Tristan, but for herself and her future with Yelland.

The *Seagull* climbed mountainous waves, shivering like a wet dog on the summits, then pitching down into bright emerald water. The helpless passengers cried and vomited, bruised from being flung backwards and forwards against the sides of the battered ship. The howling wind took up their cries when, too weak to call out, they fell silent. But as the ship lurched onward, every violent rise and shudder washed Mercy with a cold, black fear.

Water poured down into the holds making the cutter flounder heavily, virtually unnavigable as the great seas swept her nearer to the treacherous rocks off the Cornish coast. Mercy didn't know where she was or what was happening. To keep Tristan safe from the water, Mercy pushed oilcloth in an empty sea-chest and laid the baby inside. With shaking fingers she pulled the straps across his chest and buckled them tight. His little face went red with anger and his baby arms flailed in protest.

The *Seagull* was tossed like a paper ball between the two narrow points of Porthclegga cove. She hit the Spur rock with a splintering shriek which sliced her bows in half.

Mercy, and every one else in the hold was flung against the side of the ship. Someone prayed. Great black seas poured down on top of them. Blinded by salt water Mercy felt for the sea-chest, and seconds before the ribs of the ship caved in and pierced her chest, she watched as a rush of grey water took the boy through the scuttle-hole and swept him out into the darkness. She gave a half-sob and experienced a moment of disbelief as, amongst all the mayhem and carnage and chaos, she thought she saw the wings of a giant, black bird as it swooped the rolling wave-tops, as though to guide the bobbing cargo through the swells towards land and safety.

And with it went her last hope of love.

*

Mercy died with a curse on her lips. Her broken body she could no longer give. Her child was gone. All she had left was her soul. She would exchange her soul for the love of John Yelland.

BOOK THREE

MIDSUMMER EVE

ONE

Tonight it was Midsummer Eve. Tomorrow she was to be married.

In the vast cliff-top landscape John Yelland's figure seemed carved against the sky. She caught a glint of bright light as he took his spyglass off her and trained it onto a hooded figure moving along the path towards Porthclegga.

Kerry Penhale was startled back to the present and she stood up and watched as the woman approaching shimmered in sunshine, giving the impression she walked upon water. Who could she be?

So the pilchard shoals had come on an auspicious day for Yelland. Tonight he had a fortune riding on a commissioned lugger coming to Penzance from Cherbourg. But the fortune did not lie in the official cargo of pinewood so innocently stacked in her holds. No, the fortune lay in eighty half-ankers of first-class brandy, of 'Cousin Jack', and some one hundred bales of tobacco which had to be lifted off the *Jacqueline* before she docked. This Midsummer Eve there would certainly be no bright moon.

This day had been given to Kerry to allow her to prepare . . . for her wedding. The Banns had been read, and tomorrow at eleven o'clock Parson Fox would take the service in the church to which, finally, they had brought Feyther's restless bones for burial. She must prepare . . . but there was nothing to prepare. Her dress had been finished a week ago: of simple white muslin bought by Yelland, it was now hanging from the pulley in the kitchen to let the creases out. And if she went home to wait Mamma would fill her head with nagging as she tried to dissuade her daughter from fulfilling her part in the bargain.

Kerry watched from the bower of gorse as the slight, secretive figure came hurrying along the path behind her towards the cliff-top path. There was no mistaking that swinging gait, the flouncing skirts and mincing steps. It was Rosa. Not working at Trewen today? Perhaps she had been lured away by the excitement in the village. Perhaps, for childhood's sake, she wanted to be there for the catch?

But no. Rosa was in her fine red dress and beneath the cloak she carried her best bonnet trimmed with daisies. Kerry stood up and showed herself. 'Rosa! Rosa!' she called, waving her arms, knowing she could be easily seen by the figure in the distance.

She saw the hesitation, the half-turning away, the resumption of course. Was Rosa still refusing to speak to her, even now on the eve of the wedding? Rosa had been behaving most oddly lately, oddly even for one of her temperamental nature.

'Rosa!' Kerry called again. This was an opportunity to speak to the girl, to try once more to explain. Kerry didn't like this rift that had opened between them because although Rosa maddened her at times, she was still her sister.

She watched as the figure grew larger. As Rosa's face came into focus the daisies on the bonnet she held sprung to her bouncy step.

Kerry asked, 'Where've yous been? I's thought yous was workin' today?'

'You's not the only one can take a day off now 'n then, yer knows. An' I's could ask yous the same question only I's wouldn't presume to be so nosy! I's thought yous would be dollin' youssself up.'

All the bitterness was there, not just in her tone but in her stance, her glance, her very bearing.

'You's all dressed up for town?'

'An' since when carn I's dress as I's likes to go walkin' out?' Rosa threw back her hood. Kerry couldn't imagine why she was wearing it on such a warm day.

'I's not sayin' . . .'

'Well then!'

This was not going quite as Kerry had hoped. 'I's was watchin' 'em bring in the pilchards . . .'

Immediately Rosa had something to watch she seized it gratefully and gazed on the activities below with exaggerated intensity. She had done something big. She had done something very big. Something which, if it was found out, would brand her forever, hated, an outcast ostracised and despised by the whole community. She thought it might show in her face. She was overcome with the enormity of it. She had hoped she could reach home unseen but she had spotted John Yelland on the Point, and in an attempt to avoid him, had run straight into Kerry.

Kerry wondered why Rosa was being so evasive. Where had she been that she wanted to keep so quiet about it? But Kerry was more interested in smoothing things out between them. She tried. 'This is a marriage of convenience, Rosa, on both sides. There is no love . . .'

'An' yous'll go ahead and marry 'e then, with no love in yer heart?' Rosa was flushed with fear and guilt. Even her legs were trembling. She tried to concentrate on the conversation she was having with Kerry. Her sister was to blame for all this . . . for the deed she had done. Kerry was the cause of it, Kerry and Yelland

349

between them. Rosa felt like a frightened rabbit trapped in a snare, desperately trying to find a way out.

'Aye,' Kerry said slowly. 'In the circumstances . . . aye!'

'An' 'e?' Rosa went on staring hard at the bustlings below, clamping her face into a study of nonchalance.

''E wants what 'e cannot have. 'E would not be happy with any woman for long . . .'

''E would have been happy with me . . . had I's lowered myself . . .'

Ah! Rosa was getting better. There was a scorn there when she spoke of Yelland that certainly had never been there before. The sisters sat side by side in the bower, together but nowhere near each other. The breeze blew Rosa's soft curls back from her plump, pink cheeks. The effort of a long walk had left her hot and dishevelled. She placed her bonnet on the ground between herself and Kerry. She patted her favourite possession.

'As far as I's concerned good luck an' good riddance to the both of 'e,' she said with enough breath now to finish her earlier sentence. 'Have 'e! Good luck to 'e. I's wouldn't touch 'e if 'e were the last man on earth!'

This was good news. Kerry risked a glance at her sister but her face was studiedly impassive.

'I's glad, Rosa,' was all Kerry said. ''E wouldn't have made yous happy.'

Rosa didn't answer this, but raised her chin determinedly. 'Yous'll be sorry for what yous doin'. Yous'll both be sorry,' she said eventually. And Kerry was struck by the vindictiveness behind her sister's words.

She tried to change the subject. 'It all looks so small from up here. I's used to come an' sit here as a child to try an' put life into perspective . . .'

'With Tristan?'

'Aye.'

'Yous loved Tristan?'

'Aye . . .'

'Yous still love 'e?' Rosa drove the dagger home with a vengeance. Her icicle voice was cold, smooth and sharp.

Kerry bent her head and slid her fingers up a smooth stem of grass. 'I's always will. I's dream about 'e still.' She wouldn't lie to Rosa. Not now.

'But now yous knows 'e's not comin' back an' yers afraid of bein' left on the shelf, is that it?'

Kerry hunched her shoulders and sighed, but now Rosa would not be stopped. There was a great relief for her in speaking. In shouting. 'The very shame of it!' She drew herself up in obvious distaste. 'Flingin' yousself into the tavern an' offerin' yer body like that. Doan yous see . . . a gentleman has no alternative but to take yous on when yous made such a fool of yousself in front of all those people. I's wouldn't be surprised if 'e doan turn up tomorrow an' yous left standin' at the altar on yer own. 'Twould serve 'e right, it would. An' there's yous an' Mamma scoldin' me for bein' a whore! What would yous call yousself then, Kerry Penhale? Snooty cow! The tables are turned right enough now, aren't they?'

'Oh, Rosa . . .'

'Doan 'e oh Rosa me! I's couldn't care less any more. As Mamma says, yous made yer bed an' now yous must lie in it! But doan expect me to be there tomorrow! Doan expect anyone who has any sense of decency left to be there!'

And with that Rosa gathered herself together, got up and flounced off along the path, her head bobbing furiously until it disappeared over the cliff-top.

Rosa . . . !

Laughter and splashing and cursing mixed together to stir memories so pungent that Kerry began to cry.

Through her tears she watched them on the ring of shingle below the jetty. Each blue wave brought its own spray of jewels. The children were in the way, tangling and splashing, the droplets of water spangled in sunrays. With their clothes soaking wet they had given up all attempts to be helpful. The women smacked and scolded, their dresses and petticoats hitched up immodestly round their waists and their brawny arms tugging and pulling at the nets while every now and then they trod on a shell or tripped and yelped with laughter. The men attempted to be more sensible, but even they shouted and moved in a different manner today, easy . . . in holiday mood . . . stopping every now and then to form a picture that could almost have been posed for. And from the boats on the water came shouts that skimmed the surface and rose on wings of joy, smooth with the seabirds, around the cliffs, shouts that dizzied her and turned into song as she became enmeshed in the wonder of it all once again. *'Hevva! Hevva! The pilchards! The pilchards!'*

Oh, why must there be a tomorrow?

TWO

The nets were in and the sorting and packing and carting in progress. The sun dipped low on the horizon, spreading its ribbons like a sad tambourine. Kerry felt suddenly cold and drew her shawl around her. Mazey Jack had gone long ago and Yelland had untethered his horse and ridden off down the path, no doubt to make last-minute arrangements in Jessop's for tonight's big run.

Not yet. Kerry didn't want to go home just yet. She felt threatened by the oncoming night.

Midsummer Eve. When she was small she'd believed it to be a magic night. She got up and walked along the top of the cliff until she came to the little stone church. Dew fell, and the gravestones cast long shadows on the grass. Tentatively she pushed open the door. It was grey and windstripped and creaked on rusty hinges as it moved. Inside the church the air was cold, pale and yellow like wild roses. The warmth never seemed to seep through the slit windows – but the smell of the sea, like a bulky, unwanted visitor, slipped past and stayed. There were rags in the roof stuffed here and there for the drips and draughts. The little pews stood rigid like the castellated battlements of a deserted castle, waiting, always waiting for the return of their reluctant little army.

In here, silence was absolute. Kerry broke it with echoing, wooden-soled footsteps as she walked down the aisle, absorbing the particular smells of this simple place – of hassocks and prayer-books never quite dry . . . of sodden-stemmed flowers that were past their best. Of tallow candles snuffed out years ago but whose acrid aroma lingered to haunt the place. A rough wooden cross stood on a snow-white altar cloth. A small, battered prie-dieu had been dragged into position before the front row of pews ready for tomorrow. A prie-dieu where two could kneel together to take vows that would seal their lives.

Tomorrow this lonely little church would be packed to the rafters. No one in Porthclegga could resist a wedding, and despite what Rosa said, marriages were often made for more dubious reasons than this one. Once the initial flurry of gossip and criticism was over, the villagers would accept it as just one more wedding . . . a time for joy and celebration, for dancing and kissing and killing a pig, for a barrel of ale and perhaps something stronger, because her wedding breakfast would be special, held in the great hall at Trewen. Mrs Gibson the cook was doing her best, while the kitchenmaids cringed and scuttled around her. Red-faced and harassed as she worked on the bridal cake, easing out the icing by the very willpower of her curved tongue, Mrs Gibson had warned Kerry, 'Doan expect a miracle, midear, not under the circumstances . . .'

There would be many from Porthclegga would overdo the revelry and not make it home tomorrow night. They would sleep in the stables and wander unsteadily homewards after dawn, kicked out by the early-rising grooms. By then Kerry would lie in the monster four-poster bed with Yelland.

She shrank from the thought of it as she shrank from the breathy smell of the gravestones.

She never knew what made her kneel at the little prie-dieu then. The idea that it might be an ill-omen to do so before her marriage didn't occur to her, but she knelt on the left-hand side, in the very position she would take tomorrow, on the exact spot where all the local brides knelt on their wedding days and had done down the centuries.

She let her eyes wander over the edge of the dog-eared prayer-book to the floor beneath, tracing the patterns in the stone and reading the name that, worn almost away with passing feet, still declared itself in memory of one who had died, one of a hundred such stones put there over the ages. Kerry could read. She was good at names. Mamma had taught her to read by the family tree in the leather-bound Bible in Great-grandfather's trunk. She was good at reading names.

1591 TRISTAN YELLAND DROWNED

Over two hundred years ago . . . she had only once heard that unique name before but there it was – a name she loved joined with a name she hated. So there had been a Tristan in the area before The Boy came. And he had been a Yelland. How absurd! How perverse life was that the name every bride's eye must light on as she knelt to take her oath should mean so much to Kerry! It seemed to leap up out of the stone scorching as a red lick of flame across her eyes.

She fled the church with Tristan's name on her lips. He had betrayed her. He'd said he would come back. Missy had told her he would come back. He hadn't. Not in time to save her from marriage to a man she despised, from a lifetime she was doomed to spend without love.

Kerry felt as if she was dead, but without the peace that must come with real dying.

THREE

Mamma held her hand over her heart. 'I's been worried stiff,' she scolded. 'Where've yous been all day? I's sent Cassy out lookin' but she couldn't find yous.' She turned away to the fire. 'I's was afraid yous might not come back.'

'Just sitting. Just thinking.'

'Yous knows the shoals has come? The children, they all went.' Mamma looked pleased. Cath was in one of her determinedly cheerful moods.

'I's was watching from the top.'

'Ah.'

'I's met Rosa coming back from somewhere. She wouldn't tell me where she'd been.'

'To get anythin' out of that one is to get blood from a stone. I's doan bother to ask any more she'm so secretive lately. Perhaps she's been to look for a better position. She keeps sayin' she's goan to.'

So that was where she'd been. 'She's still very angry with me, Mamma.'

Cath would not meet her eldest daughter's eye. 'Well, I's fear she cared more about that black devil than we'm realised . . .'

They stopped the conversation there, both fearful of going back over old ground. To sacrifice a child for the welfare of the rest. . . . ah, Cath still struggled with the horror of it and knew that she would suffer for the rest of her days. She was only grateful she had not had to choose which one . . . Kerry had taken that decision for herself.

Cath would have sacrificed her own life if there had

been a way . . . but she had spent sleepless nights sweating under her blanket thinking about how, wringing her brain for alternatives. Cath had not accepted without a fight, she had pleaded and scolded for weeks but to no avail and she was not going to start up again now. Cath detested Yelland perhaps even more than Kerry did. This wedding was not what she had dreamed of for her eldest daughter, but Kerry would not be moved. She had always been stubborn and determined.

Catherine Penhale was appalled at what was happening to her memory of her husband, Jake. What with this marriage . . . the disastrous loan, his cruel bullying, and her sons who had followed the sot to his death . . . when she thought of Jake – which she tried not to do very often – she felt chilled and warped inside. The reality of the futile life he had left her, hardened inside her on a swell of poisonous pus. It hurt, so she tried to soften it by telling herself he had not been like that at the beginning . . . she certainly would not have married him, otherwise. She tried to remember the good times – and there had been many. No . . . she must try not to blame Jake. It was wrong to hate the dead. So she blamed Yelland instead, and hated him with a cold, ferocious energy that sometimes, she felt, weakened her against all other feeling and drove her to the edge of madness.

Of her dead sons she could not think.

For if she had picked a better man her children would have stayed safe.

This Midsummer Eve they were all together at supper for the first time since the night Feyther had died. It was because of Kerry that this was possible. Kerry looked across the table at little Mabs, rosy-faced and with a full cup of milk in her hand. She took time back

357

ten years and thought of herself. Now, to Mamma's delight, Mabs would have a childhood. She would not suffer the torments of Truro Gaol or the nightmare of work in a mill. They had come so close ... all of them ... so dangerously close! To look at them now it seemed impossible, but it had happened. Where you thought there was safety there was none. When you thought you were walking on rock it was quicksand.

True to his word, Yelland had not only rescinded the loan but had unexpectedly provided the money for Gregor to take a boat again. Now he and Jody went out with the rest and had begun to provide a basic living. Cassy was walking out with the eldest Lee boy and although she was young, gawky as a foal and impossibly clumsy and homely, Mamma approved. Cassy was happy.

Rosa had chosen to stay at Trewen, 'like a love-sick cow', Mrs Gibson scoffed. But she wasn't stopping long. 'As soon as I's can I's gettin' out of this place an' off to see the world,' she told her family. 'To travel with an acting troupe ... that's what I's dreams of doin'.'

Tonight they ate cold meat and potatoes. 'Yous'd be good at it,' put in Gregor with his fork in the air. 'You's always tellin' lies.'

'She's got the looks for it,' said Mamma, trying to smooth things over.

And the money, thought Rosa to herself, thinking uneasily of the package hidden upstairs. Her new-found freedom sat uncomfortably on her pretty, plump shoulders. The price, even for Rosa, had been high.

'She *had*,' said Cassy spitefully, 'but lately she's been goin' to seed.'

'Stop 'em Mamma, they'm always at me!' There were tears in Rosa's eyes. It was unusual for Rosa not to give as good as she gave and they all looked up in surprise.

Mamma said gently, 'Why, Rosa, yous knows they's only teasin'.'

Rosa gave a bright smile. But Rosa was jittery tonight.

The village was jittery tonight. Cath was relieved because neither of her boys had been asked to take part in the run. Gregor was inexperienced, and hadn't they recently suffered three unacceptable losses? No, the Penhales' was a blighted house, and they would be left alone for some time to come. But that didn't stop the pulse of fearful expectancy from throbbing under their own roof while they sat and waited for full night to come.

So far, Porthclegga had done remarkably well in evading the excise men. This was partly due to Yelland's contacts and undoubted expertise and also because the men he used were first-rate sailors, but far more important than that, it was because in Porthclegga the community came together as one man behind each venture. There was no fear of a squeaker from among the tightly-bound families in the village. This, coupled with the way Yelland ran his operation with a rod of iron . . . no detail too small . . . no permutation unforeseen . . . no loose end left untied, ensured success when Yelland made a run.

And unlike some of the fat-cat venturers who conducted their activities from the comfortable safety of a well-stuffed chair, a glass of porter by their elbows, to give him his due Yelland, ever vigilant, always stood in the prow of the lead boat.

Some neighbouring villages had not been so lucky. There had been fights . . . battles even . . . and over the

359

years many men had lost their lives to the musket or the gibbet, many had died from either side of the law. Everyone took part . . . from highest to lowest, from parson to most miserable sinner. The Fair Trading was not regarded as morally wrong by those who were involved. Most of them made their precarious livings from the sea – taxes were too high, iniquitous sometimes, and it was right and proper to take advantage if they could.

There were times during that long Midsummer Eve when the charged atmosphere almost took away Kerry's dread of tomorrow. The night was clear but without a moon and the sea had a black, ominous swell to it, as if it moved not with a thousand waves, but with one, great, undulating surge. From the window she could see it, glassy, black, and the Spur rock showing like a fang in the mouth of a dog tonight, for there was not a great tide.

The faces that waited so silently looked woebegone in the lantern light. The three that were missing were poignant in their not-quite-absence. Mamma's looked lost and pitiful now she could no longer wait for Feyther. The sounds outside took on eerie importance and the wind brought strange rustles and whisperings. The table was cleared, the washing-up done, the boots polished and the clean clothes pressed ready for tomorrow. No one liked to suggest bed. It would have seemed cowardly, improper, like a betrayal. But of whom?

Even inside the sounds crowded round them. The doors seemed to creak more, the floors groaned stiffly, and although it was a still, summer night the wind seemed to moan around the house. Kerry thought that the ghosts of all the gales that had blown round it, of all the terrors that had been felt inside it, of all the tears and of all the yearnings, all the wistful ghosts of the house came whispering through tonight as they sat as a family for the last time together.

And then, extraordinarily, Rosa began to cry. As, one by one, their faces turned towards her she bridled, 'I's carn help it. I's carn help it! 'Tis the strain of waitin' like this,' she sobbed, and Mamma looked over her head and raised her eyebrows at Kerry.

''Tis too much for all of us,' said Mamma, rising to comfort her daughter. 'What with all that's gone by an' all that is now to come . . . But yous, Rosa, yous'll be all right, midear.'

Rosa shook her head and grabbed the rag Mamma offered her. She sniffed then fell to hysterical crying again, looking up every now and again with angry, raw eyes. She didn't want Mamma to be nice to her.

'We's luckier than most tonight,' said Gregor, eager to quieten her. Rosa's weeping was unpleasant to behold. 'At least we's all inside an' safe.'

'Aye, what's left of us,' sobbed Rosa angrily. 'What's left . . .'

'She didn't mourn properly at the time,' Mamma sniffed to Kerry, giving a knowing nod. 'I's's never seen a child take tragedy so well. An' of course it has to come out in the end.' She bent to Rosa and spoke loudly as if to the deaf or the stupid. She shook her daughter gently. 'Y'see what's happened, child? Yous is just runnin' behind the rest o' us wi' yer grievin'.'

Affected by Rosa, and frightened of she knew not what, Cassy started sobbing from her place by the window.

'Now then, Cassy. Pull yourself together or we's'll all be at it! If anyone ought to be cryin' tonight it's poor Kerry. An' look . . . she's managing to keep herself together. We'm must all try to do the same, for her sake.'

They had spent the evening trying not to talk about Kerry. Anyone would think it was a funeral they were attending the next day, not a wedding.

'There's somethin' bad in the air, Mamma,' said Gregor. 'Rosa feels it. We's all feels it. Somethin' heavy an' pressin' but I carn say what 'tis.'

Rosa knew what it was. Rosa thought they all knew what it was and she fell to a louder bout of weeping. Look . . . here was Kerry getting the sympathy again, but because of Kerry everything had gone wrong! If Kerry had just waited Rosa felt sure that Yelland would have proposed to her in the end. She would have accepted, of course. She would have been happy, everyone would have been happy, and all would have been well. But now look what was happening. Everything was a very long way from well. She just couldn't take the sight of Kerry's long face any more! Kerry the goody-goody. Kerry the martyr. Kerry to whom they all owed such a debt of gratitude! Rosa cried tears of furious anger. And terror.

Rosa would have liked to leave the house now. At once! This minute! She would have liked to have fetched her package, made up a bundle and fled. She wouldn't care if she never saw any of them again. But she couldn't, for fear of being found out because if they knew what she'd done, they would come for her – she was certain of that. Anywhere she went they would find her, bring her back and punish her for what she had done. There were tales of squeakers being buried in sand . . . or dropped in a well with stones on their heads. This wasn't just another of her naughty, spoilt-little-girl games. Feyther was not here to chuckle and forgive. There would be none of Mamma's secret smiles. The realisation of the enormity of her action which had appeared so clear and simple, had shone with such sweet temptation this morning, had been growing within her all day. And she knew that the punishment for what she had done would most surely be death.

The night before the wedding. And they waited.

FOUR

Soft like a ghost-ship. A cloud of canvas so white it
stood against the night. It would seem that everyone
had seen it at the same time because families in awkward stages of undress and sleep – old 'Smiler' Teague
with his night-cap on . . . old Grannie Lee with her
skinny head poked through the window, in various
ways they all converged on the front. There was no
point in silence now. The smallest child in Porthclegga
could identify that shape. It was the *Hawk*, the revenue
cutter from Penryn, at full sail, her long bowspit built
for speed cutting a pearly trail through the water.

Sick! Sick! She felt sick with fear. Kerry, stifled by the
atmosphere both inside and outside the house, took one
deep breath of air and decided to go to the top. From
there she might see . . . might find out what was happening and be of more use. She needed neither lantern
nor moonlight. The course of the pathway was second
nature to her by now. Nervous, aware of a tension in
the air that resembled the interval between thunder
and lighting, she was quick and quiet like a fox. In all
the excitement she would not be missed.

Alerted by fear to the slightest sound, she heard the
muted tones of strangers' voices just as she reached her
hiding place in the bower. She crouched down and
crept across the ground, pulling her dark shawl around
her, not twenty feet away from the backs of the riding
officers and their prisoner, Mazey Jack the look-out.
They had bundled him up and now he lay like a
beached whale, helpless, behind them on the grass.

Thank God they had gagged his mouth, for his eyes widened, their over-large whites rolling in the darkness when he saw her. He would have shouted . . .

Almost at once, from further along the cliff-top, came a shot. Kerry, trembling, bent down double and covered her ears.

Down in the village, and at the same time as the *Hawk* took up her position just out from the mouth of the cove, they heard the unmistakable crack of the 'flash in the pan' . . . the all-clear signal given by Mazey Jack from high on the cliffs above them.

There was an astonished gasp of disbelief from the group of agitated onlookers. From Yelland's position far out at sea the revenue cutter might be invisible, but the glow of the powder flash in Mazey Jack's musket would carry across the water to where the men waited for the sign of a safe return.

"'E's finally gone off 'is 'ead,' screeched Grannie Lee. 'An' what a time to pick for it . . .'

"Tis not Jack.' Pengelly's eyes might be blind but they looked as if they could see and his voice was sombre with foreboding. He raised his grizzled grey head and sniffed the wind like an old hunting dog. 'God knows what's happened to Jack, for that must be the riding officers up there. Can only be they.'

All the able-bodied men were out in the boats. Only the young, the inexperienced and the old were left. Nevertheless, under the one-legged Smiler's directions, in under five minutes all who could walk behind him had armed themselves with what they had and set off for the cliff-top . . . a motley band of half-dressed cripples and boys gripping cutlasses, gaffes and broom handles.

'The dragoons . . . they'm might have brought the dragoons . . .'

'We'm must take a chance on that . . .'

'But if the dragoons are there they'm do not stand a chance . . .'

'The warning must be given . . . someone must get to the spout lantern . . .'

Voices fluttered out into the night, rising and falling, excited and muted. The fail-safe device, the spout lantern, was kept in a secret place on the opposite Point and must be used only as a last resort. No one knew where the spout was hidden save for Yelland and the ancient Pengelly. And both these men would die before giving up the secret. When lit, its harsh, brilliant fire gave out light from only one direction . . . north was the warning . . . south was all-clear. Now it was the last hope for the men who would be pulling confidently towards the shore – and certain capture. Its message would give the smugglers a chance to 'sow the crop', an essential move, now, for their safety depended on it. The half-ankers, strung together on rope, could be put over the side at a marked spot and be retrieved with creepers at a less perilous time.

Kerry did not know who had fired the flash in the pan. Certainly it had not been the gagged and bound Mazey Jack.

She hadn't the time to stop and think about it because from her hiding place in the gorse Kerry heard the little group from the village scrambling up the path in the darkness. Even their breathing sounded louder than the sea. The slates they sent tinkling down behind them would alert even a sleeping enemy, and the men who crouched, waiting, were still, very still, but far from asleep. Pengelly would lead his men straight into the arms of the riding officers. Thank God there were no dragoons.

Without a second thought Kerry gathered up her

skirts, kicked off her clogs, stood up and ran. Her movement was as startling in the silence as a screech owl's flight. She saw faces white as moons turn towards her, saw the astonishment on them, saw Mazey Jack's eyes open wider, and then all she saw was the dizzying passage of grass, boulders, bumps and hillocks as she fled like the wind away and towards the opposite Point, with the officers in close pursuit behind her. They fired, but could not take accurate aim in the chaos of the chase; all she saw was the air light up in puffs of red when she cast quick backward glances.

She ran. And ran. Her throat was burning, her sides were splitting but she ran.

All was confusion.

The watchers in the village below looked now at the cutter and now at the Point. Would the men make it? Would the riding officers, even the dragoons, prevent that imperative signal from being given? Would it be sent out in time to allow the small boats to scuttle to the safety of some hidden cove, there to bide their time until the *Hawk* gave up her vigil? Would Yelland's lugger *Jacqueline* be able to pull away and avoid a capture that would inevitably mean, by law, that she would be ignominiously cut into three and abandoned on some neglected beach to ply her trade no more? Seventeen tons, one thousand square foot of sail, and armed with nine and twelve-pounder guns, she carried a crew of thirty and was no mean adversary. She would naturally fight if she had to.

A white light shone, fiercely bright. The poorly-armed troupe of misfits could not have reached the spout, for there was no time. Even the nimblest boy following Pengelly's instructions and taking a devious course running low through the gorse could not have reached the far Point. But there it was . . . signalling safety . . . bright to the south . . . the all-clear . . . the all-clear!

'Mercy me! They'm doomed!' and Grannie Lee, white-faced and terrible, crossed herself before withdrawing.

'Who's doin' it?' Lizzie Lee's bemused voice spoke for all of them. 'Who fired the flash in the pan an' who could have known about the spout?' Unconsciously she drew her smallest children to her. Rubbing tired eyes they nestled against her skirts.

Rosa, trembling, watching with the rest, put her hand to her mouth. She, too, was astonished. The spout had provided the balm for her bad conscience. She had felt sure that somehow, someone would have made it to the spout and averted a disaster. She hadn't wanted this! She had merely wanted to scare Yelland . . . to take him down a peg or two in the eyes of the community so they would all see he wasn't such a big man, after all. The thought of vengeance had been sweet in her mouth . . . the carrying out of her plans had tasted bitter. And now . . . and now . . .

The *Hawk* turned broadsides away so that it looked like a tall white cross riding the sea. She was turning to intercept. She had spied the small boats pulling for the shore. They would have no time to sow the crop. They would be caught red-handed.

And still the spout lamp jetted flame to the south. The villagers watched it, aghast at their own helplessness.

Pengelly's men had the advantage of surprise. They followed the riding officers as they chased their prey across unfamiliar ground, Porthclegga ground, and they, like Kerry, knew every uneven inch of it.

As each officer in turn fell back to re-load, the little band creeping up from behind picked them off, one by one, until eventually there was only one man following the fleeing girl. And he, his thoughts fixed firmly on the twenty pound a head bounty, was mercifully unaware of his fate until too late.

Kerry slowed down before she reached the far Point, aware that for some reason the pressure was off from behind but far more astonished by what she saw before her.

First she saw the silver hair, blowing like a bridal veil back from the sea . . . the face so white it was almost translucent in the darkness. Before the slim figure was the spout lantern, spluttering, shooting fire, unmistakably signalling the treacherous all-clear . . .

'Missy . . . *noooo!*' Kerry started running again, her eyes fixed firmly on her childhood friend . . . her voice drifting back over her shoulder as she screamed again, '*Missy . . . nooooo!*'

In the following seconds that passed so slowly, Kerry realised beyond any doubt that it was Missy who had given that first, fatal all-clear signal, she who had fired Mazey Jack's musket. Her brain stormed with the horror and confusion of it all. Why? *Why?* Why would gentle, sweet Missy do that?

In long, slow, dream-like strides she reached her. She put out a hand to touch her . . . to show her she was there . . . for Missy had the far-off look of a sleeper, her eyes defying the very concept of past, present or future.

'Missy!' Again Kerry reached out. But Missy was too far away . . . she could not touch her. She came closer. 'Missy', she said, 'give me the lantern.' Her hand went out once more but touched nothing but air. She was in a dream. None of this could possibly be happening.

Again she tried to grab the lantern, and again. But

each time Missy seemed to float a little further away. In no way did she even acknowledge Kerry's presence.

And then a figure appeared striding forward fast across the scrub. The tall, erect figure of a man, sure and determined in movement. A stranger? Kerry squeezed her eyes in the darkness.

He came silently upon Missy from behind, easily took the lantern and simply turned it around. The danger signal flashed alarm over the dark water. He held it aloft. He held it still. It was as if he had picked it straight from the boulder. It seemed that he couldn't see Missy at all. And nor could Kerry. For Missy was not there.

'Tristan . . . ?'

Bursts of gunfire came from above and the acrid smell of gunpowder drifted down to Porthclegga, blue clouds in the damp night air. The officers would not readily give up. The villagers knew well of the bounty on the head of every smuggler caught. The old man, the boys of Porthclegga must surely be fighting for their lives up there. For those who were not taking part, time creaked past. Their gritted eyes felt strained from trying to pierce the night.

A door banged. A child cried and was comforted. A woman sobbed and was led away.

And then the miracle occurred. In the high distance they saw the spout lifted and turned to the north. Mercifully someone had managed to reach it, but were they in time? 'Curses on the darkness,' moaned Dolly Trellis. ''Tis all the more alarmin' for not bein' able to see!' Three of her men were out there tonight.

A confusion of signals . . . Something had gone very wrong.

John Yelland was not used to being bested. Not since

his father's death had he allowed anyone to make a fool of him. He could not creep home like a dog with its tail between its legs, oh no! While the other boats happily took cover having sown the crop, and the *Jacqueline* made her stately way, her holds empty of contraband, into Penzance harbour, he would take the lead boat home for all to see.

His crew, Jessop and Gumma, had characteristically opted to take a ride in one of the other boats so Yelland rowed triumphant and alone into the cove, hailing the *Hawk* as he passed her. Not only would he take his boat in so that the watching villagers could savour the moment of his return, but under the eyes of the thwarted *Hawk* he would taunt his enemy by taking a leisurely turn round the cove before eventually tying up at the jetty and calling at Jessop's to tell the tale.

And after that, and only after that would he make it his business to find out who had tipped off the revenue men about tonight's big run.

For the first time, he thought darkly to himself as he rowed, for the first time there was a squeaker in Porthclegga. He would find out who it was and make an example of the traitor. He would die such a slow, painful, lingering death that no one would ever dare betray Yelland again.

The idea that he might have been betrayed by a woman would never have occurred to him.

FIVE

Up on the Point the spout lantern flickered and died, its work well done.

Pengelly's crew began gathering up their victims and, two to a man, carted them off to a safe place until Yelland could order their fate.

'They'm saw us comin' an' they's ran like rabbits,' joked Joe Trellis, as he put his undergrown frame to lugging a burly body into a comfortable position over his shoulder. 'I's never seen anyone run so fast as those men when we sprung 'em.'

Pengelly was not so sure. He scratched his head. 'Odd, that.' But they had done good work tonight and now was not the time to reason why. Now was the time to savour and enjoy. His old blood was up and it could only be cooled by a mug of frothy brown ale. Jessop would not be down there, but his boy would, and the tavern would be open to all-comers as it always was. It beckoned. The grizzled old man licked his lips.

He could only think that one of the riding officers had fired the musket, and that another of the buggers, so far unaccounted for, had somehow stumbled across the spout lantern. His darn brain did not work as fast as it used to. He scratched his head again. 'Twas odd . . . very odd. But thank God The Boy decided to come back to Porthclegga on the very night he could prove himself useful. For without his prompt action there would have been disaster in the village tonight.

He had asked Tristan, of course he had. He had welcomed him home and then he had asked him.

'I's saw no one,' had been the straightforward reply.

'I's saw what was happening an' snatched the spout from a boulder. For some peculiar reason someone had left it burning there.'

'It doan make sense to me.' But then so much in his blind world didn't make sense that Pengelly was prepared to dismiss this anomaly from the front of his mind and push it, with all the other niggling confusions, to the back.

He heard the familiar tap tap tap of Smiler Teague's wooden leg coming towards him. 'Hows we'm doin', Smiler?'

'We's got 'em all loaded up an' nows we's off wi' 'e.'

'Leave the young 'uns to do that. They's knows where they'm goin'. We's deserve some sustenance.'

'Aye. 'Twas a queer business.'

''Twas that.'

Between the two old men who stumped and grumbled down the cliff path was stored nearly two hundred years of memory. They remembered Grannie Lee when she was pretty. They remembered the violent storms of fifty years ago when the sea had washed the floors of the cottages and the villagers had watched, terrified, out of their bedroom windows. They remembered these things more clearly than they remembered yesterday's dinner.

'But I's carn remember anythin' quite so queer as tonight's business,' puffed Smiler. 'What I's want to know is, will we's ever learn the truth of it?'

'Knowin' life as I's do, I's'd say no,' said old Pengelly. And they spoke no more but conserved their breath as the lights of Porthclegga grew nearer.

They were greeted for the heroes they undoubtedly were. They were clapped on the back, pestered with questions and followed down the path to the jetty by a bunch of grateful, exultant villagers. Children were

put onto backs and carried, for nobody wanted to miss
the first accounts of what had gone on up there on the
cliff-top while the women and children had waited in
such awful anxiety below.

Jessop's son Arny, as dubious and obsequious as his
father, was swamped in a filthy white apron tied like
a sheet around him. His thin, shiny face glistened with
exertion and he stank of horse, for he had been up and
down, up and down all night with the waiting mule
train. Up the slimy passage that led from the back of
the cellars into the large cave halfway up the cliff, and
down again, uncertain whether to leave the animals
there out of sight or bring them down to wait on the
jetty. Now he thankfully brought out jugfuls of ale to
the waiting crowd who were watching Yelland's antics
on the water.

'You's has to smile to see 'e, doan 'e? 'E's a right
devil is that one. Look at 'e now. 'E's got no fear . . .'

'Aye, the Devil doan touch 'is own. There's truth in
that.'

'Tristan Carne is back. 'E was up there with the
light. 'Twas 'e turned it round an' gave out the
warning.'

'Ned's boy?'

'Aye, that one. Grown, 'e has, since 'e went away.
'Mazin' the change in 'e so Smiler says . . .'

'Ned'll not be pleased when 'e comes in.'

'I's doan think it was Ned 'e came back for.'

'Who then?'

'The Penhale girl . . . Kerry Penhale. They's was
always sweethearts.'

'Too late then, isn't 'e? For she's to be married
tomorrow.'

'Aye. 'Tis too late.'

They drank the ale. They exchanged stories. Light-headed after the lifting of such tension, they chatted, all differences put aside and loving each other tonight. The sea breeze was cool and the swell was rising. The *Hawk* still dominated the horizon. From here its stark, dipping shape seemed to fill the entrance to the cove. And Yelland was on his first sweep, pulling strongly on the oars, the small boat sinking and rising with the waves as he determined to take his bow.

They watched. They admired. And they feared.

For amidst the celebrating, they all knew there was a traitor amongst them tonight.

SIX

Up on the cliffs Kerry wept in Tristan's arms.

'Yous came then,' were the first words she spoke, and he slipped back into his old style of talking as naturally as the way he held her.

'Didn't yous believe that I's would?'

'Five years, Tristan! 'Twas five long years!'

'Why are yous weeping? Tomorrow is my eighteenth birthday!'

Kerry shook her head. She could hardly speak. What had birthdays to do with anything? Didn't he know what had happened? He was holding her at arm's length staring at her with nothing but joy in his eyes. She couldn't hold his stare. He had changed a great deal and she supposed she must look different, too.

He had filled out and grown tall. No more the spindly lad that had taken his bundle on his shoulders and fled up the cliff path, he was a broad, firm-bodied man with wide shoulders, strong cheekbones and a quizzical smile that led from his eyes – the same amber eyes. Wiser, harder, but the same gentleness was in them that she remembered.

And she smelt the cloth of his clothes, thick, rich, well-made. She stepped back. His knee-length boots were shiny and new. Discomfited, she patted her hair and smoothed her dress. She must look wild. A mess! Did that matter?

'Things is not the same . . .' She spoke to him but kept her eyes to the ground. 'Maudie died . . .'

He nodded. 'I's knows that. I's has spoken to Parson Fox.'

'When?'

'This morning.'

'Then yous came back this morning?'

'I's was back the day before. I's had people to see. I's came here as soon as I's could.'

'Why then? If yous knew then why did yous come?'

His answer was simple. 'I's came for yous.'

Kerry faced him. Her black eyes flashed with accusation. Her hair had fallen from its cap and tumbled to her waist. Her face was pale and angled with shadows. The Queen of the Night, he thought, as he breathed her into himself, tried to gather her to him with his eyes alone. She said, 'Yous too late, Tristan. Tomorrow I's to marry John Yelland.'

What had she expected? She had braced herself. She already saw his back turned towards her as he swung on his heel and left her. She already saw the hurt on his face, the hardening of the eyes, the straightening of the mouth. So that when it didn't happen . . . when he smiled and held out his arms she was angry. Terribly angry! What was this? Didn't he understand? Had he come back to tease her?

She tried to run away. He caught her by the shoulders. He turned her roughly to face him. He kissed her.

Not like the kisses of their childhood. This kiss was slow and decisive and joined their souls together as if there had been no parting. A flow of passion swept through her body and she felt compelled to bend to him like an exultant wave . . . she knew the urgency of a flooding river . . . rushing, desiring to be taken up by his arms, to yield, to lose herself in this ocean of ecstasy for ever.

Tristan took her hand and together they walked to the bower. He shrugged off his frockcoat and laid it on the grass, then he sat down and pulled Kerry to him. She whispered, ''Tis no use. We's is playing games,

Tristan. We's is no longer children. I's has to marry Yelland or see my family starve.'

He shook his head. 'No, Kerry.' His voice was soft but insistent. He caught up her hair and let it rest like water, cupped in his hand.

'I's carn do otherwise, Tristan. A bargain was made between us.' But her heart was beating like a wild bird in her chest.

'There are things yous doan know, Kerry,' he said. 'Things that I's must try to explain to yous . . .'

'I's doan want to hear anything. Nothing can stop the heartbreak I's am feelin' now. 'Twould have been better if yous hadn't come back. Yous makes it harder to bear . . .'

He lifted a finger and put it across her lips. After silencing her he moved it, and kissed her once more. When he let her go she was trembling with a passion so unfamiliar to her that she felt afraid. She remembered, once, when she was small, daring herself to walk near the cliff-edge in a violent wind. The gusts had almost unbalanced her. She turned to touch him. She traced his face, wrapped a golden curl round a finger and said, 'Look, it fits,' just as she used to. She was trying to make it normal, as it ought to be.

'Tomorrow yous doan marry Yelland,' said Tristan as if he was stating the simplest of facts. 'The only man yous'll ever marry is me!'

Something in the way he spoke stopped her scornful laughter. She shivered and said, ''E'd kill yous.'

Tristan's words were cold as ice. ''E'd have to. For while I's alive yous'll marry nobody but me.'

'I's carn. Yous know that.'

'Kerry, trust me. I's am not the boy who went away. I's has come back to claim my inheritance. An' that inheritance lies in the house and estates of Trewen. In the name yous hates so much . . . the name of Yelland.'

378

Kerry frowned up at him. 'I's doan understand.'

'Yous will when yous knows. But now is not the time for words.'

And he bent down over her and covered her face and neck with small kisses, whispered words of love that had waited for five years to be born and to fly. She returned his passion with an intensity that overwhelmed her. She was tiny again, she let the fierce gale take her. He touched, he stroked, he kissed. He was strong but he was gentle . . . enchanting. He transported her to a state of rapture she hadn't known existed . . . he took her and, exhilarated, she soared above the cliffs right out over the open sea, whirling and drifting and screaming with the seabirds. Freed from drudgery, fear and compromise she soared to a higher pitch than Heaven itself in Tristan's arms.

She ceased to care. She ceased to think about anything so small as one tomorrow.

She was an angel. She was a mermaid. She was the very spirit of the sea itself.

SEVEN

They heard Yelland's deep voice calling from the bay.
Kerry felt her blood turn to ice. So he was down there,
mouthing insults at the *Hawk* which still hovered at the
mouth of the cove.

''E's a brave man.'

''E's an ignorant, stupid one.'

'The two, unfortunately, often go together,' said Tristan, pulling Kerry protectively back into his arms.
'Doan let's think about 'e now.'

'We's can hardly help it wi' 'e caterwaulin' down
there an' just askin' for trouble.'

She felt so right in Tristan's arms like this, and in
this place, too, which was so much their own.

'After tomorrow 'e woan matter.'

'I's carn see it bein' so simple as that, Tristan. Yous
knows what 'e's like. 'E woan give up anythin' without
a fight. Look at 'e now . . . that's 'e's fierce pride if
yous like . . .'

''E has no choice.'

'Tell me then. Tell me where yous went an' what
happened to yous an' what yous saw. An' did yous love
anyone else when yous was away?'

So Tristan told her. He stroked her and he cuddled
her as he told her about who he'd seen and where he'd
been and about how Mother Carrivick had helped him
by directing him to where he must go to get the information he needed. About how the final meeting with
Parson Fox this morning had added the last link to the
chain.

''Tis not so much about me as about my mother . . .'

'Yous mother? Yous knows, now, who she was?'

Tristan smiled at her. 'Yous know more about her than I's does.'

'How can I's?'

'Wait an' let me tell yous.'

When Mercy Geary approached Roger Yelland on that cold December day eighteen years ago he had flinched, not with surprise, but with disgust, at coming so close to a woman.

He knew he was dying. But he straight away perceived a way of punishing his son, yes, even from the grave, for his wicked, lecherous ways. For this was not the first time he had got a wench in the family way. He took the girl in and listened to her story while regarding her through dark eyes that peered sharply from deep, bony sockets and saw through all pretence.

Mercy was petrified . . . a rabbit before a bright light, mesmerised, rendered weak-limbed by the experience. Here was Power. Here was Power so malevolent it would suck her into itself and never let her go.

Wasn't this what she had always wanted . . . been looking for all her life? Hadn't she always been hell-bent on self-destruction?

Compassion? Hah! There was none to be had in this man. Just a dark, towering need for vengeance. A desire to punish and cause pain. In vain she pleaded. In vain she begged for sanctuary, but the options he gave her were a one-way ticket to the workhouse or, extraordinarily, a paper marriage and banishment to an address in London of a good Methodist household where she could work for nothing in order to pay for her keep until the boy, if it were a boy, was born.

And then? Why then, when her bastard was eighteen years old he would inherit Trewen. Yelland would sort out the papers in the morning. He would tie them so

381

tight legally they could never be untangled – she could be sure of that! Roger Yelland smiled to himself. A few years of debauchery and fine living would make the punishment all the more painful for his son when it finally came! Better to allow the fish freedom and then pull it in . . . watch its eyes . . . watch it struggle with the hook pulling against its mouth . . . a soft, tender mouth. True vengeance, thought the dying man, takes cunning and wit. Let the blighter stand for a while in the sun before the bitter winds of reality pull him down to the grave . . .

What could she answer him? He loathed her. Considered her defiled and disgusting . . . she must do his bidding. She must tell no one. If John found out he would hunt his own child down and kill him – her, too, most likely.

In a dark veil she was wed. She went to her wedding in mourning clothes.

A bride, she had knelt beside him at the prie-dieu, her tear-filled eyes lowered to the floor, not knowing whether she did right or wrong but just that she was terribly afraid of this man who was to be her husband. She trembled at the feel of Roger Yelland kneeling beside her. She trembled from the cold. The wind moaned and screamed outside. The church was in darkness save for two tallow candles set in niches behind the altar which cast eerie shadows on the walls.

She saw the name in the floor, as Kerry would see it, TRISTAN YELLAND, and Mercy never forgot it.

She answered the parson timidly. 'I will.' Roger Yelland had decided her fate and it was for her, the sinner, to obey.

'I's doan want to see hide nor hair of 'e afterwards, never, d'yous understand? Jezebel . . . Daughter of Eve, ye serpent writhing beneath the skin of man. But if it be a boy, only a boy mind, aye, I's'll have no wenches upstairs in this house, if it be a boy send 'e to the parson who knows the whereabouts of the documents . . . has the marriage licence . . . proof of inheritance. An' I's prays the bastard brat turns out to be a boy.'

Parson Fox obliged and conducted the sad little service. Well, he owed Squire Yelland his living, though the two men had little to do with each other. Yelland detested the thick-set little parson with the lily-livered religion which meant nothing to nobody. But he had his uses. And he kept his mouth shut; he understood the value of discretion, which was a rare talent in a man those days.

They walked back from the church having dismissed the witnesses, two passing beggars who were sheltering in the kitchens for the night. It was icy cold. Mercy had to run to keep pace with Yelland's stride and the cold cut her cruelly. Snow settled on the ground. There they went, leaving their footprints behind them, he a tall, wild-haired fanatic dressed all in black. She, small, fragile, in thin boots, her silver hair blowing forward over her face and her head hurting where he had so cruelly pinned the heavy, dark veil with a black lacquered comb.

He had insisted on that. 'No woman should go to church with her face uncovered,' he'd said. ''Twould be vile! Let alone on her wedding day.'

He put her in an unused room at the top of the house. 'Remember,' he kept warning her. 'If yous not quiet an' John should find out . . .'

She was terrified. Terrified of him, of the present and of the future. She shook with the cold and tried to sleep. Who knew when she would have a roof over her head again or a bed to sleep in? She wanted Daisy. But she could not confide in Daisy now. She could not confide in anyone.

She had known he would come, but when the door opened and he came to her she screamed in terror. Naked he looked more terrible than dressed. But he was strong and wiry and thin like a string bean. He raped her. Again and again he raped her. He seemed to have stored up his virility for this one night of Damnation. He tortured himself upon her. He beat her and then he beat himself with a thin-thonged whip he had brought under his gown. And the things he did to her! The things he made her do to him! The way he treated her . . . like dirt . . . something to be scraped off his shoe or stamped upon. The words he used . . . the names with which he reviled her.

Punishment . . . she welcomed the punishment.

She lay there still and cold as stone allowing these things to be done. 'For I's am yous husband for a night . . . for one night only,' he said in one of his more coherent moments. 'An you's goin' to remember who put yous wi' child . . . whore . . . I am your master. An' I's'll do with yous what I's like in the name of the Lord who is Master over all women.'

Next day she was battered and bruised and could hardly walk. She thought that her soul was dead, for she could see nothing beautiful even in her imaginings. He brought her food. He knocked at the door and left it on the floor outside. She wondered if it might be poisoned, so mad was he. She left it, although she would have quite liked to die. He returned the clothes that he had taken to keep her prisoner, and included a good, woollen cloak with one guinea in the pocket.

When darkness fell he came and told her to go.

'I need to collect some of my things,' she begged him.

'Just remember to say nothing or . . .'

He need threaten her no more. She was weary, exhausted. He was the master and she the conquered. That was how it had always been meant to be.

On that dark, snowy night after she had collected her bundle and bade farewell to Daisy, Mercy Geary had taken the road to Exeter, the start of her fateful journey. This was the third home she had left without love. She had a guinea in her pocket, and the sixpence John Yelland had so scornfully placed in her boot . . . a sign of satisfactory service. Plenty enough money to travel safely.

She did not say goodbye to Mother Carrivick, whose advice had caused such terrible consequences. Her friend had betrayed her utterly. She had denied her the help that she craved and thrown her into the arms of a monster.

So much for friendship. Friends either died, or worse, they turned their backs when you needed them. She had the address of a good Methodist house in her purse. She fought a gale all the way and reached Truro before collapsing on the steps of a tavern which was closed for the night. There she slept and in the morning was found, still alive but with every curve and fold of her cloak powdered, frozen and stiff with snow.

But John Yelland's child grew warm and strong inside her. She was growing to despise John Yelland's child.

EIGHT

'I's spoke to them all,' said Tristan grimly. 'The Newgate women, Mrs Briggsworthy, the solicitor at her trial, yes, even the ghastly Mrs Bowls. I's spoke to them all. I's knows her. I's knows that's how 'twas.'

Tristan did not know. He, like Kerry, imagined that Mercy's last act had been to try and save her son. They did not know how she planned, when her seven years of exile were up and Yelland was dead, to return and make a bargain with John: silence over Tristan's inheritance in exchange for marriage with the only man she had ever loved. But the ship went down and the last bargain was never made. No one, except perhaps the witch, knew that. So they waited, now, expectantly and with horror, as the sea churned below.

The ominous feeling in the air, on which even the thick-skinned Gregor had commented, had nothing to do with the run, or even Kerry's marriage on the morrow – with nothing so small and inconsequential. It was linked with a terrible act of betrayal eighteen years ago: it had to do with Vengeance – and with seeing Justice done.

All Mercy Geary wanted, all she'd ever wanted was her lover.

Kerry watched Yelland's progress with dread. The *Hawk* had disappeared away into the night, knowing herself to be beaten this time but they were on to the smugglers now, and there would always be a next time, and another after that.

Yelland, arrogant as ever as he rode the high swells,

was fast approaching the Spur. Tonight the rock showed itself in all its terrible maleficence, serrated, rapier-sharp, a steeple under the sea surrounded by suction as a church spire is surrounded by puffs of cloud.

Around the base of the rock the water was silver, but on its tip was a scrap of mist, a wisp of gossamer, trailing as if caught like a piece of dark veil. Even as they watched, still shaken by Tristan's story, from beneath the rock . . . from fathoms deep where the wishing coins lay, came a sapphire-blue flame, hardly noticeable at first but growing in intensity . . . growing all the time until it covered first the water around it and then spread like a phosphorescent stain out on to the sea, out as far as Yelland's boat while, in black silhouette, he rowed himself steadily past the Spur ready to head for the jetty.

'She's making sure,' Kerry whispered, moving closer to Tristan. They were unable to tear their eyes away from the small boat below them. 'Watch! Missy is making sure of your inheritance!'

And then the swallowing started. Because that's what it seemed as if the Spur was doing. It sucked the sea towards it in a whirlpool of blue, which churned and gurgled until it seemed that every inch of water rose and spun in violent motion. Yelland's boat was tossed like a straw, taken up into the turmoil and sucked towards the pulsating throat of the Spur. There was just time to see him look up, slip his oars and fall back white-faced into the bottom of the boat as it sped along the dizzying surface of the water towards the towering Spur.

He made no sound but they saw his slight figure as, at the very mouth of the maelstrom, the boat tipped on its stern up to its full height, waited for a moment, savouring the seconds, until suddenly, and with great force, it was sucked down under the waves.

The blue light withdrew, creeping back across the water like the last ribbons of sunset, circling the Spur in lazy, smoky swirls until the sea became calm again, turned once more to black, and all was as it had been before.

NINE

It was no illusion. Over one hundred people had seen it. The villagers watched from the jetty. Tristan and Kerry watched from the cliff-top.

Not one of them was sorry. But everyone was afraid.

From that Midsummer Eve, corpse lights were no longer seen around the Spur, and never again did Kerry hear a nightjar's call from the direction of the sea. She never saw Missy again, either, but the smell of lavender always seemed to evoke her memory as smells so subtly can.

From the supernatural experience came just another story of the sea . . . to be told and re-told through the generations. The audience of landlubbers was understandably cynical – for fisherfolk and Cornishmen both are renowned for their tall tales.

Mother Carrivick in her hovel at Kergilliak had seen it, and knew that she could now die in peace. Once, the house of Trewen had been doomed . . . and with its downfall would have come the downfall of the surrounding villages, which depended on it for homes and security. She had merely contrived to ensure an heir unaffected by the influences within. She had succeeded . . . up to a point . . . but even her magic could not control the sea. A spell in New South Wales would have done Mercy no harm, and at the appointed time, so Mother Carrivick's plans went, she and her son would have returned to their rightful home. Hell's teeth . . . she'd been doing the girl a favour! But after the storm the witch had known that the dark, twisted spirit released from the fathoms, a soul so tormented, so lost, so possessed, would make stronger magic than hers.

It had taken her all her powers to save the child from the sea, to persuade Maudie Carne to take it in until Tristan was old enough to be told the truth.

Yes, it was her fault for meddling. If she had not been using Mercy in her unholy way for her own scheming purposes then the tormented spirit would have found peace.

As it was, the jealousy of a woman betrayed could have destroyed everything the witch had been working for.

Up until the night of the wreck everything had been working out well.

It had started well. Old Roger Yelland had been clever. If John had lived he would have found it impossible to dispute Tristan's rights to his inheritance.

That cunning old man had carefully nurtured suspicion . . . and only suspicion, in the year left to him before he died. His watchful son never dreamed that the will had already been changed, that his father had married the serving-wench and made legitimate his bastard son. As the father became weaker the son grew in confidence, certain that it was now too late for Roger to change his will.

Mother Carrivick had not foreseen Mercy's death, nor had she predicted John Yelland's attraction to the Penhale girl.

She should have done. She knew his type. He had always perceived Kerry Penhale to be different . . . right from the time he came upon her on his horse scrumping apples from his orchard. Kerry Penhale was always different. With her vivid hair and eyes, that easy gracefulness, well – no young woman should be running about so freely without a man to command her. Hah! She was all fire and spirit! And she hated him . . . that, for Yelland, was a powerful aphrodisiac. He would see all that exchanged for a proper servility, ensure her fierce independence would be crushed into subservience. And then . . . and then . . . well, after that John Yelland would lose interest. He would break what seemed to him the unbreakable . . . after that he would leave Kerry alone.

But John Yelland had dangerously underestimated the power of a woman betrayed.

Mother Carrivick had watched the sea writhe and moan . . . had seen the corpse lights burn . . . had heard the nightjar sound in places a nightjar never should have been.

When she heard of Kerry's engagement to Yelland she knew that Mercy would act. It was nothing to do with her son's inheritance . . . it was to do with a jealousy so deep it caused the very sea to shudder and sigh.

For Yelland to be in love, to be married, was more than Mercy could stand. And she had marked Kerry down for her own son. Mother Carrivick had feared for Kerry's safety and the drowned girl had uncaringly put the lives of every man in the village at risk. But the witch should have known . . . she should have known that all Mercy wanted was her lover.

His bones, and the bones of Mercy Geary were never recovered.

So Mother Carrivick watched the wedding with great relief. She watched the Spur rock, silent and dignified, with something more akin to prayer.

The ceremony took place three weeks later. The sea was a steely blue under a breath of mist. The church on the cliff was heavy with the scent of honeysuckle which festooned the walls and the sun-blistered archway over the door.

Kerry moved in a foam of white. Her veil was flounced with layer upon layer of white netting. Between the layers Cath had secured pink rosebuds. The night before the children had filled the church with coltsfoot and violets.

Smiler Teague's peg-leg rested on a pile of prayer-books. Rosa made moon-eyes at Daniel Gulliver and meant none of it for she was about to join a travelling circus that performed tonight at Bodmin. Lizzie Lee's attitude was one of startled surprise. And for Kerry? Flower-wreathed hats of floppy straw . . . bees buzzing around the honeysuckle . . . the sense and sight of Tristan, in black, beside her. Kerry knelt at the prie-dieu where she had knelt so hopelessly just three weeks before. Now she felt nothing but happiness. Then the church had seemed cold and unwelcoming, now it was warm, alive, vibrating to the croaking of a frog in Tiggy Trelliss' pocket before he was smacked and sent out. And Kerry saw the name written in stone and wondered who he was; thought pityingly of Missy kneeling here . . .

Grannie Lee, her face a small, brown tuberous root under a riot of purple flowers was so excited by the ceremony and the promise of further celebrations that she let out a raucous squawk as Parson Fox smilingly concluded the service.

Mamma cried.

Tristan's eyes were full of love when the bridegroom kissed the bride.

One of the nicest parts of becoming Mistress of Trewen was the promoting of Daisy Wyatt to housekeeper and the flushing out of the undesirables who had turned it into nothing better than a bawdy house.

Mrs King had long left, to stay with a sister who ran a dame school in Launceston. Mrs Gibson retired to a cottage in the grounds.

Daisy wept when they told her about Mercy. 'I's knew 'er'd never come back. Secretly, deep down inside, while I's made myself keep hopin' I's always knew . . .'

'She loved yous, Daisy,' Tristan said.

'No, that 'er did not. 'Er never loved unless 'er were afraid. 'Er couldn't, poor soul, 'er were flawed like that. Things had happened to 'er.'

'She was always a good friend to me,' said Kerry. 'Right from the very beginning.'

'That were guilt,' said Daisy, sighing resignedly. ''Er were tryin' to make up for something that happened long ago, for the death of 'er little friend. 'Er always blamed 'erself for that.'

'Daisy yous bitter! Think of what she did for Tristan! Pushing him out of the boat like that and at the very last moment when she might have considered saving herself . . .'

Kerry was sorting through sheaths of wall covering designs. Trewen was a hive of activity as it underwent a transformation. From the wood behind the orchard came the sound of hammers and saws as carpenters altered dark niches and narrow corners, repaired window frames and staircases, and, almost daily a wagon arrived to bring some treasure Tristan had picked up on his journeyings and stored ready for his return. Tristan knew what he was doing. Directed by Mother Carrivick, he had taken work as a labourer on a property in Buckinghamshire and soon come to the notice of the architect, Nicholas Revett. Impressed by the lad who was so quick and adept, so intelligent in his appreciation of beautiful things, Revett had taken Tristan under his wing and cultivated his love of style and taste. Under his tutelage Tristan had eventually become an expert in pictures and porcelain. While still a youngster, he had earned large sums of money for his expertise and advise. Now, every stick of furniture, every rug, every picture at Trewan was to be replaced and the precious tapestries, carefully restored.

Only Mother Carrivick knew the truth about Mercy Geary. Everyone else preferred to see the good. 'She must have loved her son,' said Kerry defensively. 'Her last act was to give 'e the chance of life. And on Midsummer Eve she might have been the cause of a near-disaster, but all she was trying to do was ensure 'e's birthright.'

Daisy, who had known Mercy well, said, 'Yous always see the best in people. Doan yous ever wonder if 'er might have been trying to stop yer marriage to Yelland? Carn you see, Kerry, 'er loved John Yelland in spite of all 'e had done to 'er, in spite o' 'erself, right to the end.'

Kerry stared at Tristan. She searched back through her memories. 'Could that really be so?'

'We's'll never know,' he said quietly.

'Thankfully,' put in Daisy.

'She never showed herself to me,' said Tristan. 'During the search, from the time I's first realised, right at the beginning, who 'er was an' what must have happened, I's kept wondering why 'er showed 'erself to Kerry but never to me.'

'Because of my birthday,' said Kerry. ''Er died at the time I's was born an' so I's could see 'er while others could not. But how could yous keep lovin' someone who discarded you, scorned yous wi' a sixpence in yer boot, condemned yous to prostitution an' a life without hope? How could any woman love a man like that?' Kerry was angry with disbelief.

'There is no accounting for love,' said Tristan,

coming to circle her in his arms. 'An' what do it matter to us now? We's has everythin' we's ever wanted.' He raised a glass of rich red wine, one from a crate retrieved from the *Jacqueline*. He put it to his forehead, watching his wife through the ruby glow.

'But say 'tis true . . . say the incredible is true, an' that Mercy has really lured John Yelland to be with her for Eternity as the witch says she has. 'E would not make 'er happy. She could only be more miserable an' lonely wi' a brute like that . . .'

'We are shaped and fashioned by what we love,' quoted Tristan.

'More so by the way we have been loved ourselves,' said Kerry.

Daisy left the room, happy as she had never been in her life before. She was too busy to waste her time speculating on life and what might and might not have been. She only knew that what was happening to her now was good. She knew that her future was bright. Mark Gumma, the stone mason, had given her the glad eye in the kitchen only this morning and she had not looked away. She was no spring chicken, nor was Gumma, but he was a gentle man and made a good living . . .

Tristan looked at Kerry. 'There is one room in this house that the builders have not reached yet. I's suggest we's goes there an' forgets all about things we's doan understand an' concentrates on those we's do.'

'The bedroom?' There were lights in Kerry's eyes.

'Aye, the bedroom.' And Tristan picked her up and carried her up the wide staircase, past the sightless eyes of the metal visors, past the beaded glances of the mounted stags, on and on and up and up towards the reality of their love which, like Missy's, would last for ever, past death and way, way beyond.

ROWAN BESTSELLERS

OLD SINS
Penny Vincenzi

An unputdownable, saga of mystery, passion and glamour, exploring the intrigue which results when Julian Morell, head of a vast cosmetics empire, leaves part of his huge legacy to an unknown young man. The most desirable novel of the decade, *Old Sins* is about money, ambition, greed and love… a blockbuster for the nineties.

GREAT POSSESSIONS
Kate Alexander

A wonderful saga set in glamorous between-the-wars London that tells the story of Eleanor Dunwell, an illegitimate working-class girl who comes quite unexpectedly into a great inheritance. Her wealth will attract a dashing American spendthrift husband – and separate her from the man she truly loves.

THE WIND IN THE EAST
Pamela Pope

There were two things Joshua Kerrick wanted in the world: one was money to buy a fleet of drifters; the other was Poppy Ludlow. But Poppy and Joshua are natural rivals. This vivid historical drama traces their passionate story among an East Anglian community struggling to make its living from the sea.

LOVERS AND SINNERS
Linda Sole

Betty Cantrel is about to be hanged for the murder of the only man she ever loved. Once a lowly house maid she is now one of the most glamorous night-club singers in London. Two men have figured in her life: the dark and enigmatic Nathan Crawley and the cool and suave James Blair. Which one of them does she truly love – and why does she kill him?

THE DIPLOMAT'S WIFE
Louise Pennington

Elizabeth Thornton, beautiful and elegant wife of distinguished diplomat, John, has everything. Until Karl – dangerous, ruthless and passionate – turns up in her life again. Under the glittering chandeliers of Vienna, 'City of Dreams', her past returns with a vengeance and she must choose between safe love she shares with John and heady passion she feels for Karl.

THE ITALIANS
Jane Nottage

A contemporary international novel capturing the very essence of the fabulously rich D'Orsi family. Wealthy, passionate ex-playboy Alberto D'Orsi has everything – including the memory of the only woman he loved and lost during the Second World War. Now an old man, he must decide who will inherit his vast fortune: his aristocratic wife or wayward son and daughter? His decision shocks everyone.

THE RICH PASS BY
Pamela Pope

How could Sarah have foretold the bitter destiny she was choosing for herself when she vowed to reclaim her illegitimate child. But she survives – fighting to remain true to her vow and to hide the passion she feels for the father of the child. Set amid the contrasts of Victorian London, Sarah's tempestuous story is inextricably linked to that of a harsh, unequal society in this moving story of endurance and love.

FRIENDS AND OTHER ENEMIES
Diana Stainforth

Set in the sixties and seventies, the rich, fast-moving story of a girl called Ryder Harding who loses *everything* – family, lover, money and friends. But Ryder claws her way back and turns misfortune into gold.

ELITE
Helen Liddell

Anne Clarke was a ruthless, politically ambitious, beautiful and brilliant woman... passionately committed to the underground workers militia of Scotland. But did her seemingly easy rise to the post of Deputy Prime Minister and her brilliantly orchestrated, perfectly lip-glossed public face conceal a sinister secret?

THE FLIGHT OF FLAMINGO
Elizabeth Darrell

A strong saga unfolds against a backdrop of marine aviation in its heady pioneering days before the Second World War. When Leone Kirkland inherits her autocratic father's aviation business, she also inherits his murky past, and Kit Anson, his ace test pilot. She needs him; she could love him, but he has every reason to hate her.

THE QUIET EARTH
Margaret Sunley

Set in the Yorkshire Dales during the nineteenth century this rural saga captures both the spirit and warmth of working life in an isolated farming community, where three generations of the Oaks family are packed under the same roof. It tells of their struggle for survival as farmers, despite scandal, upheaval and tragedy, under the patriarchal rule of Jonadab Oaks.

THE SINS OF EDEN
Iris Gower

Handsome, charismatic and iron-willed, Eden Lamb has an incalculable effect on the lives of three very different women in Swansea during the Second World War that is to introduce them both to passion and heartbreak. Once again, bestselling author Iris Gower has spun a tender and truthful story out of the background she knows and loves so well.

THE DREAMBREAKERS
Louise Pennington

Francesca Gaeti's dream – as head of Samuels Advertising – is to take her agency right to the top. But there are four men around her who could tear that dream to shreds. *The Dreambreakers* is an exciting, glitzy contemporary novel of a sleek, beautiful, intelligent woman intent on winning in a man's world.

A BOWL OF CHERRIES
Anna King

A heartwarming family story set in London's East End, in the tradition of Helen Forrester. The story of Marie Cowley, a courageous girl growing up in a loving working class family. Marie's childhood is overshadowed by disease, but her spirit and passionate determination to make a life for herself allow her to overcome her problems – and eventually to find happiness.

ANGEL
Belle Grey

After the death of her Hungarian father in a duel, Sylvie is left to the mercy of her unscrupulous mother. Throughout her career as an actress in late-Victorian London and her involvement with Pre-Raphaelite artist, Will Mackenzie, who paints her portrait, Sylvie is seeking to avenge her father's murder and confront the ghosts of her past.

OUR FATHER'S HOUSE
Caroline Fabre

A subtly crafted saga spanning three decades, charting the slow disintegration of a family which salvages hope from the ruins. The rich and powerful Sir Edward Astonbury is betrayed by one of his children for tax evasion. To understand why the youngest must trace back over a lifetime of manipulation, deception, and mingled love and hate that has made each of them what they are.

OTHER ROWAN BOOKS

☐ Old Sins *Penny Vincenzi*   £4.99
☐ Great Possessions   *Kate Alexander*   £3.99
☐ The Dreambreakers   *Louise Pennington*   £3.99
☐ The Wind in the East   *Pamela Pope*   £4.99
☐ The Flight of Flamingo   *Elizabeth Darrell*   £4.99
☐ The Quiet Earth   *Margaret Sunley*   £3.99
☐ Elite *Helen Liddell*   £3.99
☐ A Bowl of Cherries   *Anna King*   £3.99
☐ Sins of Eden   *Iris Gower*   £4.99
☐ Lovers and Sinners   *Linda Sole*   £4.99
☐ The Diplomat's Wife   *Louise Pennington*   £4.99
☐ Angel *Belle Grey*   £4.50
☐ The Rich Pass By *Pamela Pope*   £4.99
☐ The Italians *Jane Nottage*   £4.99
☐ Friends and Other Enemies   *Diana Stainforth*   £4.50
☐ Folly's Child *Janet Tanner*   £4.99
☐ Our Father's House   *Caroline Fabre*   £4.99
☐ Fields in the Sun   *Margaret Sunley*   £4.99

Prices and other details are liable to change.

ARROW BOOKS, BOOKSERVICE BY POST, PO BOX 29,
DOUGLAS, ISLE OF MAN, BRITISH ISLES

NAME _____

ADDRESS _____

_____

_____

Please enclose a cheque or postal order made out to Arrow
Books Ltd. for the amount due and allow the following for
postage and packing.

U.K. CUSTOMERS: Please allow 30p per book to a maximum
of £3.00

B.F.P.O. & EIRE: Please allow 30p per book to a maximum of
£3.00

OVERSEAS CUSTOMERS: Please allow 35p per book.

Whilst every effort is made to keep prices low it is sometimes
necessary to increase cover prices at short notice. Arrow Books
reserve the right to show new retail prices on covers which may
differ from those previously advertised in the text or elsewhere.